silver LIES

Silver LIES

WILLA LAYNE

HEART C PUBLISHING

Printed in the United States of America.
ISBN 13: 979-8-218-31780-5 (Paperback)
ISBN 13: 979-8-218-32422-3 (Hardback)
Revised First Edition: January 2024
Originally published September 2023 (ISBN: 979-821-827196-1)

Cover Design: Beautiful Books by Ivy
Editing: Emi Janisch and Eliza Stemmons
Proofreading: Roxana at proofreadbooks.com
Map Design: Willa Layne
Character Art: Kassi Roos
For Content Warnings, please see willalayne.com

"Above all, don't lie to yourself. The man who lies to himself and listens to his own lie comes to a point that he cannot distinguish the truth within him, or around him, and so loses all respect for himself and for others. And having no respect he ceases to love."

— Fyodor Dostoevsky, <u>The Brothers Karamazov</u>

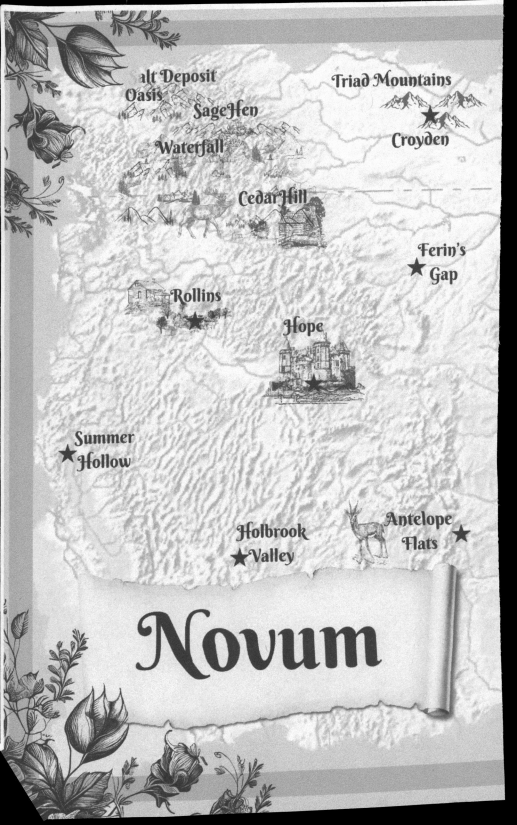

PROLOGUE
ASH

"Race ya," I yelled at the weathered old man behind me as I sprinted down the trail. My braid whipped in the breeze at my back—wind rushing across the brim of my hat, warm summer air on my face. My lips pulled into a grin when I heard him call out.

"Ash, wait!" he laughed, his breath coming in short wheezes when he caught up with me. I giggled at his struggle. His arms landed on his knees as he bent over, searching for his lost breath. Standing back up, he rubbed a sore spot on his chest. He shook his head and suppressed more chuckles as he berated me.

"I'm too old for this."

I patted him on the back with a grin. "Only trying to keep you young, Pop."

"You're a menace."

I giggled once more, putting my hands up in surrender.

"Okay, fine. We can walk. I'm just excited—I've only been to town a few times. Nan never lets me do anything fun."

428

He gave me a playful shove. "She's only trying to keep you safe."

"I know…" I sighed, and we continued on the path toward town. Cedar Hill sprawled out in front of us a short while later. Pop and I carried supplies in the bags on our backs—identical bows slung across our chests. Vendors crowded Main Street in the heat of the summer afternoon. People bartered for goods everywhere you looked. The town was brimming with people today. It was fascinating—I had never seen this many people in Cedar Hill before.

"Stay close," Pop whispered out of the side of his mouth as we entered the throng.

I stood by Pop, observing people pass as he traded the goods out of our packs for others—talking to people and knowing the right things to say to ensure a fair trade. I had watched him many times and never could figure out how he did it. Townsfolk glanced at me and turned up their noses as they passed, making me duck my head in embarrassment.

We stepped up to the booth of a man I was familiar with. Pop traded with him often. He had bushels of wheat laid out in front of him. His name was Miles, from what I could remember. Pop always did the talking, and I stayed hidden behind him, avoiding conversation—it was no different today.

"Good to see you again, Henry." The dark-haired man's voice rumbled from where he sat.

"Miles." Pop gave him a customary nod, and I peeked around his back.

"I see you brought your daughter with you today. Ash, is it?" Miles gave me a nod, as well.

Pop's face lifted in a pleasant smile.

"Yes, I could barely keep up with her on the way here."

Miles chuckled, his green eyes flashing in the sunshine.

"You're doing well, then? Staying safe up there all by yourselves?" Miles looked me over in my place beside Pop, and my adoptive father gave him a thoughtful gaze.

"You know, you're the only one that ever asks me that."

Something glinted in his eyes, and he blinked it away.

"Just bein' neighborly, friend."

"I appreciate it. We're doing well."

Miles was the closest thing that Pop had to a friend. I recalled them going fishing together a few years back.

"And Jo?"

"As stubborn as ever." Sweat beaded down Pop's smiling face as he thought about Nan.

Miles looked at me again and inclined his head.

"Teaching your daughter to hunt?" He took notice of my bow.

Pop scratched his head. "I don't know about that. She's already better than I am."

A smug smile pulled at the corners of my mouth and both men chuckled.

"What do you need today, Henry?" Miles asked, shifting the conversation.

The men traded, and the conversation bored me. I turned and watched the people around me once more. Pop knocked into me with his hip, pulling me back.

"Why don't you go get yourself a treat while I finish up here?" I straightened in excitement, and he handed me a small sack of potatoes to trade.

"Thanks, Pop." The words rushed out of my mouth and I gave him a side hug and hurried off to find something to buy.

"Don't be gone too long," he called warily from behind me. It was maybe only my fifth trip to town, and Pop had never let me go on my own before.

I strolled through the vendors, looking for something that caught my eye. My long brown braid swished against the top of my pants. At fifteen years old, I had grown tall and my clothes didn't fit as well as they used to. Someone would probably mistake me for a boy if it wasn't for my hair.

Something sweet floated through the air and into my nose, making me salivate. A cart with heaps of berries on it hid behind the popular vendors. I snuck through the crowd and up to the woman behind the cart. She wore an apron and stirred a fresh pitcher of some sort of drink with sugar and blackberries.

"Can I have a cup, please?" I asked. It was the first time I had ever bartered with anyone and my voice trembled with nerves.

"What do ya got?" Her voice had a harsher accent than most.

I held up my bag of three potatoes.

She nodded and poured me some juice in a wooden cup. Handing her the potatoes, I carefully took my cup from her hands.

"Usually I'd make you bring the cup back, but it looks like you could use it more than me."

I blanched as she turned away to serve another customer. What was that supposed to mean? Was I really that homely looking?

A commotion started down the street. People murmured in unrest as a pack of soldiers cut through the crowd. Their black clothes contrasted in the bright sun. Black caps protected their heads from the sun. Guns were attached to the hip of each soldier and some carried two weapons holstered on their chests. Each wore a blue band around their arm—the insignia of the king's men.

The crowd parted for them as they walked down the street. They were coming this way. My body jolted in terror at the sight of them. Frozen in fear, I watched as they came closer. Through the gaps in the front soldiers, I caught sight of what was behind them.

A man with blonde hair and large ears got pushed by another pack of soldiers behind him. Harsh chains covered his wrists and ankles, causing him to shuffle—his head bowed in defeat. The men passed by, and I did my best to sink back into the crowd. With a suddenness that surprised me, the leader halted the convoy. He stepped inside The Market building and disappeared.

The man with blonde hair stood not far away, his head slumped in front of him. Soldiers stood scanning the street as they waited for orders. People halted their activities, waiting in silence for what would happen next. Getting more nervous by the second, I took another step backward and bumped into the lemonade cart. The cart jostled from the impact, causing the woman to glare at me.

The blonde man's head whipped up at the sound. His eyes found me in an instant. They were bloodshot and full of pain. I gasped in shock at the resignation on his face. He looked me over for a minute before mouthing words that would haunt me forever.

"Run," he said in a soundless voice. There was no mistaking the word.

Breathing hard with panic, I forced myself to keep backing away slowly, the cup still clutched in my hand. No more attention needed to be drawn to me. When my back hit the wall of the building, I eased my way along it until I reached the corner. The soldiers were now out of earshot. I blew out a breath and turned around the corner, looking back to make sure no one was watching.

A wall of muscle slammed into my front side. Sweet blackberry juice splashed down my shirt before I even got to take a sip. The sticky concoction dripped onto the offending person's boots. I jerked my eyes up to see who it was, but before I knew what was happening, the person's hands grabbed onto my shoulders and pulled me the rest of the way around the corner.

Frightened by the move, I dropped my cup and reached for the knife strapped to my thigh, unable to get to my bow around my chest quick enough. I yanked it out and pointed it at the boy, who released his grip on my arms. He looked older than me and his face reminded me of someone that I couldn't place. He had dark hair and tanned skin. The clothes he wore fit and didn't have any holes like mine. I noticed the absence of any weapons on his person. He met my eyes, and they were full of concern.

I narrowed my eyes at him. What did he want? I had never seen him before. His face lifted into a huge grin as he looked at the knife in my hand. His white teeth glinted in the sunshine. With raised arms in surrender, he chuckled.

"Calm down. I was only trying to get you away from the soldiers."

My eyes roamed over him in question for a few moments before I decided he was okay. I slid my knife back into its sheath at my thigh.

"Thanks a lot," I said, wiping at my gray shirt that was now a shade darker. "I wanted to drink that, not wear it."

His eyebrows furrowed in apology.

"Sorry about that. You came around the corner so fast."

I rolled my eyes and turned to walk away—I needed to get back to Pop.

"Wait."

His words pulled me to a stop, and I turned—looking back at him to see what he wanted. It was rare that anybody wanted to talk to me in this town.

"I'm Diesel. I don't think we've met before."

"Nice to meet you, Diesel." I tried to be civilized, like Nan and Pop always taught me. This might be my first actual conversation with anyone other than Nan and Pop. The muscle wall, named Diesel, stepped in front of me once more as I tried to make my escape.

"You know, it's polite to share your name in return when meeting someone for the first time."

The smirk on his face made my lips tug up into a grin. I liked him already.

"Ash."

His eyes widened in shock for a millisecond before it was gone.

"Well, Ash. Since I so rudely spilled your lemonade all over you, could I buy you another one?"

I mulled it over for a moment before I answered.

"No thanks, I don't want to go back out there with the goons in town. I was about to go find my dad. He's probably worried."

Calling Pop my dad sounded strange. He had always been Pop to me, but he was also the only dad I'd ever known.

"Can I at least walk with you to make sure you find him?"

His expression was full of sincerity, and I think he felt bad for dumping juice all over me.

"Sure," I said with a shrug—for some reason, I didn't mind his presence.

We turned and walked to the back of the building and down a side street to where I last saw Pop with Miles. There were no soldiers clogging up this part of town—for that, I was thankful. Pop still haggled with Miles as we approached. He saw me and his eyes lit in relief, then my wet shirt caught his eye.

"What happened to you?" he laughed. Diesel stepped up next to me and Pop's face hardened. "Who's this?" he asked through pursed lips.

"Diesel," Mile's voice sounded from behind Pop, surprising us all.

He stood and stepped around Pop to see the boy standing next to me. They stared at each other for a long moment before Miles cleared his throat.

"Henry, this is my son... Diesel. Diesel, this is Henry Evans."

His appearance, which I couldn't place earlier, clicked into place. They both had the same dark hair and green eyes. Diesel's were a lighter shade and bright against his tanned skin.

"I didn't know you had a son," Pop sounded puzzled.

Miles nodded.

"I don't get out much," Diesel joked.

"He so kindly spilled my drink all over my shirt," I said, glancing down at the sticky mess. Miles looked at me like he'd never heard me speak before—most likely because he hadn't.

Diesel seemed embarrassed as he ran his hand through his hair. Just then, more commotion came from where we left the soldiers. We all turned our heads to investigate.

"Soldiers," I whispered to Pop, who hadn't seen them yet. He shot me an urgent expression.

"Well, it was good to see you, Miles." He shook the man's hand and inclined his head to Diesel. "And good to meet you, son. We better be going."

We took our things, and I shot Diesel one last look. He smirked at me, and I smiled right back. We left and skirted around the soldiers on our way back to the cabin.

CHAPTER 1
ASH

ALMOST FIVE YEARS LATER

Winter whispered through the pines, and the cold nipped at my fingertips. Spring was on the verge of blooming, and I couldn't wait for the warmer weather. The leftover snow made for wet and treacherous walking as I worked my way across the terrain. *Ugh, I hate the snow.* I had on a large winter coat and my customary wool stocking cap today. Winters in the mountainous north were harsh and unforgiving, requiring several layers of clothing. I gripped my bow in my hand with my quiver slung across the pack on my back.

The bit of morning sunshine that glowed through the pines today brought a blessed break from the overcast days. Birds were cackling in the trees overhead; a sure sign that spring was imminent. The creek that ran by our cabin wasn't overflowing with runoff yet, meaning we still had a few more weeks of cold to endure.

Trekking through the meadow below that cabin, I jumped over a narrowing in the creek without getting wet. The hillside opposite the cabin held deeper drifts. My knees brushed through the snow as I walked. Every step was a monumental effort with the snow this deep. It was melting, but there were spots that were still knee deep in wet, heavy snow. The southern-facing slopes were easier to navigate thanks to the sun's afternoon heat. I used them to my advantage. Snow crunching under my boots and heavy breaths of exertion were the only noises filling the brisk morning air.

I had seen the elk yesterday, when scouting for more rabbits to get us through the winter. Another reason to hate the cold months—the hunger pangs that were a constant companion. Tracking down rabbits had been my number one priority all winter, to get us through until the big game migrated back for the summer. I practically jumped for joy when I spotted the large elk herd weaving through the high mountain terrain yesterday.

The elk were back, or at least, a herd was migrating through the area—maybe spring would come quicker than I thought.

As I made a slow pace up the mountain, the pines faded into sagebrush along the slope. I grabbed a handful of sage and crushed it in my hand, only to bring it to my nose and take a deep breath of the earthy scent. It smelled like home and freedom from long winter days in the cabin. Brush mountainsides made for better rabbit hunting, but that wasn't my target today.

I left Nan alone back at the cabin early this morning. No one was around to help us anymore—it was only Nan and me.

Cedar Hill was an hour's walk west of our cabin. It was the closest civilization. There weren't many people, but enough to call it a town. Nan and I traded supplies there throughout the year.

We joined in on town celebrations and made the trip often during the summer to trade, fish, or for Nan to visit her friend. She told me I needed to stay as far away from people as possible, but living out here got lonely, so she made exceptions. I hadn't spoken to anyone other than Nan in months. The long walk through the snow to get to town was difficult on Nan's knee during the winter. For the last couple of months in the cabin, I had been content to stay put. Though, I didn't know which was worse: stuck in a dank cabin all winter or freezing to death out in the snow. At least out in the snow, the sky was visible.

As I picked my way along yet another hillside, movement caught in the corner of my eye. I drew my bow, but it was only an owl settling into a distant pine. I studied the majestic creature for a minute, but something behind the tree caught my attention. On a distant mountain, an unnaturally dark, straight line of creatures moved through the landscape. There was only one species of animal around that moved like that.

Elk. Exactly where I thought they would go, after I spotted them yesterday.

Hope and excitement burned in my chest. I moved in their direction to get a better view. I wasn't prepared for a large hunt when I saw them yesterday, with only the bare minimum of supplies in my pack. I watched them for as long as I could last night before returning to the cabin to pack my things, then I was off this morning.

Breathing hard, heart pounding from the labor of walking through the snow, I climbed up the ridge to see if their course was obvious. I knew these mountains like the back of my hand. Growing up out here with Pop and spending hours alone in these woods had served me well.

When I crested the top of the ridge, the vantage point allowed me to see which direction the distant brown specks traveled. There was another creek that ran down the valley they were meandering toward. I knew from experience that the elk often bedded down in that spot. I continued stalking toward them until I peeked over the ridge where they had disappeared.

No elk were visible at first glance, but they could have been lying under the pines—unlikely. My eyes hadn't failed me yet. I snuck down the slope and into the creek bed—signs were everywhere that they had been there recently. The musky scent of elk lingered in the pines—fresh poop and tracks muddied the area, but they left, which surprised me. There was fresh water here, and the snow had melted off in the meadow, leaving good grass underneath. It looked like something scared them, but the only tracks visible were elk. I wasn't sure what it was, but I hoped it was nothing that wanted to kill me.

The tracks wound along the creek and onto a side hill. Following the tracks was as simple as breathing. It was a large herd of about two hundred head, and snow was still on the ground—that many elk through the snow were not too hard to track.

The cover of the trees hid my presence as I followed. Close to where the tracks left the trees, the elk lay on the hillside in the thick brush for the night. The one closest to me twitched its ears, and it swung its head in my direction. The stillness of my body could rival an elk at that moment. It eventually decided no threat was around and turned away from me once more.

The temperature was plummeting, and my nose and feet ached with cold. My old hunting boots did little to keep the cold at bay and held too many holes. They were okay when I was moving and my blood was pumping, but sitting for so long had left my feet vulnerable to the cold.

The sun was getting low, and the world would be dark soon. Traveling in the woods at night had never bothered me as long as I was moving; but with the elk back, it meant the wolves would follow. They might even be here already, following the herd. A shiver raced down my spine at the thought. Predators had grown more aggressive over the years. Without guns, animal attacks grew deadly. The animals knew it too, and were more aggressive than ever—but it was either kill or be killed in the woods. There were no other options.

I didn't enjoy the killing. The thrill of the chase and outwitting the animal was the part I loved. Letting the arrow fly and killing wore on me, but there wasn't room for weakness out here.

Always make the most efficient kill. Pop's words rang in my head. *Lessen the animals' suffering as much as possible—they are giving their lives to us. The least we can do is make it quick and painless.* Advice that sank into my heart. I picked up shooting with a bow easily. Pop built me targets, and it didn't take long for me to hit the center every time without fail. Then he took me on my first hunting trip when I was ten—much to Nan's dismay. Spotting the game from a distance was easy, and I always did it quicker than Pop ever could. He said I had a gift for it. That was a memory I would always cherish. Pop taught me everything about being out in the woods, hunting, and surviving.

He believed in me more than I believed in myself most of the time. He taught me enough to keep me and Nan alive when he died in his sleep five years ago.

Pop was a man bigger than life—always telling me about his ideas for a better country. He didn't let the current state of the world get him down. Working hard alongside Nan all his life, he loved her with all he had. His smile was contagious—I couldn't help but smile anytime he was around. My fondest memories all involved him and Nan.

Nan thought that his heart gave out. Though we would never know for sure, it broke me and Nan. We buried him down in the meadow below the cabin on a cool, fall morning, sitting with him for hours, hoping it wasn't real—that he wasn't gone. Unfortunately, fall turned to winter, and we trudged on without him. Nan was so broken for so long. That was the darkest winter I could remember. I felt hopeless through the long winter days and nights, but sometimes life was just like that. A blur of days and nights where every day brings you closer to death, but you're not really living, you simply exist.

When spring came, my determination to keep us alive turned resolute—I would replace Pop. Since that day when I was fifteen, Nan had been my sole purpose. She tried to come hunting with me—worried about me out there by myself, as she still was—but she couldn't make it too long on her knee. Not to mention, she had no clue what she was doing. She stumbled through the brush like an ogre. We came to agree that it was better for me to go alone.

I owe everything to Nan and Pop. They raised me and taught me how to be brave and work hard. My adventurous spirit had been prone to wander when I was young; but when Pop died, my dedication turned to my family. I became less of the wild girl

I once was and more of a girl driven by obligation. Hunting and exploring unknown parts of the woods was what I loved the most. The thrill of the chase and finding something new was what kept me going. Taking care of Nan brought me joy, but I felt part of me was missing.

Nan and Pop both grew up in Cedar Hill and got married when they were young. Pop went hunting one day when a thunderstorm rolled in. He got lost and stumbled upon an old hunting cabin, left behind when the world got thrust back into ancient times. The cabin wasn't enormous, but it was perfect for them. They decided they should move into it and start a family. Unfortunately, they could never have children. They were happy, though—they had each other.

Until a little girl came stumbling into their lives.

I didn't know where I came from or who my parents were. I wasn't even sure of my actual age. All I had ever known was Nan and Pop and the little cabin.

Pop was on a hunting trip one day when he came across me in the woods. He said I was all alone, hiding under a tree. He searched the woods but couldn't find any trace of anyone else. I was dirty and someone had shaved my head. Pop said I clutched onto Nan and wouldn't let go when he returned. I didn't speak for a long time or even remember my name. Nan thought I went through a trauma that wiped my memories—of course, I couldn't remember any of this. They guessed I was around four years old when they found me.

No one ever came looking for me. There was never any news of a lost child. They didn't know where I came from and neither did I. Part of me felt lost. I didn't even recall the truth of my real name. The only name I had ever known was the one that Nan and Pop gave me.

Ash.

They named me after the color of my hair—so blonde it danced on the edge of silver. It started growing back soon after I arrived here. They noticed the color and swore to protect me.

I shook the thoughts of Pop out of my head so I could focus on the task at hand. Dusk crept up from the horizon, dimming the light and hiding my form as I tiptoed away from the elk. The trick now was finding a place warm enough to stay for the night.

CHAPTER 2
ASH

My guess was the elk would stay there until morning and come down to get a drink from the creek once the new day broke. If my guess was wrong, then I would have to be out here longer, following them until I got a decent shot. Archery hunting took a lot of time, patience, and outguessing your prey. Elk were fast and sneaky; capable of disappearing without a trace. They lived up to their name—ghosts of the pines. One moment they were as loud as an earthquake, crashing through the timbers and the next were gone.

As I made my way back down the creek, I spotted thick willows that would provide suitable cover for the night. Building a fire crossed my mind, but with the elk as close as they were, the scent would spook them. My bedroll was a small, foam pad with an old sleeping bag covered in canvas. My bedroll scuffed against a patch of semi-dry grass under a tree where the snow hadn't reached, as I unrolled it. Willows surrounded the spot where my bed lay for the night. If anything came in the night, I could hear it coming through the bramble.

Thanks to whatever startled the elk out of the meadow earlier, I was further up Red Creek than I had ever been. Darkness descended on the world as my backside found the soft bed. Tonight, a full moon lit the sky, and visibility was high. I had always seen well at night, even with no moon in sight, and inky blackness thicker than the shadows.

The jerky we saved for hunting trips from my pack required a lot of chewing. The silence out here was peaceful, besides the obnoxious sound of my teeth mashing together. Nights were bad out in the woods—I had a hard time sleeping, and every sound made me jump.

After a while, my jaw hurt, and I gave up on my dinner with a sigh. The cold air licked my skin, sending shivers down my spine. I could endure it for tonight... it was something I was good at—enduring. The only problem was my boots and socks were damp from today's hike and I didn't have a fire to dry them.

My boots came off easily, but my socks required tugging to release from my damp feet. The extra pair of dry socks I pulled from my bag felt heavenly against my soggy skin—at least we had a few extra pairs of socks. Nan taught me to stay grateful for what we did have. *If you complain, you will only find more things to complain about. If you find things to be grateful for, well, you'll see life a little differently.* They were words I remembered well after whining to Nan about not having any friends when I was younger.

I turned my boots upside down on a nearby log, hoping they would dry by morning. Crawling into my bedroll with my hat pulled all the way down, I settled in for the night. The only part of me that stuck out was my nose. The thought of covering it up made me feel like I would die of suffocation.

Why did nights in the forest feel like they would never end? Filled with hours of tossing, turning, and listening to the sounds of the night, tonight was no different. As I lay in bed, my body was bone-tired, but my mind was alive. Stories Nan shared over the years drifted through my mind, keeping me from the dark abyss of sleep.

The only form of education I received was from Nan. She taught me to read from old books that were left in the cabin and the few she brought when they moved from town. I could read and write well enough to get by, but most of my time was outdoors learning the basics of survival.

History lessons were also courtesy of Nan and Pop. They shared stories passed down from their parents. I had also learned a great deal from whispers in town. The world was a messed-up place. According to my adoptive parents, life was very different before it all went to hell.

Living was once a lot easier. Nan had mentioned something about lights that didn't require fire or burning candles and water running through pipes into houses—probably only a myth. Food was once readily available and little work was required to obtain it, but that was years and years ago. I wasn't even sure I believed the stories based on the world we lived in now.

A nasty virus broke out that brought the country to its knees. The sickness took millions of lives. No one nowadays knew what it was called or what happened when people got it, only that the death rate was astronomical. The virus wiped out the population in no time, forcing the world back into the dark ages.

The virus affected blonde people more. No one quite knew why the disease took so many blonde lives, but it almost wiped all of them off the face of the Earth. Something about mutated DNA, or so the rumors went.

Life changed. People had to learn to hunt and farm for their food again because everything that the country once was, had been destroyed. It baffled me that anyone wouldn't know how to do these simple tasks. What did they do all day if they weren't fighting for survival?

We lived in the northern part of a country whose name had been long forgotten. As far as I knew, the country was dotted with small towns like Cedar Hill, trying to survive. We didn't know much about anything outside of our small town.

A city popped up at the time of the outbreak—called the City of Hope. It was the new government for the new world. It was weeks of travel to the south of where we lived. Hope took claim over the continent that we lived on, the people in charge asserting it as the capital city. According to legend, messengers went out, telling any blonde person they could find that was still alive to get to Hope. Claims spread that they would help them.

In a state of panic, blondes everywhere rushed to the city. An ex-soldier, named Titus Etan, infiltrated the group that led the city. Rumor was that he killed all the past leaders before coming to power and pronouncing himself King of the new world, and everyone was too afraid to defy him. He called his new kingdom Novum, giving the country a new name, and discarding the long-forgotten one. Soldiers were recruited, new laws written, and the continent changed forever.

No one really knew what happened in Hope after that, but we knew Titus contracted the virus soon after gaining power and died. His second in command, Leon Broderick, took over. He was power-hungry and cruel. King Leon put a bounty on anyone who was blonde. He promised that anyone who brought one in would be fed, safe, and wealthy for the rest of their life. Bounty hunters flocked the country, seeking strongholds of blonde people who didn't fall victim to the virus.

The virus was wiped off the land nowadays. Anybody who was still alive had an immunity to it. Years later, we still had bounty hunters that roamed the country looking for blondes. The current King of Novum, Maximus, was a descendant of the original King Leon. I guess evil existed in one's blood, though, because Maximus was as bad as Leon. He kept rewards for blonde people high. His soldiers scoured the country, enforcing laws where they saw fit and doing the King's dirty work.

Blonde people were a novelty, or at least that was my theory. No one knew why the King wanted them so badly. My friend Marva had some wild theories about it; all I knew was blondes were as valuable as the last bit of hot tea on a cold morning. Everyone wanted a taste, but there were so few of them anymore, the truth was hard to find. That was why I had to stay hidden. The news would spread of a blonde in Cedar Hill, drawing in bounty hunters and soldiers alike.

Nan concocted a natural hair dye when they first found me to cover up my silver-blonde hair. It was full of charcoal and oak bark. It turned my hair into a dark brown color, but it only lasted for about two weeks if I didn't get it wet before the blonde showed back through again. We had tried several formulas over the years to get the dye to stay longer, but my hair just wouldn't hold it. Thankfully, my eyebrows and eyelashes were naturally dark, and there was no need to keep them dyed. Small miracles, I guess.

There might be more people out there, like me, that dye their hair, but it was hard to say.

Nan was religious about dying my hair every two weeks—I hated it. The smell was awful, and it burned my head. It surprised me that Nan had let it go this long without dye. It was a blessed break to let my hair be free for a couple of months.

The only people who knew about my hair were Nan and Pop. No one else could ever know, as long as they were still hunting for people like me.

I was always careful about only going to town right after it had been dyed, and I only had one friend who would look close enough to notice.

Thinking about my best friend brought a smile to my face.

Diesel. Five years older than me and one of the few people that dwarfed me with his size; a good six inches taller than me, with a hundred more pounds of muscle. Dark hair covered his head like everyone else, and stunning light green eyes adorned his face. Eyes a person could get lost in—not that we had ever been more than friends. I feared he saw me more as an annoying little sister than anything else.

I remembered the day we met in town, right before Pop died. He had always been there for me after that day. Diesel helped me through a lot of things in the days after Pop's passing—he was a good friend.

We hunted or fished together often, and he was always at the cabin checking on me and Nan. I hadn't seen him since the snow hit—probably the longest I had ever gone without him. I realized I missed my friend quite a lot.

Diesel lived on the opposite side of town, a short distance out. He and his dad moved into an abandoned house around the same time that Pop found me. He said that they were farmers from the South but left because the hunting and farming weren't very good. We never talked about where they came from much.

Happy thoughts of Diesel floated through my head— calming me enough to drift off to sleep.

CHAPTER 3
ASH

I got out of bed long before sunrise with my head groggy and sleep deprived. Crisp water flowed past my lips as I drank, hoping it would clear my head. The hunt required sharpness that my sleepless brain didn't possess at the moment.

My boots were still wet, with no hope of drying soon. At least my socks were dry, but the water would seep through soon enough. *Get tough or die.* Thanks, Pop, I needed the encouragement this morning. My stomach grumbled, and I ignored it for the millionth time. I rolled my bedroll and left it where I slept. I would come back for it later. It didn't serve me for it to be catching on every twig as I went through the brush.

Darkness laid over the pines like a thick blanket when I set out after the elk, thankful for the full moon and my above-average vision—I could pick my way through the trees without a problem. My footfalls were slow and measured. One snapping branch could scare the beasts into next week. Just as I came back to the spot where the elk were hours earlier, the first rays of light broke through the darkness. The elk were easy to spy in the dim light: still lying on the side hill where I left them.

I crouched down and waited for them to move. The first elk stood and shook its tan, furry coat. It was a cow from the look of it, but it was difficult to tell the difference this time of year, as the bulls shed their antlers in the winter. They were still there—great news. I stashed my pack under a bush, leaving me with my bow and the knives that were strapped to my body.

Still in a crouch, I snuck forward—hunting was like a game full of moves and countermoves. Now, I waited for the elk to make the next move.

As it got lighter, they continued to stand up, one by one. The brown beasts were too focused on picking through the foliage on the side of the hill to notice me.

Movement on the top of the ridge above them startled me. Squinting my eyes, I saw a figure low to the ground that moved with ease through the brush. *Please, not a wolf. Please, not a wolf.* The elk seemed oblivious to the intruder. They continued to meander down toward the creek and where I took my position. Perfect. Now it was my turn to make a move, but I was still worried about the dark presence behind the herd.

I glanced back up at the intruder and the light glinted off the skin of the man's face. A person—not a wolf—thank the heavens, though a man might not have been much better.

Another hunter like me, making his way down through the brush on hands and knees toward the elk, oblivious to my presence. My anger skyrocketed. What was he doing? He would scare them all away, and neither of us would get a shot.

Someone interfering with my hunt was not part of the plan today. Not to mention the elk moved away from him and little hope remained of him catching them from behind.

From my vantage point by the creek, I guessed that the lead cow would make it to me before he snuck up on the stragglers.

Good. Rage simmered in my blood, warming my frozen fingers. Food for me and Nan could be gone because of this stranger. With one last angry glance at him, I shoved the stranger from my mind and positioned myself to take a smart shot. The lead cow continued her path toward the creek not far away, taking cautious, silent steps.

The thin breeze filtered into my face, meaning she wouldn't smell my royal stink. She picked her way through the brush, stopping, eating, and sniffing every few feet. My body stiffened with stillness from my position next to a bush. In the last few steps before the creek, she turned her head away from me to look at the herd behind her. I took a split second to draw my bow before she turned back around.

She made it to the creek and put her head down to get a drink. This was my chance—there was nothing at that moment but me, my bow, and my target. I cleared my head and took a deep breath to clear the burning anger from my lungs. As the breath left my mouth, I took my shot. She stepped right as the arrow flew from my hand. Anticipating the movement perfectly, like I could see exactly what would happen—I watched my arrow stick in her heart.

CHAPTER 4
ASH

The elk lunged over the creek in a swift, graceless movement. She vanished into the brush on the opposite side—snapping branches and diving through the thickets as she went. I strained my ears to hear until no more sounds came. All the other elk scattered at the commotion, bolting across the hillside, away from me and the intruder. I stood up out of the bush and glanced at the stranger on the hill. He stood and stared off after the elk, seemingly wondering what happened. The corner of my mouth lifted at his despondent posture—served him right. He swung his head around and I felt his eyes on me. I swore internally. I should have left before he saw me. The only noticeable distinction about him was a long, dark beard as the sun peeked over the hill, forming a halo around the man's hulking form—but I could tell a very large, angry man when I saw one.

I needed to get out of there, pronto. With hurried steps, I raced to grab my pack stowed under the bush. The creek was just wide enough that it caught the toe of my boot when I jumped over, following the elk's steps.

If I was lucky, the man wouldn't come after me—unlikely. Maybe it was stupidity, but I wouldn't leave my elk to get away from him. I was growing tired of always hiding in fear. We needed this, and it was my hunt that he interfered with. Thoughts of Nan's words about avoiding strangers popped into my mind and a twinge of guilt hit me. My brain told me to run, but my stupid heart had better ideas.

The redness of the blood trail stood out like a fire in a dark forest against the snow patches that hadn't melted yet. I broke a branch and dragged it behind me, but could still see the crimson against the white snow. That wouldn't do any good—I dropped the branch and hurried on, forgetting the idea.

Annoyance and anger churned in my gut as I moved. It didn't bode well for me, being a woman out here alone with a man hot on my heels. I would stick an arrow through his leg if it came down to that. I could place an arrow well enough to know where to wound him enough that he couldn't follow me. He might die out here without help, but that wasn't my problem.

The elk made her way to the opposite side of the creek bed and then turned back toward where I stored my bedroll last night. Normally, I would wait for thirty minutes to an hour before I followed, just to give it time to die and not run off further. A wounded elk would probably find somewhere to hide and lie down until it died, but if something startled it, it could get up and run, wounded, for a great distance.

I felt confident that I had made a clean shot through the heart, and she died quickly. The trail led me to a thicket of willows—an apparent path unmistakable, right through the center. Willows caught my clothing as I waded through them on the trail. They cleared up on the other side of the thicket and the tan beast lay in a heap amongst the snow. Excitement surged in my chest at the prospect of fresh meat.

Making quick work with my knife, I sliced her throat to make sure the blood drained out. Red spilled out over the ground and it broke my heart a little. I gritted my teeth and kept working— no room for weakness. The sleeves of my coat scrunched up my arms as I got to work, dressing the carcass as I had done too many times to count.

I had barely finished pulling the guts out when a noise came from the brush. I knew exactly what or who the noise came from. Expecting it, my weapons were ready. Taking my bow and knife, I ran to the nearest tree and crouched down to hide.

Back toward the tree with my bow ready in front of me, I waited.

Thwack! An arrow ripped through the air and lodged in a tree close to my head.

I let out a string of silent curses.

"Why don't you show your face so I can stick an arrow through it," growled the man from the opposite side of the open area.

Relief washed over me, and my mouth twitched with a smile behind the tree. I would know that voice anywhere.

"Diesel, is that you?" I yelled through my chuckles.

"Ash?" Surprise and wariness battled in his voice.

I rose and spotted him in a millisecond, standing a few feet from my kill. An arrow careened right between his legs from my bow.

"That's for shooting at me."

A huge smile broke out on his face, and he charged toward me. I dropped my bow just in time for him to scoop me up in his arms in a giant bear hug. His enormous arms held me tight, and I stuck my nose into his neck, breathing him in, while giggling with excitement.

He set me back on my feet and leaned back to look at me. His arms stayed around me, and he squished me to his chest, squeezing the air out of my lungs.

"It's so good to see you, Ash," he said in a husky voice. He leaned his forehead down to mine.

"I missed you too." My voice came out much breathier than usual, with a slight tremor. The adrenaline of the hunt and the relief of seeing Diesel instead of someone else took its toll on my body. This much physical contact with him surprised me, but I didn't hate it.

He looked different. His face had sharper edges to it, like he had been grinding his teeth a lot and frowning. He had grown his beard out, and I imagined his dark brown hair was longer than usual underneath his hat. He had lost weight over the winter and gained more muscle, if that was even possible.

"Can't... breathe... D." I laughed, shoving him off me.

He released his hold, but grabbed my upper arms with his meaty hands. All the joy and relief bled out of his green eyes and was replaced with anger, concern, and something I couldn't place.

"What the hell were you thinking? What if that wasn't me? I almost shot you, Ash!" His patronizing tone made me roll my eyes. I adjusted my hat to make sure none of my hair spilled out.

"You didn't even know where I was, D. I had the drop on you," I said, not even convincing myself. "I would've been fine."

"Did you see me after them this morning? Did you know someone else was there?"

A lie almost slipped out of me, but he knew me too well. I looked away. "Of course I saw you, and it made me burning mad that you were messing up my hunt. So, I thought I would shoot first and ask questions later."

I went to walk past him and back to the elk when he reached out and grabbed my arm, turning me back into him.

"Ash," he said, too quiet. "Do you know how dangerous that was? I don't even want to think about what would have happened if that were anyone other than me." The worry and anger I saw on his face sliced through me.

"I was planning on sticking an arrow through your knee if you came after me; figured it would slow you down enough that you wouldn't bother me—if talking didn't help."

He scrubbed his hand over his face, closed his eyes, and put his fingers to his temples like I had given him a headache. I rolled my eyes and moved away. Diesel had always been protective. Sometimes, to the point of making me feel incapable of taking care of myself. I wasn't the little girl who came crying to him after Pop died anymore. I wish he could see that.

"And what were you planning on doing if it wasn't me who shot the elk?" I crossed my arms and gave him a look.

He glared but didn't answer, and I was afraid I didn't want to hear the answer, anyway. He'd come after me for a reason, and I didn't think it was to talk.

"If you see anyone out here when you are by yourself, you turn around and run in the other direction. I don't care if you are after the last deer on the continent. A piece of meat is not worth risking your life over, Ash."

My body turned to take him in once more.

"There are bad people out there; people that will hurt you if they get the chance. Don't give them that chance... please."

"Okay," I relented. "I'll be more careful."

"Thank you. I can't lose you too." He took a step closer.

I searched his eyes again. A deeper sadness haunted his gaze—that wasn't there before. I could see it in the deeper lines and sunken cheeks.

"What happened?"

The forest seemed to grow quieter as it waited for his response. He looked up at me and the pain in his eyes gutted me. We stood close enough again that we were almost touching.

"My dad died right after the first snowfall," he choked out.

"No, D." I wrapped him up in another hug.

He never knew his mom. It was always him and Miles against the world.

"I'm sorry. I didn't know."

We stayed clutched together for a few long moments.

"What happened?" I asked, my words muffled through his coat.

"He got sick last fall. I thought it was only a cold and that he would get over it, but then the temperature dropped, and it came back with a vengeance. He started lying down inside more often than he was up—coughing all the time. Eventually, he started coughing up blood. I went to town to find Anne to see if she could come look at him. She hiked out to the house, and I knew the minute she looked at him it wasn't good. She told me she thought he had pneumonia and there wasn't anything she could do to help him. He died that night, after she left." I could barely hear the last part when he finished.

Tears threatened to leak from my eyes at his broken words. "I'm so sorry Diesel. I know how much it hurts. I wish you didn't have to go through that by yourself."

I didn't know Miles well, but Diesel talked about him often. "So, you've been by yourself all winter?" I asked.

He gave a slight nod.

"You could have come to the cabin, so you weren't by yourself. I know it's a long walk, but I wish you would have come, so you weren't alone."

At that, he hardened up like nothing bothered him and his face went blank.

"I'm fine, Ash. It was a rough winter, but I got through it." He turned away from me.

I didn't understand why the sudden coldness. I was chewing it over when he said, "That's where I was going when I came across the elk."

"You were coming to our cabin?"

"I was coming to check on the elusive Ash Evans. Haven't seen you in so long—I was getting worried."

"It's been a long winter and with all the snow, I didn't feel like hiking through it to go to town."

"Is Nan alright?"

"As lively as ever." I smiled, thinking of her. "Just worried about me, as usual."

"She should be. You like to catch the attention and tempers of strange men in the woods."

I laughed. "Shut up. I could have taken you out if I wanted to."

Now we were both laughing again. It was refreshing after the earlier conversation. Miles's death was hard and wouldn't be forgotten anytime soon, but it was only another of many deaths—after a while, your heart became slightly numb to such things, but it was the reality of the life we lived. Death was like a beast in hiding, rearing its ugly head whenever it saw fit. It came without warning, stealing the people you loved most. No one wanted to acknowledge how much it took from them, because if they didn't acknowledge it… maybe the life we lived wasn't so bad.

Diesel's presence was indeed convenient—like my personal pack mule. If it wasn't for him, I would have had to stash the meat and come back for it later—in maybe two or three trips. I could pack a whole deer out by myself, but no way I could pack a whole elk. I even questioned if both of us could handle it.

I turned back to the elk. "I really am glad you're here. Now I don't have to pack all this meat out by myself."

With a grin, he asked, "How long have you been tracking them?"

"Went after them yesterday morning. I tracked them all day to that place where they like to stay back down the creek—but when I got there, it looked like something had spooked them out of there." I eyed him. "I guess that was you?"

"Yeah." He cringed. "That was me. I set out to come check on you two days ago. I was tromping across the hill yesterday trying to scare up a rabbit and wasn't paying much attention when an elk jumped up from under a pine. Didn't think they would be up here this time of year, so I wasn't trying to be quiet."

Diesel's hat shifted higher as he scratched his forehead, recalling the story.

"Anyway, I spooked them, and they didn't go as far as I thought they would. I knew I was in a bad spot this morning, but there was a yearling in the back with a broken leg. Thought maybe I could sneak up on it and put it out of its misery."

"That makes a lot more sense. I thought you were an idiot this morning for trying to sneak up behind them."

My laugh echoed through the clear, morning air, and he snapped a twig off a nearby branch and threw it at me.

"But I guess all of us can't be as excellent hunters as me." My teasing didn't bring a smile to his face like I thought it would.

"Says the girl who could have got killed or molested for putting herself in such a dangerous situation."

"Let it go," I said, exasperated. "I'm fine. It was you and I promised I would be more careful. Can we move past it now?"

"No," he growled. "I won't forget about how I almost shot you anytime soon."

"I'm not a little girl that you need to protect anymore, Diesel. I can take care of myself."

"I know you can take care of yourself, but that doesn't mean you should have to."

Did he see me as anything more than a little sister? Or his father's friend's daughter that he felt obligated to take care of?

"There aren't very many other choices out there for me, D."

"You and Nan could move closer to town. I'll help you out until you find...a husband to look after you." He glanced away.

Little sister. Definitely, little sister. Also, a husband?! Absolutely not. Especially none of the men around here— misogynistic pigs.

I shook my head. "We're fine. We love the cabin."

"Why do you live all the way out there still, anyway? There are plenty of empty houses around town. You don't have a man in the house anymore. It's not safe for you both to be out there so far."

There it was. The same thing he had told me multiple times before and the reason he came around so often.

"We are fine." I waved him off. "Nan doesn't want to leave the cabin." That may not have been the total truth. I think Nan would love to go live closer to her friend Anne, but her motherly instinct to protect me came first.

"Well—maybe I could come live with you and help out this summer. I don't have anyone else in town anymore, at least until…"

"Until, what?"

"Don't look at me like that. You and I both know that Nan is getting older. What are you going to do when…"

"Stop." I didn't want to talk about Nan dying. I couldn't even fathom the idea.

"I'm sorry, Ash. I just worry about you."

We were silent for a bit while we worked on the elk, blood staining my hands and forearms.

"I have thought about it, you know?" I said carefully.

Diesel's eyes met mine, inquiring further.

"About what I'll do after…" I didn't want to say it. Nan dying would be an insurmountable loss. "There is nothing in Cedar Hill for me. Maybe I could go find out who I really am. Maybe my parents are still alive, and I got lost or something." I left out the part about wanting to find more people like me— more blondes. If there were any more. Diesel knew enough about my backstory to know that I didn't have a clue who I really was.

"There's nothing for you in Cedar Hill?"

I didn't understand what he was trying to say. I didn't have any friends or family… except for… him. *Oh.*

I gave him a sad smile. "You have plenty of friends and you and Lily seemed close last fall. You won't even know that I'm gone." It was the truth, but me… I would miss him every day, and he would never see me the same way. His jaw flexed, and he attacked a piece of meat with savage force, hacking it away from the carcass.

"Just don't up and disappear on me one day, okay?"

"Okay."

CHAPTER 5
DIESEL

Why was Ash thinking about leaving? She had never mentioned it before. Little did she know, I'd never let that happen, not without me. I shoved my knife into the carcass a little too roughly to strip the meat from the bones so it would be lighter to carry.

Recalling the thoughts that raced through my head as I hunted her down through the willows made my stomach sour. I thought it was another man, another hunter. I had encountered plenty of other men out here while hunting, but never a woman. Ash was out here too much by herself, a situation I'd tried to remedy repeatedly to no avail. She wouldn't listen to anything I said.

She moved to wash some meat in the creek, and I couldn't help but stare. Ash was even more beautiful than I remembered. How'd she change so much over the course of one winter? I hadn't seen her since the snow fell and I had forgotten how much I liked spending time with her. She was different—in a good way. She wasn't afraid to get her hands dirty, not to mention she was the toughest woman that I'd ever met. Even at the end of this hellish winter, dressed in layers of clothing that were far too ugly and big for her, I couldn't take my eyes off her. Either she had grown more stunning, or my memory was dull. A new spark lit up my chest, something beyond the friendship we had shared over the last five years. It was a mistake to go all winter without checking on her. Even though I couldn't remember most of it, it was an oversight that I wouldn't let happen again.

I almost shot her this morning, the thought making me grimace again. I should have known it was her from the beginning. Not many people could outwit animals the way that Ash could. She was clever and ingenious about survival. I hated that she was out here alone; it wasn't safe.

We spent the rest of the day cutting up meat and sharing stories of the things that had happened to us over the winter.

We shoved our bags full the best we could and then used the skin to wrap up as much meat as we could, strapping it to the top of my pack. Ash tried to tell me she should carry it since it was her kill, but when she tried to pick up my pack, it nearly toppled her. I chuckled and picked it up, earning myself a glare. We had to leave some less desirable meat behind because there was no way we could carry anymore. The coyotes would clean it up soon enough.

We headed out and picked up Ash's bedroll where she had stashed it, continuing as far as we could until it got dark. We walked down Red Creek until we came to a branch where it ran down to two gullies. Something caught my eye further down a branch I had never followed before. "Look." I inclined my chin in that direction.

"Is that steam?" Ash asked, dumbfounded. White fog rose over the treetops, resting in the crook of the mountain.

"I think that's exactly what it is. Doesn't look like smoke."

We both looked at each other, smiling.

"Race ya," she called, taking off in the steam's direction. She dashed off into the underbrush and I smiled, following more slowly. She wasn't the one carrying hundreds of pounds of meat.

When the landscape opened into a clearing where the source of the steam originated from, Ash stood staring in front of her.

A small, rocky pool lay off to the side of the creek running by it. Steam billowed out of the clear blue depths as it dumped into the much colder creek. What luck, a natural hot pool. She walked over, crouched down, and stuck her hand in. "That feels like heaven," she sighed. "We're staying here tonight." Her lips turned up in a pleasant smile that took the breath out of my lungs. Suddenly, I imagined a future with her; I knew it was dangerous, but I couldn't help myself.

I dropped my pack with a large thud on the hard ground next to the pool where the snow had melted from the heat.

Ash's stomach growled loudly, and she clutched it like she was embarrassed. Had they not had enough food to eat this winter? I should have come sooner. I cursed my father in the grave for his untimely death and the hellish winter.

"Let's get something to eat before you get too many wild ideas," I said, gathering up any dry wood I could find. She helped me get the fire roaring next to the pool, the steam and orange flames warming our chilled limbs.

I grabbed a stick and threaded a tenderloin onto it from the top of my pack. "I think we deserve good meat after the day we've had."

"I think that sounds fantastic."

We took seats around the fire and tried to warm up as the sun fell below the crest of the mountain, taking any warmth with it. I noticed Ash staring at me as I concentrated on cooking the meat, lost in thought.

"So… How is Lily?" she snickered nervously. Guilt wormed its way into my chest, even though I had nothing to feel guilty about. She looked like she made herself more uncomfortable than me with the question by the way she squirmed.

"She's fine." I wasn't sure why she asked or what she wanted me to tell her.

Her face turned contemplative and slightly sad at my answer.

"Is that done yet? I'm starving."

I pulled the stick out of the fire and poked the meat with my finger. Then I took my knife and sliced it through the center. Satisfied it was cooked through, I took the bigger half and set it on a rock next to Ash, so it didn't burn her. She needed more food than I did.

She stabbed the meat with her knife and brought it to her lips. Her eyes closed when she took a bite, like it was the best thing she had tasted in months.

It was completely dark now, but the full moon beamed down like a comforting friend. The creek gurgled next to us, hissing where the hot water met the cold. An image played through my mind of Ash getting into the hot pool and I choked on the last bit of meat. She shot me a funny look as we both finished our dinner and continued to sit in silence and stare at the fire. The embers popped loudly, and I asked, "So, are you gonna take a bath, stinky?"

She looked up at me with narrowed eyes.

"I do not stink—that bad," she mumbled under her breath.

I covered my mouth with my hand to hide a laugh. "Whatever you say, Spitfire. My nose hairs are burned off just from our hug earlier." I hadn't called her that in quite some time, and it made her cringe. The nickname I gave her after we got into an argument about the best way to clean a fish and my stupid younger self told her she talked too much for a girl. She didn't speak to me for a whole week after that.

She grabbed a handful of nearby snow and hurled it at my

face. I ducked before it could smack me in the mouth and sat back up, grinning from ear to ear.

She glared at me with all the venom she could muster, trying not to laugh, and stood. Her angry face was adorable. "You're mean."

I swore her eyes glowed in the dark. They were bright enough you could see the blues clashing with the orange flames.

I stood up and seized her from behind in another hug. "You know, I'm only kidding. You smell like daisies," I snickered next to her ear. I was playing with fire and I knew it.

She tensed under my touch, and her breath quickened. Her hat slid up on her head from where my head touched hers. I leaned back slightly—my carefree smile instantly stalled like the echo of my heart coming to a standstill. I couldn't believe what I saw in the dim firelight and at that moment, I realized the two people I cared for the most had been lying to me all along.

CHAPTER 6
ASH

I'd known for a while that he had been with girls in town. Old Marva was the local town gossip and happened to be my other best friend, as well. She was a woman around Nan's age; the only person I talked to other than Diesel and Nan. It was where I learned all the gossip that spread around Cedar Hill when I was bored. She hung out in The Market—at least, that was what they called it. It was an old meeting building that was in the middle of town. It was where we went to trade for supplies. If you had something to trade, wait in The Market long enough—eventually, someone would come along with something worth trading for.

Lily's parents, the Smiths, owned and ran The Market. It was the local grocery store, bar, restaurant, and hotel, all rolled into one. There was a kitchen in the back part and extra rooms for Lily's family and for travelers who needed a place to stay. Lily's mom, Susan, cooked for people who needed a meal and could pay for it with a piece of silver or gold. Her dad, Rod, had come up with a secret recipe for moonshine that he sold—getting quite a lot of business, because it was the only alcohol you could find around here.

Old Marva told me about Diesel and Lily the last time I was in town. Lily was walking around the market serving tables with a huge grin on her face, and Marva had to tell me why that was. It was on my last trip to town, right before the snow fell.

Diesel deserved someone like Lily—a normal girl. I couldn't give him that because I wasn't normal. Besides the color of my hair, I wasn't like the rest of the girls.

The men in this town were about as misogynistic as they came. They kept their women tucked away in their houses, cooking, sewing, raising babies, and whatever other stuff a housewife did. Girls around my age in town didn't even know how to pick up a knife. Pop made sure I knew how to take care of myself. Men protected the women like they were gold. The only law and justice were what Maximus's soldiers saw fit to reign down upon us. They cared little about the rapists and murderers that were rumored to roam the woods. Especially since most of the soldiers fit into those shoes themselves. Mostly, those in Cedar Hill were good people, only trying to get by. We got wanderers that came through town occasionally that stole and committed other crimes. The people in Cedar Hill protected each other and served justice as they saw fit when such things happened.

A girl out in the woods, alone, was unheard of. I was always much more careful than I was today. I didn't consider myself pretty to look at, but that wouldn't matter to a man that found me out here. At nineteen years old, I was tall and lean, towering over most ladies—my body built from long days of physical labor. My lips were thin, my limbs were lanky, and my hair was the color of dirt most of the time. I only had two pairs of clothes, that usually stank because I didn't wash them enough.

Sitting inside all day and doing menial chores was against my better nature—that wasn't me. Not to mention, I had never even kissed a boy. 'Inexperienced' was written across my head in big, bold letters. I had accepted my celibacy. I never wanted to have children. The thought of bringing more blond-haired kids into the world made me sick. I wouldn't have my children suffer like I had. Why was I even thinking about it, anyway? It was obvious Diesel would never return my feelings, and I wasn't about to sit around pining for someone who didn't think I was worth it. It was easy to tell myself that, but it was harder to accomplish with his body pressed into mine.

Diesel held me from behind and suddenly let go, pivoting and staring at the fire with his head bowed.

"Well, I think I'll take a bath, then," I murmured.

"Okay," he said, still staring at the fire. "Go ahead. I'm not about to freeze my balls off just for a warm bath."

"Baby," I laughed, and he didn't even smile. Did I miss

something? "Turn around so I can get in."

He sat down next to the fire with his back to the pool, resting his arms on his knees with no snide remarks.

I stepped over to the water, peeking back to make sure his eyes were turned away. Confident he wasn't looking, I peeled off all my layers, leaving my hat on just in case. It was odd being out in the open with no clothes on. I hurried down into the pool to shake the feeling. The water felt delicious. The heat from the pool warmed me from the outside in. Baths in the old bucket at the cabin paled in comparison.

"This is the best thing I have ever felt," I moaned a little too loudly.

All I got in return was an irritated grunt. I glanced up to make sure he still sat by the fire. He hadn't moved, but the muscles in his back strained to rip out of his coat. His hands fisted in front of him with white knuckles.

Did I do something to make him mad? I dug my feet into the rocks at the bottom of the pool, raking through my memory to remember anything I could have said to upset him, but came up with nothing.

The cold air outside the water didn't sound appealing at all. I soaked in the heat for another minute, trying to enjoy the last of it before I climbed out into the chilly air.

Diesel suddenly stood on high alert. "Ash, get out." He looked beyond the creek and reached for his weapons. I didn't need him to tell me twice. I surged out of the pool and Diesel threw my clothes at me, trying not to look. That's when I heard the faint sound of footsteps crunching through the snow. My body trembled from the cold and I yanked my clothes on as quickly as possible. I slid my feet into my boots without socks or lacing them up, and picked up my bow right in time to see two men approaching from across the creek.

Their black winter clothes and blue bands around their arms caught my attention before anything else. Soldiers. I pulled my hat as far down on my head as I could. If they saw my hair, I'd never see Nan again.

"Stay behind me and don't say anything," Diesel breathed, moving closer.

The soldiers found their way across the creek before stepping into the firelight with challenging eyes. Guns held close in front of them, at the ready.

"Hello," the larger one said. A mammoth of a man, even bigger than Diesel. "We saw your fire from up on the ridge and wondered if we could join for the night?"

"No. Get lost," Diesel said, with a hard edge to his voice.

The duo stepped even closer, the larger one's eyebrows pinching together as he inspected us. Diesel retreated until the back of his arm grazed my front, leaving me only able to peek around his shoulder to see. He held his bow ready in front of him, as did I. Their eyes fell on me before turning back to Diesel.

My heart hammered in my chest. This was the closest encounter I'd ever had with a soldier, in the winter in the middle of the woods, nonetheless.

"Now, that's not very respectful of the King's soldiers, is it?"

I could see Diesel grind his teeth from where I stood.

"Where are you headed? Maybe we can point you in the right direction."

I was happy to let Diesel take this one—I wanted no part in speaking to them.

"Taking news to one of our…associates."

"Sounds urgent. Maybe you should hurry and get where you need to go."

The big one's eye landed on me. "And who's this with you?"

"None of your damn business."

I could feel the tension radiating off Diesel as they stared each other down. My hand moved to his back and offer reassurance, but he flinched away from my touch.

The large one snickered and raised his eyebrows questioningly, while the other stood staring at the pile of meat next to the fire—practically salivating.

"What'd you get?" the smaller one inclined his head to our kill.

"An elk. If we give you a few pieces of meat, will you move on and leave us be?"

The soldiers glanced at each other and nodded.

"Sounds like a fair trade. The game seems to be lacking around these parts." Or they were too poor of hunters to even find it. No doubt, they usually had everything they needed.

Diesel glanced at me before easing over to our packs. I stared at the soldiers under my hood, my face cloaked with darkness and shadows. My hand twitched on the wood of my bow, ready for anything.

The meat glistened in the firelight as Diesel handed over two large chunks of meat. The soldiers took it without argument.

"Much obliged, friend. We'll just be on our way then." His eyes flicked from me to Diesel before they strode off into the darkness once more, without further argument.

We watched and listened to them to make sure they didn't circle back. I let out a deep breath of relief when I was sure they were gone.

"What are soldiers doing way out here in the winter? I've seen men out here, bounty hunters even, but never soldiers."

Diesel pursed his lips. "Best we sleep lightly tonight."

"Not like I can sleep much out here, anyway," I mumbled, tucking my freezing body into my bedroll. Diesel was right—the instant gratification of the hot pool was only going to make this night colder and longer. Especially with how on edge I felt from the soldiers passing through our camp.

CHAPTER 7
ASH

Our feet slogged through the snow with every step—my pack felt like a boulder. The straps on my bag dug into my shoulders, causing my muscles to scream at every movement. The last few nights of not sleeping and not sleeping well had taken their toll on my body. I nearly froze to death last night and woke with frost on my eyelashes. I even considered asking Diesel if I could climb in his bed only to steal some warmth during the night, but thought better of it.

We trudged back home much slower than usual. Diesel didn't look any better than I felt—he was strangely silent. He must have slept terribly as well. Every few hours, we took a much-needed break. Plus, we stopped by the old oak tree on the way back to get some bark. It was the only one in the area, and I wasn't going any longer without it. Diesel raised his eyebrows in interest as I collected it, and I told him it was for Nan's tea.

By the time the familiar landscape of home came into view, it was late in the afternoon and my feet felt like lead. We made it to our creek—I forced my legs up the slope to the cabin with Diesel trailing behind me.

The pines shrouded the hill the cabin rested on, except for the small clearing, just big enough for the home. Our cabin stayed hidden from onlookers unless you stumbled upon it or knew where to look. The camouflaged home made staying away from prying eyes easy.

The hillside engulfed the backside of the cabin, leaving the entire dwelling looking more like a large snowdrift in the winter than somewhere to live. The kitchen was opposite the front and only door. A small table, with three mismatched chairs adorned the center of the room, reminding us every time we sat down to eat that Pop was gone. A tunnel made of earth jutted out of the kitchen, with a door covering the opening. That was where we stored our food. The earth kept it cold enough for all the produce we grew to not spoil. It also served as a great way to keep the meat away from the flies during the summer.

A fireplace was in the room's corner, built out of primeval-looking bricks. We filled our days during the summer, bringing in wood and stacking it by the cabin, so we wouldn't freeze during the winter. To the side of the main room was the only bedroom. A ladder, which was by the door, climbed up to a small loft, barely big enough for the bedroll, but I didn't mind. My bedroll ended up outside on summer nights—the stars were prettier than the thatched roof, anyway.

I pulled open the door and the smell of wood smoke and home assaulted my senses. Nan wasn't visible in the main part of the cabin. She must have been in the single bedroom she claimed as hers.

"Nan, I'm back and I've got good news," my tired voice echoed through the wooden walls.

Nan rushed out of her room at the sound of my voice. The small woman's short, graying hair stuck out in every direction. I smirked at the sight. She said there was no point in taking care of it when you live as hard of a life as we did. Though she was small in stature, she was strong as an ox and quick-witted as they came.

Nan and I were opposites in our appearance. Where she had dark skin and once-dark hair, I had fair skin and long, wavy, blonde hair. My hair was unruly most days—always in a braid or covered with a hat. Nan had dark chocolate eyes and mine were brilliant blue. She said my eyes were so bright, she could see them glowing through the dim cabin at night, the same comment from everyone who had seen my eyes in the dark.

Relief washed over her face at the sight of me. Diesel stepped in the door beside me, dropping his pack next to mine with a heavy thud.

"Ash!" She hurried to where we stood inside the door—her limp was more evident today. Nan walked around with a shuffle from a bad knee. She took a nasty tumble down a hill years ago and her knee had never been right since. She still got around, but the pain flared up and took its toll on her. I did everything I could for her, so she didn't have to work too hard at her advancing age.

"I see you found a stranger along the way." She smiled at Diesel.

"Hi, Nan. We brought you a whole elk to cook up." It made me smile that Diesel called Nan by the name I had given her. He treated her like his own grandmother.

She pulled Diesel into a hug, and he enveloped her slight frame in his massive arms.

"It's good to see you, Diesel."

"You too. Sorry it's been so long."

They released each other, and Nan stepped back. "It's good to know there's someone out there watching out for my girl."

"I'm fine, Nan, stop worrying so much," I said, exasperated at the continual argument.

"I don't even want to tell you what she did this time," Diesel joked.

Nan shot me a look. "I don't want to know. All that matters is that she's back safe now."

I narrowed my eyes. "You know that I'm a grown woman, and I'm standing right here."

"We know, dear." She pinched my cheek and turned toward the kitchen.

Diesel suppressed a laugh, with a smile that didn't reach his eyes, and I stuck my tongue out at him. His smile seemed more perfunctory than genuine ever since our encounter with the soldiers last night.

"Bring that meat over to the table and let's get it cut up. Diesel, do you want to stay for dinner?" What was she thinking? My hair was still as golden as the sun, and the heat from the cabin was already making me sweat under my hat.

He picked up his pack that was bursting with meat and set it on the table.

"I better not. I promised the Andersons that I'd chop wood for them. If I go now, I could get it done before dark."

It wasn't unusual for Diesel to do odd jobs for people around the area for extra supplies, but how did he even have the energy for that today? All I wanted was to slump down by the fire and sleep.

"Are you sure? It seems like you two have already had quite the day."

"Yeah, I better get home tonight." Why? He didn't have anyone there waiting for him. Maybe he had enough of me in the last two days.

"Okay, well, let's at least get you a few potatoes to take with you."

We didn't have much to offer, but always had plenty of brown, root vegetables to eat, which was more than some people had. Boiled potatoes had been the main staple of our diet for far too long. There was a spot down by the creek where we grew a garden. What we couldn't grow, we traded for in town. We traded potatoes, fish we caught, or meat that I killed. Nan also knitted, and we traded her projects for more yarn and other goods—like soap.

Nan disappeared into the pantry to collect the potatoes and I fished the meat out of Diesel's pack, leaving some for him. We filled the rest of it up with potatoes and he left without so much as another glance. I stared at the door after he left, thinking it was odd that he didn't want to stay after coming all this way to see us. That and he was usually always up for Nan's cooking.

I brushed it off with a shrug and peeled my soaking boots and socks, leaving my wrinkly, water-worn feet looking sad. I placed them by the fireplace to dry. Laundry was hard to do with icicles outside, so we usually lived in our stink all winter. Sometimes Nan would get enough energy to fill the laundry tub with water and give our clothes a good scrub. We would dry them next to the fireplace, but since we had so few clothes, we'd often end up wandering around the cabin in very little clothing until they dried.

The warm fire in the corner was inviting as I stood next to the blazing hearth. I freed myself from the wet jacket and left it to drip onto the wood floor from its spot hanging over the fire. My hair sprang free from my wool cap when I pulled it off—

blonde flyways tickled my nose.

An old, cast-iron stove took space in the kitchen. Luckily, it was here when Pop found the place. I didn't envy whoever had to carry it up the hill and get it into the cabin—it weighed a ton. Literally. I often wondered who lived here before. What was their story? They probably died along with everyone else, sadly.

I put a large pot of water on the stove to boil for a bath while I helped Nan with the meat. The stove housed a large center chamber for a fire. It heated, allowing for cooking on the top. A chimney for smoke jutted out the thatched roof from the stove.

"So… What happened?" Nan asked from across the table.

"I thought you didn't want to know."

She shot me a scathing look.

"Fine," I snickered. "Turns out, Diesel and I were hunting the same herd of elk. We found each other after I shot this one."

"Well, I'm glad it was only Diesel and not someone else."

Me too. She didn't know how happy I was that it turned out to be Diesel. I neglected to tell Nan about the soldiers we encountered. It would only make her worry further.

"And he didn't see your hair?"

"I don't think so."

She nodded. "Did you get more bark? We need to dye it right away."

"Yeah, it's in the front pocket of my bag and no arguments here. That was far too close for my liking. He almost saw."

We finished up the meat, and ground up the bark and charcoal for the dye, while I told Nan about Miles's death. She worked the sludge into my hair with gentle hands. "So, Miles is really gone, huh?"

"Yeah, Diesel has been alone most of the winter. I guess Miles caught pneumonia, according to Anne, right after the first snowfall."

"Anne is a good doctor. If she couldn't do anything, it must have been bad."

I nodded in agreement.

"I only met Miles a handful of times. They showed up one day and no one even knew they were there until he came to town to trade the wheat they grew. Even then, he was quiet. Never said much. I think Pop talked to him more than anybody. No one even knew he had a son until Diesel was about eighteen years old, I think."

"Not everyone gossips as much as Old Marva."

At that, she smacked me over the top of the head that she worked on. "She's only a few years older than me. If you call her old, what does that make me?"

I laughed. "You're still young and spry as a spring chicken, Nan."

Out of the corner of my eye, I saw her shake her head and smile.

She kept working the dye into my hair until it satisfied her. I used my shirt to protect my hands from getting burned and rushed to the small tub that was in Nan's room. The boiling water splashed in the tub's bottom, sending steam swirling up into the chilled air.

We kept two barrels of water in the dirt pantry. At least, that's what we called it. We hauled water from the creek and dumped it in the barrels so we could have water storage in the cabin. The water was clean, thanks to a spring feeding into the creek a short distance up the valley. We had never had trouble or gotten sick from the water. Thankfully, almost everything in the cabin was there when Pop found it. It was like it was untouched by the chaos of the world.

The water ran over my chilled hands as I collected more to cool down the steaming tub. My pants and long-sleeved shirt brushed my body as I pulled them off. These were Pop's old hunting pants, which he found in the cabin. They were the ugliest shade of camouflage that I had ever seen. It surprised me that animals didn't see me coming from a long way away. They were too big, but thanks to a string belt—they stayed on.

The last layer of thermal underwear was skintight and hard to tug off my moist legs. We traded for them when I was younger, and they didn't fit as well as they used to. The water was lukewarm and definitely not as nice as the hot pool, but my eyelids closed anyway, soaking in the feel of it.

CHAPTER 8
ASH

Three weeks later, spring was in full bloom. The runoff made its way down our creek and the water level had almost evened out. The snow had all melted except on the tips of the mountains. Green grass pushed through the soil and the temperature warmed significantly. I caught glimpses of deer moving back into the area and black bears coming out of hibernation.

Nan and I stayed busy, preparing the garden area for planting. We always let a portion of our crops seed out and we conserved the seeds for the next growing season. We grew a lot of potatoes, but we also had carrots, corn, beans, onions, wheat, and a healthy population of wild radishes. Over the years, Pop and I dug starts of berry bushes we happened upon while hunting. We planted all the bushes across the creek. We had raspberries, blueberries, and these dark purple ones. I wasn't sure what they were called, but they were my favorite. We dried the berries, at least the few that local wildlife, and I didn't eat.

Most of our produce stayed good for long periods of time in our pantry. We used vinegar and salt to preserve other things, but we had run out of that as well this winter.

Elk meat had been a blessed change to our diets over the last couple of weeks. Now instead of boiled potatoes, we could make a hearty elk stew.

We needed to go to town. Nan brought it up almost every day. We needed more candles, soap, salt, and wheat, to grind into flour, would be nice. We could make our own soap, but it was easier to trade for it. I was putting the trip off—I hated going to town. Mostly, I hated the people, except for Marva. We still had potatoes from last year, that we could trade. All of Nan's knitting projects from this winter piled up and could be traded as well. The only form of money we had was a small stash of gold and silver pieces we collected over the years, just in case. It was a rarity around here that soldiers seemed to have more of than they knew what to do with.

I woke up one morning to Nan dressed in her best sweater.

"Get ready. We're going to town." Her instructions as clear as the new day. She had wariness on her face—I didn't think she wanted to go either. With a sigh, I put on my black pants and my nicer jacket and got our packs together with all our goods.

The walk to town was slow. We stopped and rested Nan's knee a lot. The sloping trail was hard to see and shrouded in undergrowth. It made walking more challenging. We followed the creek as it flowed next to us, down to where it met the lake by town. It was easy to find the way from the cabin to town, but finding the right creek to follow back up could be tricky for someone who had never done it.

The creek that ran by our cabin flowed into a small lake at the base of the mountain. It only had enough water to be called a pond in the later summer months. Old dam remnants were on one side, but the dam had long since broken and deteriorated. Enough of it stood to keep the small lake from running out. The water that spilled out around the edges of the crumbling dam formed the head of the Paloma River. It ran down the mountains toward the sea. The only benefit of the lake was the fresh fish from its depths.

We skirted around the lake and up the slope of the hill the town rested on. I spotted the few cedar trees atop the hill dispersed throughout the houses—hence the name.

Cedar Hill only housed around two hundred residents. The town had been here for as long as I knew. There were several old houses on the outskirts and in the center of town. Most people that lived on the outskirts were farmers, utilizing the bare ground amongst the trees to grow crops, which depended on rain to grow. There were also a few families that owned beef cows, and some had horses that helped to pull the old plows to plant more crops.

There was an old timer that had a small herd of dairy cows.

On special occasions, we would get a little milk. A trader came through Cedar Hill several years ago with baby chickens, and now everyone seemed to have backyard chickens. Most of the time we could get eggs for free because people had them coming out of their ears. We had also gotten a few chicks from the trader, but a fox took out our prospect of fresh eggs.

There were often traders and random travelers coming through town. It was usual to see vendors set up outside The Market on Main Street selling exotic goods. They reserved trading inside The Market building for locals. Lily's family's vacant rooms were often filled during the warm months with people passing through, but passers-by rarely stayed long.

The outskirts of town were quiet today, with few people in sight. We turned down Main Street toward The Market. No bounty hunters or soldiers roamed the streets that we could see. We got to the front door and Anne appeared outside of it. She saw Nan and a huge smile lit up her face. She rushed over to us and gathered Nan up in an enormous hug.

Nan's best friend, Anne. They grew up together. Anne and her husband, Pete, offered to let us live with them when Pop died. She said it wasn't right for the two of us to live all by ourselves, so far away from people. Nan turned down the offer—she was trying to keep my secret hidden and keep us safe.

"JO!" she exclaimed. "Where have you been all winter?"

Nan's real name was Joanne. Both Anne's and Nan's parents

decided they liked the name Joanne, when they were born. To avoid confusion when they were little, Nan started going by Jo and Anne used her name. When I had only been with Nan and Pop for a few months, I heard Pop call Nan "Joanne". I couldn't say her name very well and it came out as "Nan". It was the first word I said, and that was what I called her ever since.

"Oh, you know me. I can't make it too far in the winter with this useless knee," she said, gesturing at the offending joint.

"We need to catch up. Let's go back to my house and have lunch. Ash, come with us?" Her eyes barely met mine before falling back on Nan. "Oh, it's so good to see you again." Her arms tightened around Nan once more.

"What do you say, Ash?"

"You go ahead, Nan. I'll go get everything we need." My smile was genuine. Nan and Anne's catch-up sessions were not something that I enjoyed. Anne gossiped about everyone in town, and they reminisced about times when they were younger. Though I enjoyed hearing stories of the past, I had probably heard them all five times over at that point.

"You sure?"

"Yes, it's been a long winter. Go have fun, Nan."

Nan looked around with weary eyes. She pulled me in close and whispered into my ear.

"It looks safe, but I don't want to leave you alone."

My eyes wandered around the open space, looking for

anything out of place.

"It should be okay. I'll be extra watchful today."

Nan gave a solemn nod.

"Don't be too long."

She patted me on the shoulder before interlocking arms with Anne. She smiled and laughed with her friend as they walked away. All I wanted was for Nan to be happy. Why wouldn't Nan come and live in town with her friend? I loved her and I wanted her around, but life would be a lot easier for her here. Watching her suffer through our tough life in the cabin tugged at my heartstrings.

Turning back toward The Market, I opened the door and stepped inside. Across the room, the locals that owned cows sat in chairs behind a table. They made the soap we used out of beef tallow—piled on the table in front of them.

"Hello, Hank, Rita." I nodded at the middle-aged couple. Having traded with me often, they knew me well.

"Hi, Ash, it's good to see you back." Rita was pleasant enough, but we never got past small talk.

"Thanks. We need more soap. Do you need any potato seed? Or Nan knit a bunch of hats and scarves this winter if you need those?"

"We'll take potato seed for our garden for five bars of soap." Hank was far less friendly than his better half. Whenever he spoke, it was short and to the point.

That was fair. The soap should last us a few months, between baths and washing clothes.

"That will work, thank you." We made the trade, and I continued working my way through the market, exchanging potato seed and knitted projects for things that we needed—not saying more than pleasantries to anyone I encountered.

I gathered as much as possible inside before stepping back out into the sunshine. My stomach grumbled from hunger. A traveling vendor outside sold food out of their wagon. I traded one of Nan's hats for a slice of bread and a piece of cheese. It was a special treat that I had only eaten a handful of times.

Across from The Market, my favorite town gossip sat under a tree in a grassy area. She gave me a toothy grin when my shadow covered her body.

"Ash, my girl, is that you?" She squinted at me in the sunlight, her hand forming a visor over her eyes so she could see.

"Hi, Marva."

"Look at you, girl, you look like you've grown taller this winter."

I laughed, settling down in the grass next to her to eat my lunch. Marva wore a brightly-colored skirt that went down to her ankles and a matching shirt. Her outfit made me smile. She was a seamstress and was always making new clothes for herself. She sat with needlework in her hands, keeping her fingers occupied while she enjoyed the spring sunshine.

"Or maybe you've gotten shorter."

She turned and gave me a scathing look. "There's no one around that's quite like you."

A big, goofy smile found its way onto my face. "What have you been up to all winter?" I asked.

"You know me, listening to everyone else's conversations and spreading rumors." She grinned at herself.

"And what are the rumors today?" I bit into my cheese. I swore in my head—*Oops, language Ash*—it was utterly delicious. Something this rich in flavor hadn't been in my mouth all winter.

"Word on the street is King Maximus is almost ready to appoint his successor to rule Novum."

"Doesn't he have a son or something that can take over?" My mouth was full of food when I responded. *Manners*, Nan's voice chided in my head.

"I'm not sure. I know he had a son, but no one seems to know whatever happened to him. Apparently, the new king will be a relative of the very first leader of Novum," she said with a flourish.

I rolled my eyes. "It all seems like a bunch of ridiculousness to me. He'll pick someone who is just as bad as he is, and nothing is ever going to change."

"At least his goons leave us alone, mostly. Rumor is, they

patrol the southern part of Novum a lot harder."

"Thank heavens for small miracles, then." Sarcasm dripped from my tone. "How big is Novum, anyway?" I had always wondered but never asked anybody—it wasn't like there was a history class and maps for that sort of thing.

"I'm not entirely sure, but I know there are oceans on either side—how far north and south it stretches, I don't know."

"And Maximus controls all of it?"

"Yes. As far as I know. All the kings before him kept extending their reach further and further—controlling more towns and gaining more soldiers."

"Do all the soldiers come from Hope?"

"No…" She looked at me like I had two heads.

"What?"

"You need to get out more, girl."

"I'd rather not."

She giggled. "No, they train all over the country. Good ol' King Maxy has advisory cities all over the place to rule the regions."

"Really? How do you know that?"

"Do you remember Dave Perkins?"

I nodded. "He's the one that signed up to be a soldier on recruitment day a few years ago?"

"Yes, and what a shame it was—thought being a soldier would be easier than starving out here like the rest of us.

Anyway, he came back through town as a soldier a while back and said he went south to train, but not to Hope."

"You mean, there are soldiers that are real people—they're not all monsters?"

"I wouldn't go sayin' that. Dave wasn't a very honorable man in the first place."

I sighed. "Will we ever be free of them?"

She looked around to make sure no one was listening. "I've heard the Far North is still wild and they still have no governing authority there."

My ears perked up. "You mean they are free?"

She shook her head. "Don't be getting any ideas. We may have to live under the King's rule, but at least we have some sort of law and order. The men up there are completely uncivilized—savage even. I've heard they're not even human anymore. They wear the skins of the animals they kill and will rip your throat out without a second thought."

"Doesn't sound so much different from us," I scoffed. "So, the King is still fighting with them to overtake the territory?"

She nodded. "Yes, as far as I know. It's not an official country or anything like Novum, only a territory, but the King is power hungry, and he won't stop until he's conquered all of it, I fear."

This was all very interesting and the first I had heard of it. Nan despised talking about politics or the King because it reminded her of Pop. He loved discussing this kind of stuff with almost anyone but me; it appeared.

"What about blonde people, Marva? Heard anything new about that this winter?"

She gave me an assessing look. "Why do you ask?"

"Well, you had some wild theories about them last time we talked, just wondered if you had more," I chuckled.

She shook her head, deep in thought. "I'm telling you, there's something strange about them—the virus did something to them. They are more capable than anyone to overtake the King and that's why he wants them so badly. He wants all the power for himself."

"But you don't know what's so special about them?"

Her face dropped. "No, but it's got to be the truth."

"I believe you, Marva," I smiled. The lie escaped my lips as smooth as silk. There was nothing special about me except the horrible color of my hair.

As we watched The Market across the street, Lily walked out the door.

"That girl is trouble," Marva said, gazing at the girl across the way. She was all long, dark hair and curves—turning the heads of all the men she walked by.

"She has been telling anyone that will listen that Diesel is going to propose to her before the summer is over."

I choked on the last bite of my food.

Marva eyed me. "Trouble in paradise?"

"No, it's fine. We're only friends." I shrugged. "He can marry whoever he wants."

"Mm hmm, sure."

"Well, I think it's about time for me to go."

Marva grinned. "Don't want to talk about it, huh? Interesting." Her fingers found her chin as she pretended to mull it over with a smirk.

"Bye, Marva." I walked away with a smile on my face.

They set vendor booths up all the way down Main Street today. In my best interest of not wanting to interrupt Nan, I wandered down the street, perusing the carts—always watchful for anything other than traders. A necklace caught my eye, and I picked it up to inspect closer. In my periphery, I could see two men coming down the street, holding rabbits and bows—like they just returned from hunting.

Luke Walters and Ty Redmond. Some of the local lowlifes. They were a little older than me and unmarried. I knew who they were, but had never spoken to them. I ignored them like I always did, expecting them to pass by, when a prickle came at the back of my neck. The feeling of their presence behind me alerted my senses before I saw them standing there.

"Look who finally graced us with her presence again," came a voice from behind me.

I turned, and both men were close to me, mischievous looks

in their eyes. Luke was tall and willowy, with shoulder length, jet-black hair, and a chiseled chin with a poor excuse for a beard growing on it. He always hung around town, looking for a job in exchange for a meal. Like too many others, he only had a dad left—his mom died when he was little.

Nan had told me to steer clear of his father, Declan; said he was meaner than a cornered mama moose. I rarely saw Declan, though Luke always seemed to be slithering around. I had heard he often went chasing gold down the Paloma River and left his son to fend for himself. What little gold he brought back, he dedicated to Rod's moonshine.

As I had observed Luke and Ty over the years, Ty seemed to be Luke's shadow, always following him. Ty had light brown hair chopped at the sides and longer on top. He was shorter than Luke, and packed a few extra pounds of baby fat that he couldn't seem to shake. I didn't think Ty's family situation was much better than Lukes, though I didn't know the finer details. Both were taller than me, but neither matured from boys to men yet. I caught myself comparing them to Diesel, who shadowed them in bulk and maturity.

"Need something?" I questioned suspiciously, raising my eyebrows at them.

"Only wondering why the filthy princess is looking at things that are way too nice for her?"

I gritted my teeth and put the necklace I was inspecting back in its place, while they snickered behind me. Marva had told me they called me the nickname behind my back, but I had never heard it straight to my face. Apparently, they said, I acted like I was too good for them, living out in my castle in the woods, rolling in the dirt. It was not my fault my hair looked dirty most of the time, thanks to the dye. I was the outcast; the dirty, orphan girl who was different from everyone else. Even the lowlifes despised me.

Luke smirked, and Ty looked vaguely uncomfortable at the whole situation. He kept looking around, wondering if anybody watched the scene. On closer inspection, the two rabbits they held looked as if they had been mauled to death. One was gut shot, and the other had a back leg blown off from an arrow.

I nodded my head at their kill. "You know, if you shoot them in the head, you'll waste a lot less meat." They didn't seem to like my helpful suggestion. Luke's eyes darkened at my jab. Obviously, their skills with a bow were subpar.

"You're too mouthy for a girl," Luke gritted out, bringing me back to what Diesel said to me all those years ago. Then, a feral smirk landed on his face, as if he had gotten an idea.

"It's probably because you never had an old man to teach you a lesson." He grinned and glanced at Ty. "I guess it's your lucky day, because me and Ty would be happy to help."

I steeled my eyes at them as he moved an inch closer. We were in the middle of town. He wouldn't do anything here, would he? Nobody would stop him if he did. I cautiously rested my hand on my knife strapped to my thigh, ready to slice off any part of his body he touched me with.

"Leave her the hell alone," seethed a voice to my left, and my eyes met ones the color of the new spring grass—filled with rage.

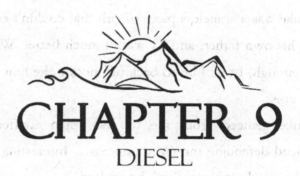

CHAPTER 9
DIESEL

I'd been watching enough to know that they were coming to town today, but avoiding her, too. Nothing made sense anymore, not after what I'd seen. Not when I knew she was lying to me. At least today, I got a change of scenery from my spot prowling around their cabin, waiting... watching.

Ash made her way down Main Street perusing the vendors, while I lurked in the shadows. A routine that I was far too familiar with. I glared at the brown braid that swished at her back. *Fooled me.* She picked up a necklace, and the turquoise glinted in the sunshine. Her eyes lit up at the jewelry. *Interesting.* I had never pegged her for a woman who cared for the finer things in life, but then again, she probably never had enough to spare to pay for such frivolities.

When Luke and Ty started hassling her, it was time to quit hiding. They moved closer to her with trouble on their faces, and I had enough. I strode down the street toward them, my body ripe with anger. What were they saying to her that made her grab the knife at her waist?

Luke was a spineless piece of shit that couldn't even stand up to his own father, and Ty wasn't much better. When I got close enough, I told him to back off, noting the hint of fear in Ash's eyes.

Luke glanced from me to Ash, then scoffed. "Lily's boyfriend defending the filthy princess... Interesting. I'm sure she'll love to hear about this," he scoffed.

He never was smart, not for as long as I'd known him. I ground my teeth together at the nickname, or maybe the fact that he called me Lily's boyfriend, in front of Ash. I scowled at both Luke and Ty, my fist twitching with the need to make him bleed.

"Come on, Luke. Let's go, man," Ty said, his eyes full of fear. Luke was an idiot, but at least he wasn't a coward like Ty.

"Yeah... Luke, leave," I glowered. These two had never been a problem before, but Ash's looks this spring were enough to turn the head of any man.

Luke made the smart decision and turned to leave instead of antagonizing her any longer after giving me one last sneer. He called back over his shoulder as he made his departure. "See you around, princess."

My nostrils flared. He and I would have to have a little chat later.

In a split second, Ash spun on her heel, walking toward

Anne's house to collect Nan. I caught her in a few strides, taking the spot next to her as she continued to walk.

"I don't need you to protect me." Anger clipped her tone. "Stop inserting yourself into my business. I told you I can take care of myself. I'm not a little girl you need to protect anymore."

This was the first time I had talked to her in weeks, and even her angry voice was like music to my ears, though I wasn't sure what she was angry about. "No, you're not a little girl anymore. I was only trying to help. I don't understand what you're so mad about?" I stopped and scratched the back of my neck, unsure of what to say. I was angrier with her than she was with me, but also, I had to keep up pretenses and another part of me couldn't help myself—I wanted to talk to her.

She stopped walking and sighed, her eyes darting down the street. "Your girlfriend doesn't look happy to see you," she frowned, gesturing down the street to where Lily strode toward us. I couldn't give two shits about her right now.

"She's not my girlfriend," I said, enunciating every word. *Where'd that come from?* When did I start caring about whether Ash thought I had another woman?

Ash shot me a derisive look as Lily stepped between us. Lily smiled brightly at me. "Diesel! I was wondering if you would be here today. I haven't seen you in a few days and figured you would be back to see me."

She needed to tone it down if we were going to keep doing

what we were doing. Ash rolled her eyes and moved away.

I snaked out my hand to grab her arm, but recoiled at the last second, remembering who she was. "Ash, wait," I said instead.

Ash turned and glared at my hand that had reached for her but changed course. Her face fell slightly in what looked like hurt before it turned angry.

"Actually," Lily interrupted, placing her hand on my tanned forearm. "I was wondering if you could come help me with something?" She fluttered her eyelashes, and I glared at her.

"Well, it looks like you have *things* to do," Ash glowered before she marched off down the street and away from us—this time I didn't follow. I'd catch up with her later. There was someone else I needed to talk to now.

"What the hell was that?" I turned on Lily, smacking her hand off me.

"Wha... What do you mean?" she stuttered.

"I told you from the beginning, Ash will always be in my life and that's never going to change, so stop acting territorial."

"But why Diesel?"

I liked Lily because she was always sweet and never expected anything out of me. Until today, that was. I wasn't sure I could look at her anymore without seeing blue eyes staring back at me, but I wasn't sure I was ready to give it up yet, either.

"Look, if you're not okay with what we talked about this

winter anymore, then we should end things right now."

Her eyes widened. "No—no, that's not what I want. I'm okay with this," she sighed, glaring after Ash's retreating back.

I nodded. "Good," I mumbled under my breath, before following Lily back to The Market.

CHAPTER 10
ASH

Anne's house was a few blocks away, and the walk was short. It was an old home, like all the others in town—small and made of faded, red bricks that were falling off in places. They had a door off to the side with a room for Anne's patients when they came—the room held all the medical supplies she had collected over the years. The sound of the wood reverberated off my knuckles when I knocked on the door. Giggling and feet shuffling came from inside, in a rush to the front door.

Anne opened the door, and I smiled down at the quaint woman with shoulder-length hair as gray as Nan's. Where Nan was all rough edges and tattered clothes, Anne dressed in much finer clothing than we would probably ever see. Anne and her husband Pete were probably the most respectable people in Cedar Hill. They were used to having whatever they needed. Most people would give Anne whatever she wanted, so she would offer medical services when they needed her. Pete had taken to people calling him the town chief. He was old enough that he couldn't do physical labor like he used to. In the last five years, he had taken to organizing town events and solving feuds between the more sophisticated townsfolk—who didn't take it into their own hands. Pete was also very good at handling the soldiers that came through and ensuring that everyone stepped in to give the soldiers what they needed, so no one got hurt.

Novum's soldiers were cruel and power-hungry. They ruled with an iron fist and took whatever they wanted when they came. If you stood up to one of them, you would probably end up dead. Most of them carried guns. Word was, the king could manufacture guns and the ammunition in Hope—something that we could only dream of. We never stood a chance against the tyranny.

Anne stood in front of me with Nan behind her, seated at the table with her hand around a glass. Nan looked at me and giggled again. It had been a while since I had seen her laugh like a much younger woman.

I couldn't help but laugh with them. I confirmed my suspicion when I spotted the bottle of Rod's moonshine on the table. Anne held a cup in her hand as well. They were drunk as skunks in the middle of the afternoon.

"What have you two been up to?" I asked, eyeing them suspiciously with a smirk on my face.

They looked at each other and burst into another round of

giggles.

I shook my head at their antics.

"Come in and sit with us for a bit," Anne said, gesturing to an empty chair by the table. "Rod gave us a bottle of his newest batch of shine to test out, and we had to try it."

I dropped my things at the door and walked in, pulling out a chair next to Nan.

The home had much nicer furnishings than our outdated cabin. There were even a few couches in the front room for guests and a dining table. A wall separated the room we were in from the kitchen.

Anne stumbled to sit back down in her chair.

"Bit strong?" I questioned, trying to hold back my smile.

"Any of it would be a bit strong when you drink a half bottle," Nan said with a chuckle.

"Let me go get you a glass." Anne tried to stand again.

Before she hurt herself, I cut in. "No, it's okay. I don't want any of that wretched stuff."

I tried it a few years ago with Diesel and hated every second. The taste was foul. Not only that, but it made me feel disoriented and loopy, which was probably the point, but I liked to stay clear-headed.

Anne eyed me up with suspicion. "What sort of young person are you? Everyone I know would jump for joy at a free drink."

I shrugged. "Guess I'm not normal."

I felt like I had wrecked their fun with my surly attitude.

Nan broke the silence when she shot me a mischievous look. "Ash just needs to learn how to have fun."

They glanced at each other with trouble in their eyes and smiles on their faces.

"What are you two up to?" I narrowed my eyes at them.

"Well," Nan piped up, "the spring festival is in a few weeks."

"Here we go." My eyes rolled, waiting for what came next. Every spring, Cedar Hill threw a spring festival, to celebrate getting through another winter and the arrival of the new spring. It was mostly a day-long party full of Rod's moonshine and food that everyone brought to share. It was always on Main Street in front of The Market. Anne and Pete went to great lengths to make sure the decorations were pristine. They had games for the kids during the day and at night anybody who had an instrument they knew how to play brought it out. There was music, dancing, and more drinking late into the night. There were also a bunch of out-of-town vendors and passersby that showed up to sell and join in the festivities. I had been to a couple of spring festivals but never stuck around for the dancing—usually, I would leave Nan to stay the night with Anne so she could have fun. I had never particularly enjoyed spending my time with the people in Cedar Hill. They seemed like they hated me anyway, so the feeling was mutual.

"Anyway," continued Anne. "We decided that because of all the single people in town, such as yourself, we'll have a dance during the night where all the young people dance with each other to get to know one another better."

My head turned quickly to Nan, eyeing her inquisitively.

"Can I talk to Nan for a minute, alone?" I asked Anne.

She laughed. "Sure, dear, but that won't get you out of this. I'll go see if Pete is back yet."

Her arm grabbed mine as I helped her out of her chair and into the kitchen.

I stared Nan down on my way back to the table. "Do you really think this is a good idea?" I asked quietly.

"I had nothing to do with the idea. They were already doing it, but I agree. I think you should come."

"Pass."

"Really, Ash, you need to get to know people in town better and make friends."

"Why the sudden change in heart, Nan? You've always told me to avoid everyone like the plague, and now you want me to spend more time with them?"

She blew out a breath. "Yeah, I know. I'm worried about you, my girl. I realize that my age is getting the better of me these days. The walk here was hard on this old body today. You need someone to be there for you when I'm gone."

I tried to cut in, but she was having none of it.

"Hush up and listen. No, I'm not dying, but you never know. I'm not saying to quit coloring your hair. You still need to be extremely careful. There are evil people out there that would love to get their hands on you. What I am saying is that there are good people who will help you and help hide your secret. People you can trust. People like Diesel. Miles was one of Pop's best friends. If he trusted him, then we can trust his son, too."

"You trust Diesel enough that you think I should tell him?"

"I've always liked him. He's a good man—always watched your back when I wasn't around. Pop told me that there were good people out there, you only had to find the right ones."

I thought back to my interaction with Diesel earlier. Something had shifted between us. He acted like I'd give him diseases or something if he touched me lately. The way he moved away from my touch with the soldiers and then the look he got in his eyes today when he reached for me, but thought better of it. Something had changed, but didn't know what.

"I ran into him today."

"And?"

I shrugged.

"He's a good one, Ash,"

"He's only my friend, and that's never going to change, Nan."

She nodded thoughtfully. "I'm not sure that's true."

"It is," I sighed. "He was talking about me moving to town

and finding a husband on our elk hunt. Plus, he's got Lily, and I'm scared it would mess up the only friendship I have." The honesty in my response made her eyes widen.

"All I can tell you is that I think the boy would lay down his life for you, from what I've seen."

I scoffed. "I doubt that."

"Stop insulting your self-worth, Ash."

Pete and Anne interrupted us, walking back into the room. Pete looked like he had too many days in the sun. Drooping eyelids shadowed his brown eyes, but his smile was still bright. He had his old hat on his head, no different than all the other times I had seen him.

"Well, she's coming to the dance, right Jo?" Anne piped up.

"Oh, she'll be there." Nan smiled back at her friend.

"Were you in on this, too?" I asked Pete.

To that, he threw his hands up in the air. "I want no part in the shenanigans of these two when they are drinking shine," he laughed.

I chuckled. He probably dealt with them way more than I did.

"If I come, it will be completely against my will."

"Well, at least you'll be there," Anne said, winking at me.

I stood. "Well Nan, since you are in no state to walk back to the cabin tonight, are you going to stay here?"

"Oh, yes, we still have more to catch up on," Anne said,

clasping her hands together.

Nan smiled at her friend. "I would love to." She looked back at me. "Will you be alright tonight?" Anne and Pete had a room dedicated to Nan for her visits. She often stayed here when we came to town; making the long walk two times a day was hard on her knee. They had offered to let me stay several times as well, but I would rather stay by myself than impose upon them anymore.

"Yes, I'll be fine. I'll come back and get you in the morning. I don't want you to have to walk by yourself."

"Nonsense. I can walk alone."

I nodded. We went through this every time, and every time—no matter how much she argued—I came to join her for the walk back. The distance wasn't that far for me—I could easily do it in under an hour.

"I'll see you in the morning." I kissed her on the forehead. "Pete," I inclined my head on my way out, "keep them out of trouble."

"Will do," he nodded.

I left for the cabin without a second glance.

CHAPTER 11
ASH

I made it back home right before dark. The sunset was a brilliant display of different hues of color. My pack thudded inside the door of the cabin when I dropped it on the wood floor. Facing the sunset, I decided to hike up to my favorite spot on the mountain above our home. Snacks for dinner that I had gathered in The Market weighed down my pockets as I ascended the slope.

Pop found the spot long ago, and we used to sit there often and watch sunsets together. At the top of the hill, the trees cleared off, providing a perfect view of the sunset and the valleys below. My favorite spot was a large, flat-topped rock that faced west, almost like it was made to watch the splendor of a sunset after a long day.

I plopped myself down on the rock and took a deep breath of the warm, spring air. The smell of pines and sagebrush lingered in my nose. The wildflowers that graced the tops of the mountains were blooming. Bright patches of red, purple, and yellow dotted the green grass. Spring might have been my favorite time of year. It was like a fresh start, filling my mind with possibilities for the future.

I pulled my knees up to my chest and rested my forearms, staring into the beauty before me.

My mind wandered to the events of the day. Why wouldn't Nan live with Anne? It was a question that was constantly on my mind. Maybe she would if I moved closer to town. Was there an empty house I could live in? The walk to the cabin was getting too hard on her, and I didn't know how much longer she could do it. Diesel asked about us moving closer to town, too. Maybe it was the safest bet or the riskiest. I still had my hair to think about.

Marva's words about Novum came to mind. It was hard to think about anything big-picture when so much of our everyday lives was solely based on survival and just trying to eat—but the thought of anyone fighting back against the King made hope bloom in my chest. Maybe one day I could truly be free and figure out what was truly happening with blondes.

The green-eyed man, who took up so much space in my head, flashed across my memory. Nan's words from earlier echoed in my ears. Could I tell him about my hair? What would he do? My adoptive parents' teachings were ingrained in my soul—trust nobody. Was I having a hard time getting over that state of mind?

Lost in thought and the surrounding peacefulness, I didn't notice that someone had snuck up on me until I heard the crunch of gravel underfoot. Rocks tumbled down the hill from my sudden stance. Diesel gazed back at me from not far away.

I stared at him inquisitively. What was he doing here? It was no secret to him that this was my favorite spot. He had come here with me often in the past. I probably should have expected it after the way we left things earlier, but then again, I didn't really know what to expect out of him lately. My backside found its spot on the rock once more. My eyes turned back to the sunset, and I ignored his existence altogether, trying to sort out my thoughts.

"Must be thinking about something important. You didn't even hear me until I was almost on top of you." He seated himself on the rock beside me, his muscle-hardened thigh careful not to brush mine.

My shoulders inclined in a shrug. His appearance destroyed my moment of silence and peacefulness.

"How'd you know I was up here?"

"Well, you weren't at the cabin, and I know how much you love watching sunsets, especially one this brilliant," he said, gesturing toward the beautiful sky.

We sat in silence longer, staring at the shadows that grew longer and the sun that slowly left the day. The sky developed from brilliant orange and yellow to a pale pink color.

Diesel blew out a breath before speaking. "I'm sorry. I didn't mean to upset you earlier. I was only trying to help." His voice was strained, like apologizing didn't come easy.

I wasn't mad at him, not really; not for standing up for me. I shook my head. "*I'm* sorry. Thank you for helping me. It wasn't you—I just have a lot on my mind." My knees met my chest, and I hugged them close. I hated that he was with Lily more than I cared to admit; and I hated that I would never be her.

"Like what?"

"Do you ever wish the world was different?" I mumbled.

"Every day."

I gazed at his profile as he took in the canyons below.

"What do you wish was different?"

"I wish I knew how to cook for one. I'm tired of eating the same thing every day," he chuckled, trying to lighten the mood.

I snorted a laugh. "Don't look at me—I'm probably worse than you. Nan does all the cooking. Maybe she can help." I pulled out the jerky and dried berries I brought with me. "You can see how well I feed myself when she's not around."

He cursed and carefully plucked some berries out of my hand. I snorted a laugh until we fell into silence once more.

"I'm worried about Nan," I whispered.

"Is this about what I said when we were out hunting? I'm sorry, Ash. I didn't mean to make you worry."

"No, it's not about that. It's more about what she told me

today."

He peered at me with inquiring eyes.

"She wants me to make more friends. She's worried about me not having anybody when she leaves."

He tried to contain his laughter, and the berries he had eaten threatened to spill out of his mouth. "You wouldn't know how to be social if it smacked you in the side of the head."

"I'm trying to have a serious conversation with you, and you're laughing at me."

I punched him in the shoulder, and he laughed, but suddenly something stopped him, and his smile fell.

"I'll always be there for you, Spitfire. Even with your lack of social skills."

"Seriously, you are the worst!" A berry flew from my hand toward his face. "I don't want to be friends anymore."

"Nope," he said, popping his lips together. "You can't take that back—we are best friends forever."

Friends. Always just friends.

"Is something going on with Nan? How come she's talking like that, anyway?"

"No... nothing more than usual. It's been a long winter and the walk to town was hard on her today."

"Have you thought about my offer at all?"

I had no clue what he was talking about, and it must have shown on my face.

"Remember, I told you if Nan didn't want to leave the cabin, I could come live with you and help out."

He was serious about that?

"No, Diesel, that's not necessary. It's fine. We are fine."

"Really, Ash. It's not a big deal. I'm in my house by myself, anyway. I'll even sleep outside now that it's warm enough. I'll probably be gone quite a bit too. I have lots of jobs lined up for this spring."

"No, I don't think that's a good idea."

"Why?"

Um. Two things: my hair and him. I wasn't sure If I wanted him to see my hair, and I was confused about him lately. Instead of giving him my very valid reasons, I spit out the first thing that came to my mind.

"I just like my privacy, I guess."

"Trying to hide something from me, Spitfire?" He raised his eyebrows and shot me a smirk. What did I say to that? *Be cool, Ash.*

"No," I shrugged. *Good one.*

"Will you at least think about it?"

I blew out a breath. "Yeah, I'll talk to Nan."

"Thank you," he breathed.

We chewed on our jerky and berries for a bit, watching the sun sink lower and the birds find their roosting spots for the night. The silence in the mountains was beautiful because it wasn't silence. The land brimmed with life, overflowing with the small sounds of the bugs and the animals around us.

"I talked to Marva today."

"Oh boy, what nuggets of information did she have for you today?" he grinned.

"She said that Novum is at war with the people in the north. That they're fighting back against the King and that they are free."

His face turned deadly serious. "I hadn't heard that."

"Who knows if it's true. You know Marva," I chuckled. "But the idea of being free does sound appealing."

"You're free here, aren't you? His soldiers don't bother us for the most part, the only time they were here last year was for recruitment."

Recruitment. I had never been, but I had heard about when the soldiers came to town looking for new prospects. According to Nan and Marva, there was never a shortage of boys and men lined up to serve the King, trying to escape our dreary existence for a chance at a better life. But if they weren't volunteering to be a soldier, then they were running away from them. Soldiers seemed to do more horrendous things than anybody else.

Tell him. Tell him about my hair. Tell him why I couldn't ever truly be free in Novum.

The words danced on the edge of my tongue, but I couldn't. He studied every feature on my face while I worked it over in my head. "Yeah," I sighed. "I guess you're right."

His eyes flashed with disappointment, and he looked away. What was that about?

"Besides, Ash. You don't want to go north. You think winters are bad here? Up there, it's like constant winter all year long."

"How do you know?"

"My dad. He knew a lot."

The sun had sunk below the skyline, casting the world in shadow. The last purple hues of the sunset shimmered over the top of the distant mountains.

"So, are you going to take Nan's advice?"

I fidgeted with the jerky in my hand. "I don't know—obviously, I'm not good at making friends. I'm probably better off by myself, anyway."

He nodded his head thoughtfully. "You still planning on leaving one day?"

"I want to know who I am, D. I want to know where I came from."

"I think you should know that I don't want you to go."

Our eyes met, and his swayed with emotion, reflecting the colorful hues of the sunset. He stood suddenly and stretched his legs, gazing down into the valley below.

"Let's get you back to the cabin before it gets too dark."

"What's your problem with walking in the dark?"

He shot me a sour look. "We're not all freaks like you, who can see perfectly at night."

My laugh echoed across the top of the hill into the cool, night air. I gathered up my stuff and stood with him. We took one last breath of the evening breeze sweeping across the mountainside and then walked down together. The shadowy interior of the cabin greeted us. I lit the fire that had gone out from being absent all day.

Crouched by the fire, stoking the small flames, I asked Diesel, who leaned against the door frame, "Do you want to stay tonight? Nan is with Anne and it's a long walk back in the dark to your house, which apparently, you hate."

A look of pleasant surprise washed over his features. The dim light and his dark beard disguised his mouth, but from what I could tell, happiness tugged at his lips.

"That would be great. Thank you, Ash."

Maybe that was a mistake. Being alone in this small cabin in the dark with him saying my name like that wasn't good for me.

He set his things down by the door. The old kitchen chair creaked when he took a seat. His large frame barely fit on the rickety, old thing, and I was afraid the legs might give out.

"Do you want something to eat or a glass of water?" I asked, unsure of what to talk to him about now.

My mind reeled with nervousness and tension. I had never felt this way around him before.

He shook his head. "No, I'm okay. Judging by what you said about your cooking, I'm not sure I would want to eat anything you would make, anyway," he said with a grin.

I took all my things by the door to the pantry to put away. Once inside, I called out, "Are you going to be planting soon?"

Diesel surprised me when he answered from just outside the pantry door. I looked up from my task and he stood in the doorway, arms raised and resting on the top door frame that was made of earth. His biceps bulged out of his shirt, and I quickly averted my eyes.

"No…" he said carefully. "Farming was more of my dad's thing. I always hated it." The pain in his face at the mention of his dad hurt my heart. It was clear that he was still grieving and trying to figure out life without Miles by his side.

"So, what'll you do for food?"

He gave a slight shrug. "Hunt, fish. I've got plenty of odd jobs in town. Anything I try to grow would die, anyway. I was never any good with the plants."

"I can help. With the plants—If you want."

"No, I'll be fine—don't need them." Surprise rang in my head at the surety of his words.

I finished putting the last of the supplies away and went to back out into the main room, but Diesel didn't move out of the way. My body had moved into his proximity, his powerful form filling up the doorway, arms still resting above his head. His intense green eyes bore into mine. He looked at me like I was a puzzle he was trying to figure out. One of his hands descended and tentatively brushed the side of my face.

I cast my eyes down. My heart raced, and my nerves had come back in full force. I think he sensed my nervousness, glancing at the fluttering pulse in my neck. He quickly dropped his hand and moved out of the way so I could pass.

I tried to get my racing heart and flushed face under control before I stepped back out into the main room. It was the first time he had willingly touched me since the elk hunt. Only the lightest graze of fingers across my cheek and it felt like an enormous leap. Diesel had pulled a chair over by the fire and gazed into its orange depths while I lingered in the kitchen.

"You can take Nan's bed."

"No way. I don't want to get on her bad side."

"Are you scared of a little old lady?" I laughed.

"You bet I am." His voice broke with laughter.

"Fine. You can take my bedroll, and I'll sleep in Nan's bed. We can bring it down from the loft and you can sleep by the fire. There'll be more room down here." The loft was tiny, and I questioned if Diesel would even fit up there.

He climbed the small ladder to grab my bed, pulling it down into the main room. I helped him get it situated, and he lay back on the worn canvas, spreading his arms behind his head. His shoulder and bicep muscles strained at his shirt again. Couldn't he find a bigger shirt? I turned and went to Nan's room to get some sleep, leaving him on the floor by the fire.

CHAPTER 12
ASH

We woke the next morning to birds chirping outside the cabin and Diesel said he was leaving, so I joined him to collect Nan.

I took the lead, and he followed behind me. About halfway there, someone came up the trail. My bow rested in front of me with an arrow ready, just in case. Diesel placed himself slightly in front of me, which annoyed me all over again.

We waited for whoever it was to step into sight. The sound of a person with a limp echoed through the forest. I put the arrow back in my quiver, stepping toward Nan. Diesel threw his hand up in front of me.

"What are you doing?"

"It's Nan." I had spent almost every waking moment with the woman for years—I knew the sound of her walk. Right as I got the words out of my mouth, the old lady came shuffling around the corner. She saw us instantly and her eyes grew wider with delight at the sight of Diesel next to me.

"Good morning, Nan." I smiled at her, stopping her from saying anything about my current walking partner. "Why didn't you wait for me?"

"Nonsense. I told you I can walk by myself." She waved me off.

Her eyes turned back to Diesel, full of mischief.

"Good morning, Diesel. What brings you out here so early in the morning?" Her eyes wandered back and forth between us.

"Just came by to see your girl."

"My, she does look quite lovely this morning, doesn't she?"

"Okay," I said, cutting her off before she could say anything further. "Let's get back to the cabin." I interlocked my forearm with hers to help her up the trail.

We walked back past Diesel, and Nan piped up again. "We'll see you at the spring festival next week, Diesel. Maybe you can even share a dance with my girl." She affectionately patted my arm. His face seemed puzzled, and I shook my head, imploring him to ignore the meddling woman.

"Bye, D." My arms pulled Nan down the trail before she could say anything further.

"I'll see you next week at the festival, then?"

"Yes, she will definitely be there," Nan answered for me.

He continued looking at me, waiting for my answer. I rolled my eyes and sighed. "Yes, I'll be there."

"Good." He turned his eyes back to Nan. "I would love to

have a dance with Ash."

I laughed at Nan's joy. "You don't know what you're getting yourself into," I teased.

His lip quirked up. "See you next week."

Something about him seemed tentative around me that wasn't there before, like our teasing that always felt so natural was now forced. When I was sure he was out of earshot, I spoke up.

"Nan, stop meddling."

She chuckled at my discomfort.

"That boy cares a great deal about you."

"We're only friends," I reminded her.

"So, you didn't destroy our cabin with your exploits last night?" she laughed.

I burst out laughing. My eyes were watering from laughing so hard at the ridiculous comment.

I raised my hands in surrender. "No, the cabin is safe."

She smirked at me, and we resumed our journey back home.

The next few days were full of working the earth and getting our seeds planted that weren't prone to frost. The weather was still warming up, and a surprise frost might still hit us. We waited until we were sure that our plants wouldn't die to plant the frost-prone seeds.

Two mornings before the festival, I left to harvest watercress that grew on Red Creek. A marshy area rested along the creek, down from where I shot the elk. Watercress grew abundantly in the water in that area. We could take it with us to the festival to share, since there was plenty of it.

I took off midmorning, leaving Nan digging radishes down by our creek. The walk was much more pleasant than it was a month ago, when I had to trudge through the snow.

The red-tinted creek ran in front of me a short while later. It was a pretty sight; all the green plants against the strange red water. I sat down to rest and get a drink out of my bottle before getting to work gathering up the plants.

As I sat next to the creek listening to the water flow, something moved a distance away—much bigger than a bird or squirrel. Unsure of what it might be, I took my stuff and clambered up the nearest pine as quietly as possible. The branches of the tree surrounded my form, hiding me from onlookers. The noise came again, much closer this time. I had my bow ready, bracing my legs on the limbs to hold myself up in case of trouble.

I peeled my eyes in the noise's direction. Footsteps got clearer as they got closer, another person, by the sound of the gait. A head peeked out of the trees on the other side of the creek. It was a man, about my age or younger, I would guess. All alone. He was small in stature and had large eyes that wandered in every direction, assessing for threats. The only weapons on his person were a few knives and what looked like a roughly-built sword that was strapped to his back over his pack. He looked too small to be a bounty hunter and wasn't wearing Novum's blue insignia around his arm like the soldiers usually did.

He didn't seem to be a threat, but I wasn't taking my chances. Luckily for me, his eyes didn't look up often enough to pick me out of the shadows of the tree. I stayed silent and hoped he would pass by.

He treaded over the ground stealthily enough that it surprised me that I had heard him from as far away as I did. The creek halted his movement, and he stopped for a break like I had.

He sat and pulled off his pack, always looking and listening for danger. He took out his bottle and filled it up with water before taking a long drink. Then he set his bottle aside and rifled through his pack in search of something. From his bag, he produced yellowing pieces of paper. What was he looking at?

His eyes tracked over the papers for long minutes. After searching them, he placed them in the grass next to him and took off his hat to splash water on his sweaty face. The color of his hair fascinated me. The shade was a similar dirty brown to mine. Did he dye his hair too? I wanted to know so badly I almost climbed down the tree and asked him, but thought better of it.

He eyed up the watercress in the creek and plucked a stem out of the water, popping it into his mouth. I imagined a peppery taste coated his tongue, and he quickly spit it out after a few bites. I suppressed a laugh at the sour look on his face. Watercress wasn't for everyone.

Where did he come from? Who was this man? What was he doing so close to Cedar Hill? All were questions that I would have loved to know the answer to, but never would, because I wouldn't leave my hiding spot to ask.

He gathered up his things and took off down the creek, looking for a spot to cross. His direction made me think he was going toward Cedar Hill. He jumped across a narrow spot in the creek not far away and I waited until I was sure he was out of earshot to climb down the tree, listening extra intently to any noises to ensure I was alone.

My feet hit the ground, and I took my boots off, rolling up my pants. Water reached my knees when I waded into the creek to gather up the abundant green herb. The creek was cool against my heated skin. Mud squished under my toes as I moved through the water. My knife sliced through the stems of the plant, easily gathering a large pile that waited on the edge of the creek, probably too big to fit into my pack.

I bundled it all up in my bag and my backside met the grass once more to put my boots on. I glanced around to make sure all my things were gathered and something caught my eye from the opposite side of the creek. I waded in once more and walked to the other side—leaning up onto the bank to snatch the paper out of the grass.

I carried it back over to the other side before opening it, to make sure it didn't get wet. The worn paper crinkled against my fingers as I unfolded it. A smaller piece of paper fell out into the grass. It was an extremely well-drawn picture of a little girl. She looked like she was maybe only four or five years old. I didn't have any idea who she was, and I felt bad that the man dropped this. Especially if it was someone important to him. His daughter maybe, but he didn't look old enough.

I set the picture aside and looked at the bigger paper. It was a map of Novum—more detailed than I had ever seen. It labeled towns and cities that I had never even heard of before. Hope was almost in the center of the map, Cedar Hill far to the north of Hope. Those were the only two places I really knew, besides the names of the outlying towns from Cedar Hill. The areas around the land where the map said 'ocean' fascinated me. What was it like living next to such a large body of water?

There were X's marked all over the map. Many of the towns held several X's. Had he really been to all these places? Was he trying to get to as many places as possible, or was he looking for something in particular? Not knowing what it really meant, I folded it back up and stuffed it in my front pocket.

CHAPTER 13
ASH

The morning of the spring festival, we got our chores done early; checking the garden, bringing water in from the creek, and collecting firewood. Small plants pushed through the soil, signaling the start of a new growing season. My knees were in the dirt when I helped brush the dust off the tiny starts. Our existence relied on these plants—it was overwhelming to think about. If something happened to them, it would be our demise.

Nan washed our nicest clothes the day prior and set them out to dry. Around noon, she said it was time to go. I begrudgingly agreed and put the clothes on that she had set out for me like a toddler. We left for town and walked into the crowded streets by early afternoon. I expected to head straight to the town center to join in the festivities, when Nan directed me down a side road.

"Where are we going?" I asked, puzzled.

"I have a surprise for you." Nan smiled secretively.

"What is it?"

"You'll have to wait and see." The smile on her face grew bigger.

I couldn't say I was excited about Nan's surprise, especially if it had to do with the foolish dance tonight. She pulled me along the street with her arm looped through mine until we arrived at Anne's house. We stepped up to the front of the door and Nan knocked. It surprised me that Anne was home with all the activities going on today.

"Perfect timing," she exclaimed, sharing a secretive look with Nan.

"What's going on here?"

They both smiled at each other as I followed them into the house. Laid out on the table were a few dresses I had never seen before. The fabric was beautiful and missing all the holes my usual clothes had. There were also stunning clips for hair, brushes, and combs. Anne had laid enough supplies out on the table to pamper a horse.

"Nope, not happening." I turned to leave, back out the door. Nan grabbed my arm before I could flee.

"Oh, hush. It won't hurt you one bit to get a little done up for once in your life."

My lips pursed, taking in both their excited faces. How could I tell them no?

"Fine, but I'm not wearing a dress," I grumbled.

Anne's teeth glinted with an enormous smile. "I thought you might say that." She walked over to the table and underneath the stack of dresses, she produced the nicest pair of black pants I had ever seen. Then, an equally stunning blouse. It was a deep red color, and the fit looked tighter than anything I owned—with a plunging V in the front to show off cleavage I didn't possess.

I shook my head. It was too much.

"Where did you get those? I can't take them from you."

"So, you love them, then?" Anne asked, smiling.

"Well, yeah. But I can't accept something that nice. It probably cost you half of a year's food."

Her steps sounded off the wood floor when she moved closer. She placed her hand on my arm and looked into my face with an affection that only Nan had ever shown me. "You can and you will, because they sure don't fit me or Jo, so if you don't take them, they will sit here forever collecting dust."

Nan had unshed tears of gratitude in her eyes. I felt my eyes soften at the sight of Nan and the selfless woman before me.

"You deserve this more than anyone I know, sweetheart. You are the only daughter I have, so let me spoil you a little bit. Go have fun tonight."

I took the clothes from her hands with extreme reverence, remembering that one of the reasons Nan and Anne had grown so close was neither of them were able to have children.

"Thank you." The earnestness in my voice rang true.

"Well, I'll leave you two to get ready. I have the kids' races to judge soon." She embraced Nan and in return, Nan thanked her again with a lone tear trailing down her cheek. "There's something there for you too," Anne whispered to Nan before she headed out the door.

"I like your best friend," I told Nan when she left.

"Me too." She stared at the door.

She turned to me suddenly, wiping away the tear. "Well, go try them on," she insisted. The fancy clothes looked expensive next to my chewed-off fingernails, which were always covered in grime, no matter how hard I scrubbed. I didn't deserve something so nice. The room where Nan stayed was small. A bed with a makeshift table next to it were the only items in the room.

The new clothes appeared pristine compared to the ratty ones I pulled off my body. My ragged underwear and bra looked silly against the delicate fabric, but they would have to do. I rarely even wore a bra, but today was an exception. The slim-fitting, black pants hugged my legs perfectly, showing every rise and fall of the muscles on my legs. Nan must have given Anne my measurements. She took them a while back, stating she would make us new clothes.

The pants stretched across my thighs and backside in a way a pair of pants never had. The high waist accentuated the curves

I didn't think I had. I put the red shirt over my head. The fabric was soft, and like the pants, the fit was snug. A deep V in the front showed enough cleavage to make people think I had a more ample bosom than I did. The outfit was perfect in every way, from what I could see without a mirror. I switched the picture and map, that had been in my pocket since I found them, into my new slacks. As perfect as the outfit was, it made me feel like a bit of an imposter. This wasn't the real me. I stared at my discarded clothes on the ground. One night wouldn't hurt, right?

I stepped out of the room and back in front of Nan.

"You look absolutely beautiful, my girl."

"Thanks, Nan." I gave her a kiss on the forehead. "I love it."

A dress on the table that appeared Nan's size called to me, and I handed it to her.

"Your turn." I winked and shooed her away into the bedroom to change. She came out wearing the cute, long, floral dress that was perfect on her.

"Nan, you look stunning."

She gave me a smile. "Now, let's get started on taming that wild hair of yours."

We spent the afternoon doing each other's hair. Nan's was harder to get done because it was so short. I did my best, brushing it to the side and adorning it with a shiny clip. She did some sort of fancy braid on the top of my head and let the rest of my long hair flow free. I rarely wore it in anything other than a long braid or in a hat, so it felt strange wearing it like this. Thanks to a recent dye job, it was dark, disguising the yellow locks. She also made me put pink stuff on my lips and cheeks. I entertained her desire to dress me up for the evening. The only problem we encountered was that I had no shoes that matched my outfit. The old hunting boots would have to do for tonight.

By the time we got done, it was early evening and dinner was about to be served on Main Street. We took the flatbread Nan made and the watercress I harvested and added them to the table with the rest of the offerings for dinner. Anne and Pete had been working hard on the festival. They decorated Main Street and The Market beautifully with wildflowers that had bloomed. Candles and lanterns were everywhere, waiting until darkness fell to be lit.

The spring festival was always situated around the first full moon of the spring, so there would be plenty of light for people to celebrate late into the night.

Vendors lined the street that had come from across Novum to sell their trinkets and food. A multitude of people were here that I didn't recognize. There was no sign of soldiers or bounty hunters, and I blew out a relaxing breath.

We stood among the crowd by the tables. Nan chatted absently with people she knew. Luke, Ty, Lily, and their other friends stood in a group close to us. They all looked at me and chuckled to themselves. I felt self-conscious and folded my arms over my chest, but turned around and ignored them. They wouldn't destroy my evening.

Anne and Pete moved through the crowd until they reached the front steps of the market.

"Welcome, everyone!" Pete's voice boomed out. "Thank you for coming to Cedar Hill's spring festival. Dinner is served. Thank you to everyone for bringing items to share. After dinner, our self-appointed band will play for us, and you can all dance the night away. I believe Anne has a surprise up her sleeve as well," he said, looking at his wife. "Please enjoy the evening." The crowd burst into clapping and cheering at the end of his speech. The band started up, playing soft music in the background.

Everyone crowded the tables to get food. Nan and I picked through the tables, snatching up anything that looked appetizing before seating ourselves on the grass across from the market. We ate and enjoyed each other's company until our bellies were bursting and I was even more unsure of the tight outfit.

I spotted Marva sitting in the grass not far away, and excused myself to go chat with one of my favorite people.

She saw me approaching and whistled. "Would you look at you in all those fancy duds."

I plopped down on the grass next to her. Marva was like the town pariah that no one liked, except for me. I guess that was why we liked one another. She rarely talked to anyone, but overheard everything. She didn't have any family that I knew of and lived in a tiny shack at the edge of town. Her house was full of fabric from the only job she knew.

"Did you make these?"

"Well, I couldn't resist making special clothes for a special girl," she said slyly. "Anne brought me the fabric, and I did what I could."

"Marva! These must have taken you ages to make."

"Nope." She winked at me. "Not even half of a thought."

I laughed. "Well, thank you, I love them."

"Anne wanted me to make you a dress," she guffawed. "You—wear a dress? Can you imagine?"

I chuckled again. "Well, I guess it's a good thing you know me better than Anne."

She gave me a wide smile full of crooked teeth. The music got louder as the sun set. People moved to dance—mostly parents, with kids who wanted to dance before it was too late, and they needed to go to bed.

"You going to dance tonight?" I asked.

"Absolutely. It's the only time I can get these old legs to move the way I want them to. Maybe I can even snag myself a young fellow."

I snickered and stood up. "Well, I'll see you later. Have fun dancing."

My mouth felt dry from all the food and lack of water. My

feet found their way over to the table to get a drink. Nan was nowhere in sight.

I stopped in my tracks when I caught sight of Diesel staring right at me through the crowd. One of his friends stood next to him, chatting idly, but he only had eyes for me. He had trimmed his beard short, making his chin even more chiseled and handsome. Dark jeans, that I had never seen him wear before, covered his legs, fitting his muscular thighs perfectly. His button-down shirt matched his eyes, making them stand out even more. He looked perfect, standing across from me, staring back. His dark gaze made me feel like I was the only girl in the world, sending butterflies dancing through my stomach.

CHAPTER 14
DIESEL

I spotted her the second I strolled into town and down Main Street. Not like I didn't know exactly where she was—I was never far away. Except when she snuck away a few afternoons ago while I was busy with a job, only to return with armfuls of watercress that was now plopped on the food table. She giggled on the grass with Marva, that crazy old coot. I swear, her blue eyes glistened in the dying sunlight as she turned her face up and laughed again. She was beautiful, and she didn't even know it. My chest twinged again, and I was disgusted with myself.

I ground my teeth together when Lily slithered up to my side as soon as I stepped into the group of friends I usually spent my time with—if I wasn't with Ash. She was harmless, but her clinginess was getting on my nerves lately. Maybe I had changed my mind about things, but she was still a perfect distraction when I needed it.

"Hi, Diesel," she said, placing her hand on my forearm.

"You look rather dashing this evening."

I quirked my lip up in response.

"Hey Diesel!" Cooper strode up. "Good to see you, man."

Cooper Benson. The man that was the closest thing I had to a friend in this shit town. He at least was a little more sophisticated that most of these backwoods' pricks. I could handle his presence, unlike many other people.

I pulled away from Lily's grip to shake his hand. He was almost a head shorter than me, with dark skin and hair. He spent his days working with wood, carving and creating whatever anyone could think of—I had to admit he was talented. I respected him for running his own business and doing well enough to take care of himself and his sister. "You too, Coop. How's the carpentry business treating you?"

"Oh, you know...interesting sometimes." His eyes strayed to Lily when he said those words and her cheeks flamed. What the hell?

"I'm just going to go see if my mom needs some help with the food," Lily said before rushing away.

"Want to tell me what that was about?"

Cooper laughed. "You don't want to know, man." He slapped me on the back, and I saw Ash stand up from her place in the grass with Marva. I hadn't noticed the clothes she was wearing before, and I nearly swallowed my tongue when I took them in. Cooper was still idly talking at my side, but my ears were buzzing from the woman across the street. She wore a deep red shirt and black pants that were far too fitted for my liking. All I had ever seen her in were her ugly, camouflage hunting pants or a baggy pair of cargo pants, but these…, shit. I could see at least three men looking at her as she passed from here. I didn't know whether to go pummel all of them or be revolted in myself for caring.

I sauntered over to her, my eyes roaming her body. She ducked her head shyly as I approached, seemingly unsure of herself.

"Ash." It was hard to form words. The contradicting thoughts inside my head threatened to make it explode.

"Better than my hunting pants?" she joked, gesturing to her tight pants.

I nodded instead of answering.

"You look pretty good yourself." She tugged at the bottom of my green shirt.

"Thanks," I said. Her blue eyes were wide and the heat in them threatened to burn me. Cooper cleared his throat by my side, and I scrubbed my hand over my face. "You remember Cooper?"

"Um, yeah. Hi," she said, shooting him a small smile. I could tell she had no idea who he was; it wasn't surprising as she didn't interact with people in town much and now I knew why.

Cooper stuck his hand out, and she put her hand in his.

"Ash, so nice to officially meet you. I've seen you around but never had the pleasure. Diesel doesn't talk about you much." Because she was none of his damn business. Then he winked at her, and I about lost it, barely containing the anger on my face. I had no right to feel this way about her—I shouldn't care.

"Yeah, same to you," she murmured.

I glared at where their hands interlocked, and she quickly pulled away, her cheeks flaming with embarrassment.

"Well, I was headed to get a drink," she excused herself. "See you guys later."

She practically ran to the drink table and poured herself a cup of water. It was getting dark, and people made their way around, lighting all the candles and lanterns. She turned to watch the candles and the moon, and her face filled with awe—the same look she got when she stared at a sunset.

"Why aren't you two a thing?" Cooper asked, and my attention on her wavered. When I looked back, she had disappeared into the shadows somewhere. I wasn't worried. She wouldn't leave without Nan, who I could still see on the grass.

I shrugged. He really needed to mind his own business.

"Well, if you're not going to…"

"I would recommend that you don't finish that sentence. Touch her and I'll rip out your throat."

I glowered at him before he chuckled awkwardly. "At least it's not Lily."

My eyes shot to him. "What's wrong with Lily?"

"Wait, you two? Oh, damn."

"What?"

He shook his head, and his eyebrows pinched together. "Never mind, man. I've got to go find my sister. I'll talk to you later."

Cooper walked off before I could ask any more questions, leaving me to work my way through the crowd listening to hunting stories, condolences for Miles, and job offers—always watching the shadow of the building where Ash had snuck away to watch in silence instead of interacting with these people. I didn't blame her—I hated this town and despised the people in it. The only person that I liked, I hated, too. Most of my interactions were forced, and I had to pretend like I belonged.

CHAPTER 15
ASH

Anne and Pete found me leaning next to the building in the dark, watching the people with no interest in talking to them. "You look absolutely beautiful," she said, smiling at me.

"Thank you. It's all thanks to you." I looked at Pete. "You have an amazing wife."

He gazed down at Anne with nothing but adoration in his eyes. "I know."

They stared at each other with so much love, it could make a person sick.

"I hope you aren't running away. Our special dance is going to start in a few minutes," Anne said.

"In that case, I better get out of here," I said in a joking voice, but I was completely serious.

She saw right through me and linked her arm through mine. "Well, I guess you'll have to walk me over to the dance floor to prevent disappearing."

"I promise I'll be good and come over."

"I don't believe you one bit, missy."

She eyed me up, and I relented, letting her lead me toward the dance floor.

I turned as we strolled away—willing Pete to save me from this torture. He only smiled and waved.

The band finished their song, and Anne gave them a signal to pause for a moment while she spoke. All eyes turned to us, and I felt extremely uncomfortable at being the center of attention. I tried to pull away from her, but she held tight to my arm.

Diesel's presence was like a beacon—I could pick him out of any crowd. He followed me over and stood at the edge of the dance floor. Nan and Marva were also in the crowd, standing next to one another. Marva's face looked flushed in the dim light. She had probably been dancing. I begged them with my eyes to get me out of this. They only smiled and laughed at me. *Useless.*

"Ladies and gentlemen, we're going to have a dance for our young people of marrying age, to help them get to know each other better." Anne's voice rose above the dull roar of the crowd. She clapped her hands together excitedly. Her grip on my arm faltered, and I took it as my chance to sidle away.

"We will have three dances. You can dance with whomever you wish. The first one will be men's choice, the second women's, and for the last I will pair you up with someone you may not have chosen for yourself."

I inched further and further away from Anne's side—hoping to slip into the shadows unnoticed.

"Everyone who is single and of marrying age, please come into the center."

She glanced to her side and noticed I was no longer there, but quickly spotted me, dragging me back with her. A few people came to the center on their own, but most got shoved and prodded by family members to join in the center. After it was all said and done, about twenty people stood in the middle of the circle—with a crowd gathered around the outside.

"Alright, I'll get things started. Since it's men's choice, would any of you strapping young men like to join Ash in a dance?" Good thing it was dark out so no one could see my beat-red face, with all the attention on me.

My eyes slid to Diesel to save me, but he was in an intense conversation with Lily, who stood too close to him. What were they talking about? Nope, I didn't care.

"I'll dance with the princess," Luke called out. This was literally my worst nightmare. He stepped toward me, but Diesel finally realized what was happening. He hurried between me and Luke and spoke to Anne. "I choose Ash."

"Sorry Diesel, but Luke spoke first. Wait your turn." Anne looked at me with genuine remorse in her eyes.

A smug smile traversed Luke's face as he moved past Diesel and offered me his arm. The idea of dancing with him repulsed me after our earlier interaction. My eyes lingered on Anne and Diesel, begging…pleading for a savior, but Anne gestured toward his arm. I reluctantly took it as he led me out onto the dance floor. I was never coming to a spring festival again. The number of times people forced me into something unwillingly tonight was ridiculous.

"Okay, the rest of you men, please pick your partners."

The rest of the couples quickly paired up, and I stood as far away from Luke as I could, waiting for the dance to start. Luke and I may be more similar than I thought. His clothes were almost as tattered as mine usually were, making me feel a little bad for him—but that was where our similarities ended. A slow fiddle song played, and Luke stepped close to me, taking my hand and my waist like the perfect gentleman that he wasn't. I avoided looking at him as we moved across the dance floor. I noted Diesel had chosen Lily as a partner, causing my insecurities to multiply.

Luke spoke into my ear, far too close for my liking.

"You look fine tonight, princess, way better when you're cleaned up than when you are skulking around in the woods."

I snorted and shook my head at his backhanded compliment.

"Someone has to feed our family. I can't sit around the castle all day and look pretty." I gave in to his taunt and instantly regretted it.

"You could marry me, and I'll bring you food. You can sit around my castle all day and take care of my needs," he smirked.

"You proposing to me, Luke?"

"Would you say yes?"

"You wish."

"I do," he said, while looking up and down my body, making my skin crawl.

I resumed ignoring him as we moved, hoping the fiddle player's instrument would spontaneously combust.

"Why don't you like me, princess? We could be so good together."

His hand slid down from my waist and further onto my backside.

Not wanting to ruin Anne's dance, I seethed at him. "Get your hand off my ass."

A filthy smile covered his face. "No, I don't think I will." His hand gave me a firm squeeze. That was it. I had enough— to hell with Anne's dance.

I stomped on his foot, and he released me. He bent down to nurse his hurt toes, and I grabbed his head, bringing my knee up to his face. A sickening crunch landed in my ears when my knee hit its mark.

"Never touch me again," I whispered into his ear before releasing his head.

"You'll pay for this," he threatened, danger lacing his tone. He pinched his nose and tried to stop the blood that poured out of it. The music stopped, and everyone looked at us. Diesel was in between us in the next instant—right in Luke's face.

"What did you do?" His voice dripped with malice—fists clenched, poised to attack.

Not wanting to make more of a scene, I put my hand on Diesel's flexed arm.

"It's okay. I took care of it," I mumbled.

Diesel's eyes turned to me. His eyes roamed my body, assessing for damage. "Are you okay?" He got to my knee, where a fresh blood stain covered my pants. He inspected it closer.

"It's not mine. I'm fine."

Anne's voice broke in as she leveled me with a disappointed stare.

"Whatever is going on here needs to stop. Take your problems somewhere else." Her angry face landed on Diesel, Luke, and I. Luke gave me one last glance, with a promise of violence written in his eyes, before he pushed his way through the crowd and out of the circle.

"Sorry, Anne," I said, turning to leave as well.

Diesel pulled me protectively to his side, laying a possessive hand on the small of my back.

"Ladies, pick your partners," Anne called out for the second dance.

Diesel didn't seem like he would let go of me anytime soon as he glowered after Luke. The song started up again. I felt weird standing there in the throng—some people danced again, but some still stared at us. Lily caught my attention—she was glaring holes through me. *Fantastic.* More people that hated me.

"Want to dance or just stand here awkwardly?" I asked, pulling Diesel out of his thoughts.

He turned toward me, his large hands sprawling over my waist when he pulled me flush against him. My skin tingled where his hands clasped to my sides. *Okay, so no more balking at touching me then.* We swayed to the music and his arms wrapped around my back, encircling me in a warm cocoon of hard muscles. I was so close to him—all I could see was his taught chest. I couldn't see his face, but I could tell by the tense way he moved that he was still ripe with anger. So was I, at the thought of what Luke did to me, but I let it go for the time being.

"What did he do?" Diesel's low growl was by my ear.

"Nothing." His hands gripped me tighter at my dismissive voice.

His head leaned back so he could study me with frustration in his gaze. "That wasn't nothing. Tell me what happened."

"He grabbed me—okay? I didn't like it, so I took care of it. You don't need to do anything about it. I told you, I can handle myself."

We glared at each other for long seconds before Diesel

glanced around with murder in his eyes, no doubt looking for Luke again. I blew out a frustrated breath and closed my eyes, leaning my head onto Diesel's chest. The scent of Diesel assaulted my senses. I breathed in the smell of wood smoke, fresh pine, and something that was unmistakably proprietary to this infuriating man.

He seemed to relax slightly at my touch as my hands moved from his shoulders to rest on his chest by my head. He gathered me closer and sighed, dropping his forehead to mine as we swayed to the music. We stayed like this for the remainder of the song. I wanted the song to go on longer—I could stay here, wrapped in Diesel's arms all night. It was nice to forget about my problems for a moment and get lost in the music and the feeling of him against me.

The music came to a halt and Anne piped up one last time, telling us she would pick our final partners. I reluctantly opened my eyes and lifted my head out of Diesel's chest. He gazed at me with furrowed brows. His eyes swirled with emotion under his long lashes.

"…and for Ash," Anne said. I pulled out of Diesel's embrace.

"How about this nice-looking young man?" The man stood at the edge of the crowd. I hadn't seen him dance before, and I would have recognized him anywhere.

"Oh, I'm not here to dance," said the man I saw two days

ago at Red Creek.

"Nonsense. Are you married?"

"Well—no," he stuttered.

"Then you can dance one time. Come on." She gestured for him to come over to me. He unwillingly stepped toward us. I moved out of Diesels' arms, wanting to dance with him, only to get answers to my questions. Diesel looked at me with confusion written on his features. Anne moved on, calling out various partners.

The hurt in Diesel's eyes made me want to change my mind. He flared his nostrils at the young man standing uncomfortably next to us.

"If you dare touch her anywhere but her hands and her waist, I'll break your hands." *Whoa*. Was that necessary?

Reluctantly, he walked to the edge of the circle to watch, not having a partner chosen for himself.

The stranger seemed like he was ready to bolt at any moment. I smiled at him, willing him to relax a little. He took my hand and my waist, making sure it wasn't any higher or lower than it should be, knowing Diesel watched from the sidelines.

"Your boyfriend's scary," he said. His voice was deeper than I thought it would be, but he looked younger up close. I was having a hard time guessing his age.

I glanced over at Diesel. "He's not my boyfriend."

The man… or boy, shook his head like he thought I was

lying to him.

"What's your name?" I asked.

"Will—and you must be Ash."

Something sparked in his eyes, like he just noticed me for the first time. He stared at me for a long second, trying to figure something out.

"Are you from here?" he asked suddenly.

"Yeah—well, kind of. For as long as I can remember, at least. Someone dropped me in the middle of nowhere when I was little, and my adoptive parents were kind enough to take me in."

Shock lit up his features and his eyes darted to my hair, scrutinizing it. I felt like he could see right through the dye. There was no way he could tell I was blonde with the dim light and the dark dye, though.

"Where are you from?" I asked carefully.

His eyes met mine again. He seemed happier then. Will was a puzzle that I wanted to figure out.

"South." His simple answer gave nothing away.

The song ended before I could ask him any more questions. He quickly turned and took off through the crowd. I followed behind him, calling after him.

A hand wrapped around my arm from behind. Diesel's firm grip halted my progress. "Just a second," I said, brushing him off and running to the spot where Will disappeared. The streets were empty, and I couldn't see him anywhere. He must have vanished somewhere in between the rows of houses. Not knowing where to go next, my feet stopped.

"Where are you going, Ash? Why are you chasing after that kid?"

Diesel was in front of me again—his eyes begging mine for an answer.

"Nowhere. I thought he was someone else, I guess." My eyes darted around, hoping to catch sight of Will again. Was he blond, like me? Why was he acting so strange?

We were on a street a couple of blocks away from the party. It was much quieter and darker here. Diesel's face was full of turmoil. "What's going on with you? Who was that?"

His guttural voice penetrated my racing mind. I felt bad for making him worry.

"I'm sorry. His hair—it looked like mine I wanted to know if—if maybe…" The words stopped coming out of my mouth as I realized what I had said. I had unwillingly told him about my hair because my mind was too scattered about Will. I waited for the shock and the questions that never came.

"Ash. You can't go around asking people about that. Are you trying to get yourself killed?"

What? My eyes widened. He knew!

He cursed loudly and grabbed my hand, pulling me into the nearest abandoned building that was crumbling with the hands of time.

My eyes darted around the space to make sure no one else had followed. When we got inside, he released my hand.

"How long have you known?" I whispered urgently. Mortification stung me and we stared at each other for long seconds. He was my best friend—he wouldn't do anything to hurt me, right? Would he turn me in for the money? I was so unsure.

"You can never tell anyone about your hair. Do you understand, my girl?"

"What about Diesel, Nan?"

"Not even him. You can't trust anybody."

The conversation cascaded back into my mind. The conversation that we had dozens of times since Pop died, but it was different recently. Nan wanted me to tell him.

He looked at me with dark, sad eyes. Barely any light streamed into the abandoned building, except for the pale moonlight that drifted through the holes in the roof.

"Since the hot pool."

"You saw? And you didn't say *anything*?"

He turned away from me with a guilty look in his eyes.

"I figured you would tell me when you were ready."

Silence fell between us. I wasn't sure what to say now.

"Were you ever going to tell me?" Sorrow filled his face, and he already knew the answer to that question.

The sorrow morphed into fury at my lack of response. "Did you think I would hurt you?" he growled into the night.

He was right—I knew he was right. He was my best friend. One of the few people I knew better than I knew myself—or so I thought. I should have told him sooner. "I—I…" I didn't have an answer for him other than Nan didn't trust him enough—I didn't trust him enough. "I'm sorry," I whispered.

His jaw flexed, and he closed his eyes, trying to compose himself.

"You're—blond?" he asked. His voice was stern and made me feel I'd done something wrong. My eyes pleaded with his for understanding.

I nodded.

His nostrils flared. "This. Changes. Everything."

"It changes nothing. I'm still the same person, just with dyed hair."

He shook his head and looked away. "You don't understand."

"Understand what?"

"How much it changes things! I'll never be able to look at you the same way again."

"Why?! I'm still me."

"That's the problem! You're still you—and blond…" he let out a string of curses and I was more confused than ever.

He stepped closer to me, his hand raising until he fingered a lock of my long brown hair.

"You dye it?" he breathed.

I nodded. "For as long as I can remember—it got away from me this winter."

He was close enough that I could feel his breath on my cheek as he softly stroked my hair.

"You're right. It was stupid to follow Will. I only hoped that maybe there was someone else out there like me."

Diesel's eyes softened at my honesty. "There's no one else out there like you."

I think he meant for his words to be sweet, but they made me feel even more alone.

"That's why you hate the King; why you want to be free." Not a question, but a statement. At that moment, I felt like he could finally see me—the real me that hid underneath the hair dye. The person who wanted to belong, who wanted to be free, who wanted more out of life. The connection between us sizzled like a tangible thing and I wondered if he felt it, too.

I leaned in closer to his lips, that were so near to mine. I wanted nothing more than to put my lips on his. It felt so right— my long-kept secret was finally where he could see it.

I moved closer, and he didn't pull away. My lips were a millimeter away when he whispered a word that made my heart sink like a rock.

"Don't."

I stepped away from him, like he had burned me. This wasn't me, begging for his attention and affection. It wasn't me. I didn't need it from him—I didn't need it from anybody. I moved further away, hardening my heart toward him.

"Ash, *wait*. Please…" His eyes looked so confused, and he put both his hands in his hair like he wanted to pull it all out.

"Soldiers!" someone shrieked as they ran past the building. No. Were they here for me? I had to get out of there. I turned and left Diesel in the crumbling building, sprinting to find Nan. Fear overcame the rejection that tasted bitter on my tongue.

I found Nan rushing away with Anne and Pete at her side.

"Nan!" I shouted, to get her attention. She saw me, eyes filling with relief.

"Come back to our house. You'll be safe there for the night," Pete offered.

"No," Diesel interrupted, having followed me. "Take Nan and go back to the cabin. They won't bother you there. Don't come back to town until I come to tell you it's safe."

My lips pursed, chewing over what he'd said before nodding in agreement. Anne and Pete looked at us in puzzlement at the measures we took to stay away from the soldiers, but said nothing.

I let out a string of curses. "I left most of my weapons at your house." My hands raked through my long hair when I looked at Anne and Pete.

"I'll bring them when I come get you," Diesel said hurriedly. He took a knife out of his belt that I didn't know was there and shoved it into my hands. "Take this, just in case."

Palming the knife, I didn't meet his eyes. Anne and Pete left for their house. Nan and I turned toward the cabin in a rush. Diesel reached for my arm before we got too far.

He took his other hand and tipped my chin up to force my eyes to his. "They're not here for you. You're safe, I promise."

I pulled out of his grasp, and his eyes flashed with hurt. "How do you know? We have to go... maybe even away from the cabin." His face lit with shock and urgency.

"Don't go anywhere. Stay at the cabin." His eyes searched my face before he swore.

"I know because—because they're here for me." His hands landed on his chest.

What? Why would soldiers come for Diesel? More shouts echoed from around us, and I glimpsed black clothing coming down the street.

"I don't have time to explain. I'll tell you everything. Just go back to the cabin. I need to know you're safe tonight."

I backed away slowly from him. He kept secrets, and I didn't like it. His eyes looked tortured when I shook my head in disgust and turned my back, pulling Nan with me toward home.

It was a long, dark walk back to the cabin. I felt naked without my pack and weapons. Every sound made me jump.

Nan was utterly exhausted when we stepped inside the small cabin, well into the night.

"He knows," I whispered. "Diesel knows about my hair."

Nan's eyes turned frantic, and she rushed to her room, searching for something at a wild pace.

"What are you doing?" I called.

She got done in the bedroom and came out to search the main room. "I'm looking for Pop's old hunting pack. We have to go."

"What?"

"He knows. I was wrong and now the soldiers are here. It's only a matter of time before they show up at the cabin. You need to disappear before they find you."

I contemplated it for a minute before shaking my head. "We can't leave. Where would we go?"

"I don't care," she replied, still searching for the pack. "Anywhere. We could wander around in the woods for the next ten years. As long as you're safe, I don't care."

"Nan, stop." My voice halted her furious search. "That's no way for you to live, and the soldiers aren't here for me."

"What do you mean? You think that it's a coincidence that Diesel knows about your hair and suddenly, soldiers show up out of the blue? I was trying to be more like your Pop, but I was wrong."

She had a point. Did I trust Diesel enough to believe him

when he said they weren't here for me? I trusted him until tonight—I would never put myself out there for him again. He made his feelings very clear, but I needed to know why the soldiers were there for him.

I shook my head. "I think we're safer here for tonight. Let's wait and see if anyone shows up on our doorstep by morning. If they do, then I promise you can shoot them with Pop's rifle, and we can live in the woods for the next ten years. Let's go to bed and decide in the morning."

She thought this over for a minute and then nodded in agreement, running her frail hand through her short, gray locks. "Henry was always better at this stuff than me. He saw the good in people and I only wanted to run away and hide."

"Pop would be proud. You're the best mom ever."

"He kept repeating something about Ash and a book."

"A book?"

"Yes. I've looked through all the books in the cabin and have yet to understand what he was talking about. My only conclusion is that it was all nonsense before he left us."

"I miss him so much."

"Me too."

Loud pounding sounded on the wooden door, shocking both of us into standing position. I pulled the gun and aimed it at the door and Nan skittered to the kitchen for a knife.

"Ash! Jo! It's just me—Open up!"

We looked at each other, unsure of what to do.

"See what he has to say." Nan gestured to the door.

With the rifle still trained at the door, I swung it open and aimed at Diesel.

He was breathing hard, and a bead of sweat dripped down his cheek like he ran all the way here. "Calm down," he said soothingly as he dropped my bow at his feet and raised his arms in the air slowly. I handed the gun to Nan and snatched up my bow and quiver, stringing an arrow but not drawing it.

"Are they gone?" I asked.

He gave me a curt nod. "They're gone, left this morning."

He carefully took my pack off his shoulders and dropped it inside the door, not making any sudden movements with a gun still on him.

"Anne put dessert in there for you, since everyone left in such a rush." Not what I wanted to talk about at all.

"Why were the soldiers in Cedar Hill for you, Diesel?"

He sighed. "Because I might be leaving with them soon."

"What do you mean?" I asked, stiff with shock.

"They came to recruit me to be one of the King's men." I whipped my bow up and drew back an arrow, aiming at his chest with shaking hands. If he was one of the King's men—if he was a soldier and he knew about my hair, where did that leave me?

"Please, it's not like that. My dad wanted more for me than this life. He's the one that talked to them. I don't know what I want yet, Ash, but your secret is safe with me. I would never tell a soul."

All this time we talked about me leaving, but never him. Never for—this. I wasn't sure who he was anymore.

"Do you know what they do to people?" I seethed. "Do you know what they do to blondes? Dragging them away to do who knows what with or killing them on sight!"

"I would *never* let anything happen to you."

"You can't make that promise, Diesel. Especially not if you're leaving."

"I can and I will. If I go, it won't be until fall. I'll always protect you, Ash."

"Why?"

"Because…" His words came out strained. "It's what my dad would have wanted."

So, that was it? The only reason we were friends? He felt obligated, not because he liked me.

"Don't do us any favors," I spat.

Nan, who had been silent this whole time, finally spoke. "You are no longer welcome here, son. Not if you are to be one of them."

He frowned.

The dance we shared and the almost-kiss had raced through my head in an endless loop last night. I shoved it from my memory and let anger and hurt flood my mind.

"*We don't need you.*"

He took a calming breath, his face an unreadable mask as he nodded. "Fine." He turned and marched down the hill.

"I'm serious, Diesel—leave us alone!" I called to his retreating back.

Nan grimaced as she dropped the gun. "What's gotten into his head?" She chewed on her bottom lip. "He looks at you like a man in love, but something is holding him back, and now he wants to be a soldier?"

"I don't know." I didn't want to talk about the current state of my feelings. I slammed my pack on the table and dug out the dessert that Anne wrapped in butcher paper at the top of my pack. I peeled back the paper, revealing what was inside. Nan came over and looked in with me.

"Is that chocolate cake?" I asked, dumbfounded. I had never tasted chocolate; only heard of the delicacy.

Nan swiped a piece out of the wrapper and shoved it into her mouth. She moaned. "Yes sirree, and it's delicious."

My fingers tentatively reached out and took a piece, bringing it to my mouth. My tongue licked at the brown dessert. Flavor exploded in my mouth at the sweet taste, almost too sugary to swallow.

"Anne's been holding out on us," Nan joked.

I grinned at her, but not even a chocolate cake could pull me out of my mood. I shoved the rest of the cake into my mouth before returning to work.

CHAPTER 17
DIESEL

After she walked away last night with a look of betrayal in her eyes, I met the soldiers at my house. My knee bounced erratically as I waited for them to finish with their fun in town before they finally showed up right before dawn.

They stepped in the door, and I shoved Barrett up against the wall, fisting his black uniform in my hands. "Why do you have to make a scene every time you come here?"

His nostrils flared as he scowled. "Have to make sure these people still know their place." Then his eyes wandered around the space as I held him.

"Looks like you've turned just as trashy as the people here," he said, looking at the mess behind me.

I shoved him into the wall one last time and released my hold on him. "What do you have for me?"

He pulled a paper out of his pocket and slapped it into my hands.

"Great, now get lost," I seethed, cramming the letter into my pocket. I'd read it later, I thought, but right then I had to make sure Ash hadn't run away.

I practically sprinted to the cabin this morning after the soldiers left in hopes her and Nan hadn't fled yet. I knew she would; she had a bad habit of hiding and avoiding her problems—if her whole life of avoiding people in the cabin was any indication. She was angry with me—angrier than I had ever seen her. I saw the look in her eyes last night—she despised me for lying to her, but she was afraid of me now, too. It was a look that I never wanted to see again.

I hadn't planned on telling her what I did, but I had to tell her something. Anything that would keep her here. She might hate me right now, but at least she was still here. The soldiers had the worst timing possible, always making a scene.

I walked toward the creek after she shouted at me and then circled back around to keep eyes on her, like I had done so many times before. I had mastered staying far enough away that she couldn't hear or see me, which was quite a feat, because she had spectacular vision.

Things had changed between us recently. We went from being friends to something more. Something that I had longed for, but knew I could never have, and the letter in my pocket secured that fate. The letter that changed so many things—it was everything I had ever wanted and yet I loathed all the same. I pulled it out of my pocket and read the words scrawled on the page. My heart sunk into my stomach, and I flung my fist into the nearest tree, savoring the pain.

The news the soldiers brought ripped me in half. I sunk down with my back against the tree, staring at the letter and hoping the words would change. I had to do this; I had to leave with them and fulfill everything my father wanted, everything I had ever yearned for. It was the right thing to do, but I wasn't sure I could do it anymore. It was as if my body was physically being torn apart and I had to make my decision right then. If I was ever going to do what I must, it was time I forgot about the steel cage she had around my heart and started hating her.

CHAPTER 18
ASH

I threw myself into manual labor over the next weeks, working hard to get the rest of the seeds planted and keep the weeds from strangling the young plants. I worked double the time to collect firewood for the coming winter. An axe accompanied me everywhere as I searched further and further away from the cabin for fallen trees, packing back the pieces one by one. I set and reset the snares, morning and night, building up our pile of jerky in the pantry. I swear I could feel eyes on me wherever I went, but never saw anything.

I had regressed back into the person I was after Pop died, going through the motions and pushing my body to the limits to distract my mind. I only saw Nan at mealtimes and at night, when I finally came to the cabin. It had warmed up enough that I pulled my bedroll outside, sleeping under the stars.

The picture and map that Will lost were always in my pocket—I pulled them out often to inspect the map, memorizing all the places in Novum. The strange man who I wished would have talked to me longer was always on my mind. I would have given him back his things. I wondered if there was more out there in the world than Cedar Hill offered. If Will could travel around with dyed hair and be okay, so could I—but I would never know for sure if my suspicions were right. If Nan wasn't there, I would take off and search for more people with hair like mine—search for my parents. I dreamed of a place where I could let my hair go free, and no one would care. A place where I could feel less out of place and alone.

Being alone most of the day helped me work through my emotions somewhat. My solitude became a comforting friend once more. Nan worried about me more as the days passed. All my progress in making friends and trusting people had been thwarted.

I came in one night after a long day of hauling and stacking wood, exhausted. Nan sat at the table reading an old book with a bottle of Rod's moonshine set before her. She made a dinner of flatbread and stewed rabbit meat. The wooden plate clinked against the spoon when I put food on it before sitting down across from her. I dug into my meal, and she peeked over her book at me.

She set her reading down and picked up the empty bottle in front of her. "I'm out," she declared, holding the bottle up. Nan didn't drink often, but she usually had a bottle of shine in the pantry for when she felt like having a few sips at night.

"I can get you more tomorrow." Susan was always good at taking a few rabbits for a bottle of the vile stuff, and as long as I didn't run into a certain person in town, it'd be fine.

"I would like that, thank you." The empty bottle clinked back onto the table.

"What book are you reading?"

She showed me the leather-bound cover. *History of Novum.*

"I didn't know there were books about that."

She flipped through the handwritten pages.

"Anne loaned it to me. She paid a pretty penny for it from a trader who came through last fall. I thought I'd read it to see if we can find any answers about blondes for you."

"Anything interesting that we don't already know?"

"I'm not very far into it, but it's much more detailed than any history I have ever heard. The first bit is a bunch of garbage about the original King Titus being an insightful and courageous ruler when he came to power. About how he set up the City of Hope and saved the blonde population."

I scoffed. "The King must have sanctioned the book himself if it says things like that."

"The only way something like this could be mass-produced is if it came from Hope. They probably have writers working day and night to copy the pages."

I nodded my head in agreement. "The book talks a lot about

how the City of Hope was set up. Apparently, it's in a mountainous place, much like here, built in the remnants of an existing city. They use solar panels and windmills to collect energy to power part of the city."

My eyes widened in surprise. "Like they have the electricity you told me about once? Automatic lights?"

Nan scrutinized her book. "Yes, apparently so. They also utilize old wells in the area to bring water into the houses."

The idea of Hope intrigued me—too bad I would never see it.

"The King set up his residence in an old government building that sits on the hill overlooking the city, so they could look to him for guidance," she read.

I snorted again, shaking my head. She continued to read quietly to herself as I cleaned up my dinner.

"Listen to this," Nan's voice sliced through the silence. "It's the story of how Titus died. When he was on his deathbed, almost ready to take his last breath, he called his first commander, Leon Broderick, into the room. He placed the crown upon his head and declared him the great King's successor. In his last moments, he made Commander Broderick promise his descendants would once again sit on the throne someday. The commander swore upon his life he would see the King's last wishes carried out. King Titus left behind his wife and two children." She looked up at me as she finished reading.

I pondered what she read for a minute, then it struck a chord with something I heard Marva say.

"Marva was talking about that the other day."

Nan's face filled with interest. "Really? What did she say?"

"Well, you can only believe about half of the rumors that she spreads, but she said that word is going around that King Maximus may appoint a successor soon. Apparently, it's one of Titus's relatives."

"Hmm, maybe there are truths in this book." She considered the idea while thumbing the pages of the book.

"Marva also said that she thought Maximus had a son that should take the crown, but she doesn't know what happened to him. Did you ever hear anything about that?"

"No, I never really kept up on the happenings of the people that lead Novum. Pop was always really interested in it, though. He would have known more."

She had a sad look, and I knew she was thinking about Pop. Bringing that up was a mistake. It surprised me that she read the book at all with how much she hated talking about such things. My hand fell on her shoulder to bring her mournful thoughts an ounce of comfort.

"Does it have any history about before Novum?" I said, trying to distract her.

"No, it started out talking about the virus that killed millions, but we already knew that. It says nothing more about the virus or blondes—only starts with Novum's beginnings."

"It's weird that it wouldn't say anything about that. That's part of the history. You would think if anyone knew about the strange virus that no one seems to know a lot about, it would be the King." I puzzled it over in my head until my skull hurt, and I didn't want to think about it anymore.

"Well, I'm going to get to bed." I left her to continue reading her book.

"Goodnight, my girl. Dream about lights that turn on with a flick of a switch and toilets that don't freeze your buns off during the winter." We shared a sad smile and I let out a soft chuckle at her joke before stepping out into the night air and bidding her goodnight.

I crawled into my bedroll and stared up at the stars, thinking about the wonders of Hope. My mind drifted to thoughts of Will and the map. There weren't any X's on the map in Hope. Had Will ever been to Hope? Did I meet someone who had seen the phenomena only to have him run off before I had the chance to ask? I wished for a second chance to talk to the strange man before I fell to sleep.

My eyes fluttered open, and the sun filled the sky with the most beautiful hues coming over the hills. I stayed in my bedroll longer, staring at the sky, not wanting to leave the warmth. The day felt bright—energy flowed through my body.

The crickets were finishing up their last songs of the night when I got up. Nan did a quick dye job on my hair and Pop's old ball cap covered the dye that got on my forehead. My long hair was braided and wrapped in leather at the end. I left Nan to her knitting when I went to get her more shine.

My long legs made quick work of the distance to Cedar Hill. The sun beat down on my skin, making me sweat with exertion. Summer was quickly settling upon us. Main Street crawled with people and the market seemed busier than normal. I kept a watchful eye out for danger as I stepped up to The Market entryway. They swung the doors open wide, letting the breeze into the muggy space.

I entered the building, ducking my head as my eyes adjusted to the dark interior. Tables were full of people eating and tables on the outskirts of the space were full of people from town trading their goods. Two burley men sat at a table closest to the bar, where Rod served his shine. They fit perfectly the description of any bounty hunter I had ever seen, long hair and beards from months of traveling, built of muscle, with beady-looking eyes that scoured over something on the table in front of them as they discussed it. One of them had a long, dark auburn braid down his back that matched his red-tinged beard. He looked like he was in his fifties and had spent too much time in the sun. His face and hands were brown, like leather. The other looked much younger—his smooth, dark skin not wrinkled with age. His black hair slicked back into a ponytail tied with leather, like mine.

Usually, I would turn right around and leave. Feeling braver than usual, or stupider—I wanted to hear what they were saying. Nan's talk of Hope last night and Will's taciturn behavior made me curious about things outside of Cedar Hill.

A table stood unoccupied next to them. I pulled my hat low on my eyes and took a seat. My back was to them, and I picked up my pack, pretending to inspect the things inside. The distance between us was so much that my ears could barely make out what they said through the buzz of noise.

"...I don't know. I still think we should head south," said red hair.

"Nah, more are around here, I'm telling you. We only need to search harder," replied the ponytail.

They pointed to places on what I assumed now was a map, probably much like Will's.

"Then why are all of Maximus's soldiers patrolling the south and barely any of them are up here?"

"It only leaves more tow heads for us to find."

Bounty hunters—now I was sure of it. Items from my pack kept finding their way to the table so I could stay preoccupied. Should I leave? My curiosity got the better of me and I lingered.

"Fine. We'll stick to the north until fall, but if we find

nothing, we go south."

"They're getting trickier to find, that's all."

Redhead grunted in response, obviously the least talkative of the two.

Ponytail continued, "Their dye jobs are getting better, hell, there could be one in this room, and we wouldn't know it."

My back went ramrod straight—time to go. I casually placed all my things back in my pack except for the rabbit meat that I had wrapped to trade for the shine and the empty bottle I brought back. I needed to act normally, or they would know something was off about me.

I strolled over to the kitchen door on the other side of the bar, peeking my head in. I was alight with nerves, willing myself not to look back at the men. Susan bustled away in the kitchen—luckily there was no sign of Lily. This woman didn't get the credit she deserved. She worked harder than any of the other ladies in town—constantly cooking and cleaning. She had always been kind to me. How did the spawn of Satan come from her loins? I cleared my throat and caught her attention.

"Hi, Susan, I brought rabbit meat. Could we trade for another bottle of shine for Nan?" The meat cloth fell open as I held it up to show her.

"Oh, yes," she said, rushing to grab the package from my hand. "That will be perfect for the stew I'm making."

She set the meat on the counter and took the empty bottle

from my hands.

"Wait right here. I'll have to run out to the root cellar to get another full bottle."

I nodded my thanks as she walked out the door. With Susan gone, I turned back around and inspected the room from my spot in the doorway. The bounty hunters were gone, and a breath of relief rushed out of my lungs. They must have left while I spoke to Susan. They knew about dye. That could mean many more people were out there, like me. Hope for a better future filled my chest—maybe I wasn't all alone.

Susan came back in with a full bottle of shine and handed it to me. "Here you go, dear, thank you again for the meat. We really needed it today."

I gave her a smile. "No problem. Thank you for keeping Nan's alcohol addiction alive."

She grinned and rolled her eyes. "Blame Rod and his experiments for that one."

I chuckled and turned to leave, expressing my thanks to her again as I went. My mind was preoccupied when I stepped toward the exit. My senses noticed the body before my mind could tell my feet to stop. A shoulder smacked directly into my chest.

"Sorry." The words fell out of my mouth before I could stop them, and a sinister face glared back at me.

"Watch where you're going, trash. Your diseases might rub

off on me," Lily mocked.

"Maybe it would make you more pleasant to be around."

She gave me a look of absolute repulsion before her face morphed into one of sly joy.

I stared her down, waiting for the comeback.

"You know, Diesel came by to see me last night."

"Good for you," I replied in a too cheery voice. I stepped around her and walked toward the door, but she followed.

"He told me I was the best he's ever had." Why was she telling me all of this?

I almost reached the door when it swung open, and Cooper walked in. He must have seen the look on my face and Lily, who still yammered on about something by my side.

"Leave her alone, Lily," he said pointedly. She narrowed her eyes at him but huffed and left without another word.

We watched her go. "I don't know what Diesel sees in her," he mused. "She's a snake."

Diesel did like her then, but Cooper didn't. It made me like him more.

"I'm glad I'm not the only one that sees it."

He snorted. "She might look good, but I'd rather live with the wolves than put up with her attitude."

I chuckled. "How come we've never talked before?"

His brown eyes flashed, and he shook his head. "Diesel."

"What do you mean—Diesel?"

He glanced around warily. "I shouldn't tell you, Diesel is my friend, but I also think he's a dick when it comes to you."

"What?" I snapped.

"He basically threatens anyone that even goes near you."

"You better be joking."

"I wish I was."

CHAPTER 19
ASH

I stomped toward Diesel's house in a fit of rage. I drew nearer, the old farmhouse coming into view. Dilapidated boards covered the house that used to be white, but only a few strips of paint remained on the weathered wood. The small house was built in a grove of trees, with open areas surrounding it, where Miles used to farm. The fields were overgrown with invading grass and re-sprouting seeds from those lost last fall.

I had been here a few times before. I knew a spring bubbled up behind the house, providing water year-round. A porch adorned the front of the house that Diesel and his dad had rebuilt when they moved in. Their house was only slightly larger than our cabin, having two rooms instead of one, and a large root cellar next to it.

The weathered wood of the steps creaked when my feet trod over them. I raised my hand and knocked furiously, wiping the sweat from my brow. My ears strained for any sign of life inside, but no one answered. A steady sound came from the back of the house, so I tested my luck there. As I rounded the corner, Diesel stood with an axe in his hands. He attacked the logs of wood with vigor—putting the pieces in a gigantic pile. The size of the pile made me think he had been out here a lot recently.

Sweat ran down his face and dripped off his clenched jaw as he swung, splitting the wood with unrelenting force. He stopped suddenly, knocking the ball cap off his head, and ripped off his wet shirt. He wiped off his sweaty face before putting his hat back on and getting back to work.

He raised the axe above his head and caught sight of me, pausing mid-swing. He looked away and dropped the axe into the wood one final time.

"Finally come to your senses," he huffed through breaths from exertion. The shadow of his hat covered his furrowed brows.

I ripped an arrow out of my quiver and shot it right past his head and into a tree behind him. He didn't even flinch—he knew my aim with a bow was exact and I intended to miss.

"You have about five seconds to explain before I shoot and don't miss."

"I thought you didn't need me." He glared in my direction. "I don't have time for this bullshit today."

His large strides ate up the backyard, and he was through the rear door before I had a chance to say anything else.

"Why are you mad at me?" I called, opening the squeaky

door and stepping inside. The smell instantly invaded my senses—a foul odor of mold and rotting food. The windows were all covered, making it gloomy. Filth and rotting food covered the countertops. A rabbit rested in the old sink, looking like he shot it, but never cared to do anything with it after. Papers littered the kitchen table, and the living area wasn't much better. Dirty clothes covered the couch like a blanket and thick dirt shielded the floor.

I swept my eyes through the room again, seeking Diesel. I found him standing in the doorway to his bedroom, a fresh shirt covering his chest. He glanced around, taking it all in for the first time as well.

He seemed embarrassed, and the anger I harbored died to a low simmer. Something was seriously wrong with him. Had it been this way since Miles died?

"I said go home, Ash."

His words said one thing, but the anger and hurt that billowed off him said another.

"No." I folded my arms across my chest and pinned him with a look. He stared right back at me, irritated eyebrows furrowed. The table caught his attention, noticing the papers strewn about it. He quickly rushed over and piled them all into his arms.

"Leave," he snarled again as he walked back to his room, chucking the papers inside and slamming the door.

I scowled at him. "No."

He cursed, raising his voice at me. "I don't have time today. I've got things to do."

"Well, cancel them because we need to have a conversation. You have no right to be mad at me! You're the one that is leaving to become enemy number one!" He looked broken. What was going on? I was still worried about him, even though he could be my downfall.

"I have no right to be mad at you?! You lied to me for years. You think that you're so perfect, but you're not. You're blond! And you never even thought to tell me."

He stepped closer, and I could feel the heat radiating from his body as he leaned in close.

"You are just as much of a liar as I am, but you're too afraid to admit it, even to yourself."

I was stunned to silence. Was he right?

He shook his head in disgust and took his bow and pack off a hook by the door. "You should be gone by the time I get back," he grumbled before leaving out the door and not looking back.

I watched him go through the kitchen window, wondering if he would come back. He continued until he vanished into the woods at the far end of the property. My heart felt heavy—I had lied to him for so long, in my own selfish pursuit to protect myself.

I stepped into the kitchen and grabbed the stinky rabbit out of the sink, throwing it out the door. The stench made bile rise in my throat enough that I suppressed a gag. That at least should improve the smell drastically. I picked old food off the counters and tossed it out the door. I scrubbed his house and cleaned until my fingers were raw. It grew late in the day, and I wondered if Diesel would ever come back. It was my form of apology, though I didn't know if it would even help. Especially with my emotions in such a tangled-up mess.

Something caught my eye outside the house, and I had an idea. Wildflowers grew in the meadow, not far from the back door. Bunches of different colors were all on display. I tiptoed through them, picking out the best ones to take back into the house, when I noticed the fresh grave dug off in the trees behind the house. I walked over to it and read the marker that Diesel must have carved out of the wood. It simply read *Miles Etan*. Had I ever heard his last name before? I placed the wildflowers on top of the grave, realizing I had watery eyes. I couldn't imagine losing Nan and having to go on by myself.

I sat by Miles, losing track of time as I pondered on the instances I met him. He loved Diesel fiercely; I was sure of that. What he had suffered this winter made my stomach churn; having to bury his dad by himself with no one around must have been heart-wrenching. I had an intense longing for Diesel to come back so I could give him a hug and then squeeze him until he told me what was really going on.

"Do you know what's wrong with your son?" I asked the dead man. I probably looked like a crazy person crouched here, talking to someone who couldn't reply, but I didn't really care.

"Probably, huh? You knew everything about him. You probably still know everything about him. Would you mind paying me a visit and enlightening me?" I mused into thin air.

A bird sounded overhead, and I internally laughed at the conversation I had with no one, or maybe a bird.

"I'll take that as a no then."

My fingers deftly played with the stems of the flowers as I sat thoughtfully next to the grave.

"I think he's pretty broken up about you leaving him. I didn't know you very well, but Diesel told me enough to know that you were a good dad."

A smile tugged at my lips. "I remember the first time I came to your house, you know? Nan told me to stay away from everyone in town after Pop died and I kept Diesel a secret from her. It was back before she let me go to town by myself, right after I met your son. Anyway, he begged me to come over. I was nervous. No one in town really seemed to like me and I worried about what you would say about your son hanging around the dirty, orphan girl. We walked in the door, and you smiled like you were genuinely happy that Diesel brought me to visit. You asked me questions about Nan and our life. You asked about Pop and what happened to him. You seemed sad about him dying—guess you were better friends than I thought. I think it was the first time I had a conversation with someone other than Nan, Pop, and D, where I didn't feel embarrassed about who I was…"

My lips pursed as memories came surging into my head.

"Diesel seemed to be so proud of us—that we got along so well or something…"

A tear slipped down my face, and I sniffed my nose, getting stuffy from emotion.

"It was always like that, every time I saw you after that. Asking about how I was and caring about my life."

"I'm sorry. I should have come over more. I should have asked more questions about you and how you were doing. I hardly knew anything about you other than the things Diesel told me occasionally. I know you loved your son, though." My words paused as I thought. "I care a lot about him too," I whispered, only being able to admit it to the dead, apparently.

"I want him to be okay or things to go back to the way they were before, at least. If you could help me out with that, it would be much appreciated."

I let out a sigh when I got back to the house. Still, no sign of Diesel, and the sun was getting dangerously low. The house was much cleaner than when I first arrived. With one last glance, I took off toward home.

I kicked myself for not leaving earlier. The last couple of

miles of walking in the dark were eerie. The back of my neck prickled like someone or something watched me. I had my bow strung as I walked, stopping frequently to watch and listen for sounds. I never saw or heard anything more than the crickets chirping. My nerves were fried by the time I got back to the cabin. I made sure Nan was safe, told her about the events of my day, and pulled my bedroll in from outside. I didn't feel like sleeping out in the inky black night.

It was hot. The kind of hot that made you wish for winter again. We woke with the sun already beating down on the world. Must be an early heat wave this year. We decided to go fishing, and I was excited to get to the lake and dive into its depths.

We packed all our fishing gear and enough food for lunch and dinner. When we got to Cedar Hill, I sent Nan off to collect her friends and arrived at the lake by myself.

The glassy surface of the lake greeted me with not a soul in sight. The lake was small enough that you could see the other side, and the side closest to town had something of a beach. It was mostly mud, but it dried out enough that you didn't slide all over. Trees and rocks dotted the edges of the other side. The lake was clear and blue today, with the sun reflecting off it. I snuck around a rocky, secluded corner where the grassy bank that went down to the water tucked back into the slope and hid from view. It was a perfect place to spend my afternoon. I leaned my bow up against a rock, sliding my bag off my back. The makeshift fishing pole I strapped to it had seen better days.

Perspiration collected on my back and forehead from the heat of the day. Fishing in the midafternoon sun didn't sound appealing. Instead, a swim sounded much more refreshing. I stripped down into my underwear, piling my hair on top of my head, careful not to get it wet. The water slowly rose over my shoulders, and I pushed off the bottom, swimming further out into the lake. Swimming was one of my favorite things. Too bad I didn't get to do it often. After a while, my arms and legs strained with fatigue from treading water, and I returned to the bank.

Waiting for my underwear to dry before I put my clothes back on, I surveyed the surrounding ground to find a spot that held earthworms to bait my hook. In a crouch, my hands sifted through the soil. *Curse this heat.* Sweat beaded on my forehead and ran down my cheek. Mud covered my hands, so I wiped my head with my forearm. Several minutes later, a wiggly, brown creature came out of the dirt. I coaxed it from its home to use as bait. I set my little pal on the rock next to my bow so I could wash my hands and unwillingly pull on a layer of clothing.

Digging my fishing supplies out of my pack, I found the hooks and line and made quick work of assembling my pole. The worm was hard to grip, sliding it onto the hook. I searched the area for a Y-shaped stick to rest my pole on. I heard people approaching, so I pulled my clothes on and walked back around the bend in the lake.

The beach we always fished at held more people than I expected. There were at least ten other people with Nan and her best friend. I didn't know whether to smile or frown at their continued antics. I shook my head as I approached them. As long as I didn't have to converse with any of these people, it'd be fine. One day, I'd leave and never have to see them again.

They had scattered makeshift chairs across the beach and people sat and chatted. Some had lines attached to homemade fishing poles thrown in the water. A couple people were off to the side, digging for earthworms to bait their hooks. A few kids ran around, playing tag, and a pang of sadness touched my chest for the times I had missed with other children when I was little. It was a sickly-sweet scene, filled with people. It made me want to turn around and leave. I wasn't cut out for interacting with this many people.

I pulled my big girl pants on and dealt with it as I moved toward Nan. She sat on an old stump with a line thrown in the water. Rita and Anne sat next to her on similar-looking chunks of wood, but instead of fishing, they were busy talking.

"I see you invited a few more people," I said to Nan, scratching the back of my neck.

She glanced up at me from where she sat, putting her hand

over her eyes to shield them from the sun.

"Yes, we're glad she did. It's nice to have a day out of our stuffy house," Rita interjected. The only time I had ever spoken to this woman was when I haggled with her over bars of soap, and she never seemed too pleased with me then. It was odd that she talked to me now. I felt vaguely uncomfortable. I smiled and stood awkwardly next to the three ladies seated before me. Nan was back to the 'making friends' thing, I guess. Since when was she even friends with Rita?

"How's the fishing?" I nodded to the lake. "Any bites?"

"Nah, haven't had one yet. Hopefully, they'll start biting more when it cools down later."

The women began discussing fishing tactics, and I took that as my opportunity to slip away, not wanting to make any more awkward small talk.

I snuck away from everyone, back to my rock and pole. The afternoon wore on. I fished in solitude, switching between bouts of sitting on the rock and laying in the cool grass, closing my eyes and enjoying the day.

Three fish made their way onto my hook. I pulled in the lake trout, gutted them, and hung them back on my string—tossing them in the water so they didn't go bad in the heat.

When the afternoon started growing cooler, I began to get more anxious. Not doing anything all day was getting to me. Why were we fishing when there was so much to be done back at the cabin?

I returned to the party around the bend in the lake—taking my catch to show Nan, so we could cook one up for dinner. The others already beat me to making a fire. A large one was alight on the beach with people surrounding it, cooking their hard-fought dinners.

Nan was still perched by her pole. Luckily, all of her friends had moved around the fire, leaving her alone.

I walked up to her, showing her my catch. "How did you do?" I asked.

She pulled her string of five fish out of the water, and I laughed.

"How do you always beat me?"

"It's all about how you bait your hook." She winked.

"I have been doing it the way you taught me from my first day with a pole in my hand. I think the fish don't like me as much as you."

"You're probably right." She smirked. "Where did you run off to all afternoon?"

"Too many people here for me." I shrugged. "Do you want to cook these up for dinner?" I asked, holding up my fish.

"That sounds fantastic, but let's cook mine. They're bigger," she winked.

I tried not to smile at her joke but couldn't help but grin at her words to cheer me up.

We found sticks and gathered around the fire, sticking our dinner over the open flame to cook. Hank, Rita, Pete, and Anne were still there, as well as a few other people that I had never spoken to before.

I pulled a stump over for Nan to sit on and crouched down, holding the stick with both our fish cooking over the fire. The group idly chit-chatted about the state of Hank's cows, and I was content to sit in silence.

The sight of the fire pulled me in, and I got lost in thought. I loosely noticed everyone had gone silent and stared at me, making me feel uneasy.

"Uh, what?" I replied dumbly to the group, not knowing who it was that spoke my name.

"We were just wondering what you thought of the spring festival," came a shy voice from across the fire. It was a woman I had seen around before, but never spoken to. She had long, black hair and squinty eyes. I didn't know her name, but I knew she helped Susan in the kitchen at the market occasionally.

"Um, it was good." What was she trying to get at?

The group chuckled at my response.

"What was the deal between you and Declan's boy?" muttered Hank gruffly.

Surprised that he got involved in the gossip and not wanting to talk about it, I simply said, "He got handsy," with a shrug.

"You could do well with a boy like him. He's resourceful."

The direction this conversation took made me clench my teeth. Hank sided with Luke. I glanced at Nan and she glared daggers at the man.

I would not back down from him.

"Don't you have cows to get home and milk?" I questioned with disdain.

He snorted. "All I'm saying is a girl like you would be lucky to get a boy like that." Rita placed a hand on his arm, as if she was trying to tell him to be quiet. He looked at his wife and shook her hand off his arm.

"Well, I think we've had enough fun for one day. Come on Rita, we're leaving." He glared at her, standing up and walking away. Rita stood, looking at Nan with an apology in her eyes, but was too afraid of her husband to say anything as she turned to follow. How you could be with someone like that was beyond me.

Only half of the sun still showed above the distant mountains. The world grew dimmer with every passing moment. Nan still appeared angry as I checked the fish on the stick and found them done. I handed her the fish to eat in silence.

"Well, I have something that will liven up this party," Anne said, pulling out a bottle of shine from behind her back. Nan smiled at her friend, but it didn't reach her eyes. I wasn't sure what she thought, but I knew I didn't want to be around this fire any longer to only disappoint her further.

I stood, taking my dinner with me. "I'm going to get my stuff."

They let me leave without comment. As I rounded the corner, someone stood between me and my weapons, leaning against the rock. I was wary as I approached, but I needed my things. Declan stood, holding a bottle of shine in his hand, staring out at the lake.

He heard me and turned, his face instantly souring.

"Well, well, well. If it isn't the trash who put her hands on my boy," he slurred. I could smell the reek of alcohol from where I stood, knowing he had probably drank the entire bottle in his hand tonight. The way he looked at me made my skin crawl. I needed to grab my stuff and leave without drawing more attention to myself than necessary.

I stepped toward my things, and he moved between us, seemingly noticing them sitting there for the first time.

"Not so fast," he sputtered, getting right up in my face. "Where do you think you're going?"

I stared into unfeeling, dark eyes, seeing where Luke got his nose and lips from, but the eyes were different. I reached for the knife strapped to my thigh, only to find that it was missing. It was on the ground, where I left it after gutting the fish.

I backed away from him, willing him to take a hint and leave me alone. He smiled an evil smile full of crooked, yellow teeth.

"You need to answer for what you did to my boy."

"What about what he did to me?" I gritted out through clenched teeth.

His nostrils flared. "You embarrassed him and me in front of everyone."

"Teach your son manners, and it wouldn't have been a problem." I knew this was a dangerous situation. I needed to turn and run or lunge for my weapons to protect myself.

His brows furrowed with anger. "Watch your mouth, bitch," he seethed.

I saw the punch coming from a mile away. His reflexes were slow from his inebriated state. He aimed right for my stomach, and I stepped to the side, dodging the punch. Then it was like his fist only moved in shadow. I saw it, but it wasn't there, like a ghost of a forethought, warning me of what was about to happen. My mind was too dumbfounded by what had occurred to pay attention when his actual fist made the same move again, landing square on my cheek. The force was enough to knock me to the ground in the mud. My cheek and eye exploded with pain—eyes watering from the blow. My ear rang, and I tried to get my wits about me to prepare for his next move.

He stumbled toward me when I heard Nan call out my name, through the ringing in my ears, from back by the fire.

"It's your lucky night," he slurred, before stumbling back up the hill toward town and disappearing into the darkness.

The sound of footsteps approaching on the lake shore

reached my ears through the ringing in my head. Still on the ground, my eyes filled with tears. I fumbled to get up and fell back down next to the rock that my stuff was on—my head spinning from the hit.

I didn't want Nan to see what happened. I quickly took my jacket out of my pack and dabbed the black fabric on my cheek, which had been split open and leaked blood. A small cry of pain escaped my lips when I pulled it over my head. The darkness and the hood would have to be enough to cover the wound for now.

My ear rang like a shrill siren when Nan stepped in front of where I sat. Only, it wasn't Nan's feet that were in front of me. The moonlight shone off a familiar pair of Diesel's boots.

"Ash?" he asked. "What are you doing?"

I couldn't handle it right now. Tears ran down my face and my cheek throbbed with pain. My eyes stayed trained on the ground in front of me. What was he doing here? I didn't trust my legs to stand or that my voice wouldn't waver if I spoke. He stood there and said nothing, and I didn't so much as glance at his face, only willed him to leave as I stared at his feet in the dark.

His boots shuffled like he was unsure of whether he should go or say something else until he finally plopped down next to me in the dirt. He had his knife in his hand and idly flipped it over and over. He fidgeted nervously and smelled vaguely of moonshine. I swore his hands trembled slightly when they weren't moving.

"I came to tell you thank you for what you did at my house the other day."

The night disguised my tears, but nothing could disguise the trembling in my voice. "Sure," I said as carefully as I could.

"Ash." I didn't look at him. I couldn't.

"Ash, look at me." My tears flowed faster. I didn't want him to see my weakness. I stood quickly, turning away from him. I wobbled when I grabbed my bow. "I've got to go. See you later."

"Ash, *stop*." His command halted me in my tracks. I breathed hard when he came up behind me. "*Look at me.*" I stood trembling with emotion, tears and blood streaking down my face.

"*Now.*"

I turned slowly toward him until my eyes were in line with his chest. He brought his hand up and placed it under my chin, raising it until I gazed into furious, green eyes. He took his free hand and pushed back the hood of my jacket. Blood dripped off my cheek and onto the dirt below, reflecting with moonlight.

His chest rose and fell with barely-contained fury. "What happened?" The muscle in his jaw ticked. I contemplated telling him the truth, but it would only cement his need to protect me and make him believe even more that I wasn't capable.

"I tripped."

"Don't lie to me!" The comment hit harder than it should have. *You're as much of a liar as I am. You just don't want to admit it to yourself.* I knew we were both thinking about his comment to me.

I pushed his hands off me and they clenched into fists at his side. "It's nothing. I'm fine."

He grabbed either side of my head in his palms, inspecting the wound in the light from the moon.

"It's not fine," he snarled before picking me up and carrying me back toward the fire.

"Diesel, put me down. I don't want Nan to see."

He kept walking toward the firelight, disregarding my request completely. When we got there, the only person left was the woman with long, black hair that spoke to me earlier in the evening. I needed to learn her name. She said that Nan had gone back to Anne's for the evening and said to let me know to have fun with Diesel. After she gave us her message, Diesel had no time for her. I hid my face under my hood so she couldn't see what happened.

"Tell Jo that Ash and I went hunting and she should stay in town until we get back. Now, leave," he commanded, and she dispersed like a leaf in the wind.

He set me down by the fire on one of the remaining stumps. I stared at the fire while he dug around in his pack, producing emergency medical supplies. He crouched down in front of me to clean the wound.

"Talk."

His hands were gentle, but his words were as sharp as ice.

"I tripped..." I started again.

"If one more lie comes out of your mouth, there will be hell to pay. *The truth. Now.*"

I sighed as he dabbed the blood off my cheek. "He caught me off guard, that's all."

His eyes turned as black as the night, and his face grew impossibly hard. "Who?"

I shook my head. "I can take care of it." Would he see me even more as an incapable little girl after this?

His hands dropped from my face, and he gathered both of my hands that rested in my lap into his own. "Please, Ash. You're killing me. I need to know who did this to you," he pleaded. His voice gutted me as his thumbs back and forth across my skin. I could feel the shaking in his hands, and I knew he deserved the truth.

"Declan," I whispered.

With my quiet confession, he was on his feet. "Come on, let's get you home and then I'll make him wish he never touched you."

"Diesel... No. What're you going to do?"

"That's not for you to worry about."

He grabbed my hand and tugged me along behind him, and I yanked my hand away. "What are you going to do, Diesel?"

He scrubbed his hand over his face. "I'm only going to talk to him about how to treat a woman."

"That's all?"

His eyes wouldn't meet mine, but he nodded. "I'll make sure that he won't touch you or any other woman like that ever again."

CHAPTER 20
ASH

The forest was bright and green today—the temperature perfect. Undergrowth snagged on my feet as I walked through the trees. I had an arrow nocked on my bow in front of me. Diesel was suddenly there, standing before me. He smiled and put his finger to his lips, hushing me and turning to look at the wild boar we hunted.

I followed him through the trees, stepping lightly so as not to scare the beast. A stick snapped under my foot and the noise caused the boar to take off into the trees. Diesel laughed. The sound was like music to my ears.

"I swear, you have bigger feet than me, sometimes," he said, through chuckles. It didn't take long for me to join in his laughter.

His laugh faded, and his eyes glowed with heat. He stepped toward me slowly, intensity burning in his gaze. The bow he carried dropped at his feet and he brought his hand up to caress my face.

The pad of his thumb brushed back and forth against the smooth skin. He tilted my chin up to meet his eyes, and I felt the concentration in his gaze. I wanted this so badly; I was desperate for his touch.

I leaned into his gaze, tilting my head slightly up. He pulled me in with his free hand on my hip. I glanced down from his eyes to his lips, begging them to touch mine. His gaze darkened, and he set his forehead on mine. He moved so slowly, careful not to scare me off.

His nose brushed my cheek before he gently pressed his lips to mine. Heat rushed through my body at his touch. His lips moved deliberately against mine in a sweet kiss.

He pulled back and looked at me, his face suddenly growing angry and distant.

"Diesel, what's wrong?"

He said nothing, but pulled me back against him and kissed me again with bruising intensity. His hands roamed my body and grabbed hard. I tried to pull away, but his grip on me was like iron. This was too fast. I struggled against him, wanting to get away.

I jerked my head to the side, releasing me from his kiss.

"Diesel," I said, shoving at his chest. "Let me go!"

When I got him off me, the person standing before me wasn't Diesel, but Declan, who stared back with an evil smirk covering his yellow teeth. Luke appeared out of the trees to his right with a matching grin.

I grabbed for my bow or knife, but they disappeared. The green trees rushed by me as I ran as fast as I could to get away from them. They gained on me. Fear ate its way into my mind. I was terrified of what they would do if they caught me—I couldn't fight them both off.

A tree root reached up and grabbed my foot, causing me to land hard on my elbows. I jumped to my feet, facing the men who sought to hurt me. A face full of someone's toned back appeared in front of me. I got a strong sense he was there to protect me. My eyes blurred and, try as I might, I couldn't blink enough to clear them to make out any of his features.

Luke and Declan's faces shone with complete clarity as they stared at the stranger with gazes full of fear. They turned and ran back the way we came, leaving me and the stranger alone. He kept his back to me, and I rubbed my eyes, trying to see him better.

When he turned, the only thing I could make out were clear, gray eyes. A strange sense of longing hit me, looking into them. Wanting to know more about him, I took a step forward, reaching out a hand.

I jerked awake and sat up. My body dripped in sweat and tears streaked down my face. *It was only a dream.* The first dim rays of sunlight made their way into the cabin windows. Feeling disgusted with myself and uneasy from the dream, I furiously wiped my face free of the tears. I quickly realized my mistake when pain lashed through my cheek and eye. My hand came from my face wet. I held it up and inspected it, gathering that the cut opened back up during the night. Blood stained my hand and the blankets I laid on. I sighed and laid back down, resting the sleeve of my shirt on my face to soak up the blood.

Anger and fear sunk into the pit of my stomach as I remembered what had happened with Declan last night wasn't a dream. Diesel walked me home and then disappeared without a trace. I didn't know what he would do to Declan, but I felt guilty for putting a target on his back, even after what he did to me. I worried about Diesel. What if he tried talking to him and Declan got the better of him?

I laid in bed for a few more minutes, trying to get my mind straight. The dream was so real—it messed with my head. I threw the blankets back and got up, thinking there was no better way than to get on with real life.

I pulled out the small mirror we owned from the drawer and inspected the damage done to my face. It looked bad. My eye was swollen, almost shut—bright red and purple bruises covered my eye and my upper cheek. The cut on my cheek stopped bleeding and dried blood crusted to my skin. My other eye wasn't much better, puffy and red from all the tears.

I dabbed at my face with a rag, trying my best to clean my wound and make myself look a little better. I gave up. It was as good as it was going to get. Blowing out a breath, I shoved the mirror back into the drawer, tired of looking at myself.

CHAPTER 21
DIESEL

I finally thought I was strong enough to follow through and leave. I drank just enough to take the edge off and went to find her, even though I knew exactly where she was all day—like I knew exactly where she was every day since I found out the truth. But instead of being angry with me like she had been, she sat on the ground, sobbing. It would have made it easier if she were angry.

Her tears and the blood on her face absolutely gutted me, even though I was trying not to care. Nobody could treat her that way, or treat any woman that way, for that matter. That was my justification as to why I was outside of the Walters house—watching and waiting like I had been the whole night after I left Ash alone at the cabin. I needed to finish this and get back to her as soon as possible. Declan needed a taste of his own medicine—everyone in town knew what he did to Luke when no one was watching. I would feel bad for the kid if he wasn't such a pig himself.

Finally, around mid-morning, Luke sauntered out of the trashy-looking home and away toward Main Street. Their house was located in the more rundown part of Cedar Hill where no one would go looking if someone screamed. I stalked closer to the house until I arrived at the front door that was hanging off its hinges. Couldn't they even maintain this pile of rubble enough to keep the rats out?

I was trying to keep my promise to Ash and only talk to him, so I knocked. No one answered for five minutes, so I swung the door open and let myself in.

The space reeked of mildew and alcohol, and I shuddered at the mess piled everywhere. I crept through the main living space and found Declan passed out on the floor in front of the fireplace. I kicked his boot with my foot, and he didn't even stir.

A jug of water on the kitchen counter caught my eye, and I grabbed it, hurling the water at his face. He sputtered and sat up, trying to catch his breath while hurling curse words.

When he spotted me standing before him with a scowl on my face, he stilled.

"What are you doing in my house, boy?"

I grasped his shirt and shoved him into the wall next to the fireplace. His breath reeked and his body didn't smell much better.

"Did you put your hands on Ash last night?"

He paused until his face lit up with remembrance. "That

filthy orphan who thinks she's too good for my son?"

I slammed my fist into his face and resumed my position, holding him against the wall. Blood dripped down his lip, and he smirked.

"She's not worth your anger, Etan. All women leave you in the end. You might as well use them for all their worth, while you can."

I knew he had lost his wife, but I hadn't expected him to be so bitter about it.

"You're a piece of shit."

He scoffed. "Maybe, but at least, I know how to treat a woman the way they deserve."

The door swung open, and Luke stepped in, his eyes widening at the sight before him. He froze for a second, trying to decide what to do, until I saw Declan glare at him, and fear raced across his face. He yanked the knife from his belt and charged toward me.

I let go of my hold on Declan and deflected his arm before the knife could slice through my back. Declan moved with shaky steps but was quick to grab a knife off the counter. They both held their weapons, cornering me into the back of the room.

"Get him, boy. This is your chance to show me you can actually be a man," Declan said to Luke.

Luke grimaced but crept closer to me, his knife ready. He swung, and I blocked his arm again, hitting him with a blow to the stomach with my fist. He faltered and stepped back. Declan snuck closer to me from the other side.

"Come on, boy!" he chided.

Luke's temper overcame him, and he started slashing out in any way possible to get the upper hand. I blocked him, move for move, without landing any fatal blows, though I could have. I recognized Luke for what he was in that moment, a broken boy who would do anything to gain the respect of his old man. I knew because wasn't I doing the same thing?

Declan finally had enough and jumped on my back when I was distracted, putting his knife to my throat. I held his arm, which shook with fatigue. Luke charged me once more, and I threw Declan off my back. He went flying through the air until his head and neck slammed into the counter with a sickening crack. Both Luke and I watched as he landed on the ground in a lifeless heap and a final breath escaped his lungs.

Luke rushed over to him and knelt by his side, shaking him violently. "Dad! Wake up!" he yelled until he finally understood what I already knew. Declan was dead.

"He's dead," Luke whispered. "You killed him!"

I didn't know what to feel; I hadn't planned on killing him, but I wasn't sad that he was gone.

"Touch Ash again and the same will happen to you," I threatened before walking out of the house and not looking back. I strode toward town in search of a moment to escape before I went back to Ash. I couldn't do it today, not if it made me like Luke.

I thought about Ash and I's annual hunting trip that was fast approaching, and I intended to go. We could take one last hunting trip together, then I would do what I had to—I still had time.

CHAPTER 22
ASH

Over the course of the day, I spent my time trying to stay busy with Nan gone. I appreciated that Diesel had enough sense to lie for me—even though I felt bad for it. The garden required little, but water would help the small plants grow faster. I pulled weeds and hauled extra water for the dull-looking ones from the creek. A few of the plants were about ready to harvest, but most of them were potatoes and they wouldn't be ready to dig until late fall.

I chopped and hauled in more wood for the winter. Mud from the creek made an excellent patch for the roof of the cabin, so no snow could get in. The berries ripened across the creek, and I picked and dried them in the sun. I made wide loops around the cabin, scouting for deer or other game to hunt. It seemed they had moved to higher ground for the summer, like they usually did. Diesel and I took a late summer hunting trip for two or three weeks up north every year. A salt deposit rested high in the mountains, maybe a two-week journey from here, that we visited every year—stocking up for the winter. We also found more game up north during that time of year and brought back loads of meat as well. I wondered if he would want to go this year. We hadn't discussed it at all, but it was still a few weeks away.

I assumed my eye had already turned black, but I refused to pick up the mirror again. I planned on giving it a few more days before I went to get Nan. Coming up with an excuse for the black eye wouldn't be hard.

I puzzled through what happened the moment before Declan hit me. It was strange, and I remembered it vividly. It was like my brain told me where he would move before he even knew himself. That couldn't be right, though. How in the world would I be able to see someone's movements before they even happened? I chalked it up to hallucinations.

That night, I built a fire next to the cabin—wanting to enjoy the summer night. It was unlikely that I would sleep, anyway. I might as well stay out in the firelight and try to sew the holes in my clothes. It was late when I heard someone approaching. I pulled my hood over my head and dropped my needle and thread. Gripping my bow, I hid behind a tree just out of the fire's glow. My heart raced with thoughts of the men who haunted my dreams. Voices sounded through the trees—two people.

"Ash," a voice croaked out as two figures stepped into the light. My head peeked around the tree. Marva and Diesel stood before the fire.

"Marva? What are you doing way out here?" I asked, stepping from the shadows. She had never been to the cabin before.

She blew out a breath of relief. "Whew! I'm glad to see you. I thought we would never make it here." She patted Diesel's arm, hooked through her own, and he rolled his eyes.

I stepped closer to the fire and to them. "What are you doing here?" I asked again, curious as to her explanation.

"You're in a lot of trouble, girl," she said, pointing her finger at me. "You made me worry."

"What?"

My eyes connected with Diesel's, the firelight dancing on his skin. He gazed at me with such worry etched in his features. "I thought you could use a friend." My heart fluttered—was he worried about me?

Marva took a seat on the log I vacated by the fire as I continued to stare at Diesel. "Thank you."

He nodded. "I'll be inside if you need me." I watched his back as he vanished around the corner and into the cabin.

Marva cleared her throat behind me, and I almost forgot she was there. "As I was saying, you made me worry." I sat down beside her as she continued.

"I saw Jo in town this morning, and I assumed she was staying with Anne again. Then I overheard Jade telling that loud-mouthed girl at the market that you and Diesel were on a hunting trip together," she said, eyeing me. That must have been the name of the woman with long, black hair. I pursed my lips— obviously, she had caught me in Diesel's lie.

"So, when Diesel showed up at the market this afternoon and Jo was still in town, I got worried. I made him bring me to see you after he told me what happened. I didn't want to tell Jo. Figured you had your reasons for lying, but I wanted to make sure my favorite gossip pal was okay."

Her thoughtfulness and the fact that she came clear out there touched me. Maybe not as many people hated me as I thought. My feelings of loneliness died down to a low simmer.

"Thank you, Marva," I said, choked up.

"Don't expect it to happen again. That was a long walk. Never thought I'd make it here."

"Do you need a drink or something to eat?" I rushed, hoping that she was okay after the ordeal.

"That would be great."

I went inside to round up a glass of water and food for her. Diesel sat on a chair in the kitchen, sharpening one of his knives.

"Thank you for bringing her here," I said again.

"It wasn't a problem. I was coming back here, anyway."

"Why?"

He looked down at the knife in his hands and I caught sight of his cut and bruised knuckles. What happened? What did he do to Declan?

"Because I'm going to stay out here from now on." There it was, exactly what I was afraid of.

"Diesel, I told you. We're fine."

His piercing gaze landed on my still-forming black eye. "You need someone to watch your back. Especially now that I know you're... blond." I didn't want to get into it right now with Marva waiting outside.

"Declan won't bother us out here."

Diesel glanced away. "No, he won't be bothering you ever again."

"*What does that mean?* What did you do?"

He shook his head. "Marva is waiting for you. You should go," he said dismissively. Later. We would talk about *a lot* of things later.

Going back outside, I sat on the log next to her and handed her the things I gathered. She took the cup and gratefully downed it all in one go. She made a gesture toward me as she nibbled on her jerky.

"That's a nasty bruise on your face."

I forgot to put my hood back on when I came back outside. My hand covered up the offending eye.

"Too late, I already saw it."

I uncovered my face, and she gave me a side-eye.

"Diesel told you what happened?" I glanced over at her. The

look on her face confirmed my suspicions—she already knew who did it to me.

"I've heard some things, but I want to hear what happened to you. Now go on."

I told her honestly about what happened that night between Declan and me and what he did—ending with gratefulness that it was nothing worse.

She gazed thoughtfully at the fire. "I overheard one of Declan's lowlife friends bragging about him putting you in your place this morning. I thought maybe you were with Diesel and he was helping you, but when I saw him." She shook her head. "I thought maybe he had done something a lot worse to you." She swallowed. "That man is full of pure malice. His poor kid has put up with his fists for years."

I felt a twinge of pity for Luke, but that didn't make up for the things he had done to me lately.

"I didn't know that," I said, inspecting my chewed-up fingernails.

"He was sporting a bruise that about matched yours a couple of days after the spring festival. Declan must have not liked what happened."

I gulped, feeling guilty for the part I played in his pain.

"Don't go feeling bad for Luke now. That boy brought it on himself. He doesn't need to follow in his daddy's footsteps."

"What if he doesn't know a different way?"

She thought through my question for a moment. "I think there's a bit of good and a bit of bad in all of us, but everyone gets to decide for themselves which side wins. That boy is letting the bad win, and he knows it, but he doesn't want to change it."

"How do I know which side of me is winning? What if I'm like him and it's the bad side, but I don't know it?"

She snorted. "You're nothing like that boy, Ash. There are people you love, and they love you. You fight for your family and take care of the people around you—standing up for yourself when you need to. The rest of the people in this town are too stupid and backward to know a strong, capable woman when they see one."

My eyes watered from her words. She didn't know how much I needed to hear them tonight.

"Is that why everyone in Cedar Hill hates me?"

She looked down at her hands. "You're different, Ash. You always have been. The men hate you because you threaten their way of life, and the women are jealous of how strong you are. But if anyone of them actually got to know you, they would love you as much as I do."

"Thank you, Marva. I love you too," I whispered. "Can you keep this between us? I don't want Nan to worry or cause more drama for anybody."

She gave me a look, like keeping it a secret was the last thing I should do. Then she finally sighed and nodded. "I won't say anything to anyone, but you stay away from them from now on. I think they both have it out for you for some reason or another. I don't want to see you hurt again."

"Don't worry about that. I want to stay as far away from them as possible."

"Keep Diesel by your side. I guarantee he won't let anything happen to you."

"Apparently he's staying, whether I like it or not."

She gave me a toothy smile. "Good to hear one of you finally came to your senses."

"What's that supposed to mean?"

"Oh, nothing. You'll figure it out one day."

I snickered and noticed her yawn.

"Want to sleep here tonight? There's a bed inside with your name on it if you want it."

"That's the best thing I've heard all day," she said, getting up and walking toward the cabin. I followed and got her settled in Nan's room to sleep, noticing Diesel had passed out on his bedroll in the main room. I guess we wouldn't be talking tonight. I went back outside into the cool, summer night to sit by the fire, brimming with unanswered questions.

CHAPTER 23
ASH

The next morning, we walked Marva back to town, showing her the proper way to get to the cabin if she ever wanted to come again. She laughed and said I had funny jokes. Diesel said he had a job and left us alone in town, so I walked Marva to her house. When I picked up Nan, she asked about my black eye—I brushed it off and told her I got caught by a tree branch. She didn't give it a second thought, because it was something that had happened before.

We got back to the cabin and if she noticed all I had done in her absence, she didn't comment. She simply asked how the hunting trip was. I told her it was good and showed her the few rabbits and wild turkeys I got while she was away, telling her all the big game had moved further up into the mountains.

We worked together, harvesting summer vegetables and storing them for winter. We spent our nights by the fire under the stars or in the cabin, chatting about things Nan learned in her book. I cherished these summer nights, especially during the winter months. Nan's words about not being around much longer settled in my mind, making me think that my time with her waned.

Diesel was like a figment of my imagination. He vanished during the day, only to return at night and sleep outside the cabin. The only trace of him was the flattened grass where his bedroll had been. I wasn't even sure if Nan knew he was there. She never commented on it.

Almost a week later, my eye only had lingering green and yellow patches under it, and I decided to pay Pop a visit one afternoon; something I hadn't done in a long time.

New grass covered the spot where we buried him, and I laid a bouquet of wildflowers fashioned around an old arrow next to the wooden marker.

"Hey, Pop," I mumbled, laying my hand on the dirt. "Wish you were here."

I gazed at the meadow with the creek running through it, envisioning all the times we spent together there, working in the garden, or coming back from hunting.

"Where'd I come from, Pop? Where'd you find me?" I sighed. I wished I'd been a little more insightful when I was younger.

"I brought you a book," I said, letting the handwritten pages fall open. It was a book of poems that Pop used to recite to me. I thought it would be fitting for me to read some to him today.

I'd never read the poem I opened to, so I began to read.

The sun sets in the west, bringing the darkness with it
An exquisite display of color that never stays
What I wouldn't give for that sunglowed sky to stay lit
I can't stand the blackness of nights that haunts my days

For the dark only brings confusion and pain
Dreams and visions that will never go away
On the outside I appear normal and sane
But on the inside I'll never be okay

I was cursed with terrible gifts from the day I was born
Only one can see through my disguise
Though, No one truly knows how inside me is torn
But that one has never been one to criticize

He shows me what it means to be loving and kind
But, I fear he does not know what is to come
Someday soon, I'll have to leave him behind
To a beautiful being I'll have to succumb

I do not fear the shackles of death
What I fear most is leaving them here
To find her way by herself from her first breath

I feel her strength and know her victory is near

Like so many before her, she'll have help at her side though it won't feel like it during war

But like the night her and I; we must go through the darkness before the light descends upon us once more
-April Miller

Someone cleared their throat behind me. I was so focused on chatting up the dead; I didn't hear them approach. I jumped up, swiping at my watery eyes, embarrassed.

Diesel stood behind me, leaning against a tree with his arms folded over his chest. He looked at me with an emotion on his face that I couldn't decipher, but most of his emotions these days were like that.

"How long have you been there?"

His eyes flashed. "Just walked up. How long have you been here?"

I blew out a breath and shrugged. "A while."

He stared at the grave with furrowed brows. "I talk to my dad too, though he doesn't listen as well as Pop, but he never did."

It was the first time I thought maybe he had unfinished business with his father that he was sour over. He gazed at the burial place for a minute longer before his eyes landed on me.

"What are you doing here, D? Why do you keep lurking and sleeping outside the cabin like a creep?"

He shook his head, and the corner of his lip lifted into a smile. "I was wondering if you still wanted to go on our late summer hunting trip?"

I shook my head. "I'm going, but you don't have any reason to. You're leaving anyway—you don't need food for the winter," I sighed, coming to grips with his decision.

"If you're going, then I'm going."

"No, I don't want you there."

"Ash, please."

"I'll consider it if you tell me the truth."

He pinched the bridge of his nose and turned away, but didn't answer.

"Is my blonde hair that disgusting to you? Is that why Cooper said you threatened anybody in town that so much as talked to me, including him?"

He twisted and faced me, staring at my confused face for a long minute.

"He told you that?"

"Yes. Is that why everyone treats me like I'm the plague? You had no right to do that." My jaw clenched with anger.

"I did it to protect you... I do everything to protect you!"

"*Why?* I don't need you to protect me anymore. You've

fulfilled whatever duty you think you had to your dad. I don't need you anymore. You are free of your obligation… You can leave and go murder innocent people now." I turned to leave. I didn't want to be here with him any longer. His hand wrapped around my wrist, and he pulled me into his hard chest. I glared up at him.

"Is that what you think? That you're an obligation to me?" he breathed.

I nodded. "You treat me like I'm your little sister."

He leaned closer until his beard tickled my face. "The way I feel about you is anything but sisterly. I can't get you out of my damn head, no matter how hard I try. You're in my every waking thought. Your face is in my dreams every night." His hand wrapped around the back of my neck and squeezed like his self-control was slipping. "I want you so bad it hurts, Ash. But I can't do that to you. I *can't* hurt you." He looked as if he hated himself more than anything else at that moment.

"What do you mean?" I whispered.

He shook his head and closed his eyes, leaning his forehead against mine. "I can't have what I want. Giving into my feelings for you would hurt me as much as it hurt you in the end. I… can't."

"How could you leave and become one of *them*?"

He opened his emerald eyes and searched for the right words. "It's complicated. It's what my dad always wanted, what he trained me for. It's what I always wanted until you came along and changed so much."

"He always wanted you to be a soldier?"

He nodded.

"Don't go. Please," I begged. "Stay—stay for me." My eyes widened at the vulnerability of my words. His eyes searched mine, his hands still on my face, thumbs stroking my cheeks. He closed his eyes and stepped back. "I can't."

Just like that, he obliterated my heart. I stumbled backward and he let me—flexing his fists at his side. He looked almost as broken as I felt with his head bowed in defeat. I turned and strode away before I said anything else.

"Ash, wait!" he called. The pain in his voice made me pause, and he placed his hand on my arm once more.

He glanced down at his hand, swallowing like he was choked up at the thought of me leaving. The grip he had on me tightened ever so slightly, and his thumb brushed against the delicate skin on the inside of my wrist. He looked at me with stormy green eyes swirling with emotion that I didn't understand. He did this to himself and could fix it anytime he wanted.

"Are you still going to the salt deposit?" he asked quietly.

I nodded in answer. The trip had always been worth it for me and Nan.

"You shouldn't go by yourself. It's not safe."

I pulled out of his grip and walked away from him. That

wasn't what I thought he would say when he stopped me—I hoped for more. He didn't get a say in what I did anymore.

"Wait," he called after me. I ignored him and continued walking back home.

I heard him coming after me again. His large strides ate up the space between us as he swore under his breath.

"Ash, hold up a second." He grabbed my arm again. I brushed off his hand and faced him.

"*Don't touch me.*" I was so furious with him for his decision. I wasn't enough for him—why was he chasing after me instead of letting me go? Why did he still care?

He blew out a frustrated breath. "I don't want you to go by yourself. I'll go with you, okay?"

"I don't need your pity," I snorted, echoing the words he told me recently.

"It's not pity," he bit out. "I can't stand the thought of you going by yourself."

"Lily is still here. I'm sure she can make you feel all better." My hand condescendingly patted him on the chest before stepping away once more. I was no concern of his any longer. I threw it in his face, the jealousy I had felt for her all this time.

His eyes darkened. "What are you talking about?"

"She told me how often you go to see her. Would she be enough to make you stay?!"

He moved closer without touching me. "She means nothing

to me." He had to be lying. I'd seen them together. Cooper said otherwise, as well.

"When are you leaving?" he asked carefully.

"When I feel like it."

"Two weeks. We'll go in two weeks," he ordered.

I glared at him. "Don't tell me what to do."

He narrowed his eyes at me.

"Sure, whatever you say," I snorted, fully intending to leave without him.

"Ash," he growled. "Promise you won't leave without me."

Thinking it through, I realized I didn't want to go alone. To the north got deep into bear and cougar country, and it would be nice to have someone there to watch my back. Even if we walked for three weeks in silence, it would be better to have him there than have a bear gnawing on my back.

"Fine. I promise," I sneered. "But stay away from the cabin until then. I'll meet you at The Market."

CHAPTER 24
ASH

Two weeks went by in a hurry. The late summer scorched the earth in unrelenting waves. The only relief we got was in the evenings, when the thunderheads rolled in and drenched the world. I loved the rain, but the thunder and lightning I could live without. Some evenings, the storms were so severe that thunder shook the little cabin. Black spots adorned the tops of the mountains where the lightning connected with the ground. Luckily, it was wet and green enough—no fires had started high in the mountains.

We spent our days busily preparing for my departure, and our nights tucked away in the cabin's safety. Nan would stay in town with Anne while I was away, but planned on visiting the cabin at least once a week to check on things and harvest any ripe vegetables and berries.

My mind spent its time stewing over my anger and hurt. I thought about breaking my promise and leaving without Diesel several times. However, every time, the survival part of my brain

224

won out over my emotions, and I knew it was better for him to be with me. Not to mention, he would know if I left. I told him to stay away from the cabin, but I could feel his lingering presence in the pines. I knew he was there, watching my every move.

The day came exactly two weeks later when I was supposed to meet him at The Market. I was reluctant to go. I dragged my feet in preparations all day. Nan gave my hair a dye job in the morning, hoping it would hold during the weeks I was away—especially with all the rain lately.

We saw a thunderstorm rolling in over the distant mountains and decided it was time to go before we got caught in it. We made it to town in the early evening, right as rain sprinkled out of the sky. I dropped Nan off at Anne's house and bid them all goodbye. Nan gave me a tight squeeze and a few words of caution before I left. I squeezed her close, my anxiety getting the better of me—I prayed this wasn't the last time.

It poured rain and the dark clouds disguised the sunset by the time I reached the market. There were no people outside on Main Street tonight. Everyone sought shelter elsewhere, enduring the storm. The lightning cracked, lighting up the sky right as I stepped in front of the door. I had my ball cap pulled low and my hood on, protecting my hair from the fat drops.

I pulled the door open and stepped inside. There were few people in here tonight and I immediately caught sight of the man

I was supposed to meet. He sat at the far back table, next to the fireplace. He had a hat, like mine, pulled low on his face. His shadowed eyes stared me down with intensity. I stared back at him, not backing down from the challenge.

He didn't move, so I brushed the drops of rain off me the best I could and moved toward him. He sat holding a cup in front of him on the table, turning his eyes down to inspect its contents.

"You're late," he rumbled, as I stepped closer. I placed myself in front of the fire—dropping my pack and bow by my feet. My hands stretch out in front of the fire, trying to soak up its heat. "You said two weeks. It's been two weeks and I'm here."

"Thought we'd leave this morning."

"Guess you should've been clearer with your directions then." My tone was glacial. He drank the last bit of whatever was in his cup—his annoyance rolling off him in waves.

"Well, now we're going to have to wait for the storm to pass, which probably won't be 'til morning."

I shrugged, turning around so the fire could dry my backside. "Got my bedroll—could ask Rod and Susan to plop right down here in front of the fire tonight. I don't think they would mind."

He glanced up, looking over to the bar. My eyes followed his. Lily leaned over the countertop, talking to Ty, who was propped on a stool on the other side.

I felt Diesel staring at me and looked back at him. His face was full of something I didn't understand. Jealousy, maybe? Was he jealous of what was happening across the room? My nose puckered in disgust.

"We're not staying here tonight."

"Not many other options, D—unless you want to brave it out in the rain."

"We'll go back to my place tonight and wait out the rain. We can leave from there in the morning—it's closer, anyway."

"Fine," I mumbled.

"Fine," he parroted.

I stood by the fire a while longer, trying to warm up and dry out from my walk here. My eyes scanned the room, taking in all the surrounding people.

I noticed a man sitting at a table near us—I hadn't seen him before. He sat alone, drinking from a cup in front of him. He had a hat and hood pulled up over his head, making only his profile visible. I couldn't make out much of his face, but I didn't think I had ever seen him around here before.

I stood and inspected him discreetly from under my hat. He was tall and seemed to be built under his baggy jacket. His large frame ate up the chair he sat in. He slid back in his seat, legs spread wide with an air of casualness about him. The large hand wrapped around his cup hosted a cacophony of scars on his knuckles. A fresh wound marred his largest knuckle. I deduced he had been fighting recently. A tattoo peeked out of his sleeve and onto the top of his hand. A large knife strapped to his thigh, and a bow sat at his feet. This man's casual presence seemed deceptive. Several things about him screamed danger, but it intrigued me.

He had a chiseled jawline, covered in scruff that jutted out from the shadows under his hat—the only part of his face I could see in the dim light. He took a drink, and the light caught his eyes. I realized he stared right back at me. Something strong sparked between our stares, and I quickly averted my eyes.

The back door opened, and Rod slunk into the room. He spotted Diesel and came over to where he sat.

"Diesel! My boy. How are you?" He extended his palm to Diesel, and they shook hands. It seemed as though Rod had been testing a little too much of his own product.

"Good, and you?"

"I'm great! I think I'm on to something. Maybe a new beverage." He winked at Diesel. Rod always was the more flamboyant of the married pair. Susan was serious and worked her fingers to the bone while Rod always seemed like his head was in the clouds. Rod noticed Diesel's empty cup.

"Well, looks like you need some more, my boy. Lily!" he shouted across the room. "Come get this man another drink." He patted Diesel on the back and moved away.

Lily's conversation with Ty got interrupted, and she sauntered over to Diesel's table. She bent over it and rested her elbows on top, so her ample cleavage hung right in his face. *Gross.*

"Want another drink?" she asked, dripping with sweetness.

Not wanting to see or hear any more of this conversation, I quietly gathered my things and slipped out the back door. Diesel could meet me at his house. Before I went, I glanced back at the stranger, only to see that he had disappeared.

I stepped out into the night. The rain slowed significantly, and only a few drops landed on my face. I only took a handful of steps out the door before I heard a deep voice rumble from the shadows.

"Hey, Blondie."

My hand dropped to the knife at my waist, prepared for a fight. The stranger from inside stepped out of the shadow of the building. It was dark out, but I could make out his features from the flashes of lightning and the dim light glowing through the windows of the market.

I was sure I had never seen him before—I would've remembered. He was the most beautifully rugged man I had ever seen. He was taller than I thought, dwarfing me with his frame. His baggy jacket disguised the cords of muscle I was sure stretched across his body. A black jacket covered his arms and torso, and black pants accentuated his muscular thighs. His bow slung across his chest, digging into the spot between his large pecs. He still had his hat on, but his hood was pulled back from his face, allowing me to see it more clearly.

He had deep-set eyes that were shadowed by his eyebrows. I couldn't make out the color of them in the dark. He had a crooked nose that looked like it had been broken before. His strong chin sported dark stubble that hadn't been shaved in a day or two. The hair on his face surrounded his perfect mouth and his full lips were pulled into a smirk. He couldn't be much older than Diesel.

I stared at him, trying to decide who he was and what he wanted. This man should scare me, but I felt more intrigued by him than anyone I had ever met. He stared back with a smirk on his face and unfiltered joy in his eyes.

"What do you want?" I asked.

He seemed amused by my question.

"Noticed you staring at me inside and wanted to say hi, Blondie." The deep timbre of his voice pulled me in.

"I wasn't staring, and why do you keep calling me that?" I said, pretending to be confused by the nickname.

He chuckled, the sound of his husky voice doing funny things to my insides. He stepped into my proximity, gazing down at me with amused eyes. "You were most definitely staring," he smirked, and it was a good thing it was dark, or he would see the redness that blossomed in my cheeks.

"You don't think I recognize dyed hair when I see it?" he said, the smirk leaving his face. He pulled his hand up from his side. I should move; I should leave, but this man had me so captivated—I froze in place. His hand nudged my hood back and pulled the hat off my head, letting my freshly-dyed hair spring free.

The rain had quit for now and no drops landed in my hair. He stared at my curls and my face, taking me in. He looked at me with such tenderness in his eyes, like I was the last piece of his puzzle. Something sizzled between us like the lightning that streaked through the sky.

"Ash," he said, his voice breaking. My name rolled off his full lips like a whispered prayer.

I finally came out of the trance he had me in. I stepped back, searing him with a look.

"How do you know my name?"

He furrowed his brows, as if my words bewildered him. Then he shook his head, looking away and into the nearby window of the market.

"I overheard it inside," he admitted.

"Who are you?"

Instead of answering, he simply handed me back my hat. I hastily shoved it back on my head and pulled my hood back on. The rain started up again, and I didn't want it to get wet.

He looked inside the market again. "Your boyfriend is looking for you."

"He's not my boyfriend," I mumbled.

He moved closer, emotion clouding his face. He was near enough that I could feel his breath on my skin. His eyes were gray, I realized, looking into their stormy depths. The familiarity I felt searching his turbulent gray pools had me questioning everything.

"I'll keep your secret if you keep mine," he whispered, pulling off his hat. Just then, another bolt of lightning screeched across the sky, brightening his face. Locks of wavy, blonde hair fell across his forehead. My eyes widened in shock. The casual smirk on his face was gone, replaced with a mask of intensity.

I couldn't form words right then. Instead, I cautiously lifted my hand to his hair. He leaned his head into my touch, and I ran my fingers through the soft locks of golden hair.

"Who are you?" I whispered, my hand still playing with the strands at the base of his head.

He hummed in approval at my soft touch on his neck. His eyes fell shut, and he pulled his bottom lip into his mouth. He breathed deeply, trying to hold back some emotion. The places where our skin connected thrummed with electricity. Then his eyes opened, and his face filled with sadness, chewing something over in his head.

His lips parted as if he was about to say something. I gazed at his mouth, ready to eat up anything he had to say. The back door opened behind us, and I yanked my hand away—willing him to cover his hair so he didn't get caught.

"Ash!" Diesel's voice cut through the night.

He moved out of the back door, looking for me. I swung my head back around to the blond-haired man, only to find he had vanished again. Pangs of sadness and longing wrecked my chest. I wanted him to come back. I gazed off into the darkness after him.

The heavens opened, mirroring my stormy mood.

"Ash?" Diesel questioned, stepping up behind me, probably wondering why I stood there, stock still, in the pouring rain.

I cleared the lump from my throat and tried to pull myself together.

"Ready to go?" I asked blandly, my mind on other things.

He stepped in front of me with a questioning face.

"You, okay?"

"Peachy, let's go," I instructed and hurried toward his house to escape the downpour. Did Diesel even say my name when we were inside?

CHAPTER 25
ASH

The thunder boomed around us as we ran the distance to Diesel's house. We were both in decent shape and made it back in under twenty minutes, would have been faster if it wasn't dark and Diesel didn't trip over every rock in his path. The only thing lighting our way were the flashes of lightning that cracked across the sky as we ran.

We crashed onto the porch, and Diesel flung the door open, ushering me inside before he followed. He dropped his pack, stepping across the floor to start a fire in the hearth. I followed suit, dropping my gear. Rainwater soaked me to the skin and my clothes dripped into puddles onto the floor. I pulled my hat and hood off, luckily, most of my hair was spared from the onslaught. Only the little bits around the edges of my face were moist. I yanked my boots off, pouring their contents of back out the door.

The bedroll that was strapped below my pack was damp and would grow mold if it didn't get dried out. Water drenched my pack, but the contents were mostly dry. I pulled everything out, setting it on the old couch.

Diesel had the fire roaring in the hearth and turned to his room to change his clothes—I assumed, since he was as soaked as me. He shut the door, leaving me in silence. I took my pack and bedroll, setting them by the fire to dry for the night. I shucked the outer layers of my clothes, hanging them up to dry as well. When Diesel came out of his room, I stood in front of the fire in my tank top and pants, shivering from the rain. He changed clothes and wore a dry shirt, soft-looking pants, and bare feet.

He gave me a quick once-over before returning to his room. When he stepped back out, he had more clothes clutched in his hand.

"Here," he said, tossing me the clothes. "Put those on before you freeze to death."

I let them fall on the floor in front of my feet. "I'll be fine."

He gave me a scathing look. "You can change in my room," he grumbled before grabbing his fully-loaded pack to check it as well.

The clothes on my trembling body would not dry out anytime soon. I snatched the clothes off the floor and stepped into Diesel's room, shutting the door. The walls were chipped and faded; a shade of off-putting yellow, dulled from years of neglect, covered them. The room simply held an old, rusted, metal bedframe with a mattress on top. A few blankets and a bearskin adorned his mattress. My mouth tipped up in a smile at the memory of how proud he was to take down the old grizzly a few years ago.

A small, wooden dresser sat next to his bed. It likely held his clothes and whatever other things he valued. My eyes immediately landed on the necklace that sat on top of the dresser. I walked over to scrutinize it. It was a simple necklace; a thin silver chain attached to a round pendant of turquoise. The same necklace I looked at that day in town when Luke and Ty started hassling me—I was sure of it.

I didn't know what to make of it. Why was it in his room? Was it for Lily possibly?

I turned away from the piece of jewelry and ripped my clothes off, pulling on the dry ones. My nose was invaded by the smell of him and it made me want to tear the shirt off. It almost hit my knees—I could only wear this, and it would cover me up fine, but no way I would risk bending over and letting the goods hang out for him to see.

I roughly pulled on the soft pants, and they were as big as the shirt. Rolling up the tops of them was a must, so they wouldn't fall down my legs. The door squeaked when I ripped it open, stomping back out into the main room and I hung my clothes next to everything else to dry before morning.

I resumed my position in front of the fire, warming up my

chilled skin. At least the house had stayed clean—there was no rotting food and dirty clothes scattered everywhere.

"Do you want something to eat?" Diesel asked from the kitchen.

"No," I said, not looking at him. I contemplated leaving him again—not wanting to see him anymore.

"You sure?"

"I'm fine."

"Come on, Ash. Don't be like that. You've got to be hungry." He sounded exasperated.

"Fine. Whatever." If it would make him stop talking to me, I would eat his stupid food.

He worked in the kitchen, banging things around louder than necessary—but I disregarded him.

I thought back to the blond-haired man. Should I stay in Cedar Hill to see if he would still be there tomorrow? Did he know who I really was? Did he know my parents? I wanted to talk to him, but chances were slim that I would ever see him again—he seemed as flighty as a rabbit. It was obvious he didn't want to be seen. He was probably dangerous, anyway. I sighed, wishing things were different, with the world, with the blond-haired man, with Diesel, but mostly with me.

Diesel stepped in front of me with a plate of food.

"You sure you're alright? I said your name twice, and you didn't answer."

"Fine," I mumbled, not meeting his eyes. I took the plate from him and sat down on the couch to eat my food. He had made a delicious-looking sandwich out of flatbread that, I wondered, if he had made himself, deer meat, and freshly-picked lettuce. The whole thing surprised me.

The sandwich was delicious. I begrudgingly devoured it in a hurry. Once I was done, I returned my plate to the kitchen and poured myself a cup of water. Diesel watched me from his seat at the table. I drank my water in silence, ignoring his presence, and returned to the couch. Pulling my knees to my chest, I watched the fire crackle.

A while later, Diesel grew tired of my silence.

"Could you do something for me?" he asked tentatively.

I made eye contact with him for the first time since we came inside. He appeared unsure of himself. I couldn't really find it in myself to care at the moment.

"What?" I snapped.

He pulled at his long hair.

"I need a haircut and it's hard to do by myself. Could you help me out?"

I blew out a breath, not wanting to get that close to him tonight. I longed to tell him no, but my stupid emotions had better ideas. Miles hadn't been around to help him do it, and I honestly felt bad for him. I nodded in agreement.

He got up and went to his room, pulling out an old pair of

scissors and a small mirror from his dresser. I slid a chair away from the table for him to sit at. He set the supplies on the table next to me and took off his shirt. I grimaced—I could cut his hair with his shirt on.

"What?" Apparently, he noticed the look on my face.

"Nothing, just sit down," I ordered, scrubbing my hand over my face.

He did as he was instructed, and I tried not to stare at the perfect muscles in his back. Lily would have a heyday if she knew what was happening right now. Shoving the thought of them from my mind, I picked up the scissors.

I trimmed up his head the best I could. I had only ever cut Nan's hair before, but they cut their hair much the same way. The pieces around his ear were stubborn, and I crouched down to inspect it closer in the dim light. My breath was close to his ear. One of my hands was on his neck to steady his head, and the other was trying to trim the last few pieces of errant hair. His body suddenly stiffened at my touch, his breath quickened, and I felt his pulse flutter under my fingers.

"Sorry," I said, pulling away. "Did I nick you?"

His hand whipped out and caught my own as I pulled it away from his neck. He tenderly squeezed my hand and placed it back on his neck, his hand still covering my own.

"No, keep going."

The pad of his thumb rubbed over my knuckles before he

finally released his hold on my hand. My stomach was in knots. His touch left my skin searing with heat. I didn't understand— why couldn't he stay?

It would be best for me to finish the haircut with minimal contact and go to sleep. I pulled my hand from his neck and finished trimming up his ears.

"Done," I said as I stood and inspected my work.

He picked up the small mirror on the table and held it in front of him. I searched the back of his head for missed hairs, and when I found none, I looked up. His eyes caught mine in the mirror. He peered at me instead of his haircut, his eyes full of longing.

The scissors slammed against the table when I put them down. "I'm going to sleep. I'm tired."

"Take my bed," Diesel breathed, from behind me.

I pivoted and strode into his room, shutting the door. I flopped onto his bed and pulled the blankets and the bearskin over me. It was comfortable and warm, and I floated off, hating him for what he was doing to me.

All I could hear were muffled shouts. People yelled all around me. I was terrified. Something chased me, but I didn't know what it was. I couldn't tell what the people shouted about.

I moved fast down a long hallway, but my legs weren't moving. Someone carried me in their arms, and I clutched tightly to the person that held me. They were trying to protect me—I knew it.

Fear thrummed under my skin, and tears leaked from my eyes. The world went black, and I was ripped away from the arms that held me. "No!" I shouted, clawing at the hands that tried to take me away from my protector. "Let me go!" I screamed.

The person fought hard to get me back, but something held them back. "No," I shouted again. "Please."

"Ash!" my protector yelled. I couldn't see his face. All I could see were the arms reaching out for me.

I wanted to go back. I wanted to go home.

"Ash!" I heard a shout again. I looked, and I saw sad, gray eyes peering back at me through the arms that were holding us apart.

"No," I cried again.

"Ash! Wake up!"

I felt my shoulders being shaken. Someone touched me and I wanted them to let go. I swatted at the arms holding me hostage and tried to run from my captor.

Large arms grabbed me around the middle again, trapping my arms underneath dense muscles. I struggled against the hold.

"Ash, it's only a dream." I heard the soft words next to my

ear. "Shh—it's just a dream."

I opened my eyes, and reality smacked me in the face. I was in Diesel's room. We stood next to his bed, and he held me against him, whispering into my ear. I relaxed into him, breathing hard. My face felt slick with cold sweat.

"You're okay," Diesel mumbled again, next to my ear, his voice raspy from sleep. "I'm going to let you go now—would appreciate it if you didn't punch me again."

I cringed as he let go. Turning toward him, I couldn't meet his eyes. The dream still rolled around in my mind, but I couldn't seem to remember why I was so afraid. Anxiety gnawed at my gut like something was wrong, but I couldn't figure out what it was.

I raked my hands through my hair. "Sorry, I didn't mean to wake you or punch you." My voice cracked with emotion.

"Ash," he said, placing a finger under my chin and pulling it until my eyes met his in the dark room. His face was filled with concern, and it made my emotions bubbling up under the surface worse. My eyes watered with unshed tears.

"Come here," he said, pulling me into him. He must have never put a shirt back on, because my cheek pressed into his naked chest and hair tickled my nose. I wrapped my arms around his ribcage, holding on for dear life. He held me for a long time, stroking my back and my hair. I tried to get a grip on reality. I felt terrified and anxious, but no matter how hard I tried, I couldn't remember what the dream was about.

Finally pulling myself out of my stupor, I recoiled from his embrace, remembering I was still mad at him.

"Thank you."

"Want to talk about it?" he asked with worry, still gripping my waist.

I shook my head. "I don't—I don't remember."

"Do you have dreams like that a lot?" His brows furrowed.

I shook my head, stepping back and folding my arms over my chest. "Only lately."

"Does Nan know?"

I pursed my lips. "No, I've been sleeping outside, so she doesn't hear," I whispered.

He studied my face for a moment before turning for the door.

"Diesel," I called shyly, hating myself for what I was about to say. He peered over his shoulder at me.

"Would you—stay?" I couldn't stand myself at that moment. The turmoil in the pit of my stomach made my heart race. The only thing that I thought would calm it down was Diesel's presence.

He contemplated it for a minute before giving a subtle nod and stepping back toward me. I lay back down in his bed and he crawled in next to me, lying on his back. He pulled me close, and I rested my head on his chest.

"Get some sleep, Ash," he whispered softly. I felt his lips move against my forehead. He put his hand over mine, which rested next to my head. A soft kiss landed on my temple before he fell back to sleep. It was a long time before I finally drifted off.

I awoke with the light of dawn. Smooth streams of daylight cut through the window and into the darkness of the room. My cheek rested on something hard. I tried to sit up, but an arm that had a vice grip around my midsection kept me down. The memory of what happened returned with rushing force. A wave of regret washed over me.

I faced away from Diesel. My head rested on one of his muscular arms. His other arm remained around my waist, clutching onto me for dear life. My back was plastered to his front, and I could feel all of him on my backside. His steady breath blew against the back of my neck, a signal that he was still asleep.

I tried to wiggle free from his grasp once more—this time prying his arm off me. He rolled and flopped onto his back, but didn't wake up. I breathed out a sigh of relief—I didn't want to face him this morning.

I tiptoed quietly across the wood floor, fleeing the room. The fire had died to embers, but at least my clothes were dry. I shucked off Diesel's clothes and put on my worn camo pants, black shirt, and jacket. Checking to see if my pack and bedroll were dry, I tucked all my things back inside and placed them by the door. I tugged on my boots and went to get a drink from the kitchen. The jug of water was empty, so I stepped out the back door to collect more from the spring out back.

The air was chilly this morning; the storm from last night cooling the forest floor. At least the rain had stopped and left the most beautiful sunrise in its wake. The orange from the sky reflected off the tiny droplets of water that beaded on the blades of grass below my feet. The ground was damp, and the smell of rain filled my lungs. There was a bit of fog lingering in the trees on the mountaintops—the last bit of the rain clouds hanging around.

I collected the water, taking one last breath of fresh. morning air. Entering the dim cabin, Diesel sat on the couch across the room. His still-naked torso bent over with his face in his hands.

"D?"

His head shot out of his hands. The misery that consumed his face turned to relief at the sight of me. His newly-cut hair appeared ruffled from sleep, but the dark circles that had been a permanent feature on his face lately were faded—like it was the first night he had slept in months.

He stood, running his hand through his hair, giving me a view of his chiseled arm. I turned away to place the jug on the counter—embarrassed about last night.

"I woke up, and you were gone. I thought you left without me." His voice cut through the silence sheepishly.

I gestured to my bow by the door. "Wouldn't leave without that."

He glared over at the offending object, obviously not noticing it until now. Silently, he left, walking back to his room and shutting the door. I rounded up a quick breakfast while he got ready, and we took off before the sun peeked through the fog on the mountaintops.

CHAPTER 26
DIESEL

I thought she was gone, that she had abandoned me. Of course, I wouldn't blame her; I couldn't make up my mind about what I really wanted. The gut-wrenching pain I felt every time I thought about never seeing her again shredded me apart. Of all the women, why was it her? Why did it have to be her?

I hadn't slept in ages, and I finally found peace last night with her in my arms. I had never seen anybody react to a dream the way she did. Something had to be eating her alive to traumatize her that much. Was she lying when she told me she didn't remember? It was hard to tell with her anymore.

We walked in silence for hours. The only sound was our footfalls and heavy breaths from exertion. Ash largely disregarded me as she set the pace, with me trailing behind her. We headed north into a more rugged country. The closer we got to our destination, the steeper the climbs would be. We trailed through the mountainsides and canyons until midafternoon when we took a break for water and to hunt for some small game for dinner.

We continue our journey until dusk, finally deciding to call it a night. We set up our camp under a large pine tree. The thunderstorms that had been plaguing us lately at least gave it up for the day.

We wordlessly laid out our bedrolls next to the fire and sat down on them as the daylight faded. I stared at her while we cooked our dinner, wishing she would say something to me, but she turned away and ignored me.

"We made good time today," I said, my voice ringing through the sounds of the night.

She didn't even spare me a glance or a word. We ate our dinner in silence, the fire popping in front of us. It was probably for the best. I laid down on my bedroll and closed my eyes, but all I could see was the relaxed smile on her face that I missed so badly.

The days went on like this. Walking, hunting small game for food, and absolute silence from her. I made small comments here and there, but she never replied. I wanted this hunting trip to be the last good memories I had with her and that was quickly turned upside down.

Her mind was on other things, but all I could think about

was her and my duty to my father.

We skirted around small settlements and villages along the way, avoiding people the best we could. There were few people this far north, but a few villages popped up every now and again, usually only comprising a family or two.

Days into our trek, I recognized the landscape we traveled through. There was a small river that flowed over the edge of a cliff near where we were, making a natural waterfall. The water dropped a small distance before it found its home in the pool below. Ash had always loved taking the afternoon away from hiking to relax and cool off in the water years prior, so we moved in the waterfall's direction.

By the time we reached the waterfall, the midday sun beat down on us with unrelenting force. The weather was hotter than it had been since we left. Sweat trickled down my red face in unrelenting streams, and I noticed Ash's face was flushed as well.

She stepped up to the bank of the pool, below the falls, and slumped down with exhaustion. Her face was beat red from the heat and probably sunburned from trekking through the sunshine for days. She laid back on her pack and threw her arms over her face, trying to block out the sun.

I realized in that moment that I missed her. She was right next to me, and I missed her like a deep ache in my chest I couldn't ignore. I couldn't handle this any longer; I needed her back. I craved her words and her smile. I needed her like I'd never needed anything in my life. I had to bring her back, and I knew just the thing to get under her skin.

I took my water bottle and sent cold water splashing down on her arms and face. She sat up, gasping from the cold water that cascaded over her flushed skin. I stood over her with my water bottle in my hand and a grin on my face.

"Oops," I said, coyly.

She picked up the nearest pebble and threw it, smacking me right in the chest. The rock was no bigger than a quail egg and it bounced right off my chest. I laughed, and she scowled in my direction. She pulled her pack off to lie back down, covering her face with her arms again.

That was it? Where had she gone? That would have been enough for her to pummel me on any other occasion, which would have been a welcome relief right now. The hole in my chest widened.

"Really?! I dump water on your head and all I get is a half-assed glare and a tiny rock to the chest! You have nothing to say to me?!"

She didn't even move or speak.

"That's it! I can't take this anymore," I said.

I hauled her into my arms, relishing the feeling of her against me, and walked toward the water. She struggled in my arms, to no avail. As the deep end of the clear depths got closer, her eyes widened.

"You wouldn't," she seethed.

"Hold your breath," I laughed.

Then we were falling into the pool. I held her to my chest as we submerged in the water. We were both still fully clothed, boots and all, and the water felt magnificent against my hot skin. The pond wasn't very deep, but enough that I couldn't touch and hold my head above the surface. I released Ash but held onto her wrist to make sure she didn't drown and swam to the surface. When her head popped up after mine, I grinned at her soaking wet form.

"Diesel!" she scolded. "You got my hair wet!"

Shit. I wasn't thinking. All I cared about was her talking to me again. "Ash... I'm so sorry. I didn't even think of that."

She turned and swam back to where our packs lay on the shore. Water cascaded off her body as she waded out of the pond and onto the bank, sitting down to take her boots off.

I followed and sat down next to her. "I'm really sorry Ash, that didn't even cross my mind," I said.

Her words had vanished again, and she pursed her lips angrily, pulling off her boots.

"Would you please say something to me?" I couldn't take it anymore. *Please say something to me.* "Or at least look at me and stop pretending I don't exist."

She furrowed her eyebrows and looked straight ahead, breathing hard. "You're leaving, and when you go, you become my enemy. You know that soldiers hunt for people like me. Either decide what you really want or leave me alone. You can't have it both ways. You can't tell me that you want me, but you're leaving and I'm not enough to make you stay—then expect us to go back to being friends for one last trip together."

She stood and ripped off her overlayer of wet clothes, throwing them on the bank by my pack. It left her in a small white tank top and underwear. I sucked in a breath at the sight of her before me. I couldn't breathe.

She snorted before diving back into the pool and away from me. I shoved my hands into the soil to try to get a grip. My self-control held on by a string, and she just shredded every last bit of it.

CHAPTER 27

ASH

I swam across the pool, leaving Diesel on the bank, staring after me. It made sense. If he left, he was only trying to spare my feelings. But why couldn't he stay? Why wasn't I enough to make him stay?

The stream of the waterfall splashed on my back, while the rocks behind it bumped into me. I pulled myself up on the rocks, basking in the peaceful roar of the water.

Soon, a dark head popped up from underneath the waterfall. Diesel swam up, pulling himself up on the rocks beside me. I glared at him for interrupting my peace. He stared back at me with narrowed eyes. His eyes glanced down at my body as his breaths turned more ragged.

"I can't do this anymore," he growled. Before he could get his last word out, his hand reached up, gripping the back of my neck. He wrenched me into him, and my lips slammed into his in a toe-curling kiss. His lips were soft and demanding. I hesitated for a moment, but he slowly coaxed my mouth open with his and I gave into him. I kissed him back, my mind clouded with anger and passion. It was my first kiss, and it was everything.

Diesel touched my body in a way that I had always dreamed of. His hand fisted in my hair at the base of my scalp, tipping my head back to give him better access to my mouth. His other hand gripped my hip, pulling me closer. My hands roamed his solid, naked chest and pulled at his hair. His short beard scratched my face, but I didn't care—I wanted to be closer. Everything that I didn't know was possible between us melded together in the heat of the kiss.

The roar of the waterfall and my blood pumping filled my ears, drowning out the world around us. The only thing I cared about was Diesel's body touching mine. Did this mean he wasn't leaving?

Out of nowhere, an arrow flew through the water of the falls and lodged itself in a crevice of the rock a few feet from us. Diesel jumped into action, pushing me down onto the rock we sat on and rolling on top of me like a human shield. I stared up at the arrow—adorned with strange fletchings like I'd never seen before. Diesel gazed out through the falls, trying to see something… anything.

"Into the water and get low. Stay behind the falls," he

commanded, rolling off me to let me escape. I cursed as I slipped into the water—someone would kill us, unarmed and half-naked. At least whoever it was got quite the show. The water from the falls hit the pond below and sent mist swirling through the air, making it impossible to see anything past the droplets assaulting my eyes. No more arrows came through the stream of water.

"Who's there?" Diesel's voice boomed over the gushing of the water.

Hearing no reply, we slipped out under the falls and swam over to the side of the pool.

"Stay here," he ordered as he crouched out of the water, dashing over to get his untouched weapons. It was strange to see our things still in the same place. If someone was trying to harm us, all they had to do was take our weapons. I wasn't about to stay behind and let someone shoot at me, though. I chased after Diesel, grabbing my bow and swinging my quiver over my back, nocking an arrow, and drawing back in quick, practiced succession.

I scanned the tree line for threats, assessing every shadow that hid from the sunlight. We both drew our bows for long minutes—waiting. It didn't escape my mind that we both stood in our underwear; probably a sight to see for whoever shot the arrow. My arm shook and sweat beaded on my brow, but I still didn't see any sign of a person.

"Get your clothes on," Diesel grunted, giving me a side-eyed glance with his weapon still at the ready.

My muscles cried with relief, letting go of my hold on the string. I crammed my wet garments back on and slipped my boots on my feet, not bothering with the laces or my socks. I pulled my ball cap on my head and my bag on my back. I had hunted enough with Diesel to sense his plan before he said anything. I re-pulled my bow, aiming for threats.

"Go," I ordered.

He knew what I meant without explaining, dropping his weapon. While I covered him, he put his clothes back on and strapped all his knives onto his body, ready for a fight.

"Let's go," he said once he was done.

I led the way as he watched my back, and we hightailed it out of the vicinity of the waterfall. We were both on edge, only dropping the hold on our bows after we had made it a good distance away from the pool. We stopped and listened for footfalls every so often. My arms and eyes were fatigued, and night came upon us before Diesel spoke.

"I don't like the idea of staying out here in the open tonight." His eyes darted around, still searching for threats.

I didn't like it either—having someone following us put me on edge. An idea sprung into my mind.

"We could go to Sage Hen for the night, probably be safer there." Sage Hen was a town to the northeast of the falls. It was a trader town, larger than Cedar Hill during the summer, but it died down to under a hundred residents during the winter months. We'd stopped there before, trading for supplies. Diesel was always the one that went into town, while I waited on the outskirts. Getting to Sage Hen meant we were almost at our destination. The salt deposit was only a two-day walk past the town.

Diesel nodded, and we took off toward the settlement.

CHAPTER 28

ASH

Wild turkeys roosted in a large pine, outside of Sage Hen. We snuck up and let our arrows fly, aiming at different birds. Diesel smiled at me in the dying light, holding up our kill.

"Maybe we can trade these for a real bed tonight."

The hard ground was my bed most nights. It didn't bother me much, but after spending a night in his lavish bed, I could see how it would appeal to him.

I made sure my still-wet hair was all tucked in my hat and pulled on my jacket, putting my hood on to disguise my identity even more. Men were usually the only ones to travel from town to town. Women were rarely seen wandering in unknown places or hunting. I needed to draw as little attention to myself as possible.

A wide meadow opened on the outskirts of town, down at the bottom of the canyon. Several fires lit up the night on the edge of the old buildings, where traders and hunters camped for the night.

"Ready?" Diesel asked.

I pulled my hat low on my head and nodded.

"Don't leave my side." He gently tucked a wayward strand back into my hat.

We walked into town. I kept my head bent low, letting Diesel led the way. We passed by the men that surrounded the fires. They laughed and made crass jokes as we went. Diesel's hand brushed mine while we walked; an insignificant thing that felt like more than it was. As soon as we passed the fires, small buildings rose up in the center of the town that seemed to be the hub of activity. There were more people here than I had ever seen in Cedar Hill, and I could tell it differed from the town I was used to.

More men made a ruckus outside a large building where a stream of people moved in and out of the wide-open doors. Music, light, and noise erupted out onto the street. A woman hurried away, getting hassled by men on her way, but she ignored them and bustled on.

The sight made me uncomfortable in my skin. It would probably be safer back in the woods. We stepped up to the door, and I peered up at Diesel. He had a hard look on his face as he took in the surrounding scene.

"Stay out here. I don't think it's safe for you to go in. Don't talk to anyone or draw attention to yourself, okay?"

I nodded in understanding and his finger brushed mine before he disappeared into the building, taking the turkeys with him. The shadow of the structure disguised my form, leaning against the wall with my eyes cast down.

I overheard hunting stories and crude comments that I would have rather not heard. Two men, slurring and tripping over themselves, walked right in front of me. I sank back into the shadows as far as I could to avoid their attention. Staring down at my feet, their boots pivoted back toward me.

"Well, what're you doing out here all by yourself, boy?" a slurred voice said in front of me.

I ignored his comment and continued glaring at my feet in silence, hoping they would leave. Instead, he kicked my boot.

"Didn't you hear what I said, boy? Where're you from?"

They wouldn't leave me alone until I answered his question. Replying in the deepest voice I could muster, I simply said, "South."

He and his comrade laughed at the sound of my voice.

"Got ourselves a young'n here, Crank," he chuckled. There was no way that was his real name—must be a nickname.

"How old are you, boy?" He insisted on keeping this conversation going. At least they believed I was a young boy instead of a woman.

"Fifteen," I lied, trying to step past them.

"Hold up." Slurry clamped his grubby hand on my upper

arm. I placed my hand on the knife at my thigh that I strapped on again after our swimming incident.

"Better keep you safe till your daddy gets back." Suddenly, his grungy face was in front of my downcast one. He leaned over, staring back at me.

"Get your hand off of me," I seethed.

His lips turned up into a sick smile. "What do we have here?" The one named Crank finally spoke as he moved closer.

I yanked my arm free and backed away from them until my back hit the wall of the building. My knife was out of its sheath and pointed toward Slurry and Crank. They both giggled like schoolgirls.

"Got ourselves a feisty one."

"Touch me and I'll cut off your hand," I said.

They didn't seem to take any stock in my words as they stepped closer. Then, it happened again. Before either of them even made a move, Crank's ghost arm snaked out to grab hold of my knife to disarm me. This time, I was ready—still dumbfounded by what happened—but I learned my lesson with Declan. When the man actually made his move, I anticipated it perfectly, swiping out and gashing his forearm. He slapped his other hand down on the wound, putting pressure on the bleeding flap of skin.

"You bitch!" he raged. "Get her."

They treaded toward me, more cautiously this time, and I

prepared myself for the fight—hoping whatever hallucinations my brain caused would stick around and help. I was curious, to say the least.

It happened over and over again, I matched their moves blow for blow until they both stood before me with wide eyes and bloody limbs.

"How're you doin' that?" Slurry said, with a slight hint of awe in his voice. Honestly, I had no idea—all I knew is it was the most powerful weapon in my arsenal at the moment. I ripped the bow off my back and drew back an arrow. I was freaked out enough; it was time for them to go. They didn't get the memo, though. They both charged toward me, and I easily avoided them—sinking an arrow into Crank's knee before stringing another arrow and putting it against Slurry's chest. His abdomen heaved with exertion where the sharp tip of my arrow sank into his clothing. He gazed at me with fury and awe, while Crank moaned on the ground beside us.

A fist came flying out of thin air and caught Slurry right in the jaw with a sickening crack, knocking him on top of Crank. A large body moved in front of me, and I dropped my bow.

"Leave," Diesel said, in a deep voice full of fury.

Their eyes filled with hate, but the monster of a man standing in front of me intimidated them too much to say anything, or was it me they were afraid of? They helped each other up and stumbled off down the street, clutching their wounds and shaking their heads in disbelief.

"Are you okay?" Diesel asked, surveying my body.

"Fine."

"Come on, let's get out of here." He grabbed my hand, leading me around the corner of the building.

"He said our room was back here."

We walked around the back of the big gathering building and behind it was another decrepit cottage with three matching doors.

"Ours is the one on the right," he said, pulling me along. We got to the door, and he produced a key from his pocket. He unlocked the knob and we stepped inside.

It was a small room adorned with one rickety bed in the middle and a fireplace on the outside wall. A single wooden chair took up a corner of the room, with a small, tin wash basin on top. It was reasonably clean, and the blankets on the bed looked warm. It hit me that there was only one bed—Diesel and I would have to share, or one of us would sleep on the floor.

We hadn't discussed what had happened earlier, and I wasn't sure I wanted to. If I brought it up and he told me it was a mistake, it would kill me. He let go of my hand and I noticed his knuckles were split and bleeding from punching Slurry.

He spun and faced me with narrowed eyes. "How'd you do that?"

"Do what?"

He chuckled nervously and scratched the side of his head. "You kicked their asses, Spitfire."

"They were drunk and slow," I shrugged. I wasn't sure why, but I didn't want to tell him the truth—he might've thought I was insane. "Is there water anywhere around here?" I asked, gesturing to his knuckles and changing the subject.

"Yeah, he said there's a pump attached to a well and an outhouse next to the cottage. Seriously, I've never seen you fight like that."

"You've never really seen me fight anyone. I usually shoot people with my bow before I let them get that close. Guess you just didn't know how much of a badass I am." I laughed it off. "I'll go get water to clean up your hand."

"I'll get it," he interjected, shaking his head and smiling. He picked up the tin basin and left before I could argue.

It was stuffy in the room, so I pushed open the single window above the bed. The cool, summer breeze filtered in through the small opening. My clothes were still slightly damp from earlier so, I placed the wood, that was stacked by the fireplace, into the hearth and got to work lighting a fire.

I was still crouched over the fire when Diesel walked back in with his bottle and the basin full of water. I finished getting the fire going and Diesel took a seat on the edge of the bed, sending the room into silence.

"Is it usually like this everywhere else?" I gulped.

"Sage Hen is worse than most. I haven't traveled a lot, but my dad and I would go out occasionally. I was glad you never wanted to come into town with me when we passed through here before. There're a lot of hunters, traders, and men out wandering the North that stay here during the summer, but women around here are scarce. Cedar Hill is different. It's safe for you to go to town by yourself, but not here."

His bleeding knuckles caught my eye.

"Let me look at your hand."

He did as he was told, and I squatted down in front of him, pulling his hand into mine. I inspected the damage and pulled off my jacket to dab at the blood. I used water from the basin to help clean it the best I could. He peered down at me tenderly as I stood up.

"All clean," I announced. What did we do now? I needed to take my clothes off and let them dry. My underwear chafed at my inner thighs. My hair sprung free from my hat, so I took it off and ran my hand through my knotty curls.

Diesel stood up and came closer, picking up a few pieces of the long strands, and inspecting them in the dim light.

"Your blonde is showing through."

"Guess a hat it is, then—until we get back."

His face turned contemplative. "You said Nan dyes it with charcoal and oak bark, right?"

"Yeah. We've tried just charcoal before, but it only holds for a couple of days. Grinding it up with the bark makes it hold a lot longer."

"Stay here. I have an idea," he said, before bounding out of the room.

I used his absence to hurry and change out of my wet clothes and into the spare ones in my pack. I placed the damp articles by the fire so they could dry tonight. Diesel returned, holding a wooden bowl, not long later.

"What's that?"

He smiled. "Coffee."

"You got someone to give you coffee?" I asked in wonder. The strong drink had only touched my tongue a few times when a trader came through town with it, and we had enough to spare to trade. Usually, in the mornings, we drank herbal tea made from the herbs we collected if we wanted a hot drink.

"Well, it's just used coffee grounds. Useless. They gave it to me for nothing."

"You think it'll work?" I questioned, with a skeptical look.

He shrugged. "I don't know, but it's worth a try. We can grind it up a little more and add charcoal—see if it works. It's better than leaving it the way it is."

I agreed with him, taking the bowl from his hands and stepping over to the fire to gather up the old charcoal that lay around the edge of the burning flames.

As I bent over, picking through the fire, Diesel took off his shirt behind me and I averted my eyes, concentrating on the task at hand. I heard him rummaging around his bag behind me, no doubt changing out of his wet clothes as well. Obviously, he didn't care if I saw him naked. I bit my lip. What did that mean?

"Got enough?" he asked.

Wait. What? Oh yeah, the charcoal. The bowl overflowed with pieces I had mindlessly stacked. I tossed the extras out before standing to face him. He was clean and dry in his spare clothes.

"Here," he said, gesturing for me to hand him the bowl. "I'll see if I can get it ground up a bit."

He seized the bowl from my hand, and I took a seat on the bed. He took out his knife and seated himself on the lone chair across the room, setting the wash bin on the floor next to him, working his blade over the contents of the bowl. I split my time between watching the muscles in his forearm work the blade and the fire crackle, so it didn't seem like I was staring. He took his water bottle and added water to the mixture, continually grinding it down until it formed a relatively smooth paste.

"Let's try this," he said, standing and pulling out the chair from the corner. He motioned for me to come take a seat in front of him.

"I can get it." I wasn't sure how I felt about him touching my head. He lightly smacked my hand with a disapproving look in his eyes when I reached for the bowl.

"Would you just let me help you?"

I exhaled and took a seat in the chair, flipping my locks over the back of it. He picked up my hair and massaged the mixture into my strands. His hands were more careful and delicate than Nan's ever were. Making his way through my hair, he was sure not to tug too hard. I closed my eyes, reveling in the feeling.

"There," he said, after a while. He moved back and inspected his work, making sure he hadn't missed anything.

"Better let it sit for a minute before we wash it out," I said.

"I'll go take the bowl back. The cook inside said if I didn't bring it back, he'd come hunt me down."

The corner of my mouth lifted in a grin. He picked up my water bottle on the way out.

"Want this filled up?"

I nodded in reply, and he once again left me alone.

By the time I got through washing my lengths in the basin, the water was murky. The dye seemed to have done its job well enough—the yellow was no longer peeked through the tips of my hair. My discarded shirt served as a towel to dry it. I sat on the bed and snacked on jerky while I waited for Diesel to return. The fight earlier crossed my mind. What was wrong with me? That was twice now that I saw someone move before they actually did. Should I tell Diesel about it? It couldn't be a fluke if it happened twice, right? I'd better keep it a secret until I knew for sure.

What was taking him so long? Should I go try to find him? I paced the room, contemplating going after him.

The door finally opened, and he walked back in with a sullen look on his face.

"Did something happen?" I spoke before he could even shut the door.

"No," he said, dismissively tossing me back my bottle. "Let's get some sleep." His mood had changed. He had gone from laughing and stealing touches to avoiding my eyes.

He laid down on the bed on top of the covers, fully clothed, and stared at the ceiling. The fire flickered as I tentatively laid down next to him and pulled the blanket over the top of me. It wasn't like we hadn't shared a bed not long ago.

"Go to sleep, Ash," he murmured.

"Do you think someone is following us?"

"I don't know…"

"Why would someone shoot at us, then leave without doing anything else?"

"I don't know."

"Did you see someone when you went inside?"

"No, I just ran into a little trouble," he said, his voice steely.

"Did the two from earlier come back?"

"No, no more questions. Please, go to sleep, Spitfire," he breathed.

All he wanted earlier was for me to talk to him, and now he

wanted me to stop talking. Feeling like my head was a jumble of emotions, I closed my eyes and tried to get some sleep.

My eyes flew open, the result of another dream that I couldn't remember. The firelight had dimmed to almost nothing. I turned my head to see if Diesel was asleep, only to find him sitting on the edge of the bed. The muscles in his back were taut with tension, and his breaths appeared labored. He bent forward and his knife glinted in the orange light, as he pressed the hilt to his forehead with white knuckles.

"D?" I whispered, my voice thick with sleep.

He jumped and hurriedly dropped the knife to the ground. "Hey—hey, what are you doing awake?" He ran a trembling hand through his hair as he turned his torso to look at me.

"Had another dream. Are you okay? What's wrong?"

"Nothing. I thought I heard something outside." He slid back into bed next to me and pulled me close. The lines were blurring between us. It was like he didn't want to care about me, but he couldn't help himself. I questioned my sanity for caring so deeply about someone who was bound to leave me and hunt down my kind.

CHAPTER 29
ASH

We woke early the next morning and avoided everyone as we headed out of town. We went back to walking in silence, except this time, Diesel returned the favor and didn't talk to me at all, either.

The landscape changed quickly after we left the outskirts of town. The mountains jutted out of the earth, steeper and rockier than we were used to. Last year, we found a small oasis hidden in the canyons between mountains—where we shot the wild boar. We spent a few extra days smoking the meat before we took it home, so it didn't go bad along the way, but it was worth it.

We called it the oasis because several small springs bubbled up out of the ground, making the earth muddy. The boars loved to rut in the swampy earth at night and sleep in caves out of the heat during the day. The mountains on either side of the oasis were rocky and filled with caves of all sizes. We spent time exploring them last year while our boar meat was smoking and had found the places where the feral pigs had made their beds. The salt deposit was up on the top of a rocky mountain that was just past the oasis.

The day wore on and the mixture of heat and the mountain climb had me feeling overheated and dizzy. We worked our way up the side of a stony mountain. The shale rock kept moving out from under our feet. I tripped and gracefully fell on my face before catching myself from tumbling the rest of the way down the hillside. Diesel was there in an instant, pulling me to my feet.

"You okay?" he asked with furrowed brows—the first words he had spoken to me all day. There were two of him. A wave of nausea hit me hard. I bent over, putting my head between my knees to stop it from spinning. What was going on? The heat never affected me this badly before.

"Sit down," Diesel said with concern in his tone, helping me sit on the ground. "Here, take a drink." He handed me my water bottle, and I brought it to my lips, taking small sips. The water from Sage Hen tasted different.

I sat for a few long minutes, trying not to crumble over onto the ground. My nausea hadn't subsided at all with the water I slowly sipped. My brain was foggy, and I had a hard time concentrating on what was going on around me. I stared straight ahead, lost in a trance.

"...Ash." A handsome face was right in front of me. His mouth moved, but the words he spoke made little sense in my scattered brain. I stared at his lips, trying hard to concentrate, to no avail.

I must've nodded off, because suddenly, someone shook my shoulders and my eyes popped open.

"Ash," Diesel commanded. "Stay awake."

All I could think about was why his attractive face looked so panicked. It was better when he smiled. At least I understood those words.

"Hey," he snapped, grabbing my face between both of his strong hands. "Look at me."

It took me a moment to concentrate, but I finally got my eyes to meet his green ones.

"What's going on, Ash? You're scaring me."

"Don't know," I mumbled. "Don't feel good."

One of his hands slipped down to my neck. He peered at my neck, assessing something.

"Your heart feels wrong." Terror filled his eyes. "Your eyes are dilated. Did you eat something?"

My brain fog settled over me like a thick soup—but I understood the gravity of the situation and fear raced through my body. I lay on my back and Diesel knelt over me with his hands still on my face and neck. I must have fallen over when I passed out.

"Ash!" My attention snapped back to him. Pain and worry clouded his features.

"Sleep. Tired." It was all I could get out.

His wide eyes darted around, eyebrows furrowed, searching for an answer. I didn't like the look on his face. Before I knew what I was doing, my sluggish arm moved until my thumb found the crease between his eyebrows. If I smoothed it out, maybe his face wouldn't look so anxious. My thumb tracked between his eyebrows and down the ridge of his browbone before my hand rested on his cheek. He leaned his face into my touch. My vision blurred. Smoky gray eyes and blonde hair stared back at me; the beautiful face of a man that I had only seen once. My eyelids fluttered, and he vanished.

"I'm okay," I told him again—whichever one held me—before my arm got tired and slumped back to the ground.

"Stay awake, Ash. Don't go to sleep," he commanded, and his voice sounded troubled.

"Okay," I whispered, closing my eyes once more. I couldn't keep them open any longer. I felt arms around me, picking me up and walking somewhere, before the exhaustion pulled me under.

CHAPTER 30
DIESEL

Her eyes closed, and she was gone. "No—NO! Ash, wake up," I shook her, and she didn't stir. Her breaths were short and labored, and her heart beat erratically beneath my palm. I frantically searched around for an answer or anything that would help. We were too far away from civilization, and I couldn't get her help—not in time.

I picked her up in my arms. I had to get her out of the sun—maybe then she'd come back to me. *She's overheated. She needs to cool down, then she'll be fine.* I chanted the words over and over in my head. I stumbled across the hill side—wildly searching for a place to hunker down in the shade. An old oak tree stood tall amongst the pines, next to a rocky outcropping, and I hurried over, placing Ash down beneath the tree. She slumped out of my arms like all the life had drained out of her.

"Ash," I said, my voice wavering. She didn't stir—not even a flinch. I checked her pulse again, and it was still there, but the rhythm was unsteady.

Something wasn't right. What did she eat? Drink? I tore into her pack and found nothing but jerky and dried berries. I pulled the lid off her bottle and smelled the water. It had a slight foul odor to it, but it always did after staying in a canteen for so long. Frustrated, I hurled the bottle into the tree and fell to my knees beside her once more.

"Ash, please wake up," I whispered, brushing a chocolate-colored lock off her face. The sweat glistened on her forehead and dampened my fingers. I'd never recover if she died—the thought rushed into my head, drowning everything else out.

Something inside me shattered. The indecision that had been weighing me down for months, suddenly, wasn't a decision any longer; I knew what I wanted. I had to keep her, even if it went against everything that I ever believed in.

I sat down behind her and pulled her unmoving body against mine, resting my hand over her heart to feel her uneven pulse.

"Please," I begged. "If there is a God above, please do not let her die."

Her heart stalled beneath my hand and panic filled my chest before it resumed beating. I stayed and felt her heart for hours, never moving my hand. Her heart stuttered and paused, and every time, I thought it might be the last beat. I had never in my life endured something as heart-wrenching as watching Ash die in my arms and having no power to save her.

CHAPTER 31
ASH

My eyelids lifted, feeling like sandpaper against my tender eyes. The sky was black, and the stars shone brightly overhead, but the branches of a tree blocked out most the sky. It was not a pine, but an oak tree, I marveled. My head didn't feel right, and I tried to remember where I was. I smelled smoke and heard the crackling of a fire. Something shifted underneath me and that's when I felt the warm body that I was cradled against. My head rested on a muscular chest and brawny arms wrapped around my front, hands covering mine. A sleeping bag was draped over our bodies for warmth. I tried to move my head and sit up.

The arms holding me moved and turned me to face the body I lay against. My eyes met tired green ones. Something about the color of his eyes confused me.

"Ash," Diesel whispered, his voice rough. "You're awake."

The memory of what happened came rushing back. I sat up slowly, my body feeling a little better, and my mind a little clearer. I scrubbed my hands over my face, trying to get my wits about me.

"How long have I been out?" I asked, my voice coming out scratchy.

"A while. It's almost morning. Your heart finally started beating right a few hours ago." He gently placed his hand on my neck to feel my steady pulse. I could sense a slight tremor in his hand where it rested on my skin. The bags under his eyes were a deep purple shade, and red rimmed his eyes.

"Are you okay?" I asked quietly.

He glanced down, closing his eyes and pulling his lips in between his teeth. His body shook. Was he... crying?

"Diesel..." I murmured, and he looked at me. A tear made a path down his face and dropped off his chin.

I brushed the wetness away with the pad of my thumb.

"I thought you were going to die," he choked.

I hugged him close, whispering words into his ear. "I'm okay. I'm right here." He cried...for me. The thought of losing me was enough to bring him to tears.

When I felt like he could hold it together, I leaned my arms on my knees, staring at the fire and trying to figure out what had happened to me. The last thing I remembered was climbing over the shale around midday.

Diesel stood up from behind me and brought over his water bottle. My mouth was dry, and I was grateful for the gesture. He took up his spot behind me again.

"Here, drink mine. I dumped yours out in case the water was bad." He shook his head. "I don't know why I wouldn't be sick too, if it was the water."

For the first time, I noticed my surroundings. We were in a small ravine, our backs to a rocky cliff and I imagined you could see a long way out in front of us, in the daylight, being up so high.

"Do you feel better?" he asked warily.

I shook out my arms and legs to assess the current situation of my body. My mind was clearer, but my body felt extremely tired and stiff.

"I think so, but I feel like I ran a marathon through knee-deep snow. You don't feel sick at all?" My voice was rough, like I had come close to losing it.

"No, I feel fine."

"Maybe it was the heat, or maybe I'm sick," I pondered, but I'd never felt so sick in my life.

We sat together, gazing at the fire in front of us in silence. Diesel idly rubbed my back, grounding me. Suddenly, the hairs on the back of my neck stood up like something was watching us. I jerked my head in the direction I thought it came from— straining my eyes in the dark to see what was out there.

Diesel was immediately on his feet, grabbing his bow and nocking an arrow.

"What?" He stepped protectively between me and whatever watched us. "What is it?"

We searched the dark, trying to find the threat. I didn't hear or see anything. The feeling went away after a while. Baffled, I shook my head. "I don't know, I thought…" I said, trailing off, lost in thought. "Thought I felt something out there." My palms smashed into my eye sockets, trying to clear my head of the fog. Diesel shot me a questioning look. He returned to his spot sitting behind me—his bow in arm's reach. My brain felt off, and I questioned my sanity.

"Go back to sleep," Diesel said, gesturing to my unrolled bed on the other side of the fire. "I'll keep watch." He probably questioned my sanity, too. I heaved myself off the ground, still feeling dizzy. Diesel helped me over to the bed before I collapsed on top of it. It didn't take long to fall back to sleep.

By the time I woke up again, it was mid-morning, and I felt better. My movements were slow and my body stiff, but I thought I was through the worst of it.

Diesel looked rough. The deep purple bags under his eyes told me he hadn't slept all night. I made him lay down on his bed and take a nap while I kept watch with my bow close. He fought with me, but eventually gave in.

I was right about the view last night. You could see for a long way in front of us from here. I sat, sipping water and nibbling on jerky, while Diesel rested. When he awoke, it was mid-afternoon. We decided to stay another night and leave for the oasis tomorrow, since it was maybe only a half-day walk away.

We needed something more to eat, so Diesel went hunting while I gathered more water. My sluggish movements wouldn't be very stealthy right now. He shot me a longing look before he left. I crept down the hill to where Diesel said the spring was and filled our bottles. I splashed the cool water on my face to get the remaining fog out of my head. The hike back up the hill was a chore. I had never felt this out of shape in my life. I panted for breath and my legs ached by the time I reached camp again. My muscles shook with exhaustion as I collapsed on my bed.

Diesel strolled back into camp right before sundown, clutching another turkey in his hand. He plopped it on the ground by the fire.

"Look what else I found," he said, pulling off his pack. He dug into the front pocket and produced a handful of juicy, red raspberries. I beamed at him with a bright smile and took the handful of delicious fruit, popping one into my mouth. I closed my eyes, savoring the taste. Diesel smiled down at me.

"I'm glad you're feeling better. You scared me last night."

"Sorry…but I'm way better now," I joked, popping another

raspberry in my mouth. He grinned at me, and it felt like old times with him again—times when there wasn't any tension, and his mood was more stable.

We laughed, joked, and had a good time reminiscing about old stories as we cooked and ate dinner. It had been a while since I had felt this relaxed and happy. Though my joints and muscles protested every time I moved, my foggy brain felt better by the hour.

I dragged my bedroll close to the fire, the night air getting nippier, this high in the mountains. Something prickled at the back of my neck again, putting me on alert. I fisted my hand around my bow and looked out into the trees again, wondering if maybe I was going mad.

Diesel noticed my shift in demeanor. He slid in close next to me with his bow on the opposite side, our backs to the cliff behind us. We both stared out into the darkness.

"I forgot to tell you," he said quietly. "When I was out hunting, I came across fresh cougar tracks a little way out."

"You think it's stalking us?"

His brows furrowed quizzically, and he shook his head.

"I don't think so. I followed its tracks for a while, to see if they came close last night—but it wandered off in the other direction like it was only making the rounds about its territory. There's one in the area, but I'm not sure it knows we're here. I feel it tonight though, something watching us."

His words were the validation that I didn't know I needed. Maybe I wasn't crazy after all.

"We'll take turns keeping watch tonight," I said.

He peered over at me with concern in his eyes.

"You sure? You're still not feeling back to normal and need your sleep."

I nudged him on the shoulder with my own. "So do you."

He gave me an appreciative smile as he gazed into my eyes. I didn't break eye contact as he looked at me—his face full of emotion. This seemed like the first time in months he didn't have a mask over his face and let what he felt spill onto it. Maybe things could be different between us. Maybe he made a mistake, and he would stay... for me.

He leaned down into me as the crickets sang their songs of the night. My eyes filled with vulnerability. This man had the power to break me in half if he wanted, and I was willing to risk it for him.

His lips met mine in a tender kiss. This kiss was the opposite of our hasty kisses under the waterfall. This one was slow and full of meaning. He raised his hand to caress the side of my face, his thumb rubbing back and forth on my jawline as our lips tangled. The kiss was full of the heartbreak he had suffered the previous night. We finally separated, and he rested his forehead on mine with his eyes clamped shut.

"I'll take the first watch," he whispered.

I nodded against him, unable to form words. He leaned back and put his arm around me, laying my head on his lap as he propped himself up against the rock behind us.

"Get some sleep," he mumbled softly, his hand stroking through my locks of dirty brown hair.

My mind was too tired tonight to riddle out what was happening between us. Instead, I closed my eyes and enjoyed the feel of his hand in my hair.

CHAPTER 32
ASH

We set out early the next morning toward the oasis—our progress slow, thanks to my recovering body. My brain was sharp again, but my muscles still seemed to be recovering from whatever ailed them. Diesel helped me along with patience and understanding. We talked all day and laughed some more, a continuation of our joyful conversation last night.

It felt nice to be us again. We walked for most of the day and by mid-afternoon, we reached the swampy area that we had seen before. Diesel put his hand out to help me over a log and I gratefully grabbed hold and pulled myself over. When we got to the other side, he didn't let go of my hand. Instead, he tugged me into his arms, turning our bodies until he pinned me against the nearest tree.

His green eyes raked over my face with hunger, and then, his familiar lips were on mine again, filled with need. I kissed him back with everything I had. My hands roamed his muscular form as he pressed me against the tree.

My mind clouded with lust, but I had a sudden moment of clarity, and I couldn't take his aloofness any longer. I needed to know if he was leaving to join the enemy before we went any further. I put my hands on his chest and shoved him backward, away from me. Surprise lined his features and his eyes widened in apology.

"Did I hurt you?" he asked immediately. "What's wrong?"

"No. I'm fine. But…"

Just then, a low snort came from down the swampy valley. We both turned to see a wild boar dashing off into the distant trees, probably startled by our presence.

Diesel searched my eyes, but the situation required urgency and we didn't have time for further talking if we wanted to take down the boar.

"I'll go around and see if I can push it back this way. Stay here and see if you can get a shot at it—okay?"

I nodded in understanding, and he kissed my cheek.

"We'll talk about this later," he threw over his shoulder, stalking away into the trees.

As soon as he was out of sight, I leaned back against the tree that he had kissed me against, taking deep breaths to get a grip on my emotions. As soon as I had collected myself enough, I snuck through the marshy soil, trying to find a trail that the pig might come out on. I found a well-worn path in a cluster of trees and dropped my pack, stashing it under the base of a large bush.

With only my bow in hand, I crept through the grass until I discovered a suitable spot to wait.

I strained my ears to listen for sounds when a twig snapped behind me. The source of the noise wasn't clear, but it came from the way I had just left—it was unlikely that anything would be over there.

The longer I sat and waited, the more I felt the sickness that had been plaguing me. The day had been too much on my tired head and muscles. I tried to shake my head of the fog and weariness.

Suddenly, something crashed through the trees to my right. I barely heard it before I felt the impact on my body. The thing tackled me, toppling me over from my crouched stance. I kicked and punched, landing solid blows before I felt the weight lift off me. I jumped up to see the perpetrator, only to find Luke standing before me.

What was he doing out here? We were a long way from home—he must have followed us the whole way. A nasty smirk covered his face, and he held up my bow in his hand. He snagged it when he tackled me. He brought the wooden weapon down on his knee, snapping it in two and discarding it a few feet from him. It fell limply on the ground behind him. That was Pop's old bow, and I wanted to strangle him only for that.

"What're you doing here?" I spat.

"Came to pay you a visit," he snarled.

"What do you want?"

"I came for payback," he said sardonically.

"For what!? I didn't do anything to you!"

I stared at him with hate and pulled a knife from my belt at his words.

"My father is dead!" he roared.

What? No. Did Diesel kill him for what he'd done to me? Was that where he went?

His eyes widened. "He didn't tell you, did he?"

"No. I didn't know," I gulped.

He scoffed. "Of course—always trying to protect the princess. Well, he killed my dad and now I'm going to kill you to give him a taste of his own medicine. Plus, Lily can have her man all to herself."

"Lily put you up to this?"

"Partially, but I wanted my revenge, too. Seeing as how the wolfsbane I slipped in your water didn't take care of you, I had to come to finish the job myself."

Things clicked into place at his words. The unexplained sickness. The odd-tasting water. My irregular heartbeat. I was lucky I was still standing.

"Coward," I raged. "You thought poisoning me when I wasn't looking was the best option? Why not face me like a man?"

His eyebrows pulled together, and his eyes became angrier.

I could see I had struck a nerve with my insult.

"I see Diesel didn't tell you what held him up so long the other night."

My thoughts turned instantly to the night Diesel went to take the bowl back and took forever. Did he know about the poison? I dismissed the thought—he wouldn't do that. Would he?

"Stupidly left your bottle out in the open, and I slipped it in while he was distracted. Seems Diesel has more secrets than all of us."

"What do you mean?"

He gave me a scathing smile. "He likes to mingle with soldiers, apparently."

"I already knew that," I scoffed.

He realized he didn't have the upper-hand, so he continued.

"Thought the wolfsbane would do the job handily, but apparently, you're tougher than you look. I wanted to vomit watching the two of you the last two days, waiting for you to tip over and die. Diesel even shed tears while he held you all night, begging with God above that you wouldn't die." He made a gagging motion.

"It was you watching us."

"Well, me and Ty. Oh, did you think Diesel was going to come to save you? Ty is distracting him, while I take care of you."

I glanced around, looking for a way out, and Luke stepped

closer to me. If I kept him talking, maybe I could think of something.

"You followed us all the way here?"

He scoffed. "No, Diesel told Lily right where you were going. All we had to do was get to Sage Hen and wait for you to show up. Wasn't hard to find you when you were stupid enough to make a scene outside the bar."

I gritted my teeth in hatred for the long-haired girl and Diesel, who seemed infatuated with her.

"She sent you here?" I said, backing up and readying myself to run.

"I told you, we both have a problem. See, she wants to get you out of the way so she can have Diesel to herself, and I have my own issues with you that I think we need to work out."

"Why not just kill me in Cedar Hill?"

He harrumphed. "Too much drama. It's much easier out here, don't you think? With no one around to hear you scream."

I didn't know if I could beat Luke in a physical fight right now. My body was weak and slow. Though he was thin, he could still beat me in strength. If I had my bow, it would be no problem to take him down, but that was no longer an option. I knew that there were caves on either side of this swampy area from staying here last summer. If I turned and ran, I might make it to the caves and hide in one of them.

A thought popped into my head before I bolted—maybe I

could appeal to him differently.

"I'm sorry about your dad. Truly. No one deserves what he did to you."

His eyes whipped to mine and a shred of humanity showed through. Then his smile faltered, and his nostrils flared with anger.

"How do you know about that?" he snapped.

"Got in the way of one of his fists. Hurt like hell. I wouldn't wish that upon anyone."

He sneered at me. "You have no idea."

This conversation was only making things worse, so I bolted toward the caves when he wasn't looking. It took him off-guard, and he took a few seconds to follow. I ran as fast as my weak legs would take me—darting around the trees and jumping over the wet spots. He was slow. I could easily outrun him if my limbs cooperated.

I heard him gaining on me. The ground under my feet steepened and became rockier. A cave was maybe a hundred feet away when he tackled me again from behind. I whipped my knife out and tried to stab his chest. My superhuman power evaded me. Where was it when I needed it? His moves might as well have been lightning strikes—I never knew where they would land. He was too quick, and my mind was too slow. He caught my arm before my knife could hit its mark. He grabbed my other hand, pinning them both above my head as he straddled my abdomen. I bucked, trying to throw him off the best I could, to no avail. My chest heaved and my brain went fuzzy from lack of oxygen.

He chuckled as he leaned over me. "Guess the wolfsbane did its job, after all."

He pinned both my hands in one of his, pulling a knife from his belt. I could feel a slight tremor in his hand, making me think he was just as afraid to kill me as I was to die. I struggled against him but couldn't get free.

"Do you know what that bastard did to me after the spring festival?" he asked. "After you so kindly broke my nose, he broke it again for embarrassing him. Do you know how bad it hurts to have your broken nose pummeled repeatedly?"

His nose hung at an odd angle that it hadn't before.

He snorted. "Don't go feeling bad for me now. I'm getting my revenge. He was still my dad, after all."

I had a sick feeling he was doing this more for Declan than himself or even Lily.

"He's dead, Luke. You have *nothing* to prove to him anymore."

That made him pause for a second and my hips bucked with all my remaining strength, knocking him off balance and causing him to let go of my hands. I elbowed him in the stomach and bumped the knife out of his hand in one fell swoop. Jumping up, I glanced back as I made my escape. Luke lunged out and caught one of my legs, slamming me into the dirt face-first. I smacked my head on the ground so hard it made me see stars. I rolled over in time to see a large rock in his hand heading toward my head, and everything went dark.

CHAPTER 33
DIESEL

I followed the boar tracks and the sound of the creature picking its way through the swamp and bramble. Something was making me uneasy about the way I left Ash, but she'd been in situations like this countless times. She knew how to handle herself; besides, I was the scariest thing lurking in these woods. It was probably the fact that I finally made up my mind after holding her the other night, while I thought she was dying in my arms. It snapped something inside of me that would never be repaired.

The boar was walking further and further away. I only caught glimpses of its black body through the underbrush. I needed to get around in front of it to see if I could scare it back toward Ash, but I needed it to stay in one place long enough, so I didn't lose sight of it all together.

Finally, a few hours later, it stopped in a mudhole to wallow. It wasn't likely that I could scare it back toward Ash at this point, but she would be ecstatic when I walked up carrying the monster pig. I inched closer and closer, using trees to hide my form until I could get near enough for a shot.

Right as I was drawing back my bow, a large crash sounded from behind me, scaring the pig out of the mud and away from me. What the hell was that? My mind instantly went back to the grizzly I had killed a few years ago. Few animals could make a sound that large.

I cursed internally at the fact that it was getting dark, and Ash was at least a two-hour walk away. But if a grizzly was here, then she would be safer where she was.

I stopped and pulled out the secret weapon I had stashed in my pack and tucked it into the back of my pants, only as a last resort. The crashing sounds continued every so often as I tracked the animal.

I crouched low to the ground to see if I could pick out any tracks in the dying light, only to find boot prints staring back at me. Something was very wrong. Who would be making that much noise in the forest if they were trying to hunt?

I stood and hurried on to figure out who was in front of me. In a rush, I spotted the perpetrator ducking behind a tree in front of me. He glanced back just long enough for us to make eye contact. What was Ty doing here? If Ty was somewhere, that meant Luke wasn't far away. My mind instantly filled with rage and my thoughts turned to Ash. I shot an arrow into the tree trunk next to the man's head.

"Stop, Ty!" I shouted, charging up behind him. He threw his hands in the air and ducked his head until I got close, aiming my bow at him the whole time.

"What are you doing here?"

"Oh, Hey Diesel. Wow, crazy to meet you out here. I was hunting." His voice had a slight quake and his eyes wandered, looking at everything but me.

"Where's Luke?"

"It's only me, actually."

I dropped my bow and sent a fist flying into his stomach. He grunted in pain and dropped to his knees.

"If you're going to lie, at least make it believable," I snarled.

Ty wasn't cut out for this sort of thing, and it didn't surprise me at all when he caved. Someone put him up to this, and I was afraid I knew exactly who it was. My heart hammered in my chest when he spoke.

"I was supposed to distract you..." he wheezed. "Luke. Ash..."

I couldn't hear anything else. Terror and fury muddled my head. I had no doubt Ash could handle Luke on any other day, but her body was in no state to fight him off tonight. I left Ty on his knees in the dark as it started to rain and sprinted off into the night, hoping I wasn't too late. That's when I heard a faint scream of pure terror that shredded my chest to ribbons. I was too far away, and I had no idea where she was.

CHAPTER 34

ASH

Was I dead? Is this what death felt like? It was wet, dark, and filled with pain. There shouldn't be pain in the afterlife—why did everything hurt? I cracked my eyes open and saw a dark sky above me. Light flashed across my vision. I was disoriented, and the light kept flashing. Something landed in my eye, and I realized it was water. Water splashed on my face. It was raining. Did that mean I wasn't dead? Why didn't Luke kill me?

I took stock of the things I knew. It was night. It was raining. The flashes of brightness were bolts of lightning streaking across the sky. I heard a rumble of thunder, bringing me closer to reality. Why did my leg hurt so badly?

That was when I felt the sensation of moving. Why was I moving? That made little sense. The sky above faded out of my vision and was replaced with dark rock. Pebbles scratched below my body as I moved. The movement was jerky, like something pulling and then stopping repeatedly. Why did my leg hurt so badly?

I finally got enough sense to lift my head. Fear consumed my body and snapped me back to reality. A large, tan animal had a hold of my leg and was dragging me into the depths of a cave. I sat up and screamed out of pure terror. Adrenaline was the only thing fueling my movement. The cougar that had a hold of my leg released me and ran off into the night.

I scrambled back toward the wall of the cave, dragging my useless leg behind me. My breath was ragged in my lungs and my heart raced so hard, I could feel it in my fingertips. My hands searched my body for a weapon; anything to help protect me. They landed on the knife still strapped to my thigh—thank the skies above that Luke hadn't touched it. Why didn't he kill me? Why not finish the job?

The cave blackened between brief flashes of light from the thunderstorm howling outside the cave. I saw well enough in the dark that even in the cave, it appeared as if it was daytime. I wasn't stupid enough to believe that the mountain lion wouldn't come back to finish me. They always came back for wounded prey. I tried to stand, but the leg that the cougar had ahold of crumpled uselessly and I fell back to the ground with a strangled cry. My only option was to stay here with only a knife to protect myself the best I could.

The cave was only a stone's throw deep, and I would hit my head if I stood. I slid all the way to the back corner, gritting my teeth in pain as I moved. This way, I would see the monster when it came back for me. My body shook wildly, adrenaline surging through every pathway in my body, frying all of my nerves.

The minutes stretched into hours as I stared at the mouth of the cave, shaking and sobbing for relief. My eyes weren't allowed to close, even for a second. I tried to slow my breathing and racing heart. The flashes of lightning brightened up the cave in short bursts. The all-consuming panic took control of my limbs and my senses. I had to breathe—to calm down.

I took stock of myself, putting my shaking hand in my soaking hair until it came away streaked red. Rain and blood soaked my hair and my head pounded with pain. I felt the lump and broken skin of a large gash on my forehead, still oozing blood down my face and into my hair.

I hesitantly felt down my leg to where the cougar's teeth had wrapped around my calf. My leg was mangled—muscle and tissue hung off my bone. Sobs wracked my body as I took my knife and cut a strip of my shirt off. I wrapped it around my leg and tied it tight—the pain made me see stars. I forced myself to stay awake—it was the only way to survive. I used a similar strip of shirt to wrap around my head and staunch the blood flow that dripped into my eyes.

It left me in a partial shirt, soaked with water and blood. Shivers and sobs tormented me repeatedly throughout the long night. My teeth chattered as I wrapped my arms around myself for warmth. Fear assailed me as I kept watching the mouth of the cave, clutching my knife with white knuckles.

I didn't want to die here—this couldn't be it. My head felt dizzy from blood loss. I continually snapped myself out of the state of shock I was in. It would be the end of me if I passed out. Darkness and terror were my only friends, as I wished for this hell to be over.

The thunder and lightning finally died down in the wee hours of the morning. The gray light of dawn seeped into the cave when I heard something outside. My heart rate spiked. Large, dark eyes peeked around the corner of the cave opening. My breath was too shallow. I could just make out the outline of the creature in the dim light. It crouched down, creeping its way into the cave toward me. I held as still as I could, waiting for its next move. It stalked closer, assessing me on its powerful legs. My hand around my knife shook violently. *I'm not going to die— You will not die today.*

When the cougar was within an arm's length of me, it stopped, lowering itself completely to the ground. We battled with our eyes. In a moment of complete shock, my gift returned. I saw the move the mountain lion made before it happened.

It leaped toward me to pounce on its kill. I reacted and swiped out with my knife, doing what I had a half-second to practice in my head. Sharp claws caught me across the chest, tearing my shirt and grazing the skin beneath. I narrowly escaped a worse fate as I felt my knife hitting its target and sinking into the cougar's chest. The animal landed on top of me, with a final terrifying scream and went still. I shoved the corpse off me, tears streaking down my face and blurring my vision.

Through sobs and quick gasps for breath, I scooted as far away from the monster as I could. My leg dragged in pain behind me. I ended up on the opposite side of the cave, staring at the cougar, hoping it was dead. For hours, I examined it, making sure it had stopped breathing. I glowered until I collapsed in exhaustion.

I ran down the hallway of a building I didn't recognize. Someone chased behind me, but I didn't feel scared. I felt excited and happy seeing the person chasing me. I rounded a corner and dove behind a piece of fabric that adorned a window. Sunlight streaked through the glass as I waited, giggling to myself.

My pursuer jogged around the corner and pulled to a stop. I giggled again.

"Hmm, I wonder where Ash could be?" came a voice I didn't recognize. He walked around the hall inspecting everything, though there wasn't much. It looked like some sort of apartment building. Doors lined the halls to the left and right.

The only thing that was different was the window that I hid under.

"I wonder if she is hiding behind here," he said, pulling back the fabric that was across the window from me. I put my hands over my mouth to suppress a giggle. He stepped closer and closer to me.

"I don't know where she could have gone," he mused.

Suddenly, the curtain that I hid behind got yanked to the side. My face broke out in a gigantic grin, and I squealed. I saw his face for the first time. It was the face of a young boy, maybe ten years old. He had charming, boyish features, and his smile radiated joy as he looked down at me. The sunlight reflected in his gray eyes and off his blonde hair.

"Gotcha," he said, reaching down and picking me up under my arms. He swung me around while we laughed together. Then I landed on his hip while he clutched me to his side. I wrapped my arms around his neck, clinging to him.

"Come on," he whispered in my ear while I rested my tired head on his shoulder. "I think you need a nap."

I snuggled in closer to his neck and closed my eyes, drifting to sleep as he carried me through the halls.

Pain. It was all I knew. All I felt was pain the next time I forced my crusted eyes open. I remembered the cave that I currently occupied. The cougar's corpse still rested on the opposite side of the cave—his chest still unmoving. The only part of my body I could move was my eyes. I rested on my side, facing the opening of the cave. It was light outside, but it looked as if it was late in the day.

I needed to move. I needed to go find help, or I would die in this cave.

Where was Diesel? Why hadn't he come looking for me? My mind drifted back to Luke's words about Ty distracting him. What had he possibly done to keep him away for so long? I needed help. My mind swam with thoughts of Diesel. He told Lily we were coming to Sage Hen. Was he in on this? Was he the one that helped poison my water bottle? I got lost in my head roaming the possibilities.

My eyes snapped open—I must have drifted off again. The light was dying, and I would have to spend another night in this cave if I didn't get out.

"Come on, Ash, get it together," I berated myself out loud with a too-raspy voice.

I tried to push myself up into a sitting position. As soon as I wiggled my arm under me enough to push, pain lashed through the upper part of my chest. Giving up wasn't an option. *Get tough or die.* Pop's words echoed through my head for the millionth time. Closing my eyes and steeling myself, I gave another shove, breathing through the pain, and finally got upright. As soon as I did, my head swam and my vision blurred. My chin met my chest to get it to stop spinning.

When I felt like I wouldn't pass out again, I slowly opened my eyes. My head throbbed from the gash on it. At least it had stopped bleeding. There was only crusty residue instead of fresh blood. Steady breaths rushed out of my lungs as I peered at the damage on my chest.

Four claw marks stretched across my upper ribs from one arm to the other. The beast's claws had gone all the way through my ripped shirt and tank top, sinking into my skin. The wounds were shallow, but made a fresh wave of light-headedness roll through me—I closed my eyes once more.

I repositioned my legs and instantly, pain shot from my hurt leg. My shirt remained tied around the worst of it. Luckily, it looked like it had also stopped bleeding. Small bits of blood dripped out, but it appeared as if the bite missed any major arteries and veins, otherwise I would have bled out by now. Other than the chewed-up muscle, my bone ached, making me think it might be broken. I remembered feeling it when I tried to stand yesterday. Was that yesterday? Time warped, and I wasn't sure how long I had been here. My bone didn't look out of place, but something wasn't right.

I needed to get up. If Diesel was looking for me, it could take days to find where I was. There were so many caves around here, searching through all of them would be no small task. I didn't know how far I was from where Luke attacked me. My bearings would be easier to find outside the cave.

Crawling was my best option. There was no way I could stand, and even if I did, the chances of me passing out again were high. I rolled to my knees, crying out in pain from my wounds. Please, let someone find me. With each step forward, my vision grew darker and darker, until eventually, all I saw was blackness.

Delirium ate into my brain. Hallucinations of a gray-eyed boy and places I had never seen before took up space in my mind. He looked down at me, smiling, beckoning me to come with him. I needed to get up.

Diesel wandered through the cave. I reached out for him, but Lily appeared behind him. His face filled with disdain as he led Lily out of the cave by the hand. I tried to yell at him, but nothing came out. I needed to get up.

Nan came into the cave and ushered me home. I needed to get up.

The mountain lion came back to life to snack on my mangled body. I cried in terror, but he kept approaching me. I needed to get up.

Voices that I had never heard before mumbled in my ears.

"Is she alive?"

"Doesn't look like it," replied another.

I heard footsteps approaching. Was this real or another hallucination?

"She's still breathing," said the first voice again. "Shit, she is torn up."

"Leave her, she's not worth the trouble," responded the second, darker voice.

A hand prodded at my neck. I tried to smack it away, but my hand barely flinched.

"Hey," said the first voice again, a little softer this time. "You still in there?" I felt a hand pat my cheek. His voice spoke again, "Come on Rex, don't be an ass. Come help me out."

I heard a grumble and more footsteps approaching.

"Holy shit!" the one named Rex exclaimed. "Look at that."

Footsteps walked away from me again.

"You think she killed this thing all by herself?" Rex asked.

"Explains why she's so torn up," replied the softer voice, that was much closer to me.

I found enough strength to crack my eyes open slightly. I looked up at a man who seemed familiar, but my confused brain had a hard time placing him. Real; this was real.

"Hey, there you are. Can you talk?"

I struggled to use my voice, but all that came out was a raspy moan.

"Hold on," he said, pulling his hand out from behind my head. He rummaged around next to him until he produced a water bottle. His hand slid gently behind my head again and he tipped the water bottle up to my lips. I took a few small sips, but my burning throat didn't work. I turned my head slightly away as a sign that I had had enough. He pulled it away.

Footsteps walked back over toward us.

"She wake up?" Rex asked.

The familiar man nodded.

"What's your name?"

I appreciated this man's kindness enough to share that information with him, but only another strangled moan escaped my lips.

"Let me clean you up a bit." I gazed at his face again, trying to concentrate harder on where I had seen him before. He lifted his water bottle and poured water onto the wound on my head, washing the blood away from my face. The water leaked down into my hair, and he cleaned the crusty locks at my scalp. His red-tinted hair was pulled back into a braid. Suddenly, a memory sparked in my brain. My eyes darted to his companion, who stood over me. They were at the market staring over a map weeks ago. Bounty hunters; the thought stuck in my brain.

I rapidly urged my body to move with everything I had. I twisted my face away from him and attempted to shove his hands away. He batted away my arms with minimal effort and pulled my head back toward him so he could keep washing away the blood.

"Hold on a second. I know it probably hurts like hell, but let me clean it up a bit more."

"Waylon, I'm telling you, it's not worth the effort, man."

The one named Waylon kept working on my head. His fingers paused right above my hairline. He stared at my head, leaning in to inspect it closer. Rex leaned in closer at the sight of his paused fingers.

"Is that—Is she—Blond?"

"Damn," Waylon whispered.

Rex had a huge smile on his face. "I told you!" His voice rose excitedly. "I told you there were more up north!"

"She won't make it if we don't get her out of here and get her help, quick."

Then Rex was there, kneeling by Waylon, looking me over. They poured water on my wounds to clean them, but the pain was too much—I let the darkness consume me again.

CHAPTER 35
ASH

The next time my eyes managed to open, I wasn't in the cave anymore. My eyelids felt rough against my eyes. I tried to blink the fogginess out of my vision, to figure out where I was.

"You're awake," came a surprised voice next to me.

The source of the voice was a woman, kneeling next to the bed I laid on. She was middle-aged, with chocolate locks pulled back into a bun. Pity for me enveloped her face. She had white gauze clutched in her hand.

"How are you feeling?" she asked in a timid voice, her eyes glancing to the side. I followed their path to see Rex and Waylon standing in the room's corner, glowering at her. The bed I laid on was in the middle of a small room. It had windows on two corners and a door on the other. A chimney jutted out of the roof on the opposite side of the door, over the fireplace. Wooden beams made up the walls, and it reminded me of the cabin I called home. A pang of sadness hit me—would I ever see Nan again? The cabin looked like it hadn't been lived in for a while. Dust and rodent droppings covered the floor. Large cracks showed sunlight between the logs of the walls. The bed was simply a bedroll, haphazardly thrown onto the ground.

"Can you speak?" she asked again from next to me.

I didn't form any words—they didn't deserve them. She peered at me with eyes full of sympathy and gave a curt nod.

"Here," Waylon said, handing her a water bottle. "Give her some water."

The woman took it and tipped it up to my chapped lips. I gulped the precious liquid down thirstily. It felt like I hadn't drunk water in days, and she pulled it away too soon.

"Not too much. It'll make you sick. I'm going to look at your leg," she explained, looking at me for permission.

"Just do what you've got to do, so she lives, and get out," Rex cut in.

I felt bad for the woman—she appeared to be here under duress. I gave her a small nod, and she breathed a sigh of relief. She loosened the shirt, still wrapped around my calf, and I winced in pain. Once she got it off, she hissed at the sight before her. She inspected the wound, poking around a little. I clenched my teeth as she worked.

"I need to clean this, or it's going to get infected." She glanced over at the men in the corner. "I'll be right back."

Rex stepped in her way. "Stay here. What do you need? I'll

go get it." She rattled off a few things she needed, and Rex disappeared from the room. She came back over to me and looked over my head and chest.

Leaning over to look closer at my head, she whispered in my ear. "I'm sorry. I wish I could get you away from them." She moved back with sadness in her eyes.

I nodded, my face contorting in pain and sadness at my situation, though I was grateful for her kindness. A tear slipped out of my eye and down the side of my face.

"These should be okay. They only need time to heal," she said, gesturing to the wounds on my head and my chest. "But I'm concerned about your leg. I think your shin could be broken, or at least cracked. It's not out of place, which is good. I think it will heal fine. Your calf muscle is in rough shape, though. I'll clean it and put it back together the best I can. I'm worried it's going to get infected if it isn't already."

She pursed her lips.

"You don't have a fever, but if you start feeling cold and achy, you might be in trouble."

Rex walked back in with the supplies. He handed them off to her, and she came back to my side. Where were we? He was gone and back in so little time.

"Here, you need to eat something," she breathed, holding up a spoon and a wooden bowl.

I nodded slightly, knowing I would need strength if I wanted to escape. She brought the spoon to my lips, and I took a mouthful of what tasted like too-mushy oatmeal. It was flavorless and stuck to the roof of my mouth, but it was the best I had. I ate as much as I could until my stomach revolted, and I shook my head when she offered more.

She placed the bowl on the floor and went back to work on my leg. "This won't feel pleasant. I'm sorry." She dumped something on my leg, and the pain was unbearable again. I let out a strangled cry and my eyes clouded with blackness.

"We need to head south to Hope," Rex whispered furtively. "What if she was with someone and they come looking?"

"She can't even stay awake for over five minutes," Waylon replied. "How're we even going to get her out of here? Carrying her here was hard enough. She won't be worth anything dead. We need to get her healed up before we take her to Hope."

I kept my eyes closed so I could hear what their plan for me was. Obviously, Diesel wasn't coming, or he couldn't find me. I would have to get out of this mess myself. Despair sank into my stomach, thinking about what would happen if I didn't get away. I hated Luke for doing this to me.

"You heard the lady doctor—she's probably going to need medicine that they don't have here. Eventually, she'll get an infection. Besides, you know she'll tell someone what we have in here and the entire village will come looking for our payday."

Village? Where were we?

"You warn her what would happen if she told anybody?" Waylon asked.

Rex scoffed. "Of course, and then some. But I don't trust her."

Waylon sighed. "Fine, let's go south. We can go as far as Rollins and hide out in the hunter's house until she is better. The town is big enough. We can probably find a doc who has what she needs, but I'm not hauling her ass all the way there on my back," he said irritably.

Rollins—I was sure I had seen that on Will's map. It was about halfway between Cedar Hill and Hope. My fingers moved along my front pocket to feel the papers tucked inside—they were still there.

"I'll see if I can find us a couple of horses," Rex said, walking toward to door, but pausing. "You think she was by herself?"

"I doubt it. I don't know what kind of idiot would let a girl like that out of their sight."

"As soon as she can sit up straight, I think I'll take a ride on that before we turn her in," Rex snickered.

My blood ran cold at his words. Escaping was the only option—I couldn't stay with these two. Waylon didn't seem so bad, but Rex's manner made my skin crawl.

"Leave her alone." Waylon sounded exasperated with his partner and Rex walked out, chuckling to himself.

Silence descended on the room, and I thought maybe Waylon had fallen asleep. I cracked my eyes open. It was dark and a dim fire burned in the fireplace, casting the room in orange shadow. Waylon sat by the door, but his eyes were closed. It took a moment to get my stiff limbs to cooperate. I moved my arms first, and the only pain I felt was from the muscles tugging at my chest—it was bearable. My body felt like someone had pushed me off a cliff.

I pulled myself up onto one elbow, leaning onto my side. My good leg swung off the bed and my body sat upright. A wave of nausea and dizziness almost toppled me. I waited a minute to get it to cease and then slowly lifted my other leg off the bed. A strangled cry caught in my throat—I bit my lip to keep any sounds from escaping. There was no way I could stand. My leg throbbed painfully as all the blood flowed down to it. I steeled myself, thinking of Nan—I needed to get home to her.

As soon as I tried to crawl toward the door, Waylon's eyes popped open.

"Lay back down before you hurt yourself, Goldilocks. You're not going anywhere tonight," he scorned. I forced myself to sit back down on the bed, grunting in pain.

"What's your name?" he asked. I laid down and faced away from him. He didn't deserve my name. He didn't like the fact that I ignored him and spoke again. "Doesn't matter, anyway. Where you're going, your name means nothing."

I wanted to cry again at his words—I couldn't go to Hope. My worst nightmare was coming to fruition. My stomach threatened to empty the bit of water and food I had today at the thought of what someone would do to me.

I rolled back over and faced him.

"Where are you taking me?"

He quirked his lips. "Oh, now you want to talk?"

I glowered at him.

"We're taking you where all the blondes go, to Hope. You're probably worth a pretty penny, too. Might be able to quit this asinine job," he muttered to himself more than me.

"What's going to happen to me? Why does the King want blondes so badly?"

A crease formed between his brows. "You really don't know, do you?"

"Know what?"

He shook his head. "Your people are freaks. I haven't noticed anything particularly special about you, but that doesn't mean it's not there, and I don't want to give you any ideas that you could use against us."

I was afraid I already knew what he was talking about, what Marva and Nan had spoken about—what made blondes so unique and made the king want them so gravely, went way deeper than the color of their hair.

I lay for hours, trying to come up with a plan—trying to think of anything that would help get me away from these men. In the early hours before dawn, I felt the first hint of a shiver creep up my spine. I pulled the blankets tighter, thinking it was only a draft. By the time the sun peeked into the room, I was freezing, and chills wracked my body. The little hope I had of escaping got crushed in the back of my mind like my leg in the lion's teeth. Even if I got away, I would die without medicine. My leg was infected from the cougar bite—I was sure of it.

CHAPTER 36
ASH

I drifted in and out of consciousness as we traveled—too weak to even move most of the time, cold sweats and shivers from the fever demolished my body. I was losing the battle with the infection, my body already weak from the poison and other wounds. How long had we been traveling? Where were we? When I was awake, I slumped over a horse, riding in front of Waylon while he held me in my seat or lying on the hard ground next to a fire. Waylon forced water and small bites of food down my throat, but I hadn't been able to keep any of it down for at least a day, I guessed. It was all a blur of confusion and darkness.

Grief consumed my mind. This might be the end of my short life. I had to spend my last moments on Earth with two people that I despised. How I wished to spend one last moment with Nan, Marva, Anne, and Pete. Thoughts of Diesel invaded my mind. What could have been between us? I wished I would have told him all that he meant to me.

Consciousness returned to me after a disturbing length of time. I was aware enough to realize that I wasn't on a horse anymore, or next to a campfire. The small room, built of rock walls, reminded me of the cave I was in not long ago. Was I back in the cave? Was it all a vivid hallucination? I wasn't sure of anything anymore. I lay on a makeshift bed. My body felt lifeless. It wouldn't move, no matter how hard I tried. Cold was all I knew—I'd given up on finding warmth.

"Go find a doctor. Now!" I heard Waylon demand from outside the room. "She ain't going to make it to tomorrow if we don't get her help."

I heard more conversation, but I didn't care to listen. This was the end. My body had betrayed me in the end, and I would join Pop soon. I found comfort in that fact and smiled, thinking of the giant hug waiting for me on the other side. I wasn't scared of death, but I feared leaving Nan alone. Blackness swirled in my mind—flashes of memories danced in my head. Pop was in front of me, beaming with a smile. I wanted to go hug him. My hand reached out for him.

"Ash. You need to wake up," a soft voice whispered, and Pop disappeared. Someone shook my shoulders and patted my face. A long string of profanities escaped the person's mouth. "You're in bad shape." His voice sounded strained, like he cared more about my well-being rather than the paycheck at the end of his time with me. How'd he know my name?

"Come on, you need to come back. You can't die! He can't live a life without you in it!" The voice was more forceful now. Hands were on the sides of my neck, lifting my head as it rolled back. Fingers pressed into my skin, and something strange happened. The places where the fingers touched felt better. My eyes wouldn't open—I had given up. I was ready to go with Pop. Steps approached, and the hands pulled back from me, taking the feeling with them.

"Can you save her?" That voice sounded like Rex's.

"She won't make it too much longer. I need to get some things. I'll be back as soon as I can," said the other voice hurriedly.

"Go with him and make sure he doesn't do anything stupid," Waylon's voice faded away.

I was in a hallway that looked familiar—except there was no gray-eyed boy around me this time. I was all alone, walking the halls. I walked and walked in what seemed like an endless maze of similar-looking corridors. All the doors looked the same. I didn't know where I went, so I kept walking.

After wandering for what seemed like hours, I arrived at a door that looked recognizable. My feet stopped while I inspected before turning the knob and slowly pushing the door open.

The door released, revealing a room—it wasn't very big, but two beds took up the floor space and a window covered the far wall in the middle. The beds consisted of pallets that rested on the floor. One had plain, worn discolored sheets, and the other had the same, but that one had a very-used, pink blanket on top of it.

A sudden urge to run to the bed and snuggle with the pink blanket came over me. I stepped toward the bed.

"Ash!" A voice from behind me sounded. "There you are. You scared me to death!" Arms grabbed me and pulled me into a hug. I wrapped my arms around a familiar neck, before pulling back and looking at the blond-haired boy that had been assaulting my dreams. His face was a puzzle of relief and anger.

"Don't be mad," I squeaked out. It sounded much younger than it should have been. I lifted my tiny hand and tried to smooth away the anger on his face.

The corner of his mouth lifted into a smile. "I could never be mad at you, but don't scare me like that again."

"Okay," I grinned back at him, my "k" sounding more like a "t."

We heard a commotion outside, and he turned us around in time to see a woman rush into the room. She was a petite, blonde woman with deep purple circles under her eyes and fine lines of crow's feet. Her blonde hair was too short, and her gray eyes matched the boy's that held me. A look of relief washed over her face at the sight of me in his arms.

She rushed inside and shut the door behind her, cautiously scanning the hall before she completely shut it.

"Where have you been, little Ashy girl?" she questioned in a sweet voice.

"Got lost," came my little voice again as I fiddled with the collar of the boy's shirt.

She moved closer and gave me a kiss on the cheek. I giggled, wiping it off.

"Auntie Izzy," I whined. The woman smiled, but we heard something out in the hall, and her face turned deadly serious.

"Keep her in here and don't come out until I come back," she ordered the boy holding me. He nodded with a serious look on his face.

The woman I had called Izzy opened the door and left. The boy carried me to the bed with the pink blanket and we plopped down on top of it together.

"Want a story?" he asked, fishing his hand between the mattress and the wall. He pulled out a well-worn book with lots of bright colors and pictures. I squealed in delight and settled myself in his lap.

The boy read, and that was the last thing I could remember.

Drip. Drip. Drip. The sound was annoying. *Drip. Drip.* Could someone make it stop so I could go back to sleep? Wait. My ears perked up again, hearing the repeated noise. Did that mean I wasn't dead? How many times did a girl have to ask that question in such a short span of time?

I finally gained enough sense to peel my eyes open. I gazed directly up at the ceiling—It consisted of several logs with boards stretched over them. This wasn't right. It was not the cabin, and the last thing I could remember was the cave. The cave. Where was I? How long had I been asleep? What happened?

A worried face suddenly appeared over me, blocking my view of the underwhelming ceiling. A face that I had seen only once before. His hair looked different. It was jet black and covered in a hat.

"Will?" I croaked out, my voice breaking. A round of coughs escaped my lungs. "Water," I coughed—my mouth felt bone dry. Will produced a small cup of water and gently lifting my head with his hand, he poured it down my parched throat. When I had my fill, I tried to say his name again.

His hand instantly covered my mouth, shushing me. He shook his head, letting me know I wasn't supposed to know who he was. He glanced over his shoulder quickly before speaking.

"Don't say my name. Pretend like you don't know who I am," he whispered urgently.

Why was he even here? Who was he? I shot him a questioning gaze, which was interrupted by loud boots stomping toward us. Will instantly busied his hands when the intruder entered the room.

"She awake?" Waylon asked.

"Yeah, she just woke up," Will replied in a completely unfamiliar voice that sounded much older than he looked. "Hopefully, she'll get better now."

"Hopefully?" Rex questioned, sounding angry. I didn't realize he stood there too.

"I can't make any promises," Will said in a stern voice. "But it looks like the antibiotics are working." He gestured his head toward my arm. For the first time, I realized there was a tube that ran out of my arm and up to a bag that hung on the wall over my head. That must be where the annoying dripping came from. Was that the medicine? I had never seen anything like that before. I felt better, though. My limbs seemed to function again, and the chills slowly subsided.

"Well, looks like you can stick around until she's better then. We ain't going to pay ya until we know she's going to live," Rex said, and Waylon didn't disagree.

Will glared at them. "How am I supposed to trust that you'll pay me? Do you think I care about her? I could put something in her IV and kill her if I wanted. That's exactly what I'll do if you don't pay me right now."

Ouch. That one cut a little deep. I trusted Will, and I didn't know who he really was. I didn't even know if Will was his real name. Why was he even here? Maybe his words were the truth, and he was only here to get paid, like everyone else. The hope I had that Will was here to help crumbled.

I couldn't trust anyone anymore—not here. Waylon and Rex both jumped down Will's throat, not liking his comment one bit.

"You kill her, Doc, and your life is going to follow hers," Waylon growled.

"Fine," Will grit out. "Half now, and half after she's better."

"Fine," Waylon said, and Rex didn't look happy. "Did you at least get her to say anything?"

"Her name is Kenna," Will lied, and the men looked slightly disappointed. Why was he lying for me?

"She told you her name?"

Will seemed to pick up on something that I didn't understand.

"Nah, she was mumbling it in her sleep. She hasn't said a word to me."

They all turned to me at that moment, and I stared back at them with hatred in my eyes. Rex looked like he was about ready to say something, then Will cut in.

"Well, she looks alright, can I leave now? I'll come back tonight and check on her."

Waylon and Rex glanced at each other, trying to silently sort something out.

Will sighed, exasperated. "I already told you two. I don't care about turning in your prized blond, I got other things to worry about. Just give me my money."

Waylon eyed Will.

"Where did you say you were from again, doc?" he asked suspiciously.

"I didn't," Will spit back. They stared each other down for a few seconds before Will said, "I don't need to bring any more attention to myself. All I want to do is get my job done here, get paid, and be on my way."

"You runnin' from something?" Rex asked.

"Something like that. All you need to know is that it's not in my interest to take your girl."

"You said you've worked for Kane before?" Waylon asked. That was the first time I had heard the name, and I wondered who they were talking about.

Will nodded. "Couple times."

Waylon stared him down for another minute before relenting.

"Alright, you're free to come and go, but if you do anything we don't like, your head is on the line."

Will stood by my side. "Give her some food and water. I'll be back later," he said, brushing by them and out the door.

He left, and I heard more voices outside the room, making me think we weren't the only ones taking refuge in this place. What did they call it? The hunters house.

Their eyes turned back to me after Will left.

"Got anything to say yet?" Rex asked. I glared up at them from where I lay.

Waylon snorted.

"They're usually a lot more talkative, begging for us to let them go and such," Rex joked. They pivoted and left the room, giving me a chance to take in my surroundings. The room was small, and the walls were made of rock. One window let the sunshine in from up high on the wall—the room's only source of light. We were most likely underground, in a basement. The window had bars over it—I probably wasn't the first person to be trapped there. The door had a lock as well. Chips and big gashes lined the walls and the back of the door. It made me cringe, thinking that someone else tried to escape this prison at some point.

I stared at the door when Waylon stepped back inside with food and water. He set it on the ground next to me.

"Eat," he commanded before leaving.

I tried to sit up for the first time after he departed. My movements were slow, and my chest still ached from the damage the cougar did. I wore the same ripped shirt and tank top I had on the night the cougar attacked. My clothes were filthy and ripped, but at least my breasts weren't hanging out, since the slashes were higher than that. The cuts appeared to be better, like they had scabbed over and healed. The only parts of my body that were clean and not covered in dirt and crusted blood were the places my wounds were. Will must have cleaned them while I was out. It weirded me out that he touched me while I was unconscious, but I was glad it was him and not the other two.

I touched my head, and it had a bandage over it. There might be a permanent scar on my forehead from the gash. My leg got the worst of it. The cougar shredded my pants to my knee. Damn, that would only leave me with one pair. My leg was wrapped in clean bandages, probably also thanks to Will.

I moved my arm and the strange tube poked further into my skin. Could I yank it out? It was annoying. I'd do it later, when I tried to escape. I needed to get my strength back first if that was where the medicine came from. My nose sniffed at the food in the bowl. Bringing it to my tongue, it wasn't disgusting. My stomach felt off—I should be hungry after so many days of not eating, but I wasn't. I forced the food down my throat until my stomach threatened to empty itself again. Dizziness crept into my head and nausea swirled from the food. Tiredness swept over my body. I was safe for now—a little nap wouldn't hurt until I felt better, then I would work on a plan for getting out of there.

When I woke again, the bowl and cup were gone from next to my bed. The window wasn't letting in any more light, meaning it was probably nighttime. My head felt clearer than it had in days, and my body stronger. I glanced up at the bag attached to the tube, and it was almost empty. Time to yank it out. I put my hand on it, about to give the whole thing a good tug, when a voice came from the corner of the room above my head, startling me.

"Don't."

Will rested with his back leaning against the door, disappointment on his face. A small lantern was next to him, lighting the corner of the room.

"Who are you?" He wouldn't get away without answering my questions this time. His face turned softer.

"Will," he whispered. "But you already knew that."

"I don't understand..." I started, but he quickly shushed me with a look. Heavy boots clunked across the floor overhead, sending fine particles of dust careening down on us. Another pair of footsteps walked past the door outside the room.

He shook his head and whispered, "I'm here to help you."

The way he said it and the sincerity in his eyes made me think I wasn't wrong to trust him.

"Why?"

"Because of who you are," he whispered.

"Who am I?" I asked carefully. What was he talking about? My blonde hair? Or did he know who I really was and where I came from?

"Someone very important." His words were ominous.

"What does that mean?"

The corner of his mouth pulled up, and he looked down at his hands. "Unfortunately, I'm not at liberty to say."

"Please, Will."

"I'm sorry. I can't. It's not my decision to make."

"Then whose decision is it? Let me talk to them."

He chuckled. "Even on the brink of death, you are a force to be reckoned with."

"And you are still not giving me any real answers."

"My only responsibility is to get you home, healthy, and safe. I'm sorry, I can't tell you anything more than that."

"Then how do I know I can trust you?"

He thought it over for a minute. "You can't, I suppose... but it's the best option you have right now." His face looked grim.

"How did you find me? The last time I saw you was this spring, weeks ago."

"You have some very powerful people looking out for you."

"What? So, you have just been following me around since the spring festival?"

He snickered again. "I didn't realize I would like you this

much—something like that."

"Stop giving me vague un-answers to my questions."

"I'm sorry, Ash. I can't give you what you are looking for." He really did look regretful that he couldn't tell me the truth.

"If you were following me around, then why didn't you save me from this whole mess instead of showing up now?"

"First of all, I never said anyone was following you around. You did. Second, if anybody was following you, they probably got there too late to help." He let too much slip. I could see it written on his face. He wasn't supposed to let me know there was someone else with him.

"So, you were following me?! Wait—They?"

He winced. "Forget I said that."

"Yeah, I don't think so. Who is they, Will?"

He took a pretend key and locked up his lips. He had to be younger than me. There was no way someone older would have done that. He reminded me of a younger brother that I had always wanted.

"Will," I scolded.

"Ash."

"Will."

He stared me down, trying not to let his lip twitch up into a smile.

"How old are you, anyway?" I asked.

"Seventeen."

"I'm the older person here. That means you have to tell me everything."

He laughed and blew out his breath. "Fine—it was Jackson." He eyed me warily.

"Should that name mean anything to me, or are you making up names to get me off your back?"

His posture slouched slightly, and he snickered. "Well, in this fictional scenario, that you have constructed in your head, where someone was following you; Jackson would be my brother."

"Why were you and your brother following me around?"

"Orders," he shrugged. "I can't tell you anything more. I have already said too much."

The number of people that had followed us from Cedar Hill to the oasis was astounding, and we didn't even know it until we got past Sage Hen. Wait...

"The arrow at the waterfall—was that you?"

His eyes grew wider.

"It was you! Why did you try to shoot us?"

"We weren't trying to shoot you."

"Um—I beg to differ."

Will finally shut his mouth and I didn't think I would be getting anymore answers out of him. I lay there staring at the ceiling for long minutes, hearing Will breathe from the corner in the darkness.

"You should know that you're a terrible liar, Will."

I heard a muffled laugh from the corner. "Maybe I wasn't trying to lie. Maybe—I was trying to bend the rules to help you understand."

"Can you tell me something real?" I whispered.

The silence grew between us, and I didn't think he would answer my question.

"I'm blonde too," he whispered, quiet enough that the wind would have blown it away.

I sat up and looked at him. I knew it—I knew it from the first time I saw him at the creek. Footsteps sounded again from above our heads. I opened my mouth to say something, and he cut in, glancing at the door warily.

"I'm not going to tell you anything more. Go to sleep. It's the only way you'll get better.

CHAPTER 37
ASH

The days carried on and on in an endless cycle of the same events. Sleep. Eat. Hate everyone. Repeat. I scratched marks on the wall for the days I had been there. Seven. Will pulled the thing out of my arm and said that it looked like I was healing well. He kept tabs on my leg and my other wounds. I lounged around the tiny room, every day hoping to escape. Waylon and Rex came in to bring food, but said nothing to me other than rude and crass remarks. I think there were several other people staying in the house. Several voices filtered down from above and heavy footsteps constantly sounded overhead.

Will came every day to sit with me for long periods, monitoring my progress and changing my bandages. The only thing we talked about was how I had obtained my wounds. My story about the cougar made his eyes widen. I kept waiting for him to say or do something to help me—I had about given up hope for that. He acted cagey and I couldn't get a read on him. I tried to say things to him, but he quickly shut me down with looks that said "not now." His hands were always gentle on my wounds, and his eyes were full of kindness one moment, but the next, they hardened, and he acted like a completely different person. Occasionally, he acted odd. He would change a bandage and then lay his hand on my leg and stare at it, like he was trying to concentrate. I would move my leg away and question him with my eyes, and he would always pull back sheepishly, saying nothing.

After seven long days, I could finally put weight on my leg without it making me want to cry. My body healed unusually fast, maybe thanks to the medicine that I had never had before. I tried to move my body more, in between people coming into the room, to get my strength back up to where it was, so I had a fighting chance. The gloomy room made me want to pull my hair out. I chewed my nails to almost nothing. I missed the sky— I found myself trying to squeeze my head through the metal bars, just to get a glimpse of the sunsets. Home—all I wanted was to go home. I didn't know how long I had been away. The days after the infection set in were a blur. I could barely remember any of the time between when the cougar attacked and when I woke up there. Was Nan worried about me yet? Had Diesel gone home? I missed him like the moon misses the darkness.

My hair had fully turned back to its natural color, and I still wore the raggedy-clothes that were on my body when Luke and the cougar attacked me. Blood stained my clothes, and my shirt was torn from staunching the blood. I stank so badly I couldn't even stand the smell of myself in the tiny room. Between me and the bucket in the corner that I had to call the bathroom, I wanted to scream.

On the eighth day, I couldn't take it anymore. Waylon came in to bring me breakfast.

"I need a bath," I said disgustedly to him.

He looked at me for the first time in days, taking in my appearance. He nodded, turned, and left the room.

My fists met the back of the door he had gone through, beating my frustration out on the door. The solid wood didn't budge. The only thing I managed to do was hurt my hands. I tried the knob for the millionth time, and it still didn't turn. Breathing heavily, I slumped down the back of the door until I sat on the ground—my head hung between my knees. I couldn't give up. *I wouldn't.*

The doorknob rattled, and someone pushed into the room. I moved out of the way and Waylon stepped in.

"Come on," he said gruffly. "I got a bath and found new clothes for you. Be better if you didn't smell like a pig when the soldiers come and get you."

"What! When?!"

He shrugged his shoulders. "When Doc says you're ready."

Will. He was the only thing stopping them from turning me

in right now. Waylon grabbed my arm roughly and pulled me out of the room.

"Try anything and you'll regret it," he grumbled.

It was my first time out of the room. The door led out into a larger room with a cement floor. My prison cell was the only room in the basement, constructed crudely from large rocks. Not much was down there, except for two bedrolls that looked like they had been slept on—probably Rex and Waylon's, and on the far side of the room laid a set of wooden stairs.

He hauled me up the stairs and opened another door at the top. It led into a hallway with three doors. At the end of the hall, was another door that looked like it led outside. He noticed where my eyes had landed and gripped my arm tighter, opening the second door and shoving me inside. It was a small washroom. There were no windows, and I cursed this place for the millionth time. It held a small bathtub and a sink. Clothes draped over the sink and the bathtub held water.

"Wash yourself up and don't do anything stupid," Waylon commanded before stepping outside the door. I could still see his shadow lingering under the door, so I knew he was waiting right outside. I sighed. It could be worse—it could be Rex. He would probably insist on watching me bathe.

I limped over and felt the water. It was cold, but at least I could get rid of my stink. I took my time pulling off my clothes—uneasy with the knowledge that Waylon could open the door at any minute. I peeled my pants off my legs, and something fell out onto the floor. The papers I carried in my pocket were long forgotten. The picture of the hand-drawn little girl and Will's map stared back at me. I tucked them in the pocket of the new pants that were on the sink.

My leg remained wrapped in bandages—best not to get it wet. I slid into the tub, propping my bad leg against the edge, and quickly washed myself off in the cool water. I wished I knew what the weather was like outside. Was it still hot or was fall coming on?

I winced when I ducked my chest and my head under the water in quick succession, the cool water sending pins and needles through my wounds. I hurried and scrubbed my hair of all the blood and filth and climbed out of the cool water, shivering, but at least I was clean.

With no towel, I got the remaining water off the best I could before pulling on the clothes that were on the sink. It was a simple pair of black pants that were slightly too big, and a shirt that drowned me. It almost went down to my knees, so I tucked it into my pants. A pang of sadness hit me at the memory of putting on Diesel's clothes, which were roughly the same size, not long ago. There wasn't any underwear, unfortunately, and my old ones were too disgusting to put back on—but at least there was a clean pair of socks. It was important to find joy in the little things in such circumstances, or the despair and grief would swallow you whole.

I pulled my boots back on when Waylon knocked on the door impatiently. "Hurry, Kenna, I don't have all day."

Who was Kenna? Oh. Right, that was what Will told them my name was. Why did he lie for me? Thankful that Waylon didn't walk in on me, I made sure I tucked away the picture in my pocket and opened the door.

Waylon looked me over and nodded in approval before grabbing my arm and taking me back toward the basement. Thinking quickly but not smart, I elbowed him in the gut, trying to make an escape out the back door. He grunted but was mostly unfazed by my attempt—only gripping my arm tighter and putting his other hand behind my neck, and shoving me back down the stairs and into the dank room without a word. I fought him the whole time, trying to get a shot off that would give me a moment to run, but he was too strong.

Breathing hard, I slumped back down on my bed. Anger and frustration seeped out of me. I was still weak. The fight with Waylon took its toll on my fragile body. My leg ached and a wave of exhaustion settled over me, so I closed my eyes and drifted to sleep.

Sometime later, Waylon barged in and threw food down on the floor for me with his auburn eyebrows pulled into a scowl. I glowered right back at him and he left, slamming the door behind him. I watched as he went, and the door slammed, but didn't catch the lock. It swung back an inch after hitting the jamb. I waited for him to pull it all the way closed, but it never happened.

This was it—this was my chance. My heart rate spiked, and I crept over to the door and peered out the crack. Waylon disappeared at the top of the stairs and no one else was down in the basement. It was now or never. Since there were no windows down here, my only option was up the stairs. I pulled the door open enough for me to fit through. Trying not to make any noise, I limped across the floor as quietly as I could.

The light shadowed at the base of the stairs. I held my breath, listening for footsteps. Hearing no sounds, I made my ascent. The wooden stairs creaked under my feet as I moved. I stopped every couple of stairs and listened for sounds. The door at the top was shut but not locked. I stepped out into the hallway and Waylon's voice sounded from around the corner. I dashed to the second door, praying no one was inside. No one was in the small bathroom, so I quietly shut the door behind me, leaning against it and listening for sounds as I tried to quiet my breathing. Waylon's voice came again, but I couldn't make out what he was saying, and the footsteps faded down the hall. I held my breath as they walked by and turned down the stairs. I cursed myself for not shutting the door of the room behind me. He would know I was gone as soon as he got to the basement.

I made a mad dash for the door I saw earlier at the end of

the hall. My leg pulsed in pain at the sudden movement, but I ignored it and lunged forward. I yanked the door open, running outside to freedom. The fresh air hit me in the face—I might get away. The sunlight was bright on my face, and it took a moment for my eyes to adjust to the bright light from being inside the dark basement for so long. I only made it about a few steps out the door when something jerked my hair. The forward momentum of my legs, mixed with someone grabbing my hair and yanking me backward, caused my whole body to fall back. I fell flat on my back, knocking all the air out of my lungs and smacking my head on the hard dirt.

My head must have still been fragile. Stars filled my eyes, and blackness crept at the edges as I tried to get my breath back. When the stars disappeared from my eyes, I peered at a man whom I had never seen before standing over me, with a smirk on his ugly face.

"Going somewhere, Goldilocks?"

I scowled up at him from my spot on the ground. "How original. Did you come up with that nickname yourself?"

My good leg kicked out, taking his legs from under him, and he landed on his butt next to me. I was up in an instant and on the move again. My vision swayed from the knock on my head, slowing my retreat. An arm grabbed me from behind, wrapping around my biceps and my middle, caging me in. I could feel his sour breath on my neck. We faced the crudely-built house once more, and two more men leaned up against the edge of the building. They were probably all there when I escaped out the door, most likely why I didn't see them in my haste. All bounty hunters. They eyed me up suspiciously while the one that held me kept his grip firm.

I fought his hold but could not free myself. I heard steps and shouting from the house, quickly approaching. Waylon and Rex appeared through the door and stopped in their tracks when they caught sight of us.

Waylon spewed curses, running his hands over his face.

"How'd she get out?" Rex demanded from his partner.

"I don't know. I went back down, and she was gone."

"You left the door open, stupid bastard," I bit out, not able to control my temper. I quickly bit my tongue. That was the wrong thing to say—he surely wouldn't make that mistake again. The other men laughed at my comment, and Waylon gave them a dark look.

"Thought you were supposed to be leaving, Webb," Waylon spit at the man holding me hostage.

Webb chuckled from behind me. "We were on our way out when we caught ourselves a little snack. This is what you have been hiding in the basement, brother?"

Brother? Why would Waylon be with the likes of Rex if he had a brother with the same occupation?

"Give her back," Rex barked. Webb's two cronies from the

wall leaned forward with their hands on knives at their sides, ready for a fight.

"I don't know. I'm pretty sure it's finder's keepers, and since you can't keep track of your belongings, maybe we should turn her in for you. She seems pretty special to me, and will probably fetch a good price." Webb sniffed my neck, sending prickles down my spine.

I looked at Waylon, hoping he would save me—wondering which was the lesser of the two evils.

"Webb," Waylon threatened.

"Fine, but only because I don't want the boss's wrath if you go and whine to him again." Webb threw me forward out of his grip, and Rex caught me in a similar hold. I saw Webb's face for the first time and the similarities between the two brothers were astonishing. They could be twins. The only difference was Webb had a gnarly scar down the left side of his face and years of anger in his eyes.

Rex pushed me back toward the house. I fought his hold, trying to free myself. The panic that flooded my body lit every nerve on fire. I was so tired of this. So tired of fighting; but I wasn't about to give up now.

When we stepped back through the threshold of the house, I elbowed Rex in the side and ducked my head out of his arms in quick succession, freeing myself from his hold. He reached out and grabbed my arm, yanking me back and slamming me into the wall with his body. I saw it coming, just like before, with the cougar and Declan. I saw his hand come to my face, but my body was too weak and slow to defend myself. His palm ricocheted off my face, the noise bouncing off the cabin walls. Thoughts of someone else doing this to me not long ago whirled through my mind.

"Stupid girl," he spit in my face. "Do you know the trouble you've caused us?"

Rex huffed angrily and almost yanked my arm out of its socket, hauling me back downstairs. He pushed me into my room and onto the floor in a heap. I heard the lock click shut behind me. Tears streamed down my face, and I pulled myself over to my bed, sat down, and pulled my knees to my chest. Sobs wracked my body. I feared a worse fate awaited me. I felt so far removed from myself; a shell of who I used to be. I was weak, and I hated myself for it.

CHAPTER 38
ASH

Sometime later, Will arrived, and I sat in the same position. His presence in the room didn't even faze me. My mind sank into a dark place, and I ignored him.

"Can I look at your leg?" he questioned gently.

His words might as well have been the wind. I hated him. I hated this place. I hated the men holding me hostage.

"Ash?" he prodded again.

My eyes jerked to him in anger. *"Don't call me that."*

His eyes landed on the bruise that I was sure had formed on my cheek and flashed an emotion that appeared to be anger.

"What happened?"

I narrowed my eyes at him. I didn't owe him any answers.

"Go away." My body shifted away from him as I resumed staring at the concrete floor.

He leaned closer, and suddenly, his hand was on the back of my head. "Your head is bleeding. What happened?"

I snapped. Slapping his hand, standing, and shoving him

away from me with my hands on his chest. I backed into the corner and yelled at him. "Don't touch me!"

He stood with his hands up in surrender and shot a look at the door, waiting for someone to come in at my outburst. When no one entered, he turned back to me, eyebrows furrowed.

"I won't hurt you, but you need to tell me who did."

My fists clenched at my side. "Who do you think?"

His nostrils flared, and his eyes narrowed. "Can I look at your head, please?" he asked through gritted teeth.

"No, leave me alone." My voice was hard. I pulled the picture and the map out of my pocket and threw them at him. "Take your stuff back, while you're at it."

He squatted, picking up the things on the ground. His fingers held the items gently, and he examined them with affection in his eyes. He peered up at me like he knew something that I didn't understand.

"Where did you get these?"

"You left them by the creek you stopped at, outside of Cedar Hill." I had no reason to lie to him like he obviously did to me.

He stood back up, gazing at the picture in his hand.

"You were there?"

I nodded.

"You can keep them," he said, setting them back on the bed.

"I don't want your trash."

He closed his eyes, like he was trying to gain his composure.

"Can you please let me look at your head?"

"No."

We stared at each other for a few more moments—I wouldn't back down. The last thing I wanted was for another man to touch me.

"Fine," he breathed. "Get some rest. I'll come back in, in a bit. I'll be right outside if you need me."

I scoffed. "Just tell them I'm good to go, doc. Might as well get the show on the road."

He glared at me before turning and leaving the room. Voices came from outside the door when he stepped out.

"She all healed up?" Waylon asked. "Seemed pretty lively today."

It was quiet for a minute, then Will spoke.

"If you two bastards would keep your hands off of her, she would be a lot better."

Tense silence took up the space on the other side of the door before Will spoke again.

"The infection in her leg could still come back, give it a couple more days."

He lied. I was certain that my leg would be fine. It only needed time to heal. I saw it when he re-wrapped it a day ago. The part he put stitches in didn't even look pink and puffy.

"We don't have that kind of time," Rex growled. "Apparently, whoever was with her when we found her tracked

346

us here and is sniffing around Rollins. We need to move or get the soldiers here now."

Diesel! He was there. For the first time in days, a sliver of hope shone in my head. He came for me! He found me!

"Look," Will replied. "Just wait until tonight. I'll go grab medicine you can take with you in case something comes up."

They must have agreed without words, because two sets of boots went up the stairs. So much for Will sticking around. I stared at the map and the picture still sitting on the bed and slid them back into my pocket for safekeeping.

About an hour later, a door slammed upstairs. Someone must have been furious for me to hear it all the way down here. Shouts and angry stomping came down the stairs.

My back hit the rear corner of the room for protection against whoever came down to greet me. The only weapon in my hand was the rusty fork they provided with my food that I hid behind my back.

"Kane, wait," Rex called. His voice sounded scared. Waylon must have never left, because his voice echoed from the other side of the room. "Kane! What're you doing here?"

Kane. Their boss, from what I had picked up. This man must be the epitome of evil if he had bounty hunters working for him. The angry boots stomped past Waylon, toward me. My hands trembled in fear, and the door swung open wide.

In front of me stood a furious version of the man I met

347

weeks ago in the rain. The man that made me feel things I had never felt before. The man with gray eyes and scarred knuckles. My eyes went wide in shock. This was a completely different version of the man I encountered. His cropped hair and short beard were jet black. Did I mistake his hair for blond? I vividly remembered his golden locks falling into his eyes, but the black matched the man before me. All the softness of the night we met was gone, replaced with furious rage as he looked me over. He wore dark pants and a dark shirt that hugged his muscles in all the right ways. Everything about him seemed dangerous. The bit of his tattoo I saw on his hand that night was now on full display. It snaked down the length of his arm and onto the top of his hand—looking like some sort of tribal marking. He didn't have a bow slung across his chest; instead, he carried twin guns holstered on his chest like I had only seen once before. His name was Kane, leader of the bounty hunters.

His eyes scanned over me, and mine filled with fury. He assessed me from head to toe until his eyes narrowed on the newly formed bruise on my cheek. Waylon and Rex's faces appeared in the doorway behind him. He stepped closer and my breath became more labored, clutching the fork behind my back. His hand came up to my chin, lifting my face to his, and I didn't flinch away from his touch. Anger settled in my chest, and I defiantly stuck out my chin, not wavering under his dark gaze. His fingers were gentle on my skin, sending chills racing through my body. Gray eyes peered into mine and I felt like he could read every emotion on my face. The longer he gazed at me, the darker his eyes became. My thoughts turned to the fork hidden behind my back, and I jerked my arm out, aiming for his throat.

"How could you do this to your own…"

The hand that held my chin slammed over my mouth, cutting off my words, and he caught my other arm before it could meet its target with little effort.

"It would be wise if you kept your mouth shut," he murmured.

He moved even closer until our noses almost touched, his hand still holding my mouth hostage. He had backed me into a corner with no escape. I felt his rough skin as it moved down the length of my arm, causing goose bumps to form on my skin. His large warm hand wrapped around my own that had a solid grip on the fork.

"Let go, Blondie." The corner of his lip barely twitched when he spoke. My grip on the fork was solid, and I wouldn't be letting go. His hand gently squeezed mine, fingers working in between my own, until the fork clanged to the ground. He didn't release my chin or my hand, even when the fork was silent on the floor. Kane was the most dangerous man I had ever met, yet I savored his touch. How could someone so vile be so handsome? I despised myself for even admitting it. His eyes searched mine until he finally nodded and pivoted toward the room's entrance. The door slammed in his wake before he yelled at Waylon and Rex to follow him, and their footsteps faded up the stairs. How could he do this to his own people?

I stood still in the corner, trying to catch my breath. Kane's assessment of me made me feel alive again and ready to fight. I couldn't picture the person I met in Cedar Hill and the person who just came in as the same. Was he scouting me out when we met that night in the rain? So many unanswered questions.

I shook my head, picked up my weapon once more, and tried the doorknob for the hundredth time. To my dismay, it stayed locked.

CHAPTER 39
DIESEL

I had been walking day and night for so long, I wasn't even sure how many had passed. It was all I knew, putting one foot in front of the other, like the beat of her steady heart. It drove me onward. Rollins—I had to get to Rollins. That's where they took her.

I pulled at my beard that had grown too long and my hair that cascaded past my ears, remembering the way Ash cut it right before we left on this damned hunting trip. I remembered the way her fingers felt against my skin, not soft but calloused from days of hard work. I remembered how much strength she possessed and drove myself onward; she wouldn't give up on me.

There was so much blood. Puddles of blood stained the cave floor when I finally found it, far too late. The body of a cougar lay heaped in the corner with a fatal wound to its chest. There were so many caves in the area, and I searched day and night until I finally spotted her pack under a bush, where she must've hidden it.

I hated myself for leaving her side and I hated that I was so incompetent, I couldn't even find her until she was gone. But she was still alive. She had to be. I'd almost lost her once—I wouldn't lose her again.

Three sets of tracks left the cave, none of which were hers. They had to have carried her out and they wouldn't have bothered if she was dead. I followed them until they reached a tiny village, not far from the salt deposit. A woman there told me that she helped a blonde girl that was with bounty hunters, but she wasn't hopeful that she would live with her injuries— said they stole their horses and headed to Rollins. I didn't have such luck with a horse. My feet were my only mode of transport. So, I walked; walked until I was so tired, I could hardly see straight. Then I slept for mere minutes and continued. She was my sole purpose; without her there was nothing. I couldn't ask soldiers for help—they would laugh in my face.

I finally arrived in Rollins, weeks after last seeing Ash. My heart and my feet were broken beyond repair. I gazed up into the starry night, wondering if Ash could see the stars from wherever she was.

I entered a bar full of obnoxious drunks with no place to go. It was a start. I questioned everyone, asking if bounty hunters had traveled through with a blonde girl, but no one had any answers. I asked everyone until, finally, I slumped down in a chair, feeling absolutely hopeless.

"Hey, sorry, but we're closing for the night. Either get a room or get out," said the man that had been serving drinks.

I nodded and began to collect my things.

"You're looking for a blonde girl?"

My eyes snapped to him as he casually washed a table with a rag. "Yes."

His eyes drifted around the room, assessing anyone who remained in the building. "The bounty hunters—they have a house right outside of town on the east side. There's always a hoard of them staying there, and they bring blondes through from time to time. If you're looking for a blonde girl, I'd bet good money that she's there, but you didn't hear it from me." He shot me a look that told me to keep my mouth shut.

"Thank you," I murmured, rushing out of the bar.

I rushed east as fast as my exhausted legs could carry me. Rollins was much larger than Cedar Hill and I dodged houses and people along the way. When the houses began to thin on the east side of town, I slowed my pace, realizing I had no idea which house it was.

I heard two men arguing in hushed whispers in the alleyway next to a building as I walked by. I glanced up to see one in a hood walking away—his back to me as he retreated. The other watched until he was gone, and then turned toward me. I recognized him instantly and drew my knife, charging toward him. He didn't see me until the last second and I slammed him into the wall of the building, pressing my knife into his throat.

"Where is she?" I snarled to the man Ash called Will. He was in Cedar Hill not long ago. If he was here, then he was probably the one that took her.

"Stop..." he choked out. "I'm trying to help her."

"You know where she is?"

He nodded, unable to speak until I moved my knife slightly away. "Where?" I didn't care why, all I wanted was to get to her.

"I'll show you if you let me go."

It was my only option, but I didn't trust him one bit. I moved away, and he gasped, rubbing his throat. I glanced at his hair, wondering if Ash's suspicions about him were right, but it was as black as the night.

"This way," he muttered, walking away, and I followed with my knife still gripped in my hand.

We wove our way through the remaining houses and out into the forest beyond, through the trees. Will moved with surprising agility and stealth. He ducked down behind a line of trees, and I followed suit, crouching down next to him. A house laid in the clearing, faint candlelight flickering from the windows.

"She's inside," he whispered.

I stood, ready to march inside and kill whoever had taken her.

"Wait!" Will said urgently. "It's Diesel right?"

I nodded.

"There are fifteen bounty hunters in there right now. If you barge in there, you are as good as dead."

That made me want to charge inside more, fifteen men... alone with her.

"How do you know? And while you're at it, you'd better start explaining why you're here and helping me really fast?" I snapped, tipping my knife toward him.

"I'm a doctor," he said, his eyes dropping to my knife. "I know because I've been in there with her, taking care of her."

"She's alive?" I breathed.

"Yes, I'm hopeful she'll make a full recovery."

After weeks of terror, I finally felt like the air reached my lungs again. I could breathe—she was still alive.

"What are her injuries?" I gulped.

"She has a contusion on her head that has healed, but I'm afraid I could do nothing about the scar it'll leave. She said someone hit her with a rock. She has a few shallow gashes across her chest from the claws of a mountain lion, I believe, again scars that I can do nothing about. The worst is her leg. When I first saw her, I wasn't sure she would make it. She had a severe infection, but I was able to bring her back from the brink of death with antibiotics. Her leg was gashed open severely, and the bone fractured, but with time, it will heal."

I closed my eyes, trying to gain my composure. I should've ended Luke when I killed Declan, and this would have never happened. My eyes flicked open and back to Will. "That doesn't explain why you're here or why you were in Cedar Hill this spring."

"I'm from around here. Someone came looking for a doctor and I answered the call. I was as surprised as you when I saw Ash laying there. As far as this spring, I was searching for a missing person. The fact that we are meeting now is purely coincidental."

"You expect me to believe that?"

"Believe it or not, it's the only truth you're getting if you want my help."

We glared at each other, trying to find the other's weakness, but I didn't have any other options. Storming inside would probably only get me killed and Ash taken to Hope.

"Fine," I growled. "What's the plan?"

CHAPTER 40
ASH

Footsteps creaked on the floor again, and this time, I had a plan. I tucked myself behind the door, waiting for someone to enter the room. The door pushed open softly. I lifted my fork, ready to stab whoever approached. After my encounter with Kane, I was ready to fight again, no matter what. The person on the other side paused for a moment, noticing my absence, until Will's head peaked around the door. My fork aimed toward him.

"You're going to stab me with a rusty fork when I'm here to help you get out?" His black eyebrows raised.

"What?" I was wary of his true motives.

"Come on, they won't be gone for long. Hurry." He ushered me to come out of the room. I followed him up the stairs and he stopped at the top, gesturing for me to stop as well. We heard words being shouted outside.

"We'll have to go out the back door," he whispered. "Be as

quiet as you can." He looked at me, assessing. "Do you need help?"

"I'm fine, I can walk." Was this real or an elaborate scheme?

He nodded and crept forward. We would have to go past the door where all the shouting came from to get to the other side of the house. We snuck up the hall and rounded the corner. The house opened into a large room with a kitchen and a sitting room. The room was trashed and could use serious cleaning. A door adorned the opposite side of the house, next to the fireplace.

"Head north. Diesel is out there waiting for you."

What? Diesel was there? Did he know Will? I wanted to cry with relief, but what if he was lying?

"He's really here?"

Will observed me tenderly and nodded. "It was all I could do to hold him back from barging in here and getting himself killed. We had to wait until we had an opening. All the other hunters left earlier today."

"Other hunters?" I had met three of them in my unfortunate encounter this morning. Were there more?

"There were about fifteen other bounty hunters staying in this house until this morning. I couldn't help you until now." That explained all the footsteps I had heard over the last several days. He pulled a knife from his belt and forced it into my hands—it was the same knife Diesel had given me once before, and I knew Will told the truth.

"Take this. Now, you need to go," he whispered urgently, showing me out the door.

"Wait." I turned to him. "What about you? Where are you going? Am I ever going to see you again? Who are you, really?"

He looked at me like I imagined a brother would look at a sister.

"I'm going in the other direction to lead them off your path. We'll see each other again someday."

I wrapped my arms around him, surprising him with a hug.

"Thank you." His arms found their way around me.

"Take care of yourself, Ash. You're more important than you know. Diesel has medicine in case you need it. Stay with him. He'll keep you safe."

We pulled away from each other.

"Thank you," I whispered again. "For everything."

I turned to leave but thought better of it. He was halfway back across the large room when I called to him.

"Will, wait!" He turned back toward me. There were so many questions I had that had gone unanswered. Who was I, really? Where did I come from? Why were he and his brother following me? On whose orders? What was I supposed to do now? Who was Jackson? How could I go home and live with this information?

He must have seen the uncertainty in my eyes. He moved

back toward me.

"It's not your battle to worry about, Ash. Just go home and be happy. Live the life you always wanted. Forget everything I told you. It's not your problem."

"How can I just forget?"

"Pretend I never existed."

"I can't, Will."

He shook his head. "All anybody wants for you is to be happy. It's the least you deserve—try to find that."

My eyes pleaded with him for more, but he shook his head and walked away without another word.

The shouting outside raised an octave, and I knew I had spent too long there. I opened the door and stepped outside. It was nearly dark now. Trees surrounded the house a way off. They weren't pine trees like I was used to, and I squinted, scanning them for signs of Diesel. I tried to get my bearings as I moved toward the trees. Will said go north.

I caught movement out of the corner of my eye—a group of soldiers approached the house. There were about ten of them from my guess. They spotted me the instant I spotted them. I didn't take my time looking at them any longer. I sprinted as fast as my limping body could go toward the tree line.

"There she is!" one of them shouted.

"Get her!" yelled another. Did they already know I was here? Were they coming for me?

They all ran after me, and my leg slowed my progress significantly. I heard more shouts and commotion behind me. Glancing back, Kane and Waylon rounded the house—Kane's face full of fury. They all rushed in my direction, with Rex nowhere in sight.

I ran faster, trying to find my escape in the trees.

Suddenly, an arrow whizzed by, finding its mark in one of the soldier's legs behind me. I turned toward where the arrow came from and could barely make out Diesel, standing by a tree with his bow drawn, loosing arrows at the men behind me in the dying light. The sight of him made me want to cry.

"In the trees, get him!" a soldier yelled. That was when they pulled out their guns and the shots started ringing through the air. I didn't look behind me anymore. I ducked my head and ran harder, hearing bullets and arrows fly by me.

The trees approached, and I dove behind the one nearest Diesel. Breathing hard, I could tell it had been a while since I had exerted my body that much. Diesel shot one last arrow and lunged at the tree I ducked behind. Tears swelled in my eyes. Green eyes, blazing with rage and relief, found mine. He scooped me up into his side, and I reveled in the feeling of him against me. We gazed at each other for a moment, and he placed his forehead against mine behind the safety of the tree.

"You're here," I hiccupped out through tears that had spilled onto my cheeks.

"I'm here Ash—I've got you. I'm never leaving you again." His voice broke with emotion and his lips found mine in a hurried kiss. He was much leaner and covered in dirt, but I couldn't care less right now. He was here.

"Hold your fire!" Kane's voice boomed out from beyond the tree line. "You might shoot her!" The shots ceased—obviously, he had authority over the soldiers.

"You shoot her, and you die!" I heard him seethe to the men. "I want her brought back to me alive."

"We've got to go," Diesel said quietly. It was fully dark now, and I doubted they would see us sneak out through the trees. "Come on."

I leaned my weight into him, and he helped me move through the trees on my bad leg, holding up my side as we went. The trees swallowed our figures as we walked off into the night. Footsteps sounded behind us, closing in quickly. Diesel stopped suddenly, placing me between a large tree and a thick bush.

"Wait right here for a minute," he whispered.

He saw the look on my face before I could even get any words out.

"Don't test me right now, Ash," he said in a haughty tone. He crouched down in front of me as the soldier behind us passed by. As soon as he passed, Diesel stepped up behind him and wrapped one arm around his neck and the other over his mouth. A sickening crack filled the night air, and the soldier slumped down silently. Diesel took his gun and shoved it in his pants before returning to me.

"Did you just—kill him?" I had never seen Diesel with so much wrath.

"Don't ask questions you don't want the answer to." His voice was unapologetic.

We hurried onward, but didn't get very far before someone found the soldier's body and shouted. We heard several more footsteps headed in our direction. Diesel looked around as we moved, searching for our next option.

Out of nowhere, someone rammed into us from the side, knocking me to the ground. Diesel smashed his fists into the soldier's face, but two more appeared out of the dark. However, only one was a soldier—the other was Waylon. The soldier moved to where Diesel and the other soldier tussled on the ground, and Waylon came toward me.

I stood, ready to fight, pulling the knife that Will had given me out of my pants as Waylon descended upon me.

"I was nice to you. This is your fault," he said, his voice dripping with malice. What had I done to him? His arm swung out to deliver a blow to my face, but I ducked under it, kneeing him in the back as he turned. It was nice to know my weird superpower had my back. He growled at the blow and came after me harder. I looked at Diesel, and he still fought with one soldier. The other seemed to be slowly peeling himself off the ground.

In my moment of distraction, Waylon grabbed me around the back, pinning my arms to my sides. Feeling stronger and angrier than I had in days, I threw my hips back into him and my upper body toward the ground, causing him to lose his grip. I fell to the ground and rolled away from him. Leaping up once more, I ran toward Diesel. Ignored the stabbing pain in my leg with all the adrenaline racing through my body.

Diesel's eyes caught mine in the dark and he must have not liked the look of panic I surely had on my face. He tossed the soldier away from him and whipped off his bow from across his chest, drawing back and aiming for the man on my heels. His arrow rested on his bow for too long, and Waylon was suddenly on top of me again, knocking me to the ground. With Waylon on top of me, Diesel finally had a clear shot, but a gunshot rang out from somewhere close by, throwing off his aim. Another soldier charged him right after the shot. The arrow stuck Waylon in the thigh. I used his surprise and abrupt pain to my advantage. I rolled over on top of him and pulled my knife up to finish the job. He deserved this for all he had done to me, but I hesitated. I had never killed a man before.

I was on the verge of deciding his fate, with my arm raised, knife in hand, when a steely grip landed on my wrist. Time skidded to a halt. A breeze blew my loose hair into my eyes as I peered up at the person attached to the hand gripping my own.

Lightning danced across my skin where his skin touched mine. I kneeled over Waylon as Kane peered down at me with a stony demeanor.

I stared back, my lip curled into a sneer. Waylon seemed to be slightly delirious and moaning in pain underneath me. He glanced down at him but looked instantly back to me, like he couldn't care less if the man lived or died. His thumb gently stroked my wrist once.

"It'll do more damage to you than it will to him," he stated. His voice seemed too gentle for the moment, like the wind that whispered through the trees.

He gave my wrist a squeeze that wasn't painful, but made me drop the knife onto the ground. Feeling suddenly very vulnerable, I stood, shaking out of his hold. He didn't fight— didn't even reach for me again as I turned and ran away from the man, who both terrified and intrigued me, before he changed his mind.

Two quick, successive gunshots echoed in the stillness of the night. Two soldiers crumpled to the ground and Diesel let the gun fall to the forest floor. The shot placement was impressive for someone who had never used a gun before.

Diesel ran toward me and lifted me off the ground in his brawny arms, unaware of Kane's presence in the dusky night— But I could see through the darkness like no one else. I could still see him watching us. He stood over Waylon, who moaned

on the ground, but his eyes were on me as Diesel raced us off
into the night.

CHAPTER 41
ASH

Diesel ran as fast and as far as he could until he finally slowed to a walk.

"You can put me down," I breathed. "I can walk. I don't think anyone is following us anymore."

His only answer was squeezing me harder to him.

"Diesel," I said again, louder. "You can't carry me the entire way."

"The hell I can't," came his coarse voice.

"D, please," I said softly. "My leg is hurting." It was the truth—the way he was holding me made my sore leg uncomfortable.

He sighed and stopped, looking around for something before changing his direction. He halted and gently set me down on a fallen tree.

The night was fully dark, and the only light came from the stars and the sliver of a moon that was out tonight. A chilly breeze rustled through the forest. I may have been unconscious for longer than I believed. The days in between the cave and showing up at the hunters house were fuzzy. I shivered at the wind on my skin and wished for my jacket.

Diesel noticed my discomfort at the chill in the air. He crouched down, pulling off his pack. He fished around inside of it before pulling out my black jacket, the one that was stashed inside the pack that I left under a bush when I last saw him.

"Here, put this on," he said, helping me into my jacket. He pulled the hood up over my head, tucking my hair back into it. His hand didn't move after all my hair was tucked in, but remained on my cheek, stroking my skin as he gazed at me.

"You found my pack?"

He nodded, anguish filling his features.

"How did you find me?"

He shook his head and closed his eyes, like it hurt too much to talk about right now.

"Not now, we need to keep moving," he whispered delicately to me. "Let me look at your leg."

He took his hand away from my face and pulled my wounded leg into his lap with extreme care. The bandage was darker than it should have been. His breathing intensified the longer he glared at my leg.

"Diesel? Is everything okay?"

His eyes glinted with murder. "I should have killed every one of those bastards for what they did to you," he snarled. The pure malice that laced his tone took me by surprise.

"It's okay. I'm out now." I ran my fingers through his scruffy beard, forcing him to look at me.

He peered back down at my leg, none of the anger dying out. "It's bleeding. I need to unwrap it and look at it, but we need light. We either have to build a fire or wait until morning." He ran his hand through his hair, not liking either of those choices.

"Don't build a fire. We're not far enough away. It's probably fine; the stitches that Will put in probably got pulled out."

His eyes flashed at the name. He stood and tugged at his hair, trying to regain his composure. At this rate, he would make himself bald before he turned thirty. I gave him a minute and let him breathe to work through his anger.

"Diesel, it's fine. Let's just keep going."

I stood, and he was there in a second, pushing me back down to sit—his haunted eyes filled with pain.

"Where else does it hurt?" he whispered, his voice breaking with emotion. I hid the truth from him to save him from the pain that I had endured these last weeks.

"Nowhere, I feel fine." It was a lie. I knew it and he knew it, but he didn't push me any further.

"How long has it been?" I asked, uncertainty filling my tone at the lapses in my memory.

"A little over a month," he said, his voice wavering.

My brows rose in shock, and I grieved for all the time I had lost. A questioning grimace covered his features.

"You didn't know?"

I looked away, trying to hold back my emotions. "No—I can't remember most of it. Nan is probably having a heart attack."

"She'll be fine," he said dismissively. Then, he gathered up my chin in his hand and turned me back to face him.

"The only thing I am worried about is you." I pulled him into a long-awaited hug, and he gripped me tightly. My body trembled with adrenaline and the emotion of seeing him again. After my body ceased quivering, I said, "Let's go. I don't want to get caught again."

"You're not walking on that leg. Get on my back, I'll carry you."

I shrugged him off and took a shaky step forward. "I can walk."

His bulky frame stepped in front of me, stopping me in my tracks and forcing me to look up into his enraged eyes once again.

"Ash..." he snarled. "I swear, if you argue with me one more time right now, I'm going to lose it."

He saw the defeat in my eyes and turned around so I could climb on his back. He took the bow off his chest and held it in his hand while he continued to walk.

My nose tucked into the crevice by his neck, and I breathed

in the scent of Diesel that I had missed. He walked for a few more hours until he couldn't go any further. We found a place to settle in for the night in a thick bramble of bushes. Without lighting a fire, he unrolled the one bedroll that he still had attached to his pack.

"I'm sorry. I couldn't carry both our packs. I took everything out of yours and put it in mine, but left your bag and bedroll."

I nodded in understanding. Exhaustion overwhelmed me, and all I wanted to do was fall over and go to sleep. The day had been too much on my beaten body.

"... Ash." I realized Diesel had been talking to me, but I didn't know what he said. He looked at me with a softness in his eyes as he grabbed my hand and pulled me toward him.

"Come on, let's get some sleep."

He helped me ease down onto the bedroll and sat next to me. We both took off our boots, and without hesitation he opened the bed and laid down, pulling me in next to him and covering us up. I was too tired to over think anymore. I snuggled in next to his warmth with his front to my back and my head resting on his arm. It was the first time that I had felt safe in weeks. I clutched onto his arm that wrapped around my middle, pulling me into him, hoping this wasn't a dream. A tear welled up in my eye and slipped down my cheek.

"I didn't know if you would come," I whispered into the darkness, and he tensed at my words. "Thank you for coming after me. I missed you. I've never been happier to hear your name than when Will told me you were waiting outside for me."

He clenched me tighter when I mentioned Will's name.

"I would never abandon you, Spitfire. I already told you—I'm never leaving you again." His breath was hot in my ear, and he brought his hand up and ran his fingers through my hair. He placed a gentle kiss on my neck below my ear, the rough whiskers of his beard scratching my sensitive skin. My eyes drifted closed as he continued to play with my hair. Right as I was on the brink of sleep, I heard him whisper words I thought were only a dream.

When I awoke, I was alone in the bedroll. I slept fitfully for the few hours we had of darkness before dawn. Every time I moved to get comfortable, Diesel was there, pulling me back into him like I would disappear if he let go.

I sat up in the thin light of morning, scrubbing my hands over my face to wash the sleepiness from my eyes. Diesel sat not far away, with his arms propped on his knees in front of him. His green eyes pierced holes in my blue ones, and I had a hard time reading the look on his face. I was sure I looked terrible, with all the wounds and lack of sleep.

"Sleep okay?" he asked in a rough voice.

"Yeah, you?" I pulled my knees to my chest to conserve the warmth from the bedroll. When I did, my leg smarted, and I winced in pain. Diesel was next to me before I could even get my legs all the way up.

"I'm going to look at your leg now," he said with a troubled look on his face. Without asking, he pulled back the top cover of the bedroll and took my bad leg out of the warmth as he inspected it.

Brown patches of dried blood stained the white bandage wrapped around the wound. It looked worse in the light of day. He took out his knife and pressed it gently against my leg, with the sharp part up, to cut the bandage. Before beginning to cut, he hesitated.

"If anything hurts, you tell me."

He ran the knife up under the bandage, being careful not to pull too hard or touch my skin with the blade. He peeled the bandage back and glared at my leg.

"I didn't know it was this bad," he said in a dark voice full of anger.

"I guess that's what you get when you mess with a cougar, lots of teeth marks." My joke did little to lighten his mood. His eyes shot to mine, and he gave me an incredulous look. My leg didn't look that much worse than when I last saw it. There were a handful of stitches at the top pulled out—probably the source of the bleeding. Though, it didn't look infected, only irritated by all the movement yesterday. Diesel inspected it and must have come to the same conclusion.

"Let me re-wrap it," he said, pulling out supplies from his pack. These must be the things that Will gave him, and that brought a whole new line of questioning to my mind. As he worked on my leg, I asked again, "How did you find me? How did you meet Will?"

His hands stilled on my leg, and he grimaced like this was the last thing he wanted to talk about. Finally, he took a breath and kept working as he told me his story. His fist clenched after he ripped off the last piece of tape holding my bandage in place.

"Did Ty tell you that Luke poisoned me?" I asked, curious as to his explanation for that one.

His eyes flashed in rage and shock, and I knew he didn't know about the poison. I let out the inner breath I had been holding for weeks. *He didn't know. He didn't know.*

"What?" he snarled, trying to contain his temper.

"That's why I got so sick after we left Sage Hen. Luke said he put wolfsbane in my water bottle the night before we left."

I looked at him pointedly, waiting for an explanation. He was the one that took my bottle out that night and didn't return for a long time. His voice turned steely. "I didn't know about the poison or that they were even there."

I believed him, but his eyes turned guilty as he searched his memory for something.

"I'm sorry. I might have left our bottles on the counter for a minute, unattended. I got—distracted."

That's all the explanation he gave me, and it was not enough.

"By what?" I bit out.

He shook his head. "It's not important," he said, brushing me off. My nostrils flared in irritation at his non-answer.

"The only thing Ty told me was that Luke was after you, and I left before I heard anymore. The only problem was that it was dark and raining, and I got turned around on my way back to where I left you."

Anguish filled his eyes.

"When dawn broke, I realized I had been going in the wrong direction. I doubled back, but by the time I got back to where I last saw you, you were nowhere in sight. The rain washed away all the tracks and I couldn't find you or any of your stuff."

His voice was full of emotion, and he put his hand on his head, trying to push the memories out of his mind.

"I looked for days. I searched through all the caves, but I was on the wrong side of the valley. I kept going back to where I last saw you, praying for a sign. That's when I found your pack stashed under a bush."

"Did you find my bow?" Maybe I hadn't lost one of Pop's last gifts to me.

His brows knit together. "No, I'm sorry."

I nodded, crestfallen at the loss.

"When I found your pack, that's when I went the other way, trying to think like you. I eventually found a cave with a dead cougar and so much blood," he choked out.

The pain in his words made me reach out and put my hand on his leg for comfort. My emotions battled. I wanted to kiss him, to ease his pain, but throttle him for holding things back and keeping secrets. Luke's ominous words danced through my head—*Diesel has more secrets than anyone.* I thought of that night in the cave; the most terrified I had ever been. He peered at me with so much hurt and regret in his eyes.

"What happened?" he breathed.

I recalled the events of that terrible day—how Luke attacked me and how I awoke to the mountain cougar hauling me into a cave. It was hard for me to get out of how I killed it. The fear crept back into my mind from that night. I relived darkness from the days that followed, and the hallucinations that would haunt me forever. I left out the part about my abnormal human ability to see the cougar's move before it made it, like I could see the future. I wasn't ready to share that with anybody.

Diesel gathered me into his lap and sat down on the bedroll, taking the spot that I had vacated. I realized a few tears had slipped down my face. He held me tightly against him, pressing his head to mine.

"Luke was there to kill me. Why didn't he finish the job?" I murmured.

"I bet he got scared after he hit you with the rock and ran. He's not Declan, no matter how much he was trying to prove himself. He's not cut out for killing."

I hated Luke, but I couldn't help feel bad for him too.

"I can't believe you killed that lion all by yourself. You're the biggest badass I have ever met." He faked a chuckle for my benefit, trying to make me feel better—but I could tell what I had to endure alone was eating him alive.

I continued to tell him about how Waylon and Rex showed up and the days that followed. I told him about the gaps in my memory and Will showing up to save my life. Diesel took deep, calming breaths against me as I finished my story.

"How did you find Will?"

"Fate. A lucky mistake," Diesel said, with a hard edge to his voice. "I was raising hell in Rollins, looking for you. I saw him last night and recognized him from when he danced with you at the festival. I about killed him when I first saw him. I thought it was him—that he had done it to you. He told me he knew where you were, and that he was trying to help, right before I ripped his throat out."

I turned in his arms and looked at him with wide eyes. "Diesel!"

He didn't look apologetic at all. His face simply hardened.

"I won't apologize. I'm indebted to him for helping me get to you, but I will kill anybody who hurts you or tries to take you

377

away from me again."

"Did he say how he found me and why he was there? Or who he was?" I was curious if Will had told him.

Diesel shook his head. "All he said was he was a doctor that lives here, and it was a coincidence that he found you. He said he was looking for a missing person and that's why he was in Cedar Hill this spring, but he wouldn't tell me anything else."

Will's story to me was different and made a lot more sense than what Diesel said. He was lying to one of us and I had a feeling it was Diesel. Was I the missing person he was searching for?

Should I tell him about all the things Will told me? Though honestly, he didn't tell me much other than I was important, and he and his brother had been following me for an unknown reason. He told me to go home and try to forget him and be happy. Should I do that? Try to forget?

"I would have followed any lead to find you. It could have been the devil himself and I would've followed him to hell to get to you," he whispered.

I decided it was best to keep it from Diesel. Emotion played over his face, and I glanced down at his lips, which were so close to mine. Before I knew it, his lips landed on mine in a scolding kiss. My lips melded with his, his kiss full of longing and the heartache we had both felt for the last few weeks. I poured back into him the love that I felt for him. The love I had worried wouldn't be returned.

He pulled me closer, and I kissed him harder, his beard scratching my face in the best way. He put his arm around my back and picked me up, laying me down underneath him. He paused to sit me up and pull my jacket off my torso. The second he got it off, he stopped with shock on his face, staring at the still-healing wounds on my chest from the cougar's claws. They peeked out from underneath my shirt.

Diesel grimaced and stood immediately, pulling me up with him and placing me on my feet. He shook out my jacket and put it back over my head before he cursed and yanked at his hair as he walked away. He left me standing there, feeling crushed and unsure of what I did wrong. I closed my eyes, holding back unshed tears.

He paced for a minute before returning. His feet stepped into view of my downcast eyes. He placed his fingers under my chin, forcing me to look up at him.

"Don't for one second think you did something wrong. We just—I can't do that to you right now. I'm an asshole. I'm sorry." His eyes implored mine, searching for forgiveness.

"It's okay, I'm fine," I lied through my teeth, because I felt anything but fine.

He shook his head. "We better get going."

CHAPTER 42
ASH

We walked for days. My leg ached from overuse, but I didn't tell Diesel. All I could think about was getting home to Nan. We walked, and we slept. Diesel hunted for food, while I rested at the fire. The trees morphed back into the familiar pines and the landscape became hillier. We continued to head north toward home. We skirted around any towns or people that we encountered, crossing rivers and streams along the way. I kept my hair in my hood, even when it got warm out. No one followed us, as far as we could tell, but that didn't mean we were out of the woods yet. Fall came on strong, and I worried about Nan and our crops which I hadn't been able to harvest with her.

Diesel and I shared details of our time apart with each other, but said nothing further. He fussed over my leg and the amount of food I ate. We slept together at night in his bedroll, and he clutched me tight. He was always touching me: holding my hand, or helping me navigate the terrain. I felt desperate for him to tell me he wasn't leaving—that I was enough to make him stay. I needed him to shed light on all the lies that surrounded us. After he pushed me away, the morning after he rescued me, I was too afraid to ask—too afraid to hear his answer. How could he still want to be a soldier after he fought and killed them so easily? It would be him who was hunting down people like me. I couldn't stand the thought. Why was he so adamant about becoming one of them?

One night, when we were close to being home, I sat by the fire when Diesel came walking back into camp with a rabbit clutched in his hand. We cooked dinner, and as we ate, I found the courage to ask a question that had been bothering me for days.

"What happened that night in Sage Hen when Luke slipped poison into my bottle?"

He stopped chewing mid-bite and closed his eyes.

"Do you remember the two soldiers that we ran into at the hot pool this spring?"

"Yes," I responded warily.

"When I went back to give the bowl back, the smaller soldier from that night, Carter, was in the bar. We had a conversation and while we spoke, I left your bottle on the counter."

"You knew them?" I blanched in shock.

"Yeah," he cringed. "They were coming to talk to me this spring when we ran into them. I didn't want to tell you because

I wasn't sure what I wanted yet. That was the night I saw your hair for the first time, and I didn't want to put you in any more danger. The soldiers knew better than to discuss private matters in front of you."

"Explains why they didn't hassle us more. I always thought it was strange that they just walked away. You didn't want to put me in more danger, or you were afraid to tell me the truth?"

"Can you blame me? You tried to shoot me when you found out that I was interacting with soldiers. Twice!"

"If I wanted to shoot you, you'd be dead."

He shook his head, and his lips turned up in a smile. "I'm sorry I didn't tell you sooner."

"Why was Miles so adamant that you work for the King? Please, help me understand, D. Why do the soldiers want you so badly?"

He sighed and chose his next words carefully. "It's a long, complicated mess. Our family used to be highly regarded in Novum. Miles thought if I went back and worked for Maximus, then he would remember who we were, and I could be somebody important one day. That we could have power enough to lead and change the country."

"Is it only Miles that wanted it or you, too?" He had to want it. Otherwise, why put me through such hell?

His eyes turned down as if he was ashamed of his response. "Yes, I want it to."

Not wanted, as in the past. Want, as in he still yearned for it.

The next afternoon, we reached the expanse of the headwaters of the Paloma River. We weren't far from the lake it ran out of at Cedar Hill. My excitement built, and I moved faster up the banks of the river. Not long later, I saw the sun reflecting off the glassy lake. I moved faster, running to get to town.

"Slow down," Diesel called from behind me. "You're going to hurt your leg more."

I was too excited to listen—we were almost home. I had missed it so much; the smell of pines, and even the nasty mossy scent coming off the lake in the late summer. I made sure my hood covered my head as we made it to the outskirts of town, pushing back any stray hairs. I turned down the street toward Anne and Pete's house, with Diesel hot on my heels.

I saw Nan before she saw me. She and Anne walked down the road, away from the house, as if they were going somewhere.

"Nan!" I called. She turned the instant she heard my voice and tears started flowing down my face. She raced toward me as fast as her old legs could take her. I ate up the rest of the distance in a flash, scooping her slight frame into a hug.

"Ash!" she cried through tears of her own. "You're here.

You made it back. I was so worried." We held each other and sobbed for long minutes, trying to get our emotions together.

She finally pulled away from me and looked me over. I was sure there was still a fading bruise on my cheek, and a healing scar on my head from where Luke had taken a rock to it. The other injuries she couldn't see, but I knew I looked worse for wear. I was filthy from a lack of bathing and clean clothes, and I had lost weight from the days of not eating. My collar and hip bones protruded more than normal. She placed her hand up to my cheek, inspecting my face.

"What happened, my girl? You've been gone for so long," she choked out.

Anne stepped up at that moment, and I noticed her and Diesel standing next to us.

"Let's go inside and get these kids rested, and something to eat, while they tell us what happened, Jo," she said sweetly to Nan.

Nan nodded, tugging me along by the arm and back to Anne's house. She immediately noticed my limp and pursed her lips. Inside, she pushed me into a chair. It felt good to sit. My leg ached constantly now, to the point where I wasn't sure I could handle it. I had ignored it until now but sitting here finally home, I realized the pain that I was in.

Anne and Diesel followed us in, and Diesel pulled out a chair next to me, scooting in close and resting his arm on the back of my chair. Nan looked at me with a questioning gaze. Anne came back from where she had disappeared in the back with a medical kit in hand. She set it down and ducked into the kitchen to produce two cups of water and crusty bread, placing it in front of us on the table.

"Well?" Nan insisted.

I gave Anne the side eye. She might as well know if she was going to be part of this. I pulled the hood off my head, revealing my blonde hair. But she didn't act shocked.

"I've known for a while, sweetheart," she said. Nan had a sheepish look on her face. Well, I guess that solved that problem.

"Oh," was all I said, stupidly, before regaling them with the tale of what happened. They listened in shock and horror at the events I had been through the last month. I took sips of water and bites of the delicious bread between words and questions from the older women. Diesel sat silently by my side.

I got to the end of my story, and the women continued to ask questions. Diesel fidgeted by my side impatiently.

"Ladies," he cut in. "I think that's enough questions for now. Anne, will you please check Ash out so we can go home, take a bath and get some rest?" Clearly, he was no longer interested being here.

"You can go home. I'll be okay here," I told him.

"Not without you." The way he said it made me think it was totally out of the question.

Anne interrupted our staring contest when she pulled another chair over and asked me to prop my leg on it so she could take a peek. She hiked my pants up and cut the bandage free, hissing at the sight of my mauled leg. It looked a lot better than it did two weeks ago, though. The wound had healed over, leaving deep, jagged scars.

"I'll have to cut these stitches out," she said, before proceeding to do just that. It wasn't a painful experience, but was slightly uncomfortable.

"You said you thought it was broken?"

I nodded. "That's what Will told me. It feels broken."

"I'm going to push along your bones. You tell me if something hurts, okay?" she explained.

"Okay," I replied nervously, not wanting more pain in my leg.

She began by my knee and worked her way down. When she got to a certain spot, I cried out in pain at her touch.

Diesel sprung into action. He stood and grabbed Anne's hand, holding it away from my leg and glaring at her menacingly.

"Don't hurt her," he threatened, giving her a look that would make a grown man shrink.

Pete chose that moment to come walking in the door. He saw Diesel holding Anne's hand and glaring at her.

"I suggest you get your hand off my wife," he warned Diesel.

"It's okay, D," I soothed. "She's only trying to help."

Diesel looked up, noticing Pete's presence, and dropped Anne's hand.

"Be more careful," he said under his breath as he stepped behind me, placing his hands on my shoulders protectively. Pete came in and shut the door. It filled the room with silent tension as Anne continued her inspection.

"It's definitely broken, and I'm sure the walk here only made it worse." She brought her finger up to her chin and pursed her lips in thought. "I think it might only be a crack, but if you keep walking on it the way you are, it could slip further and be a more serious break. You need to stay off it for at least two weeks, and then only light use for another two, to give it time to heal properly."

"What? No!" I gasped. "No way, I can do that. It'll be fine."

"Ash!" Diesel and Nan both scolded, making me feel like a scorned child.

"You need to listen to Anne," Nan said.

"She's coming home with me. I'll make sure she stays off of it," Diesel chimed in.

Excuse me? My eyes darted to him. We hadn't discussed this.

"No, Nan needs me," I said adamantly.

"*Yes.* I'm not leaving you again. My house is closer to town anyway, in case we need anything. Nan can come too," he pointed out logically.

"Sounds like the girl doesn't want to go with you," Pete

piped up.

Diesel shot him a disdainful look. "Stay out of this, old man."

"Stop it, both of you," Nan scolded.

She came and sat on the chair next to me and looked at the people in the room.

"Can we have a minute, please?" she asked kindly.

Anne nodded and pulled Pete out of the room, but Diesel didn't budge.

"I promise I'll look after her," Diesel told Nan.

"Just give us a minute, please," Nan said. His green eyes searched mine before he nodded and stepped outside.

"Ash," Nan said softly, pulling my hands into hers as she spoke. "Did something happen between you two?"

I shrugged. "I don't know. There's so much that happened in the last month. I don't know how to feel. All I wanted was to come and be with you again, Nan."

Nan looked down at our hands before she said, "I think you should go home with him."

"What! Nan, no! I want to go back to our cabin with you."

She appeared crestfallen.

"Things are changing for me, my girl. I don't think I can go back there with you."

"Did something happen while I was gone?" My voice sounded frail.

"No—Well, yes. I don't think I can make the walk anymore. We tried to go back to take care of things, but on the way back, I had some sort of episode and couldn't get out of bed for three days. Anne thinks it has something to do with my lungs, but if I don't exert myself too much, I'm okay."

My eyes clogged with tears, and my voice filled with emotion.

"Nan, I'm so sorry I wasn't here."

Hearing her say she didn't want to go back to our home felt like a dagger in my heart. The home I dreamed of coming back to was crumbling around me.

"Don't be sorry—you have dealt with enough. It's time to let someone take care of you. That boy out there loves you. Let him take care of you, Ash."

"Maybe, but I think he wants other things more," I sniffled.

"You can't see the way he looks at you. No one would walk across the country until their feet were bleeding if they didn't love you."

I wiped the tears from my eyes.

"What are you going to do? Stay here with Anne?" I asked, broken inside.

She nodded.

"They are the closest thing I have to family, besides you. I love Anne like a sister and she and Pete have agreed to help me. I want you to find happiness, Ash. I think you can find that with

Diesel."

She reached up and wiped a stray tear from my cheek.

"Don't cry, my girl. Just remember all the good times we had in that little cabin."

Contrary to her wishes, I cried harder—flashes of Nan, Pop, and me running through my memory. She pulled me into a hug until my tears were dry.

"It'll be okay," she whispered. Tears streaked down her cheeks as well. "We'll still see each other, and you can come visit me every day when that leg heals, and bring my grandbabies to visit."

I choked out a laugh.

"That's not happening," I promised her.

She smiled. "I love you, my girl. More than anything. Go with Diesel now."

"Can I at least stay here tonight with you?" I didn't want to leave her tonight. I had been away for too long.

"Of course, I would love nothing more."

The door opened and Diesel stepped back inside. His eyes softened when they met mine, his face full of understanding. I was sure he heard every bit of that conversation. My face turned pensive as I looked at him. I *really* looked at him, and saw the man standing before me. His clothes were tattered, and his hair and beard were long and scraggly from weeks of searching for me.

Anne and Pete returned, breaking our eye contact. Anne came over to where I rested and handed me a bag.

"Take this. It's dressings for your leg, and I slipped a little something else in there as well, just in case."

I reached up and pulled her into a hug.

"Thank you for everything," I whispered into her ear. "Can I stay here with Nan tonight?"

She looked at me, surprised that I wasn't leaving with Diesel. "Yes, that would be fine." Anne gave me a kind smile and Diesel stepped closer.

"Ash, please just come home with me tonight." His tortured eyes made me feel bad for refusing him, but I needed some time with Nan.

"Tomorrow."

"Can I put my bedroll on your floor tonight?" he asked the owners of the house.

My eyes shot to his, and he frowned at me pointedly. Was he really that adamant about not leaving me?

"I suppose that would be fine," Anne replied. Pete stayed silent, assessing the man that had threatened his wife. The room descended into awkward silence, and I couldn't bear it. Diesel wasn't going to give up, and I didn't want them to have to suffer through tonight because of me.

"Never mind," I mumbled. "I'll go with Diesel."

Pete came to my rescue. "Leave her be for tonight. You can

come back and get her in the morning, boy."

Diesel glowered at him and pursed his lips. We all awaited his answer. His fingers found his hair again in a practiced move of agitation.

"Fine," he grumbled, given no choice. He walked straight over to where I sat and tried to plant his lips on mine, for everyone in the room to see. I turned my face away, embarrassed, giving him my cheek instead.

"I'll see you in the morning," he muttered into my ear before stomping out of the house.

The night wore on and we all sat around the table, eating and exchanging stories. Nan was different. She was more tired and much less lively than she had always been. Her breathing seemed labored and movements slow—it made my heart ache for her. I felt a pang of longing for Diesel; I had spent the last several nights sheltered in his arms, and I craved them again tonight.

I took a bath and washed all the stink off my body from the weeks of traveling, smelling better than I had in days. Anne let me borrow some clothes that didn't fit right, but they would work.

When the night fell, Anne organized a bed in Nan's room for me and I laid my exhausted body on top of it, bidding them all goodnight. I woke early in the morning from another unsettling dream and scrubbed my hands over my face.

Everyone in the house still slept, so I left Nan a note saying I went to Diesel's house so she wouldn't worry. I limped out the door in the early morning light with Anne's bag she had given me strung across my back. A hat and hood were pulled low on my head to disguise my still yellow hair. A noise came from beside the house, and I spun to see what was there, hoping the soldiers hadn't found me.

CHAPTER 43
ASH

"Where're you going?" Diesel's rugged voice sounded from his spot against the house. His back leaned against the brick and his forearms rested on his knees.

"I was coming to find you, actually. Have you been there all night?"

He nodded solemnly. "I was worried."

My heart soared at his words. I loved him. There was not a doubt in my mind that after all we had been through, I had fallen hopelessly in love with him.

"I needed some time with Nan."

"I know." He stood and came toward me. "Can we go home now?"

"Back to cabin or your house?" I really wanted to go home—back to normalcy. I only wished Nan was there with me.

"Wherever you want, Spitfire. Your home is my home." He reached out and laced his fingers through mine, and our eyes locked. My heart soared, nearly coming out of my throat. "I want to go back to the cabin." I swallowed hard.

"Then that's where we'll go." He scooped me up and carried me back to our little cabin. I rested my head on his chest, holding tight to him.

Walking back in after so much time away felt surreal. Everything was the way we had left it the morning we departed on our trip. He pushed the door open with his foot and carried me across the threshold, setting me down gently on a chair in the kitchen.

Diesel slumped down into a chair next to me and rested his forearms on his knees. He looked like a man in pain. Not physical pain, but the kind of anguish that only haunted your mind in the darkest parts of the night, when no one was around to distract you from your suffering. I knew too well that agony; it was impossible to run away from.

"I'm sorry... for everything," he murmured into his hands. "I've done so many things wrong when it came to you. I—need you, Ash. I'm sorry if you didn't want me here after everything, but I'm so afraid of losing you again."

He looked up, and I saw the anguish in his eyes.

"It's not that I don't want you here, D. The only other person I want to spend my time with besides you is Nan. I need to know where you stand, though. I need to know if you're leaving me," I choked out. Being without him last night had almost been too much to handle—the dreams ran wild without him there.

I gazed at him with such vulnerability. Last time I was here he crushed me, and I closed my eyes waiting for it to come again. Warm hands slid around mine and Deisel knelt on the ground at my feet.

"Ash," he mumbled. "Will you please look at me?"

I opened my eyes and stared into a face that burned with a raging fire of regret and love.

"I love you." His green eyes penetrated into my very soul and his confession lingered between us. "I couldn't leave you if I tried, and I know because I tried. I tried pushing you away and hating you, so I could do what I thought was right, but I— couldn't. When I lost you…" He paused, bringing his fist to his mouth to control his emotions. "Those days I searched for you. I couldn't stand myself; I couldn't stand that I'd pushed you away instead of treating you the way you deserve. I promised myself if I found you and you were still…" He gulped. "Alive, that I would never let you go again. I was trying to please a dead man, but that's a fool's pursuit. It's time I started living for me and since you are *my everything*, I'll live—for you."

A tear slipped out of my eye, and I bit my lip to keep it from quivering. "But you said you wanted to go. You wanted what Miles wanted for you."

"I did, and I do because it's what he raised me for, drilling it into my head every day. Think of how much I could change if I got close to Maximus, but I need you too. I can't breathe when you're not around. I'm terrified that if you leave, you'll never come back. I. Can't. Let. You. Go." It was hard to breathe—I didn't think I was capable of feeling so much in a single moment.

"You can't have both, Diesel. They'll never let me go with you. Are you delusional? Have you seen my hair? Nobody even knows what they do with blondes?"

"If in an alternate reality we could go to Hope together and you'd be safe, would you come with me?"

"I'd go anywhere with you, D. I have dreamed of seeing the wonders of the City of Hope since this spring, but that's not the reality of our lives."

He nodded. "You're right. It's only a dream anyway," he whispered.

"I love that you want to change things, but I need you to choose. It's either me or the King, because I'm sorry, but I won't be associated with anybody who works for him or his soldiers and bounty hunters. And I don't understand how you could kill them so easily and then want to become one?"

"It was all so much clearer before I found out that you're blond."

"What? Because dragging innocent people to the unknown just because of the color of their hair, which is something they have no control over, was okay?"

"No, it was just easier to overlook. I choose you, Ash. Please remember, *everything* I do is to protect you. I. Love. You." Both of his hands were on my face, fingers digging into my cheeks— the emotion in his voice had me falling and I knew everything had changed.

I did the only thing I could think of and put my lips on his. His lips had never felt as right as they did right then. Knowing he loved me, that he finally chose me, sent my mind into a tailspin I'd never recover from.

"Do you want to know the only thing I regretted when I was dying?" I whispered coarsely.

"What," he breathed.

"That I didn't tell you that I love you."

He tugged me into his arms, holding me tight. I wrapped my arms around the back of his neck, wanting more. He released my lips and made a trail of kisses down my neck, burying his nose in the spot between my neck and shoulder. His lips made their way back up, and he kissed my lips a few more times for good measure. He moved away and leaned his forehead on mine.

"As much as I love this, you really need a bath," I grinned. It had been a long time since such a large smile had graced his face. It was a beautiful sight that made my knees weak. He looked slightly less broken. He was still covered in grime from the long trek, and from spending the night next to Anne's house.

"Oh, yeah?" he questioned, raising his eyebrows with a glint

in his eye. He lifted his arm and shoved my face into his armpit.
I burst out laughing and pinched his chest to get away from the
stench. He chuckled with me—the deep husky tone like music
to my ears, and he pushed my hand away with minimal effort.

"Not fair," he cried, laughing. "I'll go start a fire and boil the
water." He gave me a quick peck on the lips before standing. I
stood to help, and he grabbed my shoulders, gently pushing me
back down with pursed lips.

"Sit down. You're not standing on that leg for two weeks."

I rolled my eyes. "I'll be careful."

"If you walk on that leg *at all* in the next two weeks, I will
take great pleasure in tying you to the bed to make sure you stay
put." His look was full of promise, and I knew he would do it if
I didn't listen. Tingles ran down my body at the thought of his
threat.

"This is going to be a long two weeks, isn't it?"

The corners of his mouth slowly rose until he gave me a
brilliant smile. "I'm looking forward to it."

He turned and left to go gather the water. Sunshine blazed
into the cabin windows, and I relished the feel of it on my skin.
Diesel lit a fire in the hearth and hung a pot over it to boil. I
stayed seated on the chair, per Diesels' request, though I hated
when he told me what to do.

Diesel brought me food, while we waited for the water to
boil. Once it simmered, he took it to Nan's bedroom—adding a

few more buckets of cool water. He carried me into the bedroom and set me carefully on the bed.

"You need to rest. It's the only way you'll get better," he said, kissing my forehead. I laid down on the soft blankets and gazed back at him. My hand reached up and cupped his face. His hand covered mine on his face and he kissed my palm.

"Go to sleep," he whispered before tugging off his clothes and sliding into the tub, which was entirely too small for him. When he pulled off his socks, I noticed for the first time the large blisters and unhealed wounds from walking for so long. My breath caught in my throat; he hadn't complained once. He walked until his feet were raw and bleeding just to find me.

I gazed at him while he washed his body, entranced by the muscles working in his arms and back. For the first time, it was okay to stare, so I drank it all in, behind the cover of blankets.

He muttered curse words to himself before finishing and standing up in all his glory. He grabbed the towel and made quick work of drying himself off and pulling on underwear. He came over and laid down beside me. When I scooted over, my shirt moved aside, revealing the skin underneath. Diesel glared at the newly-formed scars across my chest.

"It's okay," I whispered, bringing his hand up to my chest to trace his fingers down the lines. "It's over now."

His eyes filled with sadness that I didn't understand before he brought his lips up to kiss every inch of the red gashes.

"I'm never letting you go again," he breathed. The air simmered between us. The moment was like everything—everything that I had ever dreamed of with Diesel. Everything that I thought I ever wanted. To have someone want me and feel like I belonged, and for only a moment, not feel tarnished.

CHAPTER 44
ASH

It turned out that the "something extra" Anne had put in the bag was thistle tea, which all the girls around here used for birth control. I immediately drank it the next morning, after we found it in the bag. My last cycle was some time ago, long before leaving on our hunting trip gone bad. I must have skipped one because of the stress, sickness, and malnutrition, I decided.

We stayed inside the cabin for the next three days, only leaving for bathroom breaks and water. We couldn't keep our hands off each other. We defiled every part of the cabin, which made me laugh, because that was exactly what Nan was worried about. Nan; I missed her. We were too far away.

"Can we stay at your house?" I asked Diesel that night, while we laid in bed.

He rolled to look at me. "I thought you wanted to be home?"

"It doesn't feel like home anymore with Nan gone. I want to be closer to her to help."

"Of course, we can go tomorrow." I nodded in agreement, and we snuggled close to fall asleep. A tear slipped out of my eye. It was the end of the life that I knew in the cabin with Nan.

"Should we be worried about bounty hunters and soldiers showing up in Cedar Hill looking for me?" I whispered.

"Did you tell them where you were from when they—had you?"

I stroked my hand across the muscles in his chest. "No, I didn't tell them anything."

"Then there's no way that they know where we are. They found you way up north, and if they go looking there, they'll never find you."

Kane flashed across my mind. He was the only one that knew where I would have been. He didn't know where I lived, but the first time I saw him was in Cedar Hill. Surely, he could find me if he wanted. Something about the way he just let us go in Rollins made me uneasy. Were we really safe here? I had yet to tell Diesel about my encounters with Kane; as far as Diesel knew, he didn't even exist. I wanted to keep that information to myself. I also kept all the things Will had told me to myself. Did that make me a liar? Diesel's words from this spring popped into my mind. *You are as much of a liar as me...* But who was I trying to protect by lying? Myself? Diesel? Will?... Kane?

"What about Will?"

I recalled him telling Rex and Waylon that he had worked

for Kane before. Did that mean he had helped other people like me slip out from under Kane's nose? It was the only explanation. Will was good; there was no way he would really work with Kane. What about his brother, Jackson? Why were they following me? Who was I? I wanted to know that answer more than anything.

"Why would he be a threat when he helped us?"

I shrugged. "There's just so much we don't know about him. He's blonde too."

Diesel's mouth dropped in shock at my confession. "Are you sure?"

I nodded. "What if there's more people out there like me than we realize? Maybe we could go north in a few years and be free, figure out how to change things from there, like you wanted."

"I don't think going north is the answer."

I scrubbed my hands over my face. "Maybe not, but you got me thinking about life. I feel this burning in my chest now to think about more than myself. I want to change things too, D. I want to help people like me and figure out what's really going on with the blondes."

"Maybe it's not all as black and white as it seems, Ash."

"Do you know something that you're not telling me?"

He shook his head. "I'm only saying there are two sides to every story."

I gave him a long look. "I want to be free. I want to live my life without having to look over my shoulder all the time."

"I know and I'm sorry, but that's why you have me now." He rubbed my back. "I'll keep you safe. You don't have to worry anymore."

I was afraid his idea of keeping me safe meant locking me inside and throwing away the key. *Go and live the life you always wanted.* Will's words rang in my head. Was this it? Was this what I wanted?

We woke the next morning and cleaned out the small cabin the best we could. We packed all the things that were mine, and the things that I wanted to take to Nan. Diesel harvested all he could from the garden while I sat on a chair right out the front door and watched, per his demands. By mid-afternoon, we had piles of produce and possessions by the front door, including all of Nan and Pop's books. No way we would be moving it all in one trip. Diesel decided it was best to take me tonight and come back for subsequent loads the following days. We visited Pop's grave one last time, and I remembered the conversation we had last time we were here together. How things had changed. Diesel held my hand as I told him goodbye. Tears streamed down my face as we walked further and further away from the cabin that I had called home for the last sixteen years.

The next week and a half felt like the worst kind of torture. The only thing Diesel would let me do was sit on the bed or the couch in his house. I fought him at every turn, hopping around the house on one leg. My leg hurt less and less every day. I gained back all the weight I had lost, thanks to Diesel constantly feeding me and my poor physical fitness. The bright part was the constant affection from Diesel, that only left me wanting more.

We dyed my hair back to its ugly brown color right away, concealing the blonde once more. I conceded to the fact that it would probably be the reality of my life until the day I died.

We had a few visitors stop by once we got back to his house, while Diesel was gone, hauling loads of stuff from the cabin. Old Marva came by a few days after we got back. I had to tell her my story, and she was happy to see Diesel and me together. She filled me in on all the things that had been going on in Cedar Hill while we were gone. Including the fact that neither Luke nor Ty had shown back up. I noted this to Diesel after she left, and he only gave me an aggravated grunt in return.

Anne came by every few days to check on my healing. She was happy with how well I seemed to heal. She brought Nan with her one day and she stayed with me all day with me, leaving me with books to read in my boredom. Besides being bedridden, this might be the happiest I had been in a very long time. I didn't feel lonely with Diesel by my side and the constant visits from people I considered family.

On day fifteen of my purgatory, Anne declared I could start using my leg lightly. The news was like music to my ears, while Diesel chewed on his lip, like he didn't trust her advice. I began walking around the house on my leg, but Diesel regularly reminded me not to strain it.

It was odd, going from living with Nan to suddenly living with Diesel. He was surprisingly clean, but I thought it was only because he was as bored as I was. We cooked, cleaned, whittled, joked around, and got lost in each other, day in and day out. I didn't know if I had ever seen Diesel smile as much as he had in the last fifteen days.

The morning after Anne declared I could get out of bed, Diesel surprised me with one of his old bows from when he was younger. It fit me well and I fell even more for him at the sentiment. He set up targets for me outside to practice on, since it was the only thing I could shoot right now, seeing as how he wouldn't let me more than a few feet out of the house.

He took off the next morning to the cabin to get the final load of harvested potatoes for winter, leaving me in the house alone. I milled around, not knowing what to do with myself and feeling antsy. This was probably the longest I had ever been inside, fully conscious, at least.

In the evening, when Diesel still hadn't returned, I went outside to shoot my bow. I pulled arrows from the target when I heard someone coming around the side of the house, calling

Diesel's name in a very feminine voice.

I made sure my bow was in hand and an arrow was ready when Lily stepped around the side of the house. She looked the same as the last time I saw her and carried a basket with bread. The moment she saw me, her face warped into disgust. I stood rooted to my spot as she stepped closer.

"I heard you were back, but I didn't know you were here... living with him," she said, disgusted. She looked around, making sure Diesel wasn't near before continuing.

"Too bad Luke wasn't man enough to finish the job," she seethed.

I knew it! I knew she was in on it! How I wished Diesel was there to hear this load of garbage.

"But he hasn't shown his face back here to even tell me what happened."

"Why do you hate me so much?" I asked her sincerely, wondering genuinely about the answer.

She snorted. "Because Diesel will never be with me while you're around, jerking his chain."

"Isn't that Diesel's decision?"

She smirked like she knew something that I didn't.

"You would think, but you're not what he really wants. I can tell. He's only with you out of some sort of obligation that I haven't figured out yet."

I didn't want to believe the words she said, but something

tickled at the back of my mind, like she was right, breaking the happiness coma I had been in.

"What did he tell you?" I hated asking her about his secrets, but I wanted to know.

"You're nothing more than a means to an end for him. Once he's done with you, he'll discard you like the trash you are."

"What is it that he wants from me?"

She pursed her lips and looked away. She didn't know. Was she lying about all of it, or was there a thread of truth to what she was saying?

"And you think getting rid of me would solve all your problems?"

"I know it would. I would watch my back if I were you."

"Are you threatening me?" I glared at her, and she was right up in my face. Enough was enough—my hand balled into a fist, and I punched her square in the nose. Man, that felt good.

She dropped the basket of bread by her feet and cried out in pain, covering her face with her hands. She shrieked in a decibel high enough to shatter my eardrums, tears streaming down her face. I chuckled as she ran away. Served her right.

I stared after her, chewing over her words. It was probably only a ploy to get into my head; an attempt to rip me and Diesel apart. I couldn't let her win, but the doubt crept in.

The basket of bread landed on the counter to await Diesel's return. He got back a little after dark, and I rested on the couch, staring at the fire with tea in my hand when he walked in. His pack was full, and two large bags of potatoes weighed down each hand. He set them on the counter next to the bread, eyeing it up.

"Where'd that come from?" he asked before anything else.

I glanced at him before looking back at the fire.

"Lily," I stated plainly.

He muttered curses under his breath before coming across the room and sitting next to me. He took my mug from my hands and placed it on the floor. I protested, but he ignored me and pulled me into his lap. He leaned down and gave me a deep kiss before coming up for air.

"I missed you," he said, tenderly.

My eyes softened at his words.

"Let's hear it," he said

"Oh, you know, she came here to tell me about how she knew what Luke was up to and how she wants me out of the way, so she can have you all to herself."

He paused, chewing over my words. "She really said that?"

"Yes, you don't believe me?"

"I believe you. I just can't believe she'd actually be behind that."

I laughed caustically, shaking my head and walking away from him toward the kitchen.

In an instant, he was there, picking me up and placing me on the counter, his body resting between my thighs. I glared at him for manhandling me again.

"Sorry, I didn't mean it like that. I spent a lot of time with her last winter. I don't think she is capable of what you're saying."

I grimaced at his words and looked away from him.

"Is that supposed to make me feel better?"

"No." He cursed. "Let me talk to her, okay?"

Yeah, him talking to her was the last thing I wanted. He ducked his head for a moment before meeting my eyes.

"I killed Declan," he said firmly, without a hint of remorse. Hearing him say the words sent guilt racing through my body.

"I know, Luke told me. That's why he wanted me dead—to get back at you."

His nostrils flared in rage. "This world is a vicious place. He didn't deserve to live after what he did to you. What I did was an accident, but I've seen men kill for less. The world is better off without him. Luke should have been thanking me, but he wanted revenge, so he went after you. I don't think Lily had anything to do with it."

I scrubbed my hands over my face in frustration. He caught my hand in his, glaring at my bruised knuckles.

"What's this?" His voice was strained, coming out through his clenched jaw.

"She deserved it," I mumbled.

"You hit her?!"

"Never felt better about hitting someone." My face challenged him to say something more against my actions.

"You can't hit everyone you don't like."

"I don't know. I think hitting you would make me feel much better right now."

Diesel blew out a breath and rolled his eyes.

I fiddled with my fingers, unsure whether I should bring up what else she had said.

"She said you're only with me because you feel obligated—that I'm just a means to an end."

His eyebrows furrowed. "And you believed her?"

"I don't know… Is it true?"

He remained between my legs, his hands resting on either side of my hips.

"No. I'm with you because I love you. You're it for me."

I nodded. I wanted to believe him so badly. He scooted the pack on the counter toward me, and I opened it, looking at the contents. It was the rest of my clothes from the cabin. I grabbed it off the counter and went to our room to unpack my measly amount of clothes. It would be nice to have something that fit better than the ones I had been borrowing from Diesel.

I glanced at the door on the other side of the bathroom—I had yet to see the inside of Miles's room, and I wondered if Diesel would ever go in there.

Diesel left me alone as I unpacked my stuff, placing it in one of his dresser drawers. Once I was done, I slumped down on the bed and closed my eyes, drifting to sleep.

I dreamed of Waylon and Rex chasing me and not being able to get away. This was the first time since we got back that a nightmare had assaulted me. I woke up in a cold sweat and I was in bed alone. Hurt settled in my heart at Diesel's absence. I got up to see where he was and found him at the table, writing something on a blank piece of paper.

"What're you doing?" I asked, puzzled.

I could tell I startled him—he jumped at the sound of my voice. He quickly stood, coming over to me.

"Hey, you okay?" he asked with concern in his voice. "You have a bad dream?"

"Yeah, just wondered where you were."

He soothed his hands down my arms.

"Go back to bed. I'll be there in a minute," he whispered.

I nodded and went back to bed, but even when he came in, pulling me close, it took hours to get back to sleep.

I awoke early the next morning and pulled my clothes on. Diesel appeared to be sleeping soundly, so I went to the kitchen and found breakfast. I picked up my bow and decided to go see

Nan today.

At that moment, Diesel stepped out of the room wearing only the boxers he slept in. His hair was disheveled with sleep, and he looked at me, confused.

"Where are you going?" he said in a gravelly voice, full of sleep.

"Going to visit Nan," I told him, taking a step forward.

He lunged out and grabbed my arm.

"No, Ash."

I thought his overbearing protectiveness would fade away after a while and after my leg healed, but it only seemed to be growing worse.

"Yes, Diesel," I mocked, yanking my arm from his grip. "It's not that far, not a big deal. Don't tell me what I can and can't do."

He narrowed his eyes at me. "Fine," he relented through gritted teeth. "But I'm coming with you."

I rolled my eyes but stepped back inside and closed the door, waiting for him to get his clothes on.

He hurried and got his things together, and we made our way to town on the bumpy path. I was slower than usual because I tried to be careful with my leg, but it felt so good to be out of the house.

The walk was silent, and Diesel dropped me off at Anne's house, saying he had things he needed to do in town, and left—

fine by me.

The visit with Nan sealed in all the cracks of homesickness of being away from her. We talked and laughed and joked. Anne came home from seeing patients in the afternoon and we made lunch together. Nan got tired after we ate, so I left so she could take a nap. Sadness tugged at my heart as I left. I should be the one taking care of Nan after all the years she took care of me. I wondered if she would consider coming and living with us.

I thought over a plan for it when I turned toward The Market to see if Marva was around. I walked up to the back door, memories flooding my senses from the last time I was there. A pang of longing made its way through my chest at the man I met that night. I shook my head, realizing that man no longer existed, only Kane.

I reached for the doorknob as the door pushed open, so I stepped out of the way, letting whoever it was out. Lily. No doubt running more errands for her parents with a basket clutched in her arm. I ignored her and waited for her to step out of the way so I could go inside, internally smiling at the sight of her black eyes and swollen nose. What caught me off guard were the puffy red eyes like she'd been crying all morning. She didn't move, instead started to run her mouth again.

"Look who finally made it out of the house."

"Yeah, finally healing up from all the things that you, I mean Luke, did to me," I replied dryly.

She turned to face me, and I was surprised she didn't learn her lesson last time. Right then, Cooper rounded the corner behind her and looked at us with surprise in his eyes. Lily didn't see him and kept talking.

"You're right," she seethed. "I am the one who gave Luke the idea to go after you and I would do it again in a heartbeat to get rid of you," she hiccupped, like she was about ready to cry again.

She stepped closer to me, and I let her, not the least bit intimidated by her physical threats. She pointed her finger at me.

"I have other ways of getting rid of you. Just wait."

Cooper sauntered up next to me and slung his arm over my shoulder like we were old friends. Why did he always seem to show up when Lily got in my face?

"What's happening ladies?" The words slid out of his mouth, smooth as butter, and he quirked a brow at Lily.

"Stay out of this, Cooper," she spat. "Ash and I are catching up."

The smirk on Cooper's face turned downright evil. "Unless you would like me to tell the whole town who you've been sleeping with, I suggest you make yourself scarce, and leave Ash alone."

Her eyes widened. Cooper had some dirt on Lily, apparently.

"Fine," she scoffed and rushed away.

Cooper smiled at her retreating back, and I chuckled.

"Please, do share."

"I went to do a carpentry job for Tim this spring, and you would never believe who was inside with him, in very little clothing, I might add," he laughed.

"Tim? Like the loony, old guy who has all the goats?"

"The same." His laugh was infectious, and I found myself giggling with him.

"What was she doing with him?" I cackled.

He shook his head. "I don't know. He said it was payment for some sort of weed he got for her."

"Weed?"

"Yeah, what did he call it? Dogsbone? Nah, that wasn't it. Wolfsbone?"

The smile instantly fell from my face.

"Wolfsbane?"

"Yeah! That was it!"

CHAPTER 45
DIESEL

Ash wasn't at the Thompson's house with Nan. She left after I specifically told her not to leave without me, but she never did listen to anything I said. It wasn't safe for her to be alone right now, not until I received the message that I so badly wanted to hear. Until then, our lives were in a limbo that she didn't even know about. I hurried toward The Market—the only place she would have gone besides back home, probably to gossip with Marva again.

I had already been there once this morning, right after I dropped Ash off at the Thompson's, seeking out Lily. I found Susan busy in the kitchen, like always.

"Diesel!" she exclaimed. "I heard you were back. Where have you been?"

"Hunting trip."

"Ah, that explains why I haven't had any help around here. I hope you enjoyed the bread I sent out with Lily yesterday."

I shot her a lazy grin. "Yes, mam. Thankyou."

"Do you have any time today? We could really use some help with the roof. It's leaking in one of the guest rooms."

"I'm sorry, I don't have time today. I was wondering if Lily is around?"

Susan gave me a weighted look. "Of course, dear. She's just in her room."

"Thanks," I said before turning around and sauntering down the hallway. I knew where her room was. I pounded on the wooden door, and Lily pulled it open from inside.

"Diesel! You're back. I missed you." Lily shot me a demure look, and I charged into the room and slammed the door.

"What were you doing at my house yesterday?" I fumed.

"My mom wanted me to take you some bread. I didn't know Ash was living with you." She puckered her nose when she said the name and glared at me.

Might as well cut straight to the point. I had no time for her shit today. "Did you have anything to do with Luke coming after Ash when we left?"

She snorted and looked away, but didn't answer.

I strode over and grabbed her arm, forcing her to look at me. "Did you send Luke after us to kill Ash?"

A flicker of alarm played in her eyes, and I knew the answer before she spoke. "I thought it's what you wanted," she breathed.

I shoved her away. "What I wanted!" I bellowed. "You

nearly killed her!"

She shook her head with her mouth slightly agape. "You fell in love with her, didn't you? What about everything you told me last winter?"

"Things have changed. I'm not the same man I was last winter. There are things that you don't know. Speak of this to anyone or threaten Ash again, and it will not end well for you."

The first tear slid down her face. "You've lost yourself in your own lies." Her nostrils flared in disgust. "You don't even know who you are anymore."

Her words were like an arrow through my chest that filled with fury. She wasn't right—I knew who I was.

"Where's Luke?"

"I don't know."

"If he shows his face here, you better tell him to run because if I ever see him again. I'll kill him—Leave Ash alone," I raged before leaving and slamming the door in my wake.

That was this morning before I left to go blow off some steam, chopping wood. It didn't help take the edge off very much. Lily's words stuck in my head like a bad memory.

I made it to the backside of The Market and turned the corner, only to find Ash standing in the alleyway with Cooper—his arm slung over her shoulders as they laughed together. Jealousy ripped through my chest like a ferocious beast and my eyes focused in on where his arm touched her.

I strode up and pulled her to my side and away from Cooper, tamping down my anger. "Something funny?" I scowled, eyeing them suspiciously.

"Nothing you want to know about, man," Cooper said and winked at Ash. He wanted to die today. "But I would keep a careful eye on my girl if I were you. Lily was just here, threatening her."

"What did she say?" I snapped.

"Might want to ask Ash. All I heard was something about Lily sending Luke after her and she would finish the job herself if she had to."

Obviously, Lily had not heeded my warning earlier. Ash didn't know I had already spoken to her. She most likely thought this was the first time I heard this information from someone other than herself.

"Well, I better get going. I have to get out to Tim's place and finish a job," Cooper snickered, and Ash tried to chuckle as he left, but it fell flat.

I stayed rooted in place, working everything over in my head, then slowly turned toward Ash.

"I'm sorry, D," she said. What did she have to be sorry for? I backed her into the wall, caging her in my arms. "That was probably hard to hear. I know you spent a lot of time with her last winter."

I had, unfortunately, and it was probably why I didn't believe

Lily was capable of something like that. She was sweet, but now I realized what else she was. Ash hated Lily and yet she apologized for the hurt she had caused me.

"Don't you dare apologize. Nothing about this was your fault." No, it was mine. I never should have led Lily on for as long as I did. A deep ache in my gut took over as I thought about the things I had said, and the promises I had made back before everything changed between me and Ash. It piled on to the knots already in my stomach from other things. I closed my eyes and swallowed, feeling the heat from Ash's face radiating on to mine.

"It was her who got the wolfsbane for Luke."

My eyes shot open. "What!?"

"Cooper said that Tim told him she—traded him for it."

My fingers dug into the brick building until my bones throbbed. I thought Lily had only talked to Luke about this, but she had given him the means to kill Ash. Pure wrath simmered under my skin.

"I'm so sorry I didn't believe you…"

She put her hand on my face, her thumb stroking across my cheek and tickling my beard. "It's okay," she said in understanding. "I love you, Diesel."

I covered her lips with my own, never tiring of hearing those words from her mouth.

CHAPTER 46
ASH

When we got back to the house, I plopped myself down in Diesel's lap. He pulled me in, and we snuggled close.

"How come you didn't wait for me to come get you today?" he asked.

I snorted. "Because I'm a grown ass woman who can walk home by myself."

He nuzzled into my neck, which seemed to be his favorite spot. "Don't bite my balls off. I'm only trying to keep you safe," he said playfully.

"Thank you. I appreciate your concern, but I can do things by myself, you know."

He nodded into my neck. "I know," he said, blowing out a breath. He placed a soft kiss on my neck, and I melted into him.

"Did Lily threaten you last time?" I stiffened at his question.

"Yeah," I said, not wanting to lie.

"Why didn't you tell me that?"

I shrugged. "Didn't think you'd believe me." I quickly backtracked, "But it doesn't matter now. It's in the past."

"It matters," he stated, tilting his head up to look at me. "I'm so sorry. I can never tell you that enough, and it matters because she still has it out for you."

"I'm not afraid of her," I huffed. "You didn't kill Ty, did you? They're still not back."

"No, but I should have."

I cringed, remembering Declan. We hadn't talked about it since I found out. I didn't want to know how he did it. That was the fourth person I knew he had killed for me. How many people was he willing to slaughter for me? Did he regret it like I did? Did he feel the weight of their deaths on his shoulders?

"You told me I can't punch everyone I don't like. Well, you can't kill everyone who threatens me."

"Watch me."

A long breath escaped my lungs. "I still feel guilty about it every day. I know he wasn't a very good person, but it was my fault," I admitted quietly.

"He hurt you, Ash. He hurt his own son, and we don't even know how many other people. It wasn't your fault, it was mine. I was the one who did it. I didn't tell you because I knew you would feel guilty."

I nodded, resting my head on his shoulder.

"Is it true what Cooper told me about you warning everyone

to stay away from me?"

I felt him tense underneath me and his thumb started drawing circles on my hand.

"It's true."

"Why?"

"Because I couldn't stand the thought of you sharing your smiles with any other man."

I gazed at the fire dissecting his words, not knowing whether to feel flattered or upset. "You took away my freedom by doing that, you know?"

"What do you mean?"

"You didn't tell me the truth or tell me how you felt about me, just like you didn't tell me about all the things happening with you leaving to be a soldier. You fed me partial truths, enough so I wouldn't write you off completely, but you thought you knew what was best for me. You didn't even give me a choice."

I was such a hypocrite. There were so many things I was still holding back from him, too.

"I did it to protect you." He wrapped his arms around me tight like I'd get up and leave him at any minute.

"You lied to me too," he breathed, tugging on a strand of my hair.

"I know, and I'm sorry. How about let's try to be more honest with each other?" I spoke to myself more than him. I felt guilty for all the things I kept from him. I opened my mouth to tell him about Kane, Will, and the thing I was most afraid of about myself, but the words wouldn't come out. Diesel was right—I was a liar. At least I could admit it to myself now. I lost every bit of righteous indignation I had toward him for lying to me. We were both made of the same thing, lying to each other under the guise of protecting the other, when really, we were only guarding our own selfish beliefs. I wasn't any better than he was.

Marva was right—there was a little bad and a little good in everyone, but there wasn't a winning or losing side. The good and the bad all swirled together, making us who we were and driving our belief of what we thought was right. In the end, I'm not sure Diesel or I would ever abandon those beliefs for each other. I loved him, so much so that my heart yearned for his presence, but there were some things that, if broken, could never be repaired.

"What if you'll hate me because of the truth? What if I lose you forever because of the truth? That's what I was afraid of," he said.

"Then... I guess we were never meant to be."

My words lingered between us as we sat in silence for a moment or two until Diesel picked me up and set me to the side.

"Stay there; I'll be right back." He hurried off into his room and I stayed seated in anticipation. He strode back out with the necklace that I saw resting on his dresser, so long ago, dangling from his fingers. Sitting down next to me, he held the necklace up.

"I got this for you. I saw you looking at it one day and I couldn't help myself."

Tears welled up in my eyes. It was always for me—the thing I had thought was for Lily. I turned, and he placed it over my head, pushing my hair out of the way as he did up the clasp with fumbling fingers. He gave me a soft kiss on the back of the neck.

"It's beautiful, thank you."

"I'm so sorry for everything," he murmured. "None of what I did was fair to you. Promise me you'll love me, no matter what happens," he whispered.

"It's okay," I murmured. He had a vice grip on my heart and had since the day I met him. "I love you, D."

"No, *promise* you'll always love me, no matter what," he pleaded, green eyes full of vulnerability.

"I promise," I whispered, hoping I didn't make a promise that I couldn't keep, and he swallowed my words with a kiss that consumed me.

CHAPTER 47
ASH

The days wore on, and I slowly got out of the house more. We went hunting together and gathered food for the coming winter. Diesel was always with me—he never let me leave the house alone. He seemed to grow increasingly protective. I was not sure if he was on edge about Lily's threat, but I needed to figure out what was going on soon, because I couldn't take being caged up much longer. We fought more and more about his controlling, overprotective behavior. He went off to do things while I visited Nan, but never actually told me what he was doing. I was more confused than ever. Should I tell him about Kane? Were they coming to find me? Most importantly, I had to tell him about the biggest secret of all that I was keeping. I just had to find the right time.

Insecurity grew in the pit of my stomach with every passing day. *Go and live the life you always wanted.* What did Will mean? Was this what I wanted? I had always wanted Diesel and the security of someone else in my life, but I wasn't so sure anymore.

My nightmares gradually grew worse, every night filled with pain and terror. Dreams of Waylon, Rex, and cougars constantly assaulted me. I even dreamed of Kane, but those dreams were different. Diesel was there to soothe me back to sleep, but sometimes when I woke, he wasn't there. He liked to write at the table in the middle of the night. I always tried to get him to tell me what he was doing, but he brushed me off. I was constantly tired and irritable. The good news was my cycle came and went, meaning I wasn't pregnant. I blew out a breath of relief when it came.

I thought about Will often. I still carried his map and picture in my pocket everywhere I went. It was like a piece of him, bringing me comfort to know that I wasn't alone. I wished I knew who he was and why he helped me. Most of all, I wished I knew the biggest secret—who I really was.

I badly wanted to clean out Miles's room to clear the weight of it hanging over Diesel's head. Also, it would be nice to have an extra room. Maybe Nan could even come stay with us. Every time I pushed the issue or tried to go in, Diesel's temper got the better of him. Was he still grieving for his father so much that he couldn't part with his things, or was there something in there he didn't want me to see?

Fall was in full swing, and the leaves turned colors. I visited Nan often and made sure Anne and Pete had help whenever they needed it. I begged her to come to stay with Diesel and me, but she laughed and said she didn't want to interrupt anything.

Diesel's birthday was coming up on the first full moon of the harvest. I mentioned it to him one night, and he looked at me like he had forgotten. It was the next week—I told him, and he only got moodier at the prospect of it. A birthday party was what he needed to pull him out of his funk. I consulted with Anne and Nan, and we came up with a plan.

On the day of Diesel's birthday, he was more on edge than ever. He refused to leave me alone all day, constantly holding me and telling me sweet things. I told him we were going to town to celebrate by midafternoon—he agreed only after lots of begging.

On our way to town, Diesel never let go of my hand. His eyes wandered everywhere, like he was searching for something. His behavior was strange.

"Are you okay?" I asked when we got into town and headed down the street toward the market.

He gave me only a nod in answer and kept walking. I stopped, giving his arm a tug, stopping him as well.

"D, what's wrong?" I asked, squinting in the warm, fall sunlight.

He chewed on his lip, thinking about something.

"I have something I need to tell you." He looked around as a few people passed us in the street. "But I can't right now. We will talk tonight when we get home."

"Promise?"

His eyes softened as he gave me a gentle kiss.

"Promise."

I felt nervous about what he had to share with me, but I pushed it to the back of my mind until tonight. We turned and walked up to the market's front door. There was no one out on the street out front, which seemed weird, but, I knew everyone was already inside, per our plan.

I opened the door and led Diesel inside. The room was bursting with people who knew Diesel from Cedar Hill.

"Happy Birthday!" they all shouted when we walked in. I smiled with glee at the look of pure shock on his face. It was better than I expected. Friends and neighbors gathered around, smiling, and celebrating the handsome man at my side. They all gathered around, wishing him a happy birthday, and pulling him into hugs and handshakes.

I stepped back into the corner to give them room. Nan sat on the far side of the room, so I went to join her.

"It's perfect!" I said when I reached her, pulling her into a hug. "Thank you."

"Don't thank me. All I did was invite a few people. You know how Anne loves to throw a party," she chuckled.

"Is someone talking about me?" Anne said from behind me.

I smiled and pulled the woman into a hug. "Thank you again, Anne."

"Oh, it was no trouble at all, dear," she said, squeezing me back.

"What do you need help with?" I asked.

"Let's go get the food to set out?" she said, heading toward the kitchen. I followed, leaving Nan sitting in the chair.

I was thankful that Susan let us commandeer the kitchen for the night. Rod was out in the main room, pouring drinks, but Susan and Lily had disappeared for the evening, and I couldn't be more grateful. When we got to the kitchen, Anne handed me a knife to slice up root vegetables and put them in the oven. She took a pan that was finished out of the oven and into the crowd outside. It left me alone in the kitchen—the laughs and conversations from outside the door filtering in. I smiled, knowing Diesel enjoyed the conversations, while I enjoyed the silence in the kitchen as I sliced the vegetables.

A commotion came from outside the kitchen and Anne yelled over the top of the crowd, "She's in the kitchen."

I set the knife down to see what was going on, and Diesel was there, filling up the doorway, breathing hard. He breathed a sigh of relief when he saw me, stepping over and wrapping me in a hug with a worried look on his face.

"Hey, what's going on?" I asked, concerned, muffled by his hug.

"Nothing," he mumbled. "I just couldn't find you."

A chuckle escaped my lips. "Where would I go, D? The place

isn't that big."

Pain covered his face, and he opened his mouth like he was going to say something when Anne walked in the door behind him with an empty tray.

"Better get back out there, lovebirds," she chimed, breaking us apart. "I'll finish this up." She gestured to the vegetables I was about to finish cutting. I nodded my thanks to her and Diesel pulled me out of the kitchen by my hand. He was tense and something was definitely going on with him.

Music started up as we made our way through the crowd. Diesel spoke to people, but was short with them as we went. He never released my hand again. He was constantly glancing at me, making sure I was still there. I reassured him as we went, giving his hand a gentle squeeze. He finished up a conversation and tugged me into a corner of the room, sitting in a chair and with me on his lap. He put his arms around me and stuck his nose in his favorite spot.

"Can we go home?" he mumbled into my neck.

"You don't like your party?" It wasn't like him to not enjoy the company of other people. That was more my thing. He leaned back, gazing at me.

"No, Ash. I love it. I just want to be alone with you."

"I haven't even given you my present yet," I told him with a sly smirk. Surprise filtered over his features.

"You got me a present?"

"Mm-hmm, and if you wait here, I'll go get it." I placed a kiss on his cheek before trying to stand. His brawny arms wouldn't release me.

"I don't need a present. I only need you," he whispered into my ear, sending shivers down my body.

"The sooner you let me go, the sooner we can go home," I breathed into his ear.

"Hurry," he said in a strained voice, releasing me. I chuckled as I walked away from him, feeling his eyes on my backside the whole way. I turned and smirked at him, noting the way his green eyes tracked me across the room.

Nan stood in the kitchen. "I'm going to take Diesel's cake out to him. You want to come to watch?" I asked her. Nan and I worked for hours in Anne's kitchen yesterday, baking this cake. Neither one of us had baked much before, so we spent our time making sure it was perfect. We flavored it with vanilla bean and sugar from a trader that came through last week, and decorated it in edible flowers. Nan gave me a sweet smile, but her eyes were wary.

"Is something wrong Nan?"

"I don't want to ruin your night, my girl. Let's talk about it later, okay?"

"You sure?" What was with everyone wanting to talk later?

"Of course," she said. I gazed at her with questioning eyes and finally gave a nod.

"I'm going to run to the bathroom really quick—be right back." My bladder was about to burst. I gave Nan a kiss on the cheek and left out the kitchen door, to the outhouse behind the building.

As soon as the sunlight touched my skin, I saw a figure across the street.

Kane stood before me, his gray eyes pinched together. Why did he keep showing up? My pulse skyrocketed. He looked every bit as menacing as the last time I saw him; sporting black hair and guns strapped to his chest. The only difference was that this time he had a hooded coat over his head and pulled over his guns. They found me. I darted away and back through the kitchen door. Nan was still in there, working on the food.

"I'm sorry Nan, I don't have time to explain, but I've got to go. Stay with Anne. I love you, so much. Thank you for everything tonight."

I pulled her into a quick hug, then, turned and ran into the main room with Nan yelling after me, trying to get away from the ominous man outside. I ran right into the hard chest of Diesel as people chanted around us. "Dance! Dance!"

He grabbed hold of my arms and swept me onto the dance floor before I could utter a word.

"Dance with me," he whispered into my ear, pulling me close and swaying to the music.

"Diesel," I exclaimed. "We need to go!"

He held me tight as we continued to sway, but gazed at me full of alarm. "What's wrong?"

Suddenly, the music and the chanting paused, shouts echoing across the room. I tried to turn to see what was happening, but Diesel wouldn't let me go. He seethed curses under his breath. "Not yet!"

"What's happening, Diesel?" He knew something that he wasn't telling me.

Soldiers filed in through the front and back doors of the market. They spread out in formation with guns holstered. Two soldiers stepped in through the kitchen door behind Nan where I just came from. I went to step toward her, but Diesel snatched my hand, pulling me back and stuffing me behind him. Had Diesel lied to me? Were they coming to take him away to be a soldier?

A commotion came from the front door and a man walked in through the line of soldiers. He wore pristine black clothing, nicer clothes than any of the other soldiers sported. He was well-groomed and appeared cleaner than any person in this room. Sharp features covered his face, and his hair slicked back into a rat tail behind his head. His entire persona screamed slimy to me. It caught me by surprise when I spotted guns that were holstered to his chest, just like Kane's.

"Ladies and Gentlemen," his shrill voice boomed over the room, silencing the murmurs. "My name is Captain Ian Peters.

The First Captain to the great King Maximus." His eyes scanned the room as he spoke.

"We have come today to collect the future King of Novum and his betrothed."

My eyebrows knit together in confusion. Why would a future King be in Cedar Hill? I glanced at Diesel for answers—his eyes were wide with alarm and his mouth slightly parted.

"Upholding a promise made by King Maximus's ancestor, the second King of Novum—Leon Broderick. He calls upon the descendant of the great first King Titus Etan on his twenty-fifth birthday."

Etan. Titus Etan. My mind finally connected the dots. Diesel Etan. *Our family used to be highly regarded in Novum.* Understatement of the century. No. No, this couldn't be happening, that couldn't be right. My eyes filled with shock, and I stared at Diesel and our hands clasped together in horror. He held tighter to me, not meeting my eyes.

"Son of the late First Captain Miles Etan and Granddaughter of King Maximus."

Captain Peters's eyes finally landed on me and Diesel, standing in the back of the room. His lips lifted in a sly smile.

"Future King of Novum, Prince Gabriel Diesel Etan, and his betrothed, Princess Asha Broderick."

He gestured toward us, and the room exploded in gasps of shock. People parted in front of us, clearing the way to the front of the room.

A million questions raced through my head. I was Maximus's granddaughter—I was a Broderick. I stared at the side of Diesel's head, willing him to look at me. The only way the Captain would have recognized him was if he had seen Diesel before. I yanked my hand from him, and he finally brought his tortured green eyes to mine. *He knew.* He knew all along. Everything he said to me was a lie. I backed away from him. Lily's words rang in my head. *He is only with you out of some sort of obligation that I haven't figured out yet.*

"No," I choked out, my voice breaking.

"Ash…" he whispered, his voice full of emotion.

I looked away from him and to Nan's horrified face—she didn't know either. My eyes connected with hers in a moment of love and sorrow.

"Run, my girl," she mouthed in desperation.

I turned to Anne, who clutched Nan's side with matching horror.

"Take care of her," I mouthed, still backing away from Diesel.

She gave me a solemn nod before I turned and ran to the least-guarded kitchen door to make my escape. I shoved into the two soldiers, knocking them off balance. They reached for me, but I saw it coming and evaded their grasp. The orange sunset glinted off my skin when I made it outside. I lunged away from the lies following me. Arms wrapped around me from behind. Arms that I had become so familiar with. The arms of a man who betrayed me.

"Ash. Please, stop."

"No," I cried. "You lied to me—you knew! Let me go!"

His grip might as well have been a steel cage. There was no escaping. Did Will know who Diesel really was? Did he work for the King too? Was everyone under that evil man's thumb?

In between my struggles, a figure caught my eye across the street, hidden in the shadows. Stormy, gray eyes met mine. Kane had a part in this—I knew it. There was no other explanation as to why he would have been there. I had never felt as much hatred as I did right then; hatred for the man holding me prisoner in his arms. The one man that held my heart, and then crushed it in his hands. And the other man across the street—whose secrets needed undoing.

CHAPTER 48
ASH

"Let's get her back to your house," Captain Peter's slimy voice spoke from behind us. Diesel's arms continued to cage me in. How did he know where Diesel's house was? Of course, he had probably been there before. I recognized the smaller soldier from this spring, Carter. Luke was right. Diesel—or Gabriel had more secrets than all of us. My chest, that had been full of love for him not long ago, burned with hatred. It hurt to breathe—how had he kept this from me? Maximus was my grandfather. I was betrothed to Diesel, and we were supposed to be married. He was possibly the future King of Novum. My mind tried to process all I had just learned. His real name was Gabriel Etan. Relative of the first King, Titus.

The gray eyes across the street connected with mine, and I poured all the venom I could muster into my stare. They didn't need Kane to find me when they knew right where Diesel was. His troubled face turned away, leaving me alone in the arms of the man who ripped my heart out.

"Ash, please." Diesel's voice was in my ear—he sounded broken.

"Let me go, D. You don't have to do this."

"I...can't," he breathed. "Please, don't make this harder than it needs to be."

If he thought that I would actually listen, then he didn't know me at all. He carefully took the knives strapped to my body, tossing them on the ground behind us. I kicked my leg out behind me, slamming my boot into his shin. The impact made both of us cringe in pain. My still-sore bone jostled shooting pain down my shin bone.

"Stop it, Ash. You'll hurt yourself."

"Like you actually care about hurting me!" I said through gritted teeth.

"Etan," Peters said more forcefully.

Diesel turned us around. The soldiers filed out the door and formed a semicircle around us. The rest of the crowd of Cedar Hill folks pushed in behind them to get a glimpse of what was happening.

"Leave! Unless you all have a death wish!" Peters shouted. The soldiers turned on the townsfolk, training their guns on innocent people. I stared in horror at the guns on Nan, Marva, Pete, and Anne all clutched together wide-eyed, with faces full of panic.

"Diesel, please," I begged him. He must have some power to stop the madness.

"Just walk and stop fighting me. They'll be fine."

I caught Nan's eyes one last time, begging her to turn and leave before something terrible happened. Then I stepped toward Diesel's house, to get the guns off the people I loved, my head bowed in defeat.

His firm hand held my arm with unrelenting force as we walked. Soldiers moved in front of and behind us as we shuffled down the path, forming a barrier around us. I refused to look at Diesel and kept my eyes trained on my feet.

"You couldn't have sent word about *this* before now!" Diesel fumed to Captain Peters, who walked on my other side.

"The king's orders," he shrugged.

"*Why?*"

"I don't dare to speak for the King. I'll let him explain himself when we get to Hope."

"What?" I cried, jerking to a stop. "I'm not going to Hope."

Peters stepped into my space, and I glared into his black, soulless eyes.

"Princess Asha, my dear, you most certainly are. Whether you like it or not."

He was too close to my face. I brought my free hand up, punching him square in his slimy mouth.

"I'm not your dear," I spit at him.

Diesel grabbed both of my arms from behind again. "Ash, stop!"

Peters chuckled, rubbing away a drop of blood from his lip with a finger that had never once seen a hard day of work. His fingernails were too long, and it disgusted me even more.

"You're lucky you're a princess, and I'm under orders to not touch you. I fear if you lash out like that at any other man in Hope, your fate will not be so kind."

Diesel pulled me closer to him.

"Are you threatening my fiancé, Peters?" His tone was full of ice.

"No sir. Only giving her a warning for the future."

I couldn't see Diesel's face, but I could imagine the glare he shot at Peters. Obviously, he was still trying to protect me—why didn't he think of that when he lied to me for the last five years? *I need your words, not your protection.* Apparently, he had not listened to anything I said. I felt relief. All this time, the guilt of not telling him my secrets had been eating me alive, but he was every bit as guilty.

"Walk, Ash," Diesel said from behind me, pushing me forward again. We walked in silence the rest of the way to the house, my mind questioning everything that I knew.

The house that had felt like home this morning went cold. The love that held me there with Diesel was gone, dying along with my trust in him. It felt as dreary as the day I cleaned it this spring. A dead rabbit might as well have been in the sink again—it would match my feelings. Was anything that he told me ever since I met him even true? Pure sorrow and hatred filled my chest for all the time I had lost with the liar. We were perfect for each other. Neither of us knew how to tell the truth, but he didn't know my truth yet, or possibly ever. I had to protect it at all costs.

Diesel pulled me into the house and opened the door to Miles's room. I had never stepped foot in there, fearing I would break Diesel's trust—now I wished I would've, so I could've seen what secrets lay inside. He pushed me inside the dank room carefully and let go of his hold on my arm. I felt his eyes on my back, but I didn't turn to look at him. He didn't deserve that for what he had done. If he truly loved me, he would have told me long before now.

The room was dark and dreary, and no windows covered the walls—only worn, yellowing paint. That was probably why he put me in here and not in this room; to lessen the chances of my escape. He knew me too well—he knew that I would run at the first opportunity. Diesel was no better than the men that kidnapped me not long ago, trapping me in a room only to drag me to Hope—to an unknown future.

A tiny bed was pushed against the far wall. It had no frame, like Diesel's. Unlike the other rooms in the house, they had packed this one full of objects. Chests and drawers full of things ate up the space of the room. A small path led to the bed, but the rest of the floor space was covered in junk. Odd trinkets and fine clothing bled out of the drawers.

What did Peters call Miles—the late First Captain? Like the First Captain to the King, much like Captain Peters? If Miles held such prestige in Hope as the descendent of the first king, why was he here? Why was Diesel even here?

"Ash," Diesel's pained voice came from behind me, startling me from my thoughts. Apparently, he hadn't left.

"*How could you keep this from me?*"

"I'm sorry—I had to." His hand brushed my lower back, and I moved away from him, further into the room.

"Etan!" Peters called from outside the room. How had I not put it together when I noticed the last name on Miles's grave? The door snicked shut, trapping me in the room, with reminders all around me of where Diesel and Miles had come from.

I was a princess. Maximus was my grandfather. Where were my parents? Was I so unlovable that they cast me away? Did Miles know who I was the whole time? If the King knew where I was, why didn't he bring me back? I had so many unanswered questions, but one thing I was sure of—I didn't want to go to Hope under duress and leave Nan. This was the only home I had ever known, and I planned on staying with her until her last breath. Did Maximus know the true color of my hair? What happened when the dye faded?

The door had no lock. I swung it open to see two soldiers standing at the threshold. Peters, Carter, and Diesel spoke at the table, with the rest of the soldiers scattered about the room. They looked so out of place in the space that held so many memories. I tried to step out of the room, but the soldiers by the door grabbed me by either arm, pushing me back inside. My eyes connected with Diesel's.

"Please, don't do this." He had reduced me to begging. His face looked pained, but he turned away, avoiding my piercing gaze. "Lock the door," he instructed. The soldiers pushed me back inside and shut the door. My hand met the handle again, and it didn't budge—they had managed to lock it from the outside. How could he do this? My fists met the back of the door with fury pounding on it until my knuckles came away bruised. Memories flashed in my head and the room morphed back into the rock basement in Rollins. No. I couldn't be back there. All I could see were rock walls, and I could smell the stench of the room once more. My breath wouldn't fill my lungs. My chest ached with the torment of being trapped. I fell to the floor, covering my eyes with my hands so I couldn't see it.

I felt like I was dying all over again, except this time, Pop wasn't there for me. No one was. It was only me trapped in that little rock room with no sunlight shining through the bars. My heart raced and my frantic breaths wouldn't fill my lungs, no matter how hard I tried.

This had never happened to me before. Not even all those days I was trapped inside the rock room. Why was this happening now? Something inside of me snapped. I felt it, like a thread that was barely holding on. These feelings had been there all along, but I was strong enough to control them until now.

I squeezed my head between my hands to quiet my thoughts and take a moment to breathe. Just this morning, I had been lounging in bed with Diesel, happier than I had ever been. And now, it was all crashing down around me. The panic slowly subsided, and I turned my eyes up once more, bringing me back to Miles's cluttered room. My hands were covered in bruises from hitting the door in blind panic and rage. I stretched them out and stood, pacing the room.

My eyes worked their way over all the things in the room. Fine clothing, that I had never seen either of them wear, spilled out of the drawers. Fine silverware and China riddled with dust from under-use sat atop every chest and shelf. Why have all these things if they never used them?

Did this mean that they moved from Hope to Cedar Hill? But why? The answer was obvious, but I didn't want to believe it. Me.

Something caught my eye between two wooden chests, an empty space on the otherwise-cluttered floor. A corner of paper peeked out from underneath a worn, wood floorboard. I crouched down and pried the board up. It released easily, probably having been removed and replaced several other times. In the small space under the board rested hundreds of papers all embellished with the King's insignia.

I pulled the one on top up and it crinkled as I opened it. It was dated from early this spring, right after the spring festival.

Gabriel Etan,

Maximus sends his regards for your father's passing. Based on the writings from your last letter, he updated you on the situation in which you find yourself before he passed. Miles was one of Maximus's most trusted men. He expects that you are still the man the King trained—with obligations only to Novum. He was rather impressed with your duty to your country and to your assignment when you visited last year. Your training has served you well.

As your father told you, Maximus has run out of options for his next successor, and would like to honor the promise of his ancestor. Leon Broderick promised, that one day, Titus Etan's descendants would sit on the throne of Novum. Because you are of noble lineage and bear the Etan name, Maximus would like to give you a chance to serve as the next king of Novum. You will be given the title of prince until he decides whether you are suitable for the position. With this honor comes many duties and obligations, which we will discuss further when you rejoin us in Hope.

Maximus has been fruitless in the search for his dishonorable son,

Liam, over the last several years. It is apparent Liam does not know where his daughter lives as we do. Our attempts to lure him to her for Captain Etan and yourself to capture have proven disappointing.

Yes. She is blond. Maximus did not feel that information was pertinent to your assignment. He instructed your father to withhold that information so you could grow closer to Ash without bias. He is aware of the hatred that runs through your blood for their kind. You were only to watch her to see if her father ever returned and listen in case Henry ever told her the truth. She poses a great threat to the kingdom, especially if she finds out her true identity and disappears. Her worth to the King has expired. Maximus would like you to dispose of his granddaughter discreetly as soon as possible. Please finish your mission in Cedar Hill and return to Hope by your twenty-fifth birthday to work under the King for a time before you take the throne as your own. If you cannot complete the assignment by your twenty-fifth birthday, we will send someone to do it for you. Barret and Carter said you seemed rather close with Ash this spring when they came to bring news.

Regards,

First Captain Ian Peters

ABOUT THE AUTHOR

Willa is a debut author, native to the great state of Idaho. Ranch wife by day, she turns to writing to channel her creative energy when she is not chasing her herd of children and cows. If Willa isn't on a horse, she is probably dreaming up her next book. Silver Lies was the product of boredom after having her third son. When she couldn't go out on the ranch and ride her horse, she escaped into writing to cope with the house fever. Willa loves the change that comes with new adventures and challenges, it keeps life interesting! She enjoys writing stories with strong capable women and the realities of living life without modern conveniences.

www.willalayne.com
Instagram: @authorwillalayne
Facebook: Willa Layne
Tik Tok: @authorwillalayne
Email: willa.layne@outlook.com

Please consider leaving a review if you liked the book!!

WILLA LAYNE

ACKNOWLEDGEMENTS

Thank you. Thank you. Thank you. I can't say it enough. Most importantly, thank you to my husband and kids for all the time they let me spend on a computer over the last few years. Thank you for all the dinners you cooked and the house you cleaned when I was stuck in my own world.

Thank you to all my beta readers for all your time reading and the ideas to improve my story.

Thank you to my cover designer for putting up with my crazy ideas and approximately one hundred emails to get the cover right. I absolutely love it!

Thank you to my wonderful editors, Emi and Eliza who jumped right in and fixed everything. I couldn't have done it without you!

To all my wonderful ARC readers, thank you for giving me a chance. You'll never know how thankful I am for all your support.

To Kassi for trying book cover art for the first time, you totally rocked it!

Bookstagrammers and Booktokers. You are the real heroes—teaching and supporting me through it all! <3

BOOKS IN THIS SERIES

GOLDEN
SECRETS:
BOOK 2 OF
THE SILVER
LIES SERIES

KEEP READING FOR A SNEAK PEEK AT BOOK 2 IN THE
SILVER LIES SERIES: GOLDEN SECRETS.

CHAPTER 1
ASH

My eyes moved over the page, reading and re-reading the words.

Dispose of his granddaughter.

The oxygen left the very air I breathed. My chest heaved with effort to take a lungful. Dispose of... Kill me. Diesel was supposed to kill me.

The letter fell to the ground, the shuffling of paper the only noise in a soundless room.

Kill me.

Diesel worked on an assignment for the king. My stomach dropped. What a fool I had been for ever believing what I had with him was real. *It was all a lie.* Everything he had ever told me was a lie. I was his assignment and nothing more. Diesel was supposed to kill me. I felt like I would be sick. Why wasn't I dead? Why was I now a princess with a fiancé that I wasn't sure if I loved anymore?

I pulled out another letter. This one was much older and

addressed to Miles.

Captain Etan,

I trust you are well. Your last letter about Asha was very informative. The king requests that you keep sending updates on her current situation and if her father ever shows his cowardly face. The king also wishes for more information on the people that are raising his granddaughter. Please continue with your assignment and stay true to Novum.

Regards,

First Captain Ian Peters

I dropped that one and picked up another. This one was different—Diesel's handwriting covered the page. The paper was crinkled and flattened out again. Lines scratched out several of the words.

Peters,

~~*SHE IS BLOND! Did you know she is blond?? This changes everything!*~~

~~*Princess Asha is BLOND. Why was I not informed of this? Did you not know? He knew, didn't he? Miles knew! Why did no one tell me?*~~

This letter had to have been right after the elk hunt this

spring—the night we got back to the cabin and he left in a rush. He came back to write to the king's commander. Tears threatened to spill out of my eyes. Had any of our friendship ever been real? I threw the letter by the others and pulled up another. Reading through them was like a drug—I knew it was bad for me, but I had to keep going. I had to know the truth.

Captain Etan,

Maximus thanks you for your diligence in this assignment. Your son has completed his training under the guidance of myself and the great king. He was top of his class in school and in combative training—showing great potential. He lives to serve the kingdom of Novum, earning the rank of a captain. He oversees his own unit of soldiers. As promised, he will be returning to live with you in Cedar Hill and join you on your very important assignment.

Diesel will be returning in a month's time with a unit of soldiers coming through Cedar Hill. He will enter separately, to not draw undue attention. His mission is the same as yours. Find Liam. We believe he may be getting close. He has been briefed on this and knows the importance of the task.

Regards,

First Captain Ian Peters

The paper slid out of my hands and dropped onto the wood floor. I stared at my hands in shock and horror at the words on the page. My mind slid through all the conversations with Diesel and Miles. The hours I had poured my soul out to him, wondering who I was and where I came from. He knew, and he never let it show. *He knew.*

It explained why Miles was so happy to see me every time I went home with Diesel and why he asked me so many personal questions about my life. It wasn't because he cared or liked me. It was because he fed the information to Maximus. The realization hit me like a bullet to the heart. Everything that I believed about these men was founded upon a lie.

Memories came crashing back to me of the day we met. The day that he first came to Cedar Hill. He came with the soldiers that passed through that day—I was sure of it. It explained why no one had ever seen him around before and the shock on Miles's face when he saw his son for the first time in years.

My mind swirled with the black pits of hatred. Everything that he had ever told me was a lie. He was only friends with me per the demands of my *grandfather.*

My father. Liam. He was still alive. Peters mentioned him in the letters. What did he do to earn the title of disgraced and dishonored? Why had he abandoned me? Where was my mother?

I wanted to scream and rage at the injustice of it all, but I was a prisoner with no power to resist. My life was full of secrets, and I only knew a small part of them. My heart ached for the man that I loved, the man that I had yearned for all these years. The man that didn't love me back. If he did, he would've told me the truth.

I ripped the rest of the letters out of the small space, my eyes racing over the hand-scrawled words. Questions. There were so many questions about my life and the people in it. My well-being, living situation, and relationship with Nan and Pop. All questions that I was sure Miles and then Diesel had replied to with answers.

The nights I awoke, and he was writing at the table now made sense. The unanswered questions about what he was doing. He probably filled them in on every minor detail of what we did together. Disgust burrowed its way into my stomach, making bile rise in my throat again.

He is only with you out of some sort of obligation that I haven't figured out yet. Lily's words echoed in my head. She was right all along. Did she know? Did he tell her?

The door creaked open behind where I sat on the floor. I still held the letters in my hands as I turned to look at Diesel with hatred glowing in my eyes. Pure panic flashed across his face.

"*It was all a lie.*" The ice in my voice could rival the coldest of winter days. "*You were supposed to kill me.*"

Diesel stumbled over his words. "Ash…please, no…it's…it's not what you think. Please let me explain." His voice was low and full of emotion as he glanced at the door behind him.

I stood and hurled the papers at him.

"You told him everything about me. You fed him every little detail he wanted! But you couldn't bother to even tell me who I was!" I shouted.

"I...couldn't. You don't understand. Please."

"You couldn't? Or you wouldn't? Was everything a lie? Our whole friendship? Was anything you said to me in the last month real?" My vulnerability gutted me. I wanted him to tell me I was wrong, to tell me this was all a stupid mistake. I gave him everything—my heart, my body. I had never felt more foolish in my life. The pain of regret made me want to melt into the shadows and disappear.

"Ash..." His whispered words told me all I needed to know.

"*Get out.*" My voice was deathly quiet.

He stepped toward me, his green eyes imploring mine. He reached for me, but my only response was to yell at him.

"Get out!" I screamed again. I couldn't stand to look at him any longer. I would rather deal with Peters at this point. He crushed some papers he had caught in his hand and left me alone in my misery.

As soon as the door shut, the first tear escaped my eyes. I lashed out, swiping at it furiously. Diesel had managed to rip out my heart in one fell swoop.

Sometime later, the door opened again as I rifled through a chest of shiny trinkets. My useless brain searched for answers to all my questions. A gray-haired woman that I loved with all my heart was pushed through the open doorway. Her face filled with fear. Diesel appeared behind her. Had he brought her to tell me one last goodbye as a show of good faith?

"Nan," I said, rushing to her side. I glared at Diesel, waiting for an explanation.

"Maximus requested she come with us." His voice sounded a bit broken, but I couldn't care less. Making Nan come with us on the trek to Hope would surely be a death sentence.

"Diesel, please... She can't."

"I'm sorry. There's nothing else I can do." He looked genuinely remorseful.

I stepped in front of Nan. "If you make her come, you are sentencing her to death," I growled. "If she doesn't make it, I will *never* forgive you."

Diesel shoved his hand through his dark locks. "I'll see what I can do." Our eyes met for a charged moment. I missed his strong arms around me already. The bit of safety he provided when he was near. The remorse in his eyes spoke to my soul, but if he caused Nan's death, I would rip his heart out myself.

He exited the room quickly with one last longing look. My hand grasped Nan's as we sat on the single bed. I let out a shaky breath.

"I'm so sorry Nan. I should have figured it out sooner... I should have..."

"Hush up, my girl. This is not your fault."

"Nan." My voice broke. "You can't walk that far. You can't go."

She squeezed my hand. "Ash, my girl. I have something I need to tell you." I searched her face for what she was about to divulge. She didn't know who I really was, did she?

"Is this about what you didn't want to tell me earlier?" Her face was a riddle of sadness.

"Yes. I found something this morning in one of Pop's old books that Diesel brought to Anne's from the cabin a few weeks back."

My eyebrows furrowed, waiting for her to continue. She produced a yellowed piece of paper out of her pocket. I hated all the letters that I had read today and didn't want more secrets from another. She handed it over to me and my eyes landed on the words.

My Dearest Joanne,

If you are reading this letter, then I have probably gone to the other side. I have felt the pangs in my chest recently making me think my time with you is short. I am a coward, and I'm writing to tell you things that I should be man enough to say to your face, but can't.

I am so sorry for the way I treated you when we were younger. I never deserved you. You were always more grounded than me and an altogether better person. I love you with all my heart and regret the choices of my past, besides the fact that they brought Ash into our lives.

I'm sorry for leaving you for such long stretches of time. I told you I was hunting, but it was a lie. I think that you knew, but you never questioned me. Cedar Hill was never enough for me, and I craved more. I love you so much, but I felt my parents forced me into marriage much younger than I wanted.

The times I left to go hunting… I was actually exploring the world. Wandering from town to town, meeting new people. I left you at home in the cabin alone, far away from civilization, and there is nothing that I regret more than that.

I met someone on my travels. His name was Liam, and he had the same sense of exploration as me. We talked for hours about the world we live in and new discoveries. We mapped out a plan for a new government that didn't include a single man in power. Liam was convinced he could see the plan through. We met several times after the first, planning to meet in different cities. He was a strange man, always seemed to be hiding something and never indulging much about himself. I didn't divulge anything about you or where I was from either to protect us.

I had planned to meet him one time in Brocket, a little village just outside of Hope. I waited for a time but he was late. When I went to leave, he ran up out of nowhere with a large cloak covering his figure. He had a bundle in his arms covered in blankets. He was terrified and told me I was the only person he could trust. He placed the bundle in my arms and our little girl stared up at me with her large blue eyes. That's when he told me he was the prince of Novum, sworn to serve the crown. He told me his daughter was blonde and must be protected from his father. Maximus was hunting him for treason, and he couldn't let him have his daughter. I looked into those beautiful eyes and knew I had to protect her Jo. He said her name was Ash.

I swore I would protect her and keep her hidden. Just then, soldiers appeared in the village after him. He gave Ash one last kiss with tears streaming down his face before he disappeared. I had to help, Jo. I had to. He ran away before I ever told him where I was from. I have never seen him again since that day. It was my one chance to give you what you always wanted: a child. I could never give that to you, and this was my chance.

I am so sorry that I have lied for all these years. I was afraid you would turn her away if you knew the truth. We must protect her. Liam will return for her one day, he will find his daughter and we need to keep her safe until that time comes. She is the best thing that ever happened to me besides you, my love. I love you more than anything in the world. I hope my confessions don't destroy you or our daughter. She can change the world simply because of who she is. Please tell her when she is old enough and the time is right. Give her the book that I tucked this letter inside. She can change the world with its contents.

With all my love,

Your beloved Henry

A tear fell down my face and splashed on the paper, smearing the ink. The salty taste of too many tears and betrayal lingered in my mouth. My real name *was* Ash. I had hoped to one day know the truth and now that I did, it felt like someone had stuck a knife in my heart. I looked at Nan's tortured face. Pop lied to me all those years, too. Was he any better than Diesel? Was there anybody in my life that wasn't there because of a lie?

"He was never around before you came along. He would leave for long stretches of time, claiming to be hunting, but rarely did he come back with any game. I knew something was off, but I never questioned him. In our world, to be married meant to be taken care of. I'm not like you Ash—I was afraid if I confronted him, he would leave me. I always had food and warmth and I couldn't lose that.

"The day that he came back with you was the day everything changed. He never left for more than a few days and always came back with game. He turned into the husband that I had always wanted and the father that you needed. I never wanted to tell you any of this because he was your hero, and I didn't want to destroy your memories of him."

I hated letters—they ruined everything. "I'm so sorry you had to go through that, Nan. I had no idea." My arms wrapped around the woman who grew more tired and thin every day.

"I wish we could have found it sooner. We would have been

more careful. We could have left and never trusted another soul."

"It wouldn't have changed anything. Diesel would have found me. I was his and Miles's assignment from the first day they stepped foot in Cedar Hill."

Shock filtered through her features. "What?"

"They knew who I was. Miles was Maximus's captain. They followed me here. I'm not sure how they found me after Pop took me, but it was me. They were using me to try to find my father. Diesel was supposed to kill me, per my *grandfather's* request. When their plan didn't work." I spit out his name like a curse.

I stood and picked through the letters on the floor, handing her the more detailed ones. She read and closed her eyes when she finished.

"I thought he loved you..." She looked more heartbroken than me. "Maybe he still does. He was supposed to kill you and you're still here."

"All I ever was to him was a job. A job that brought him a crown." Pain sliced through my chest at the callousness of my own words. "I don't know why I'm not dead, but it's not because of love." I wasn't even sure I believed in the word anymore.

"I love you, Nan. You don't deserve this. I'm afraid if they make you come that your heart won't make it," I whispered.

"Don't worry about me; I'll be okay," she said sadly. "Whatever happens, I'll be with the people I love the most. You or Pop."

"You're all that I have left, Nan." My voice broke into tortured sobs. I couldn't lose her. She gathered me close, stroking my hair.

"Shh, shh. I'll be there always, even if I'm on the other side. I will be with you. Now, put on your brave face, my girl. You won't get anywhere with your pain. Put your strength first. You can be your own strength. Use it."

Tears ran down my cheeks and I wasn't sure how long we sobbed together before the door flew open again. Diesel gazed at me with a troubled face.

"Nan can stay with Anne, but we'll leave five soldiers to stay with her. The King needs eyes on her."

"Why?"

"I don't know…" I couldn't tell if he lied or not, but I guess that was my downfall from the very beginning.

My chest hurt from the pain of my broken heart. Nan was my strength and would have to stay. My relief from her not having to walk all that way morphed into heartache. Would I ever see her again?

"Thank you," I whispered.

"We leave for Hope in the morning." I hated how defeated his voice was, and I hated that I still cared.

"No, I won't let Ash go alone," Nan spoke from my side with wrath in her voice directed at Diesel.

"It's already been decided." Two soldiers stepped into the

room behind Diesel. "It's time for you to go."

Diesel held up his hand to halt them while I said goodbye to the only mother I had ever known, for maybe the last time. Tears streamed down my face as I clutched her tight.

"I love you, Nan. Thank you for everything you did for me."

"You have a world of secrets that you have yet to face, and when you do, you must stay true to who you are. Be strong, my girl. I love you more than anything." She slipped a small book into my pocket. The book Pop must have told her to give me. The same pocket that still held Will's picture and map.

The soldiers took Nan away, and I let them go without a fight. It was better for her to stay here than come with me, no matter how much I wanted her to. Everyone departed the room, leaving me alone with my tears and suffering. I let them flow, knowing that they had to be dry tomorrow to face my future.

9 798218 317805